PRAISE FOR *THE VIXEN*

"Combining elements of mystery and romance, Prose's novel is a sly indictment of Cold War paranoia."
—*The New Yorker*

"Prose holds up a mirror to a fractured culture in this dazzling take on America's tendency to persecute, then lionize, its most subversive figures. . . . This is Prose at the top of her game."
—*Publishers Weekly* (starred review)

"No one states problems more correctly, more astutely, more amusingly and more uncomfortably than Francine Prose. . . . Her insights, the subtle ones and the two-by-fours, make me shake my head in despair, in surprise, in heartfelt agreement. The gift of her work to a reader is to create for us what she creates for her protagonist: the subtle unfolding, the moment-by-moment process of discovery as we read and change, from not knowing and even not wanting to know or care, to seeing what we had not seen and finding our way to the light of the ending."
—*New York Times Book Review*

"A pleasingly intricate plot that hinges, inevitably, on lies and betrayal, both personal and political. There are spies here, and traitors. But in the richly textured place and time that Ms. Prose portrays with her usual skill, there are few clear distinctions."
—*Wall Street Journal*

"Depending on the light, it's either a very funny serious story or a very serious funny story. But no matter how you turn it, *The Vixen* offers an illuminating reflection on the slippery nature of truth in America, then and now."
—*Washington Post*

"Prose is a master of language, and her captivating words are all the more striking in contrast to the novel's intentional profanity. Good fiction entertains and asks questions, gesturing to truths beyond the novel itself. *The Vixen* does just that, with an extra note of fun."

—*BookPage* (starred review)

"I know book people are wont to throw around the phrase 'compulsively readable,' but in the case of Francine Prose's *The Vixen*, I can't help myself. I read it with compulsion. . . . Come for the propulsive mystery and sentence-level tautness, stay for the 1950s publishing mise-en-scène."

—*Literary Hub* (38 Novels You Need to Read This Summer)

"Like a fable, the story is animated by the tug-of-war between principle and personal ambition. Prose has crafted an inspired work of fiction that, while staying within a realistic framework, does for an invented New York publishing house what Ira Levin did for a certain Manhattan apartment building in *Rosemary's Baby*."

—*Shelf Awareness*

"Prose ingeniously takes on publishing, the fallout of WWII, and McCarthyism in a gloriously astute, skewering, and hilarious bildungsroman. . . . Mordant, incisive, and tenderhearted, Prose presents an intricately realized tale of a treacherous, democracy-threatening time of lies, demagoguery, and prejudice that is as wildly exhilarating as the Cyclone, Simon's beloved Coney Island roller coaster."

—*Booklist* (starred review)

"*The Vixen* is a deeply and unexpectedly funny book. Prose, with her signature brand of humor, is arguably the only person who could have written this book well."

—Shondaland.com

"Prose's exuberant, lighthearted novel immerses the reader in 1950s ambience, yet it's full of winks and nods to the current political climate. Simon, our overheated narrator, pulls us along as he stumbles into Cold War intrigue, and we're never sure which way the plot will turn until literally the last sentence. What a delightful read!"

—*Library Journal*

"Smart, assured fiction from a master storyteller and thoughtful social commentator."　　　　　　　　　　　　　　　　　　*—Kirkus Reviews*

"Francine Prose has brilliantly used the Rosenbergs' story as the foundation for a captivating coming-of-age tale about ambition, love, family loyalty, truth and lies, and the publishing business. . . . There are many moments when one can imagine Philip Roth or Joseph Heller smiling at Prose's ingenuity and verve. She long ago secured her literary reputation, and *The Vixen* will only serve to burnish it."　　　*—Bookreporter*

"Prose is a powerhouse. *The Vixen* will fascinate and complicate the histories that haunt our present moments. Like Coney Island's Cyclone, this story tumbles and tangles a reader's grip of reality. It's told with the heart, humor and daring of a true artist. Prose's *Vixen* is a triumph and a trip though the solid magic that books make real."
　　　　　　　　　　　　　　　—Samantha Hunt, author of *Mr. Splitfoot*

"Only a writer as deft and ingenious as Francine Prose could tell us the story of the American present, slantwise, through the McCarthy past. A bright Coney Island Jew tries to rise in the gin-soaked world of WASP publishing, where his job is to mash the tragedy of the Rosenberg executions into pulp. I relished every page of this hilarious, cunning and utterly engrossing novel, and came away with a startling recognition of the place we now call home."
　　　　　　　—Danzy Senna, author of *Caucasia* and *New People*

"A rollicking trickster of a novel, wondrously funny and wickedly addictive."
　　　　　　　　　　—Maria Semple, *New York Times* bestselling author of
　　　　　　　　　　　　　　　　　　　　　Where'd You Go, Bernadette

"Can a novel be wildly intelligent, deeply compassionate, politically astute and utterly absorbing? In her dazzling new novel Francine Prose accomplishes all of this, and more, as she explores the fate of the Rosenbergs and the travails of an editorial assistant new to both publishing and love. *The Vixen* is irresistible."　　　—Margot Livesey, author of *The Boy in the Field*

"In an enthralling new novel, Francine Prose, a maestro storyteller, interrogates the murky symbiotic relationship between history and individuals: Is it the senselessness of history that undermines and rewrites each person's life story, or, is it a collection of cruelties from individuals that change the course of history? Equally suspenseful and philosophical, *The Vixen* is both a page-turner set in an era of espionage, conspiracy, and mistrust, and an exploration of one of the sustaining factors of civilization that also has to sustain perennial attack from politics and history: human decency."   —Yiyun Li, author of *Must I Go*

THE VIXEN

ALSO BY FRANCINE PROSE

FICTION
Mister Monkey
Lovers at the Chameleon Club, Paris 1932
My New American Life
Goldengrove
A Changed Man
Blue Angel
Guided Tours of Hell
Hunters and Gatherers
The Peaceable Kingdom
Primitive People
Women and Children First
Bigfoot Dreams
Hungry Hearts
Household Saints
Animal Magnetism
Marie Laveau
The Glorious Ones
Judah the Pious

NONFICTION
Peggy Guggenheim: The Shock of the Modern
Anne Frank: The Book, the Life, the Afterlife
Reading Like a Writer
Caravaggio: Painter of Miracles
Gluttony
Sicilian Odyssey
The Lives of the Muses: Nine Women and the Artists They Inspired

NOVELS FOR YOUNG ADULTS
The Turning
Touch
Bullyville
After

THE
VIXEN

A NOVEL

FRANCINE
PROSE

HARPER  PERENNIAL

NEW YORK • LONDON • TORONTO • SYDNEY • NEW DELHI • AUCKLAND

HARPER ● PERENNIAL

This book is a work of fiction. References to real people, events, establishments, organizations, or locales are intended only to provide a sense of authenticity, and are used fictitiously. All other characters, and all incidents and dialogue, are drawn from the author's imagination and are not to be construed as real.

A hardcover edition of this book was published in 2021 by HarperCollins Publishers.

THE VIXEN. Copyright © 2021 by Francine Prose. All rights reserved. Printed in the United States of America. No part of this book may be used or reproduced in any manner whatsoever without written permission except in the case of brief quotations embodied in critical articles and reviews. For information, address HarperCollins Publishers, 195 Broadway, New York, NY 10007.

HarperCollins books may be purchased for educational, business, or sales promotional use. For information, please email the Special Markets Department at SPsales@harpercollins.com.

FIRST HARPER PERENNIAL EDITION PUBLISHED 2022.

Designed by Bonni Leon-Berman

Library of Congress Cataloging-in-Publication Data has been applied for.

ISBN 978-0-06-301215-8 (pbk.)

22 23 24 25 26   LSC   10 9 8 7 6 5 4 3 2 1

For Howie

AUTHOR'S NOTE

To paraphrase one of my characters, this is a novel and not a work of history. Certain events, like Joseph Welch's takedown of Senator Joe McCarthy, more or less follow the historical record, but it should be clear, for example, that *I Love Lucy* and *The Adventures of Ozzie and Harriet* were not broadcast on the same TV channel, on the same night: the night of the Rosenberg execution. Eleanor Roosevelt's remark about the fish is now said to have been made by someone else on her boat.

THE VIXEN

The shades are drawn, the apartment dark except for the lunar glow from the kitchen and, in the living room, the flicker of the twelve-inch black-and-white screen. My parents and I are silent. The only signs of life squawk and jitter inside the massive console TV. My mother and I have been watching all day, and now my father has come home to join us.

Dad and I share the love seat. It's comfortable, sitting close. Mom lies on the couch under a brown-and-orange crocheted blanket that she found in a secondhand shop. Sewn onto the blanket is a hand-embroidered silk label that says: *Made especially for you by Patricia.*

"Look, Mom," I say. "Your blanket's lying."

"Who isn't?" my mother says.

Though it's not especially hot outside, our air conditioner is blasting. We're chilly, but we can't leave the room or adjust the thermostat. Changing channels is beyond us. We'd have to get up and fiddle with the antenna. My father is exhausted from work and the long subway ride home. My mother's migraines have grown so unpredictable, her spells of vertigo so severe, that she'd have to cross the carpet on her knees like a *penitente*. I can't even speak for fear of hearing the reedy, imploring voice of my boyhood: Hey, Mom, hey, Dad, what do *you* think? Would another channel be better?

Another channel would not be better. The Rosenbergs would still be dying.

ALL DAY, THE networks have been interrupting the regular programming with news of the execution, which, without a miracle, will happen tonight at Sing Sing. It's like New Year's Eve in Times Square: the countdown to the ball drop.

In between updates, we're watching *The Adventures of Ozzie and Harriet*. Ozzie and Harriet Nelson are comforting their son Ricky, who hasn't been invited to the cool kids' party.

A reporter interrupts Ozzie and Harriet to read a letter from President Eisenhower. He's stumbling over the hard words. The *abominable* act of treason committed by these Communist traitors has *immeasurably* increased the chances of nuclear *annihilation*. Millions of deaths would be directly *attributable* to the Rosenbergs' having stolen the secret of the A-bomb *detonator* for the Russians. An *unpardonable* crime for which clemency would be a grave *miscarriage* of justice.

Miscarriage isn't a hard word. The reporter must be rattled.

It's the third time today that Mom and I have heard the president's letter. Earlier, the reporters got the words right. Maybe it's harder for them too, as zero hour approaches.

There's an interview—also replayed—with the doughy-faced Death House matron, who wants the TV audience not to judge her because of her job. This is her chance to tell us that she is doing God's work. "Ethel was an angel. One of the kindest, sweetest, gentlest human beings I ever met in my life. You don't see many like that. Always talking about how much she loved her children. Always showing photos of those two little boys. She was very sad."

"Damn right she's sad," says my father.

Back to Ricky Nelson sneaking into the party and being tossed out by the cool kids.

Cut to an older reporter explaining that the attorney general visited the Rosenbergs in prison. Their death sentences could have been commuted if they'd consented to plead guilty and name their accomplices. But the *fanatical* Soviet agents refused this generous offer.

"They were stupid," Dad says. "They should have said whatever the government wanted. They should have blown smoke directly up Dwight D. Eisenhower's ass."

"Ethel was always stupid," Mom says. "Stupid and proud and full of herself and too good for this world. She wanted to be an actress. She studied opera. She sang for the labor strikers, those poor bastards freezing their behinds off, picketing in the dead of winter. So what if they didn't want to hear her? She had a *beautiful* voice. She was kind. *Brave!* They shouldn't have killed her."

I say, "They haven't killed her yet."

My parents turn, surprised. Who am I, and what am I doing in this place where they have learned to live without me? We hardly recognize one another: the boy who left for college, the son who returned, the mother and father still here.

TWO WEEKS BEFORE, I'd graduated from Harvard, where I'd majored in Folklore and Mythology. I'd written my senior thesis on a medieval Icelandic saga. I'd planned to go to graduate school in Old Norse literature at the University of Chicago, but I was rejected. I'd had no fallback plan. The letter from Chicago had papered a wall between the present and a future that looked alarmingly like the past.

In a way it was a surprise, and in another way it wasn't. College was always a dream life. My parents' apartment was always the real one. The new TV and the air conditioner were bought to keep my mother entertained, to stave off the heat that intensifies her headaches, and to console me for having wound up where I started.

My parents had so wanted me to live their parents' immigrant dream. If I'd had a dollar for every stranger they told I was going to Harvard, I wouldn't have needed the scholarship they never failed to add that I'd gotten. They'd assumed I'd become a Supreme Court justice or at least a Nobel Prize laureate.

Somehow I'd failed to mention that I was learning Old Norse to puzzle out the words for decapitation, amputation, corpses bristling with spears. I told them about my required courses, in history and science. With every semester that passed, my parents felt less entitled, less *qualified* to ask what I was studying. What, they wondered, would they—a high school teacher, a vendor of golf clubs—know about what I was doing at Harvard? During the summers, I'd stayed in Cambridge, mowing lawns, washing cars, working in a second-hand bookstore to pay for what my scholarship didn't cover.

WE'RE BACK TO Ozzie and Harriet telling Ricky he should throw his own cool party. But none of the cool kids will come.

"Ridiculous," says Dad. "The kid's a celebrity teen heartthrob. Everyone goes to his parties."

Outside the White House, protestors wave signs: *The Electric Chair Can't Kill the Truth*. Or *Rosenbergs! Go Back to Russia! God Bless America*. A reporter intones, "The Rosenberg case has excited strong passions. It's incited an almost . . . political crisis at home and around the world. Demonstrators were killed in Paris while attempting to storm the US embassy."

Then it's back to Ricky moping on his bed until Harriet assures him that one day he'll be a cool kid and give the coolest parties.

Someone in the control room must have gotten something wrong. Or right. The Nelsons vanish. Blip. Blip. Fade to black. Filling the screen is a photo of an electric chair, so menacing and raw, so honest about its purpose—

"God help her," my mother says.

"We're not supposed to be seeing that. Someone just got fired," I say.

"Holy smokes," says my father.

"Hilarious," says Mom. "Funny guys."

"I wasn't joking," I say.

"Sorry," my father says.

"Two boys," Mom says.

Dad says, "I apologized, damn it."

"Not you two. Not Ricky and David. Michael and Robbie Rosenberg. Those poor boys! Not Ozzie and Harriet. Ethel and Julius. Look how people live on TV. Teenage-party problems."

"It's not real," says my father. "The Nelsons live in a mansion with servants."

And now a commercial: A husband growls at his wife until she hands him a glass of fizzy antacid. There's a jingle about sizzling bubbles. *Sizzle sizzle*. The husband drinks, it's all kisses and smiles. It was just indigestion!

Here's John Cameron Swayze reminding us that, without a last-minute commutation, the Rosenbergs are scheduled to—

"Sizzle," says my father.

"Stop it," says my mother. "Simon, make him stop it."

"Dad's nervous," I say. "That's what he does when he's nervous. It's not as if you just met him."

"Two hours and fifty-four minutes," chants John Cameron Swayze.

My mother says, "Where are they getting fifty-four?"

"They know something," says Dad.

"Gloomy Gus," says my mother.

"Look who's talking," says Dad.

"Are you okay, Simon darling?" my mother asks me. "Are you feeling all right? You don't have to watch this, you know."

But I do. I have to watch it. I have left the glittering world of ambitious young people bred for parties and success, students who had already succeeded by getting into Harvard. I've lost my chance to become one of them. They have all gone ahead without me. I've said farewell to the chosen ones with their luminous skin and perfect teeth. I have returned for this summer or forever because—I tell myself now—this is where I am needed. Watching TV tonight with my parents is my vocation, the job I was born to do.

"Anyone hungry?" my mother asks. "I can't eat."

"You'll eat later," says Dad.

"*Later*, after Ethel is dead, we'll grill steaks on the fire escape."

"That's not what I meant," says my father.

WE'VE MISSED THE opening of *I Love Lucy*. Lucille Ball is telling her friend Ethel about a mystery novel she's just read.

"Ethel," murmurs my father. "Not Lucy's Ethel. Our Ethel . . . "

"No one will ever have that name," says Mom. "All the Ethels will change their names. Already there are no Rosenbergs. Ten years from now you won't meet one Ethel. You won't find a Rosenberg in the phone book."

"Don't tell me the end of the mystery," Lucy's Ethel is saying.

Lucy says, "Okay. I promise. The husband did it."

"That's the end!" says Ethel.

"No," says Lucy. "They arrest the husband. *That's* the end."

"You can say that again," says Dad. "The husband did it."

"We don't know," says my mother. "Nobody knows what Julius did."

"Julius did it. He and the brother-in-law were in bed with the Russians. She typed some papers because the baby brother asked. Those guys wouldn't trust a woman with sensitive information. The brother sold them for a plea deal. And the Feds threw Ethel into the stewpot for extra flavor. It's spicier with the housewife dying. The mother of two with the sweet little mouth."

"Not everyone thinks that mouth is sweet." Is Mom jealous of a woman about to be executed? Ethel had a beautiful voice. Ethel sang for the strikers. Maybe my mother envied Ethel, but she doesn't want her to die.

"Look, Simon. It's Jean-Paul Sartre. Hush now. Quiet. Listen."

Why is Sartre at Lucy and Ricky Ricardo's? But wait, no, he's in Paris, in a book-lined study. And how does Mom recognize Sartre?

I can never let my parents suspect what a snob I've become. My mother is a teacher. She knows who Sartre is.

What did I do at college that raised me so far above them? I'd studied the university's most arcane and impractical subjects. Each semester I'd taken classes with a legendary professor, Robertson Crowley, an old-school gentleman adventurer—anthropologist—literary theorist who had lived with Amazonian healers, reindeer herders in Lapland, Macedonian bards, Sicilian witches, and Albanian sworn virgins who dressed and fought like men. I'd studied literature: English, American, the Classics, the Russians and the French, with some art history thrown in and the minimum of general education.

While I memorized fairy tales and read Jacobean drama, my father was selling Ping-Pong paddles at a sporting goods store near City Hall. And like the angel guarding Eden, my mother's migraines drove her from her beloved high school American history classroom and onto our candy-striped, fraying Louis-the-Something couch.

The interpreter chatters over Sartre's Gallic rumble. "United States . . . legal lynching . . . blood sacrifice . . . witch hunts . . . "

"Blowhard," Dad says.

"Sartre says our country is sick with fear," says my mother.

"Everyone's sick with fear. That's why he's a famous philosopher?"

Mom says, "To be honest, I haven't read him. Simon has. Have you read Sartre, darling?"

"Yes," I say. "No. I don't know. I don't remember. In high school. Yes. Probably. Maybe."

"I know you read the Puritans. I gave them to you, right? I

remember your reading Jonathan Edwards, Cotton Mather. And look, the Puritans have come back. Like zombies from the dead."

"They never died," says Dad.

I say, "I wrote my college essay on Jonathan Edwards. Remember?"

"That's right," my mother says. "Of course. Didn't I type it for you?"

No, she didn't. But I don't say that. I'm ashamed of myself for expecting my mother to remember the tiny triumphs that once seemed so important and were always nothing.

RICKY RICARDO IS keeping secrets. Someone delivers curtains that Lucy didn't order. The husband in the mystery novel wrapped his wife's corpse in a curtain. Is Ricky plotting a murder? Close-up on Lucy's fake-terrified eyes jiggling in their sockets.

Cut to a commercial for Lucky Strike, long-legged humanoid cigarettes square-dancing. "Find your honey and give her a whirl, swing around the little girl, smoke 'em, smoke 'em—"

"Smoke 'em," says my father.

"Please don't," says Mom. "I'm begging you."

Did Ricky kill Lucy? We may never know because the Rosenbergs' lawyer, Emanuel Bloch, is reading a letter from Ethel. He's read it aloud before, but it hasn't gotten easier.

"You will see to it that our names are kept bright and unsullied by lies."

You will see to it that our names are kept bright and unsullied by lies.

The attorney's voice is professional, steady, *male*, until it breaks on the word *lies*.

"Ethel's dying wish," says my mother.

Dying wish. So much power and urgency packed into two little words: superstitious, coercive, freighted with loyalty, duty, and love. A final favor that can't be denied, a test the survivors can't fail.

My father says, "How come her dying wish wasn't, Take care of the boys?"

"We don't know what she told her lawyer," says Mom.

THE NEWSCASTER TELLS us yet again how the state's case hinged on a torn box of Jell-O that served as a signal between the spies. The Communist agent Harry Gold had half the box, Ethel's brother the other half. Gold's handlers instructed him to say, This comes from Julius. The jagged fragments of the Jell-O box fit, like jigsaw puzzle pieces.

"She should have stayed kosher," Mom says. "Observant Jews don't eat Jell-O. Cloven hoof, smooth hoof, the wrong hoof, I forget what."

"Some rabbi ruled that Jell-O is kosher," says Dad. "Probably the Jell-O people found a rabbi they could pay off."

"Was Ethel kosher?" I ask.

"Who cares? There *was* no torn Jell-O box," my father says. "Except in someone's head."

ROY COHN, MCCARTHY'S right-hand man, appears on screen, grinning like the mechanical monsters outside the dark rides on Neptune Avenue.

"In *his* head," says Dad. "The strawberry Jell-O is in Roy Cohn's head."

My mother curses in Yiddish.

I say, "Did they specify strawberry?"

"Is this a joke to you, Simon?"

Flash on the famous photo of Ethel and Julius in the police van. How sad they look, how childlike. Two crazy mixed-up kids in love, separated by their parents.

Then back to Lucy. Ricky isn't plotting to kill her. He's throwing her a surprise birthday party!

"Birthday secrets, atomic secrets. Everyone's paranoid," says Mom.

"Rightly so," says Dad.

"Two hours to go," says my mother.

"There's still hope," says Dad.

"There's no hope," says my mother.

The air conditioner is pumping all the oxygen out of the room. I want the Rosenbergs to live, but meanwhile I can't breathe. I want them to be saved. I want the messenger to hurtle down Death Row, shouting, Stop! Don't throw that switch! Meanwhile some secret shameful part of me wants them dead. I want this to be over.

Lucy and Ricky wear party hats. Lucy blows out the candles, and the camera swoops in for the big smoochy kiss. How can anyone not think of Ethel and Julius?

THE NETWORKS STOP the sitcoms. The action is at the jail. The two Rosenberg boys get out of the car, holding the lawyer's hands, tugging him forward, the younger boy more than the older, trying not to run from the shouting reporters, the popping flashbulbs, the rat-tat-tat of the cameras.

"The Rosenberg sons," says the newscaster. "Going to see their parents for the final time."

"The older boy understands, not the little one," says Dad.

"They both do," says my mother. "We're watching two kids whose parents are about to be murdered. Real children. Not child actors. Murdered on TV."

The camera finds some carpenters checking the new fences around the prison. Protests are expected, and the workers keep looking over their shoulders to see if the angry mob has arrived.

Where *is* the angry mob?

Union Square. The silent protestors hold signs: *Demand Justice for the Rosenbergs, Stop This Legal Murder.* Close-up on a pretty girl in tears, then a sour old hatchet-faced commie with a sign that says, *If They Die, The Innocent Will Be Murdered.* Then back to the barricade builders, who have finished, though no one has come to test their work.

A FLASH, AND two newscasters appear like genies from a bottle.

"For those who have just joined us . . . This afternoon our attorney general informed the president that the FBI has in its possession evidence so *damning,* *conclusive,* and *highly sensitive* that, for reasons of national security, it could not be introduced at the trial."

The dark walls of Sing Sing bisect the screen. Another man gets out of a car.

"Our sources have identified the man as the Rosenbergs' rabbi—"

My mother says, "The rabbi. *That's* the case against them there. The Dreyfus Affair, Part Two."

"Ethel and Julius were hardly Jewish," my father says. "Their god was Karl Marx. Remember *him?* Opiate of the people. Jewish Communists don't think they're Jews until Stalin kills them."

"*Killed* them," I say. "Stalin's dead." Why am I correcting my father? Who do I think I am?

"Blood is blood," says my mother. "Ethel and Julius were Jewish."

"*Are,*" I say. "*Are* Jewish."

"Optimist," says Mom. "And *you?* Still Jewish? After four years among the Puritans?"

"Of course," I say. But what does that mean? I'd wanted Harvard to wash away the salt and grime of Coney Island. Now I feel as if a layer of skin has been rubbed off along with it. At school I'd copied out a quote from Kafka: "What do I have in common with Jews? I hardly have anything in common with myself and should quietly stand in the corner, content that I can breathe." Only now do I realize how far that corner is from my parents.

What kind of Jews are my mother and father? We don't keep

kosher or go to temple or celebrate the holidays. Do they believe in God? We don't discuss it. It's private.

On Brighton Beach, on the boardwalk, you see numbers tattooed on sunbathers' arms. Whatever we believe or don't, Hitler would have killed us. Had Kafka lived, he might have discovered how unfair it is, that the murderers who hate us are what we have in common.

My parents are Roosevelt Democrats. They believe in America, in democracy. They believe that Communists were willfully blind to the crimes of Stalin. But America is a free country. Go be a Communist if you want, just don't try to bring down our republic. My parents believe that McCarthy is the devil. *He* is the threat to democracy. His investigations are the Salem witch trials all over again, this time run by a fat old drunk instead of crazy girls.

My parents long for Franklin and Eleanor Roosevelt's sweet voices of reassurance and comfort. They never miss Eleanor's syndicated column, "My Day." Lately she's been reporting from Asia, visiting orphanages, lecturing on human rights, meeting refugees from Communist China.

"Come to administer last rites—" the newscaster says.

"Jews don't have last rites," Dad says. "Moron."

"Maybe the rabbi can give her some peace," says Mom.

"Forty-five minutes," says Dad. "The rabbi better talk fast."

A man in coveralls enters the prison. It's the electrician who will see that "things" run smoothly. Shouldn't he have come earlier? Maybe he'd rather not hang around, contemplating his crappy job. A few beers in a commuters' bar in Ossining sounded a lot better. Several reporters have noted that, due to the expected influx of protestors and the press, local businesses will stay open late.

Another reporter says we're seeing the two doctors who will pronounce the Rosenbergs dead.

"Nazi doctors," says my mother. "How is this different from Dr. Mengele?"

I remember Mom covering my eyes with her hand at the movies during a newsreel about the death camps. I peeked between her fingers at the living skeletons pressed against a fence, staring into the camera. My mother's ring left a sore spot on the bridge of my nose.

"Not every doctor is Mengele," says my father. "The prison docs aren't experimenting on twins."

Mom says, "Franklin and Eleanor would never let this happen."

Twenty minutes. Fifteen.

Ethel Rosenberg is reported to have kissed the prison matron goodbye, a sweet little peck on the cheek. A photo of Ethel and Julius kissing flashes onto the screen. If we can't see them strapped in the chair, at least we can see their last embrace.

IN THE KITCHEN, the light above the table blinks.

"That's that," Mom says. "*Adios, amigos.*"

"That's not possible," my father says. "Scientifically speaking."

Blink blink blink. What was *that*?

WE STARE AT the walls of Sing Sing. A helicopter drones overhead. Up in the tower, a prison guard waves both arms like an umpire ruling on a play. Safe!

The reporters have revived. "A guard appears to be signaling that the execution is over. Ladies and gentlemen, I think everyone would agree that it's been an extraordinary day for Americans everywhere and for those following this dramatic story from all over the world."

My mother is weeping quietly. My father perches on the edge of the couch and tries to put his arms around her. He hugs her, then hoists himself up and, groaning, sits beside me.

A man appears in the prison doorway. "Reporter-columnist Bob Considine witnessed—"

Reporter-columnist Bob Considine looks shaken. His clipped robotic delivery makes him sound like a Martian emerging from a flying saucer. We come in peace, the Martians would say, but that's not what Bob Considine is saying:

"They died differently, gave off different sounds, different grotesque manners. He died quickly, there didn't seem to be too much life left in him when he entered behind the rabbi. He seemed to be walking in time with the muttering of the twenty-third Psalm, never said a word, never looked like he wanted to say a word. She died a lot harder. When it appeared that she had received enough electricity to kill an ordinary person, the exact amount that killed her husband, the doctors went over and pulled down the cheap prison dress, a little dark green printed job—"

"A cheap prison dress! Ethel was such a clotheshorse!" my mother says, through tears.

"—and placed the stescope . . . sterscope . . . I can't say it . . . stethoscope to her and looked around and looked at each other—"

"All those doctors and electricians," Dad says, "they can't even get that right."

"—looked at each other rather dumbfounded and seemed surprised that she was not dead."

"Her heart kept beating for her boys," says Mom.

"Believing she was dead, the attendants had taken off the ghastly snappings and electrodes and black belts, and these had to be readjusted. She was given more electricity, which started the game . . . that . . . kind . . . of ghastly plume of smoke that rose from her head and went up against the skylight overhead. After two more jolts, Ethel Rosenberg had met her maker, and she'll have a lot of explaining to do."

"*He'll* have a lot of explaining to do," says my mother. "In hell."

"He's doing his job," Dad says. "Explaining why two murders should make us feel safer."

I CAN'T GET past that one word: *game*. *Started the game of the ghastly plume of smoke* coming from Ethel's head. *The game.* Did Bob Considine really say that? Did I hear him wrong? I can't ask my parents. *Game* is what I heard.

"Please don't cry," I beg my mother. "It's bad for you."

"It's good for me," she says.

"Go out," Dad tells me. "You're young. It's early."

I go over to the couch, lean down, and kiss my mother goodbye. She reaches up to cradle my face. Her hands are soft, unroughened by years of dishes and laundry, and, as always, cool. Cooler than fever, cooler than summer, cooler than this cold room. Once her hands smelled of chalk dust, of the dates she wrote on the blackboard: 1620, 1776, 1865. Now they smell of lavender oil. Soothing, my mother says.

I put my hands over hers. Her graduation ring, which I've always loved, presses into my palm. In the center is an onyx square, studded with diamond specks spelling out *1931*: the year she graduated from high school. Microhinges flip the onyx around, revealing its opposite face, a tiny silver frame around a tinier graduation photo of Mom: smiling, hopeful, prettier than she would ever be again.

"Poor Ethel," says my mother.

"Poor Ethel." I'm still thinking of her in the present tense.

"Be safe, sweetheart," my mother says.

"I love you," I tell my mother, my father, the room.

"Have fun," my father calls after me. "Just stay off the Parachute Jump."

DEPENDING ON THE stoplights, the traffic on the corners, and whether I take the streets or the boardwalk, it's between a twelve to fourteen minute walk to the amusement park. I can do it with my eyes closed, like a dog, by smell, into the cloud of hot dog grease, spun sugar, sun lotion, salt water. I can follow the rumble of laughter, the demented carousel tunes, the screams carried on the wind from the Cyclone. I could find my way by the soles of my shoes sticking to the chewing gum on the sidewalk, rasping against the sand tracked in from the beach.

Thousands are weeping in Union Square, in San Francisco, London, and Paris. But in Coney Island, it's a regular fun Friday night. Guys plug away at shooting galleries, massacring yellow ducks while their girlfriends squeal because they are about to win the stuffed animals they'll have to lug around all night like giant plush albatrosses. Their kid brothers slam their skinny hips into the pinball machines, while the children stuffing themselves with cotton candy look first happy, then glum because the melting candy is tasteless and sticky and getting all over their faces.

I buy three hot dogs, double fries, a lemonade. Clutching the bag to my chest, I take the food up to an empty bench on the boardwalk. I gulp down my dinner, gaze at the sky, and try to recall where I'd read a passage about the sky turning a glorious color for which there is no name. In the story the sunset reminds the hero that everything in the world is beautiful except what we do when we forget our humanity, our human dignity, our higher purpose.

The only thing the sky says to me is that the third hot dog was a mistake. I feel anxious and queasy. The spectacular pink and cerulean blue purple into the color of a bruise, and the wispy charcoal cloud is the plume of smoke rising from Ethel's head.

To my right the Parachute Jump flowers and blossoms and drops, flowers and blossoms and drops, like a poisonous jellyfish, a carnivorous undersea creature.

Just after the Second World War, for reasons never made clear, my father's little brother, Mort, was parachuted into Rumania, where he disappeared forever. His body was never found. I can't leave the house without my father warning me to stay off the Parachute Jump.

It's a tic. He can't help it.

I'd avoid it without his advice. The height has always scared me. The fragile canopies, the probable age of the suspension lines.

I head along Neptune Avenue, past the dark rides. The Spook-A-Rama, the Thrill-O-Matic, the House of Horrors, the Devil's Playground, the Den of Lost Souls, the Nightmare Castle, the Terror Tomb. Then along the Midway, past the crowds waiting to see the Chicken Boy, the Three-Legged Girl, the Lobster Baby, the Human Unicorn. Then on to the thrill rides, the Wild Mouse, the Thunder Train, the Rocket Launch, the Twister, the Widowmaker, the Spine Cracker.

How could any of it be scarier than Ethel's death? Not the goblins, the pirates, the skeletons and laughing devils, not the shaming of the freaks, the plunging freefall, the vertigo, the fear of flying off the track, of being launched into space, the fear of the parachute failing to open and of the eternity before you hit the ground.

As always, I wind up at the Cyclone. The line isn't long. The ticket taker knows me. Hey, Simon. Hey, Angus. How's it going. Fine, thanks, and you? Same old, same old.

I give Angus two dimes. He hands me a ticket. I walk through the gate in the fence surrounding the wooden roller coaster. I fold my long legs into the compartment in the middle of the little train. I lower the safety bar over my lap.

I wait for the ride to begin.

CHAPTER 1

In the winter of 1954, I was assigned to edit a novel, *The Vixen, the Patriot, and the Fanatic*, a steamy bodice-ripper based on the Rosenberg case.

The previous year, Ethel and Julius Rosenberg were executed for allegedly selling atomic secrets to the Russians. The horror of the electric chair and the chance that the couple were innocent had ignited outrage in this country and abroad. Protestors took to the streets in sympathy for the sweet-faced housewife whose only crime may have been typing a document for her brother, David Greenglass.

But according to the manuscript that landed on my desk, the Rosenbergs (in the novel, the Rosensteins) were Communist traitors, guilty of espionage and treason, eager to soak their hands in the blood of the millions who would die because of their crime.

The Vixen, the Patriot, and the Fanatic, Anya Partridge's debut novel, portrayed the Rosensteins as cold-blooded spies, masterminding a vast conspiracy to destroy the American way of life. Esther Rosenstein was a calculating seductress, an amoral Mata Hari who used her beauty and her irresistible sex appeal to dominate her impotent husband and lure a string of powerful men into putting the free world at risk of nuclear Armageddon.

It was strange that I, of all the young editors in New York, should have been chosen to work on that book. My mother grew up on the Lower East Side, in the same tenement building as Ethel—Ethel

Greenglass then. They went to the same high school. They hadn't been close, but history had turned Ethel, in my mother's eyes, into a beloved friend, almost a family member, the victim of a state-sanctioned public murder. Perhaps my mother's sympathy was unconsciously spiked by our natural human desire for proximity to the famous.

My being assigned *The Vixen* was, I thought, pure coincidence.

No one at work knew about the family connection. The only person who bridged the distant worlds of home and office was my uncle Madison Putnam, the distinguished literary critic and public intellectual, who had used his influence to arrange my job. If he knew that his sister-in-law had been Ethel's neighbor and classmate, he would never have said so.

Joseph McCarthy, the senator from Wisconsin, was still conducting investigations, accusing people of being Communists plotting to destroy our freedom. There were no trials, only hearings. McCarthy was the prosecutor, judge, and jury. To be accused was to be convicted. Once you appeared before the committee, your friends and coworkers shunned you. Most likely you lost your job. There were betrayals, divorces, suicides, early deaths brought on by panic about the future. Refusing to cooperate with the investigation could mean contempt citations and prison. The cooperating witnesses who agreed to "name names" were despised by their more courageous and principled colleagues.

You didn't mention someone you knew in the same sentence as a Russian spy. You definitely didn't admit that your mother or wife or sister-in-law grew up with the woman who committed the Crime of the Century. Those were not the celebrities whose names anyone dropped, not unless you wanted the FBI knocking on your door. If someone found out that Mom had known Ethel, my father could have been fired from his job managing the sporting goods store, and Mom would likely have been barred from going back to teaching when the doctors cured her migraines.

A tawdry romance loosely based on the Rosenberg case, *The Vixen, the Patriot, and the Fanatic* was intended to be an international best-seller. It was not the sort of book that would normally ever appear under the imprint of the distinguished firm of Landry, Landry and Bartlett.

Landry, Landry and Bartlett published literary fiction, historical biographies, and poetry collections, mostly by established poets. The company was founded just after the Second World War, though it seemed to have been fashioned after an older, more venerable model: a long-established family firm. Since the retirement of its ailing co-founder Preston Bartlett III, one heard rumors—whispers, really—that its finances were shaky and its future uncertain, rumors that my uncle seemed delighted to pass on.

The hope was that the money *The Vixen* generated might allow us to continue to publish the serious literature for which we were known and respected, and which rarely turned a profit. It was made clear to me that publishing a purely commercial, second-rate novel was a devil's bargain, but we had no choice. It was a bargain and a choice that our director, Warren Landry, was willing to make.

...

Perhaps this is the point to say that, at that time, my life seemed to me to have been built upon a series of lies. Not flat-out lies, but lies of omission, withheld information, uncorrected misunderstandings. Many young people feel this way. Some people feel it all their lives.

The first lie was the lie of my name. Simon Putnam wasn't the name of a Jewish guy from Coney Island. It was the name of a Puritan preacher condemning Jewish guys from Coney Island to eternal hell-fire and damnation. My father's last name, *my* last name, was the prank of an immigration official who, on Thanksgiving Day, in honor of the holiday, gave each new arrival—among them my grandfather—the surname of a *Mayflower* pilgrim. Since then I have met other descendants of immigrants who landed in Boston during the brief tenure of the patriotic customs officer. Brodsky became Bradstreet, Di Palo became Page, Maslin became Mather. Welcome to America!

And Simon? What about Simon? My mother's father's name was Shimon. The translation was imperfect. In the Old Testament, Simon was one of the brothers who tried to murder Joseph.

I hadn't (or maybe I had) intended to compound these misapprehensions by writing what turned out to be my Harvard admissions essay about the great Puritan sermon, Jonathan Edwards's "Sinners in the Hands of an Angry God," delivered in Massachusetts, in 1741. My English teacher, Miss Singer, assigned us to write about something that moved us. *Moved*, I assumed, could mean *frightened*. I wanted to write about *Dracula*, but my mother paged through my American literature textbook and told me to read the Puritans if I wanted to understand our country.

I wrote about Edwards's faith that God wanted him to terrify his congregation by describing the vengeance that the deity planned to take on the wicked unbelieving Israelites. It seemed unnecessary to mention that I was one of the sinners whom God planned to throw into the fire. I was afraid that my personal relation to the material might appear to skew my reading of this literary masterpiece.

I had no idea that Miss Singer would send my essay to a friend who worked in the Harvard admissions office. Did Harvard know whom they were admitting? Perhaps the committee imagined that Simon Putnam was a lost Puritan lamb, strayed from the flock and stranded in Brooklyn, a lamb they awarded a full scholarship to bring back into the fold. *That* Simon Putnam, the prodigal Pilgrim son, was a suit I was trying on, a skin I would stretch and struggle to fit, until I realized, with relief, that it never would.

The Holocaust had taught us: No matter what you believed or didn't, the Nazis knew who was Jewish. *They* will always find us, whoever the next *they* would be. It was not only pointless but wrong—a sin against the six million dead—to deny one's heritage, though my uncle Madison had done a remarkable job of erasing his class, religious, and ethnic background. I tried not to think about the sin I was half committing as I half pretended to come from a family that was nothing like my family, from a place far from Coney Island. If someone asked me if I was Jewish, I would have said yes, but why would anyone ask Simon Putnam, with his Viking-blond hair and blue eyes? My looks were the result of some recessive gene, or, as my mother said, perhaps some Cossack who rode through a great-great-grandmother's village.

...

When Harvard ended, in June, I'd returned to Brooklyn without having acquired one useful contact or skill my parents had hoped would be conferred on me, along with my diploma. Another lie of omission: My mother and father were astonished to learn that I had majored in Folklore and Mythology. What kind of subject was that? What had I learned in four years that could be useful to me or anyone else? How could eight semesters of fairy tales prepare me for a career?

Freshman year, I'd taken Professor Robertson Crowley's popular course, "Mermaids and Talking Reindeer," because it was a funny title and it sounded easy. After a few weeks, I knew that the tales Crowley collected and his theories about them were what I wanted to study. Handed down over generations, these narratives were not only enthralling but also seemed to me to reveal something deep and mysterious about experience, about nature, about our species, about what it meant to tell a story—what it meant to be human. I wanted to know what Crowley knew, though I wasn't brave or hardy enough to live among the reindeer herders, shamans, and cave-dwelling witches who'd been his informants. I wanted to be like Crowley more than I wanted to sit on the Supreme Court or win the Nobel Prize or do any of the things my parents dreamed I might do.

Despite everything I have learned since, I can still remember my excitement as I listened to Crowley's lectures. I felt that I was hearing the answer to a question that I hadn't known enough to ask. That feeling was a little like falling in love, though, never having fallen in love, I didn't recognize the emotions that went with it.

By the time I took his class, Crowley was too old for adventure travel. He'd become a kind of Ivy League shaman. Later, he would become the academic guru for Timothy Leary and the LSD experimenters, and soon after that he was encouraged to retire.

Every Thursday morning, the long-white-haired, trim-white-bearded Crowley stood at the bottom of the amphitheater and, with his eyes squeezed shut, told us folktales in the stentorian tones of an Old Testament prophet. Many of these stories have stayed with me, stories about babies cursed at birth, brides turned into foxes, children raised by forest animals. Most were tales of deception, insult, and vengeance. Crowley told story after story, barely pausing between them. I loved the wildness, the plot turns, the delicate balance between the predictable and the surprising. I took elaborate notes.

I had found my direction.

At the start of the second lecture, Crowley told us, "The most important and overlooked difference between people and animals is the desire for revenge. Lions kill when they're hungry, not to carry out some ancient blood feud that none of the lions can remember."

He kept returning to the idea that revenge was an essential part of what makes us human. Lying went along with it, rooted deep in our psyches. He ran through lists of wily tricksters—Coyote, Scorpion, Fox—and of heroes, like Odysseus, who disguise themselves and cleverly deflect the enemy's questions.

It was unsettling to take a course called "Mermaids and Talking Reindeer" that should have been called "Lying and Revenge." But after a few classes we got used to all the murderous retribution: the reindeer trampling a man who'd killed a fawn, the mermaids drowning the fisherman who'd caught one of their own in his net, the feud between the Albanian sworn virgins and the rapist tribal chieftain. Crowley told so many stories that proved his theories that I began to question what I'd learned from my parents, which was that most human beings, not counting Nazis, sincerely want to be good.

What little I knew about revenge came from noir films and Shakespeare. What would make me want to kill? No one could predict how they'd react when a loved one was threatened or hurt, a home destroyed or stolen. But why would you perpetuate a feud that would doom your great-grandchildren to a future of violence and bloodshed?

I was more familiar with lying. How often had I told my parents that I'd spent the evening studying with my friends when the truth was that we'd ridden the Cyclone, again and again? Lying seemed unavoidable: social lies, little lies, lies of omission and misdirection. I wondered where I would draw the line, what lie I couldn't tell, and I wondered when and how my limits would be tested.

I wrote my final paper for Crowley's course on a tale told by the Swamp Cree nation, about a Windigo, a monster with a sweet tooth and a skeleton made of ice. In revenge for some insult, the Windigo uproots huge trees and tosses them around, killing the animals that the Cree depend on for survival. Finally the people lure the monster to their village with the promise of a cache of honey, and the warriors kill it with copper spears, heated in the fire and thrust into the Windigo's chest, melting its icy heart and bones.

Lying, revenge, the story had everything. I wrote my essay in a fever heat even as I used words I would never normally use, translating myself into a foreign language, the language of academia, clotted with phrases like *thus*, *nevertheless we see*, and *consequently it would seem*, with words like *deem*, *furthermore*, and *adjudge*. The A that I received was my only one that semester, *thus further* strengthening my desire to study with Robertson Crowley.

At the end of the term, students called on Crowley for individual conferences, and he advised us on what we might want to focus on, at Harvard.

He stood to greet me as I entered his office, deep in the stacks of Widener Library. The furry hangings and snarling wooden masks with bulging eyeballs and bloody incisors reminded me of the mechanical clowns and Cyclops outside the Coney Island dark rides. I was ashamed of myself for recalling something so vulgar in that hallowed place of learning, in the office that I so wanted to be mine someday.

Crowley said, "Mr. Putnam. Good work. While you are at college you must study 'The Burning.'"

"Great idea," I said. "Thank you."

"You're welcome. Now will you please send in the next student?"

I'd watched other students go into his office. Several had stayed much longer. I tried not to dwell on this or to wonder if I'd failed in some way, and if his friendly compliment and his advice were a way of rushing me out. I chose to ignore this distressing memory when, three years later, I asked Crowley for a graduate school recommendation.

Leaving Crowley's office, I'd had no idea what "The Burning" was. It took all my courage to ask his pretty assistant, who later became a respected anthropologist and disappeared in the Guatemalan highlands in the 1980s. I pretended to know what he *could* have meant, but . . .

"Obviously," she said, "*Njal's Saga*. The only thing he *could* mean."

I read the saga that summer. When I got to the end, I reread it. The world it portrayed was merciless and violent, but beautiful, like a film or a dream, a world of cold fog rising off the ice, of mists that engulfed you and separated you from your companions. I read other sagas, but I kept going back to that one. Why did I like it best? I wrote my senior thesis about it, as if the answer would emerge if I only read the text more closely and wrote about it at greater length and depth.

Running through the thirteenth-century saga is a long and vicious dispute between Njal and a man named Flosi. This kinsman kills that kinsman; one soldier kills another. Each death is payback, brutal death repaid by brutal death. Under attack, Njal takes refuge with his clan, in the family longhouse. Flosi's men surround them. They let the women and children go, but when one of Njal's sons tries to sneak out, disguised as a woman, he is recognized and beheaded. Flosi's men set the building on fire. Eleven people die. Near the end, Njal's surviving son kills a man for mocking his brother's failed escape.

I wrote about revenge. I had to. Crowley was on my committee. I wrote about truth and honor, about masculinity, and how even sworn enemies knew that it was evil to slander the innocent dead. I had a scholar's curiosity, a deep love for my subject. I loved research. I loved the way that one text led me to another, the way that each book suggested the next I needed to read.

After my thesis was accepted with high honors, I passed Crowley in the hall, and he said, "Congratulations."

Later I went to see him after I'd been rejected by the University of Chicago. I thought he might know why. I knew it was pathetic to ask, but I couldn't help it.

He seemed not to remember me. He nodded as he listened to my story, which took two sentences to tell.

He said, "I'm sorry. Good luck."

...

Back home that summer, I slept a lot. My parents said: He's catching up on sleep. He worked so hard for four years. I liked napping on the love seat with the television on. I woke to the strident voice of a Belgian chef teaching American housewives how to prepare frangipane tarts and veal stews, dishes that, she clearly believed, American women were incapable of making. During the commercial breaks, my mother sighed so theatrically that I couldn't pretend to nap. The advertisements were her signal to say, Cheer up, Simon, have patience. There's so much to live for. Life is full of surprises.

It would have been cruel to point out that not all surprises were good. Last year—surprise!—Mom's migraines had forced her to quit teaching. Now she spent her days on the couch, an ice pack on her forehead. Once, during an ad for a bathtub cleanser, she said, "Simon, your mother predicts: Everything you learned in college will come in handy. Your life will get better and better." Across the room, cartoon soap bubbles costumed as Vikings chanted a threatening baritone jingle as they swirled down the drain.

My mother said, "You know so much about the Vikings. Maybe they could use someone like you in the advertising business."

I longed to share her faith, her sweet optimism. I got up and left the house.

...

The only time I felt awake was during my daily walk to Coney Island. I craved the noise, the crowds, the salt air, the sideshows on the midway.

Rain or shine, I stood in line to ride the Cyclone with the giggling couples looking for an excuse to grope each other, the kids gearing up to cry and vomit. As the train chugged up the incline, I felt the husk of my life drop back to earth, like the stages of a rocket. After that first plunge, all that remained was the bright kernel of soul—authentic, pure, fully alive—exploding inside my head. I wanted to feel my hair blown back, my skin stretched over my bones. I wanted to think I might die, that death might solve my problems. I wanted to feel my brain pressed against my skull. Mostly, I wanted to feel grateful and happy to be alive when the train leveled and slowed. The Cyclone was my prayer, my meditation.

In July my father timidly suggested that he could find me a job at the sporting goods store. My mother and I wheeled on him, horrified by the thought of me spending my life comparing tennis rackets. Our distress made my father seem to shrink, and I too felt smaller, reduced by my own ingratitude. I wanted my father normal-sized again. I wanted him to know that my love and respect for him didn't mean that I wanted to work where he worked.

All that time, in secret, my mother was also working hard, working on her brother-in-law, my uncle, the influential literary critic and public intellectual Madison Putnam, who—through his prolific writings, relentless social climbing, strong opinions, quotable bons mots, and eagerness to enter the fray of every literary controversy—had risen above his working-class origins. By the fall, my uncle had secured an entry-level position for me at Landry, Landry and Bartlett.

***

By the time I was assigned to edit *The Vixen, the Patriot, and the Fanatic*, I had been at Landry, Landry and Bartlett for six months, much of which I'd spent trying to figure out what I was doing there. Officially, my job as a junior assistant editor involved going through the "slush pile" of unsolicited manuscripts, rejecting hopeful first-time authors and waiting to be fired. The sense that every day could be my last made me feel like the medieval monks who kept skulls on their desks to remind them of their final end.

I liked some things about my job. I liked the free books I could steal from the carts in the hall and from people's offices. I liked reading the modern poets and novelists we published, writers who hadn't been taught at Harvard, many of them European, nearly all of them alive.

I liked the smell of coffee that greeted me in the morning, unlike my coworkers, who ignored me and who seemed to think I wouldn't be there long enough to bother getting to know. After I'd been there for months, they treated me like someone whose name they were embarrassed to have forgotten. They looked past me, or through me, as if I were a ghost, and I began to feel like one, haunting the office. I imagined that my colleagues closed their doors as I walked past them along the labyrinthine corridors, but that would have meant that they were acknowledging my presence.

Only the mailroom guys and the messenger called out, "Hey, Simon!" If my fellow editors were present, they looked surprised, as if they'd seen someone warmly greeting an apparition. Sometimes I imagined that my colleagues were hiding something from me, and later, when my work required hiding something from them, I was grateful for my cloak of invisibility.

I felt lucky to have the job, though it wasn't what I'd planned. I still longed for the library carrel smelling of dust and mold, for the warm dark cave where I could spend my life reading sagas about honor killings, about women with thieves' eyes bringing disaster down on the men who ignored the warnings. Somewhere my authentic self was being acclaimed for his original research, even as my counterfeit self was stuffing envelopes with rejected novels about Elizabethan wenches, aristocratic Southern families with incestuous pasts, the plucky founders of small-town newspapers, and inferior imitations of *The Wall*, John Hersey's bestselling novel about the Warsaw Ghetto.

On my first day at work, a young woman named Julia, who'd had my job and was leaving because she was pregnant, showed me how to log in submissions and write a two-sentence comment—if, and only if, a stamped self-addressed envelope was enclosed. I was supposed to return each manuscript, gently marred by coffee stains to prove that

I had read it, together with the form rejection letter, retyped with a personalized salutation and, if I felt moved, a brief handwritten note at the bottom of the page.

In her soon-to-be-former office, Julia opened the desk drawers and slammed them shut. Then she snapped her hand at the tower of manuscripts stacked against the wall. She hadn't looked at me once. I was sorry that she resented me and sorry for feeling irritated that she didn't try to hide it. It wasn't my fault that she'd been fired. If they hadn't hired me, it would have been someone else.

Under the circumstances, I kept thinking that it was wrong to notice how pretty she was, wrong to be attracted to her haunted, dissatisfied air—to some brave, reckless spirit that I thought I saw in her. I sensed there was something she wanted to say, that she almost said, then decided not to say, something weightier than suggesting I compile a list of adjectives—positive but not too positive—to use and reuse in those scrawled postscripts on the manuscripts I returned.

I assumed that Julia's secret had to do with the rounded belly clearly visible under her tight black dress, a daring choice at a time when pregnant women were expected to wear flowered smocks suitable for the babies they were about to have. Her outfit was even more defiant because, as I soon learned, Julia wasn't married.

Julia shrugged, miming boredom as she glanced at the toppling stacks of folders and envelopes, the mountains of unsolicited manuscripts. I felt like a combination of a clerk in Dickens, the girl in "Rumpelstiltskin" forced to spin straw into gold, and Hercules facing his thirteenth labor: Kill the lion and the Hydra. Capture the dog that guards the underworld. Muck out the Augean stables—and oh, when you're done, read the slush pile at Landry, Landry and Bartlett.

Julia said, "Do you know what those are?"

"Manuscripts?"

Julia shook her head.

"Wrong. That pile of shit is the hourglass your life is about to trickle out of."

Did Julia always talk like that? I wished she was staying on. We could work side by side. We could get to know each other, and she wouldn't hate me. I wanted to see her again. There was no point asking if I could get in touch with her in case I had questions.

"Have fun, Mr. Ivy League Hot Shit," she said.

"Please call me Simon," I said.

"Please don't tell me what to do," she said and burst into tears. Her tears blotched the form rejection letter, which seemed only right, preparation for the writer's tears that would fall on it later.

Julia wiped her eyes with the back of her hand. "Just read the first twenty pages. That's enough to tell if it's any good. Otherwise you'll go insane. But you should probably skim till the end. Some writers purposely leave out pages. Sometimes they glue pages together. That's so they can claim that their books weren't read. A few writers have tried to get our readers fired, which will never happen. Warren's got our backs. But don't let Warren fool you. You think he cares about you, he *sees* you, he understands who you are, and then you look, and your wallet is gone."

"My wallet?"

Julia rolled her lovely eyes. "Obviously not your wallet. Something you care about more. Plus he's got a lot of crazy ideas about politics he knows enough not to mention."

"What crazy ideas?"

Julia said, "Why would I tell *you*?"

I understood why she was angry. She'd been fired. She was pregnant. But nothing she said about my new boss, Warren Landry, could have diminished the excitement I felt after our first brief meeting, when he'd welcomed me to the firm. I was in awe of Warren, the way only the young can be in awe of a powerful and charismatic older person.

On the long circuitous walk from one end of the office to the other, from Warren's regal suite to Julia's cell—now mine—I fantasized exchanges in which I impressed him with my brilliance. But in his actual presence I'd sounded like a jerk.

"Are you okay?" asked Julia.

"Yes. Why wouldn't I be?"

"You turned red and sort of . . . grunted."

I knew why I'd blushed and made that sound. I was reliving an excruciating moment from my talk with Warren. He'd asked why I wanted to go into publishing. I should have expected the question, but all I could say was, "I've always liked books!" He'd smiled slightly (or was it a smirk?) and raised one perfectly arched silver eyebrow.

Julia detached a key from a ring and handed it to me, holding it between her fingertips, as if it were covered with germs.

"The bottom desk drawer locks."

"Why would I need to lock it?"

"You can leave your purse when you go to lunch."

"I don't have a purse," I said.

"Too bad for you," Julia said. "By the way, I'm taking the typewriter. I'll need to make a living somehow."

"Sure," I said. "Go ahead. Take it. I'll report it missing." I had no idea how I would do that, or what excuse I would make to get a new typewriter from the firm. Would I get in trouble? I'd figure it out. It seemed like the right thing to do.

. . .

Despite Julia's advice, I felt I owed it to the writers to read their work to the end, and to express my sincere hope that their book would find a better fit, a more suitable home, than Landry, Landry and Bartlett. I tried not to think about the recipients of these letters. I couldn't have gone to work if I did.

I made notes about the manuscripts in the same notebook in which I would later rewrite sections of *The Vixen, the Patriot, and the Fanatic*. I still have the child's composition book with its marbleized black-and-white cover. These are some of my summaries and responses:

The Igloo Lover: Arctic explorer infatuated with an Inuit woman
 "lent" by husband; couple dies on separate ice floes.
I, Barbarian: "Have I passed the test, O Hunt Master?"
The Bridge and the Pyramid: Dissolving suburban marriage.
 Autobiographical? Neglected wife finds portal to a past life:
 Cleopatra.
The Second Mrs. Windfall: *Rebecca* with names changed.
Mary M.: Magdalene loves Jesus. Unrequited.

I began each manuscript in a state of hope that curdled into disappointment, then boredom, annoyance, anger, then remorse for the anger that the writer didn't deserve. Why had these people *made* me disappoint them? Then I'd feel bad for feeling that way. It wasn't their fault that life was unfair, that talent and luck were unequally distributed.

I typed the personalized form letters on the battered Smith Corona that I'd got from the firm when I reported that Julia's typewriter had died from overwork. I explained to an old man named Andrew, a longtime employee who signed checks and dispersed petty cash, that I'd brought the company typewriter to the repair shop. I'd been willing to pay for it to be fixed, out of my own pocket, but the repairman told me that it was hopeless. I was afraid that the part about my offering to pay would reveal that I was lying, but Andrew was hardly listening, and that same day one of the mailroom guys lugged in the replacement typewriter.

...

I often dozed off in my office. A syrupy warmth would seep up my spine, weighing down my eyelids, pulling my chin toward my chest. How delicious it felt to surrender where no one saw or cared, where my mother wouldn't wake me and beg me to be patient.

My dreams were pitifully transparent. Storms at sea, shipwrecks. The *Titanic*. I was alone in a raft. Above me the ocean liner, like a sleek Art Deco whale, tipped and vanished under the water, then re-emerged as a Viking longboat, its deck crowded with warriors demanding their enemies' hearts and livers. Until that ship too hit an iceberg, with a boom and then another boom and then—actually . . .

Knocking. Someone was knocking on my office door.

I stowed the remains of the chicken sandwich that my mother had so lovingly assembled (dry white meat, white bread, mustard) in the top drawer of my desk just as my boss, Warren Landry, bounded in without knocking again.

Standing in my doorway with his arms braced against both sides, Warren was partly backlit by the low-wattage bulbs in the corridor. He had a Scrooge-like obsession with keeping our electric bills low. His white hair haloed him like a Renaissance apostle, and the costly wool of his dark gray suit gave off a pale luminescent shimmer. He was a few years older than my parents, but he belonged to another species that defied middle age to stay handsome, vital, irresistible to women. I'd spent my first paychecks on a new suit and tie, cheap versions of Warren's, or what I imagined Warren would wear if the world we knew ended and he no longer had any money.

Often, on his way back from lunch, Warren lurched down the hall, all jutting elbows and knees, chatting up the typing pool, leaning on the front desk, stepping into the offices of people he liked. Sometimes he lost track of who worked where. The worst insult was having him pop in, look at you, blink, shake his head, and pop out.

I was always excited to see Warren, though *excited* wasn't exactly the word. *Petrified* was more like it. I was ashamed of my craven desire to interest him, to impress him, even a little. Was it his confidence?

His mystique? Or was it simply because he was my boss at a job I'd gotten because of my uncle, who was widely disliked and feared for the power of his journal, *American Sketches*, which created and ruined careers in politics, literature, and art?

I liked the idea of having a boss. Just saying those two words, *my boss*, made me feel like a grown-up.

Everyone knew Warren's history. During World War II, he'd gone undercover for the OSS, running a psychological warfare department that spread rumors behind enemy lines. He was responsible for the spread of disinformation warning German soldiers that their wives were cheating on them with draft dodgers and Nazi bureaucrats, inspiring the soldiers to desert and go home and throw the traitors out of their beds.

Shortly after the war he and his Harvard classmate Preston Bartlett III started a small exclusive publishing company in a modest midtown suite. By the time I was hired, the firm's office—divided into spaces ranging from windowless cells like mine to Warren Landry's baronial chambers—occupied half the fourteenth floor of a limestone building with a view (for the lucky ones) of Madison Square Park. I imagined that Warren, always so frugal, must have hired the least expensive architect to design the maze of cubicles, larger offices, and minimal public spaces linked by passages in which, after working there for years, one could still get lost.

Our founders had decided that three surnames sounded more impressive than two. But Warren also liked saying, "I am the one and only Landry!" He said it with a Cheshire cat smile, owning up to his egotism, charmingly but defiantly asserting his right to name two-thirds of a business after himself. Somehow he conveyed his freedom to do whatever he wanted, perhaps because he'd grown up in a warm bath of privilege drawn by servants, a bath cooled somewhat by his contempt for all that privilege meant, which isn't to say that Warren didn't look and act like a very rich white Protestant person.

Preston Bartlett had provided the startup funds and later the fallback money. Unfortunately, the bulk of Preston's fortune now went to the private sanitarium to which he'd been confined since suffering the breakdown that was never mentioned around the office. The firm had taken a hit without Preston on board to make up the deficits and shortfalls.

Meanwhile Warren Landry had become a publishing legend for his persuasiveness, his decisiveness, his impeccable taste, for the boundless energy with which he oversaw the entire process, *A* to *Z*. He kept track of the numbers, costs and sales. He'd been known to hand-deliver books when a shipment was late. When a novel appealed to him, he read it in a weekend, though he preferred our nonfiction list: books about Abraham Lincoln, modern Europe, Napoleon, World War I; Calvin Coolidge and Woodrow Wilson, men who could have been, and probably were, Warren's distant cousins.

Even the lowliest job at Landry, Landry and Bartlett carried a certain cachet. Within days of taking the job, I began to receive, in my office mailbox, invitations to Upper East Side literary parties, where stylish young women grew more interested in me when they learned where I worked. I didn't want to be liked because I'd been brought in to tackle the flood of unsolicited manuscripts inundating the mail room. But I welcomed the attention. Once again I was content to let people believe what they wanted about who I was and where I came from, though I did mention Harvard quite often. I tried not to dwell on the idea that encouraging a misunderstanding was first cousin to a lie. I felt disloyal to my parents, ungrateful for their love and care, but I told myself that they would approve of my need—it was time, after all—to separate my history from theirs.

I affected the carefree air of a recent Ivy League graduate, Simon Putnam, a literary aristocrat born for the job he'd rightfully inherited. The people I met at parties were eager to assume that I was the real thing, perhaps because *they* were the genuine article, or because they wanted to be. I never talked about my childhood. When strangers asked where I came from, I said, "New York," which was, strictly speaking, true. I tried to seem mysterious and enigmatic. At that time, in that world, any man who didn't talk nonstop about himself and his ideas was thought to be hiding something. Which, I suppose, I was.

...

Since I'd been there, Preston Bartlett had twice come into the office, though no one could figure out why. Once, I'd been in the reception area when he arrived. I registered the wheelchair, the plaid ship's blanket, the curved shoulders, the trembling lips.

Violet, the receptionist, picked up the phone, and Elaine, our sweet-natured publicist, came out to greet the company's ailing cofounder.

She leaned over and took his hand in hers, but he snapped it back.

"I want to see the boss," he said.

"Warren's in a meeting," said Elaine.

"I want to see the real boss," he said, louder.

"Warren's in a meeting," Elaine repeated, calmly. "I'm so sorry, I really am."

Preston raised his hand in a gesture that signaled either objection or acceptance, I couldn't tell. His attendant, a burly Viking in pure white scrubs, turned his wheelchair around just sharply enough so that the invalid slapped back against his pillow. From where I stood I could see the old man smile, and I thought of how the force of gravity stretched my lips into a frozen grin, in freefall on the Cyclone.

If only I had listened to what our mad cofounder was saying, if only I had been brave enough to breach the circle of dread around him, I might have averted what happened, or at least saved myself the trouble it took to fix it.

...

Knock, knock.

"Mr. Landry! Good afternoon!"

"Warren. Please. Call me Warren." Warren Landry wanted us all, from the chief editors to the mailroom guys, to call him by his first name. Apparently this would prove that the company was an enlightened democracy and not a dictatorship ruled by ambition, intimidation, and fear. Except for a few intrepid souls, we couldn't bring ourselves to do it. Even the women he slept with called him Mr. Landry in public. The irony was that when he wasn't around, we all referred to him as Warren. Did you hear what Warren had done? What Warren said at that meeting?

"How goes it, Simon, old boy?" Warren called all the men *old boys* and *dear old boys* and all the women *sweetheart*. His diction and accent combined the elongated vowels of a New England blueblood with the dentalized plosives and flat *a*'s of a Chicago gangster.

After I'd been on the job a few months, wrangling the slush pile that kept growing, no matter what I did, Warren began stopping by my office, an airless sarcophagus barely big enough for a chair, a desk, and the stacks of manuscripts. Each time he seemed surprised by the institutional grimness that was partly the result of my refusal to put up one photo, one image or personal object. Deciding what to put on the walls would have required knowing who I was, or how I wanted others to see me. Family photos and personal totems would have marred the blank surface I hoped to project.

My boss regarded the stained green carpeting, the metal furniture, the heaps of wheat-colored envelopes. Did such squalor really exist in his airy Olympus?

By then I'd learned that Julia, my tearful predecessor, had gotten pregnant by a married biographer on our list, the author of a critically acclaimed life of Pancho Villa. I also heard rumors that Warren was the father. When Julia decided to keep the child, ignoring those who advised her to get an illegal abortion in Puerto Rico or at a secret clinic in New Jersey, she'd been "encouraged" to resign. Several co-workers told me this, separately, my first week on the job. Their tone was confidential, as if we were old friends. They told me what they thought I should know, then never spoke to me again.

Sometimes Warren looked surprised to find me at my desk—instead of Julia, I feared. And sometimes I thought that he stopped by my office just to annoy my colleagues.

He gazed past me at the bare walls, then up at the low buzzing ceiling.

"My God! How can one have room to *think* here? A few weeks in this cell, and we'll have a full confession out of you."

"A confession of what?"

"Joking, old boy," he said. "I was just winding you up." Warren used a lot of Briticisms—*taking the piss*, *having you on*, *winding you up*—that I assumed he'd picked up in the OSS. He smiled. "Or did you think I meant it? Hold on, dear boy. What *do* you have to confess?"

"I was too," I lied. "I mean I was joking too. I was joking."

"Ha. One *joking* would have sufficed."

I would have offered Warren a chair if I'd had one. It was too awkward to give him mine. So he remained standing uncomfortably close to my desk.

This was before I understood why Warren stopped in so often, what he wanted from me. At the time I imagined that he might be one of those Harvard graduates (I have since met many) who harbor a reflexive, misguided respect for their fellow alumni.

Our having gone to the same school meant nothing. We'd had different educations. Warren had hosted the Fly Club's black-tie parties, to which swan-necked women wore cocktail dresses and their grandmothers' pearls. He'd edited the literary magazine and assembled a staff that bridged the gap between rumpled poets with fake British accents and old-money legacy students.

And me? An undergraduate Caliban, I'd hunkered in the lowest level of Widener Library, which I left on weekends to see my Radcliffe girlfriend, Marianna, an Asian Studies major with whom I had friendly, tentative sex in my dorm. I preferred my room to hers, where I felt inhibited by her statuettes of the Buddha and Hindu gods watching what we did. At my all-male high school, I'd learned nothing about women. Marianna had gone to boarding school, where she'd learned a little more than I had. She'd decided that she was my girlfriend, and I'd seen no reason to object.

One autumn weekend we visited her parents in Cape Ann. The rambling farmhouse was as foreign to me as Kublai Khan's palace. Her parents liked my being a Harvard student—and the fact that Marianna and I had no plans to stay together. Her father showed me to my room, in a chilly wing of the house, far from Marianna's. His stern face said: No sneaking around. He needn't have worried. It wasn't that sort of affair. I wouldn't be lying awake all night, tormented by lust for his daughter.

Just before the end of senior year, Marianna was awarded a graduate fellowship to study Japanese art at Yale. It was humiliating to admit, even to myself, how bitterly I resented her getting the future intended for me. I told myself that it was all about who she was and who *I* was: further evidence of the inequality, the unfairness of the world. I wanted to be one of those to whom success came easily. All you had to do was be born into a particular family, in a particular place, and the Three Kings rode up on camels, bringing you frankincense and myrrh, opportunities and riches.

I'd been happy at college. I'd liked my classes, my girlfriend, my roommates and friends, all of whom had scattered after graduation. Marianna and I promised to call or write, but it never seemed like the right time, and all that summer I'd had nothing to say. We'd lost touch. Every so often, I met a former classmate at one of the literary parties. We talked about getting together, but we never did.

When I tried to imagine Warren's college experience, I felt a sense of loss, of having missed out on something, a regret that bordered on grief. I'd gone to the wrong parties. I hadn't had as much fun.

"Working hard?" asked Warren.

It took me a moment to understand what he'd said, then another to make sure that it was a question and not a crack about catching me napping. In fact the work *was* hard: steeling myself to read and reject the manuscripts piling up in my office. It was disturbing to realize that, after six months, I still felt overwhelmed. Each day I labored to reduce the stack of envelopes that kept growing despite my attempts to shrink it. Boredom and pity and anger still warred in my heart when I read submissions like *Herod's Daughter*, a novel set in Biblical times about a young woman's struggle to save Jesus; *Prairie Dogs*, a shoot-'em-up cowboy saga; *Tears in the Apple Pie*, a memoir by a housewife whose husband ran off with his great-aunt; and *Pinocchio-land*, a dystopian fantasy about a future in which everyone's nose gets longer when they tell a lie. This last one struck too close to home, and I decided to omit the consolatory postscript from my rejection letter.

"It's . . . fun," I said. "I enjoy it." I touched my nose, involuntarily. My face turned mandrill red.

"Fun, is it?" Warren said. "Nonstop fun, I'm sure."

I believed (or wanted to believe) that Warren had a natural sympathy for bookish guys like me. People said he admired intelligence, that he helped young people, mostly young men but occasionally women, even some who weren't pretty, even some he didn't sleep with. He'd stayed cordial with several former girlfriends at the office. He had a wife and five sons at home in Darien, a family no one at work had ever seen, and, people said, a formal portrait of himself aging in his attic.

His employees knew not to worry if he didn't look us in the eye. During the editorial meetings, at which I was never offered a seat at the table but relegated to the chair symbolically nearest the

door, Warren didn't look directly at anyone except our chief publicist, Elaine, with whom he was rumored to be—or to have been—
romantically involved. Often Warren seemed half asleep, then roused
himself to deliver a remark so perceptive that the room fell silent and
everything stopped. I remember him doing that, but I can't recall
even one of his famously incisive remarks.

I do remember him turning in his swivel chair, facing the wall, and
saying, "The young no longer study history, so we're doomed to repeat it. In ten years, no one will remember the war, or what we fought
for. Hitler? Who was he? We must become their memory, *be* their
memory, because ours was nuked out of existence when we bombed
Hiroshima." He had a repertoire of speeches he used to fill a silence
or change a subject.

His favorite words were *democracy* and *an educated electorate*. Those
were his deities, his ideals, though early on I sensed that those words
had a different meaning for Warren than they had for me. His people
had been in this country for generations before mine. I wondered:
Why should it matter so much if a family came from somewhere and
not from somewhere else?

"So, Simon, old boy, what are we working on? What keeps us
burning the midnight oil?"

We both knew that no midnight oil was being burned. I was hardly
about to stay up into the wee hours reading *The Emperor's Concubine*
or *I Married a Minister.* After all that pointless and discouraging reading, I'd finally been given an actual book of my own to shepherd
through the final stages of production.

Autumn Light was a slender volume of watery nature poetry by a
woman named Florence Durgin, who'd had a very modest success
with *The Burning Boy*, a suite of inspirational sonnets about adopting
an orphan boy badly scarred in the atomic bombing of Nagasaki. The
Japanese kid, now in his late teens, hadn't adjusted well to his new life
and was facing a gun possession charge, so a sequel seemed unlikely.

But Warren cared about Florence, who had a two-book contract. Warren hadn't said much when he gave me the manuscript, except to warn me that Florence's meditations on the forest would likely sell less than two hundred copies.

For a heartbeat I forgot Florence's name, though she was my only writer. I felt guilty for not having read her first collection. I'd promised myself that I would. I could visualize the cover. The title, the author's name. That was as far as I'd gotten.

"You know . . . that book of poetry."

"Poor Florence." Warren's sigh suggested that Florence's sad fate linked us: two decent men whose hearts brimmed with manly sympathy for a damsel in distress.

"I admire the woman," he said. "Be kind to her."

"I always am." I'd never been *unkind* to Florence, but I didn't exactly fake joy when she dropped by the office with variant drafts of her book, indistinguishable poems to be added and subtracted. I promised myself to be kinder. I'd invite Florence for coffee. I didn't have the nerve to ask Warren if the company would pay me to take her to lunch. I would read her first book. It was the least I could do.

"A suffering human," said Warren. "As we all are. Remind me: What's the new one's title?"

"*Autumn Light*," I said.

"Good God," said Warren. "Who in the holy Jesus hell came up with that one?"

It struck me that Warren might have exceeded his customary two lunchtime martinis. He listed slightly to one side. His upper lip stuck to his teeth.

He brandished a thick cardboard folder the color of dried blood.

I prayed: Let it be a manuscript. Let it be the book that will show Warren what I can do.

. . .

There are moments when our desire is so powerful and so focused that the object of that desire seems to float before us, a shimmering mirage. Our longing is so intense that we can almost persuade ourselves that the hoped-for event has occurred, the dream has come true. Fate has figured out what we need and decided to hand it over.

I had such a clear, strong idea of the book I *wanted* Warren to be holding that it was almost as if I'd already read it—or written it.

The manuscript I imagined was a historical novel set among the Vikings, as stirring and eventful as the greatest sagas, but with a simpler narrative line for the modern reader without the time and patience for archaic locutions, genealogies, and subplots. This book had been written expressly for me. I was its ideal reader, the perfect choice, the *only* choice, to edit and improve it, to help it find its audience. My seemingly impractical education would turn out to be useful in a wonderfully unpredictable way.

I pictured myself with my briefcase, taking the blood-colored folio to the 42nd Street public library, where I could work without distraction as editor and fact-checker both. I felt the joy of looking forward to work I respected and enjoyed. For the first time it seemed likely that I might come to love my job. At least I'd be back in the library.

Warren said, "Let's put *Autumn Light* on hold, okay? Push Florence's poems till next season. I have something better for you. Something that might actually be, as you say, *fun*."

Since then I have learned to be on guard whenever anyone suggests I might have fun with something. But all I thought at the time was that Warren was offering to pay me to have fun. *Paid* and *fun* defined a good job. My life was about to change for the better.

Warren suspended the blood-colored folder above my desk, holding it with both hands, goggling at it, mock-warily, as if dropping it might damage the gunmetal surface. He laughed his bark-laugh (he had several fake laughs) and dropped the folder on my desk so hard I flinched and was embarrassed.

"Relax," Warren smiled. "It's a novel. Not a hand grenade. An interesting piece of fiction by an unusual new writer. When you get around to reading it, I hope you'll tell us what you think. No rush, I would normally say. But in this case . . . well, if we dither, one of our rivals might recognize its sales potential, *pounce*—and snatch it from under our noses."

Why did I never wonder why Warren would entrust such a potentially popular book to a beginner? Beneath my youthful diffidence and insecurity lurked the egomania of a Roman emperor.

"I'll start reading this afternoon," I said.

"Very good then," said Warren. "It'll require a bit of effort, but not major work. And if I may say so, it's a damn sight better than *Pinocchioland*."

How did he know about *Pinocchioland*? Did he really read every word that came through the office? The manuscripts piled up on my floor always seemed to have been unopened.

"Two months. Two and a half. It's the middle of February now, so May Day at the latest. The international Communist holiday—what could be more appropriate? I'll expect this on my desk by then."

"Sure," I said. "I can do that."

He looked hard at me as if I was supposed to know what his look meant. Then he gave up and said, "Dear boy, aren't you curious? Don't you even want to know what this literary sensation is called?"

"Yes! Of course!" I pried the manuscript out of its folder and read the title page:

The Vixen, the Patriot, and the Fanatic
   A Novel
   By Anya Partridge

"Quite a title," I said.

"Hot stuff, am I right?" Warren hooked his thumbs under his

lapels. "I thought of it myself. The author wanted something rather *artsy* and inappropriate for a book of this sort." Was he winking, or was the fluorescent light playing tricks with one eyelid?

"What was *her* title?"

I watched Warren pretend to think. "Our author wanted to call it *The Burning*. Yes, that was it. *The Burning*. Dear boy, are you feeling all right? You've gone quite pale."

"The Burning" was the title of my undergraduate thesis about *Njal's Saga*. I'd focused on the scene in which a wise man named Njal and his family are burned alive in their home. Had I mentioned that to Warren? I didn't think so. Maybe it was a coincidence. Not such a strange one, really. *The* and *burning* are common English words. There was also a chance that I'd blabbed about it at the drunken office Christmas party that I barely recalled. I hoped I hadn't, but if I had, I was flattered that Warren remembered and was joking, or testing me in some way.

"I thought *The Burning* was a brilliant title compared to the other one she suggested, which was, let me think, *A Simple Box of Jell-O*. I assume you know she was referencing the torn halves of the Jell-O boxes that identified the spies in the Rosenberg ring."

The Rosenbergs? Had I heard Warren right? Was he telling me that this novel, with its potboiler title, was about Ethel and Julius? My throat had swollen shut. I couldn't trust myself to speak. But I had to say something.

"I do," I croaked. "I do know."

"Of course you do. An amazing detail, no? Who could make that stuff up?"

Warren waited for me to agree. "Amazing."

"Most readers—*our* readers—will get the reference, but who in God's name would buy a spy thriller called *A Simple Box of Jell-O*?"

Warren waited. It was my turn to speak. "Maybe we could call it *The Vixen, the Patriot, the Fanatic, the Burning, and a Simple Box of Jell-O*."

Warren tried another laugh, louder and more explosive. "Good! That's *very* good. You're catching on. How about *The Vixen, the Patriot, and the Fanatic Burn a Simple Box of Jell-O?* Better, don't you think? Go ahead. Give our little vixen a look-see. Read me that *marvelously wild* first sentence."

I turned past the title page and read:

Like a handsome ocean liner slicing through the waves, the attorney general sailed through the prison hallway. He seemed confident, but he was on edge. He was finally meeting Esther Rosenstein, the notoriously buxom and beautiful Mata Hari who'd almost slithered through the dragnet the FBI dropped around her.

I felt like a spelunker crawling through the opening of a cave that I already knew would be too narrow to squeeze out of. I imagined my mother reading this. No, I thought, I can't do this. I felt a shiver of dread.

"Esther Rosenstein?" I said. "*Really?*"

"I know, I know. Esther and Junius Rosenstein. Maybe you can persuade Miss Partridge to change her characters' names. If you can manage that, our lawyers will be breaking out the champagne. Our readers will know who the author means no matter what she calls them. I know the Rosenbergs are a sensitive subject. But in a way, that's the whole point. Timely! Trust me. The book's not bad."

I wanted to believe that. One paragraph wasn't enough to be sure that the writer was slandering Ethel. *You will see to it that our names are kept bright and unsullied by lies.* In January, the Rosenbergs' lawyer, Emanuel Bloch, had dropped dead of a heart attack. When I thought of him reading Ethel's letter, how his voice had broken on *lies,* I felt I was hearing the voice of the dead with a message from the almost-dead: a client who predeceased him by months.

"I know, my dear boy. It's not *War and Peace.* Okay, maybe it *is* bad, but it's not *bad bad,* and it could make some sorely needed money.

It's *a little bad*, in a few places. Your job would be to make those places *less bad*. You could even make them *a little good*."

So what if Anya Partridge, whom I pictured as a bookish woman in late middle age, had decided to make her Esther Rosenstein prettier than Ethel Rosenberg? In her photos Ethel looked like a kindly, girlish, dumpy mother of two, not a sexpot Mata Hari. But already I sensed that beautifying Ethel/Esther would be the least of the novel's problems.

Warren sighed. "My boy, can I be honest?"

"Of course, Mr. Landry."

"Please. Call me Warren. *Totally* honest?"

"Of course." This was not going to be good news. "Warren."

"Look around."

It was awkward, pretending to look around my tiny office in which there was nothing to see.

"Not in here. Out there." He gestured toward the corridor. "May I close the door?"

Even with the door closed, he lowered his voice. "Would you like to guess how long it's been since the rent has been paid on all that talent and brains out there? Let me give you a hint. *Reputation* doesn't keep the lights on. *Distinguished* doesn't fend off one's creditors. Care to take a wild guess?"

Any answer would have been wrong. "I have no idea."

"Good. Save your ideas for Miss Partridge's novel. The point is, we are hoping that the sales of the little *Vixen* will get us over a rough patch and allow us to continue."

Warren could be vague and elliptical, but now he couldn't have been clearer.

"I understand."

"Oh . . . And one more *amazing* detail."

He picked up the folder and dug around, then pulled out a photo that he placed ceremonially on my desk.

"Presenting . . . Miss Anya Partridge!"

A startlingly beautiful woman looked up at me. Her huge dark eyes were ringed with kohl, her black hair bobbed like the star of a 1920s silent film. She wore a trench coat, not entirely concealing a filmy black slip dress. Smoking a thin black cigar in an ivory holder, she lounged against the pillows of a canopied, elaborately carved Chinese bed.

Ever since the outrageously seductive jacket photo of a sleepy-eyed Truman Capote had helped put his debut novel on the bestseller list, our industry was awakening to the commercial value of the author portrait.

I said, "This will blow Capote out of the water."

"Smart boy! My thoughts exactly. What would you call her look? Hong Kong brothel meets Berlin cabaret? Lotte Lenya? Pinch of Marlene Dietrich? Soupçon of Rita Hayworth? Let's find a more literary model . . . Let's say . . . Colette, only juicier. To coin a phrase . . . a bad-girl hothouse tomato!"

Warren and Anya watched me extricate myself from her force field.

"Simon, old boy. One caveat. Our author is a bit of a recluse. She may not agree to meet you. That shouldn't pose a problem. But some editors might find it tricky to work with a voice on the phone."

"I can deal with that." I didn't want to work on this commodification of Ethel's tragedy. It was morally indefensible. But I had agreed. I'd succumbed to my lowest—my least admirable—impulses. I wanted to meet its author. And I couldn't say no to Warren.

"Well! Good to hear. It would mean a lot to me, and"—he cleared his throat—"it will likely speed your exit from this coffin of a so-called office and into some more desirable real estate at Landry, Landry and Bartlett."

"That sounds great," I said. And it did. I wanted a successful—an enviable—career. I wanted to rise in the organization. I wanted to find my place in the literary world. I wanted to *be someone*. Preferably someone like Warren.

"Great," said Warren. "Well, then."

He stopped on his way to the door and spun, a sharp Fred Astaire half circle that ended in a momentary totter. "One more thing. The most important thing. I almost forgot." He put his forefinger to his lips. "Tell no one about this book. Not yet. I don't want the word to get out. Not your mother. Not your girlfriend. Not your best pal after three scotches."

"I don't have a girlfriend, and I don't drink scotch."

"Not even your mother, Simon. *Not even your own mother.*"

"No worries about that." Of course I wasn't going to tell Mom that we were publishing a bodice-ripper about the Rosenbergs. But Warren's warning was disturbing. I considered every likely and unlikely explanation, but none of them—other than his somehow knowing about my mother's connection to Ethel—made sense. It had to be a coincidence, like Anya Partridge wanting to call her book *The Burning*. Like my being asked to work on it. Me, out of all the aspiring young editors in New York.

Warren said, "I always think the ends justify the means, but this time the ends *completely* justify the means. One popular novel, in let's say *questionable good taste*, won't destroy our reputation. It's a funny thing, Simon. Usually I only care about means. I give two shits about consequences. But in this case it's the consequences, *the hoped-for consequences*, that should make all of us give *less* than two shits about the means. The gods of literature are just going to have to take a step back and appreciate the economic realities of our business."

That was the moment, *way past* the moment, when I could have refused to work on the book. Without incriminating anyone, without disclosing a family secret, I should have explained that *The Vixen* wasn't my kind of novel. With all due respect, I hadn't gone into publishing to work on commercial fiction based on recent events. There was no need to say—in fact it was as if I'd forgotten—that I'd gone into publishing because it was the only job I could get. Nor was there any reason to add that I felt the novel was beneath me, that it horrified me to imagine how my parents and Uncle Maddie would react if they knew what I was doing.

I said nothing. I didn't protest. In those days, declining to work on a book about the Rosenbergs' guilt might have seemed suspicious, not that I imagined Warren reporting me to the authorities. I should have had the courage of my convictions and said no because it was wrong to devote myself to refining this grotesque insult to the Rosenbergs' memory.

Saying that might have gotten me fired. But that wasn't my fear. Not entirely.

I complied out of laziness, passivity, and because agreeing is always easier than refusing. I had complicated feelings about Warren. I was embarrassed by my abject desire to earn his respect. My longing to be admitted into the club of men like Warren Landry, to grow up to be a man like Warren, was in conflict with my uncertainty about who he was underneath that glossy hair, those magnificent suits, all that charm and charisma.

"Too bad," Warren said. "About the girls and the scotch. We'll fix the girlfriend-and-scotch problem. I mean, the *lack* of girlfriend and the no-scotch problem. Meanwhile, not a soul. Can you swear to that? Scout's honor?"

I hadn't been allowed to join the Boy Scouts. Too military, too fascist. My parents didn't want me wearing a uniform of any kind. The Boy Scouts weren't Hitler Youth, but my parents were unrelenting.

My father had been in the navy, at Okinawa. I found an old photo album with a faded shot of Dad standing with a group of men, looking down at a tangle of corpses in Japanese uniforms. No matter how I begged, how often I asked, he would never talk about the war. I'd stopped asking. It was his past, his history. He could keep it to himself. Did he and Mom ever talk about it? I assumed they did.

I held up my hand. "Scout's honor."

"So I'll wait to hear from you about this," Warren said. "Great chatting with you."

"Me too," I said, nonsensically. Me too? I was waiting to hear from me too? It was great for me chatting with me too? After Warren's footsteps faded down the hall, I went to the men's room and looked in the mirror to see what someone this awkward—this *embarrassing*—looked like.

CHAPTER 2

I brought the manuscript home and hid it under my bed, though my parents never entered my room without knocking, not even when my mother—lately, my father—needed to vacuum. I had no reason to put off reading the book until they were asleep, but it seemed right. I felt like a kid smuggling porn into the family sanctum.

Esther Rosenstein appeared on the first page.

The prosecutor sensed her presence from all the way down the corridor, overpowering the usual prison smells—disinfectant, sweat—with the crazed perfume of estrous animal passion.

Estrous animal passion? I read on:

Most of the prisoners hid in their cells, curled up in their bunks, but Esther wound her arms around the bars like the serpent in the Garden of Eden and positioned her body in a way that best displayed her ample, shapely breasts. Let the lawyer come to her. She had plenty to tell him. How the Communists were right, how Russia had a better system than our sham democracy.

It got worse in places, presumably the places that Warren wanted me to improve. Esther was a "raven-haired beauty" with "Elizabeth Taylor–violet eyes."

You will see to it that our names are kept bright and unsullied by lies.

I dropped the manuscript on the floor and fell back against the pillows.

After a while, I drifted into the living room to compare what I'd read to my mother's bookshelf shrine to Ethel. A half dozen photos floated in store-bought frames. If a stranger walked in, we would have hidden them, but no strangers ever walked in.

Here was Ethel and Julius's last kiss. Ethel's back was twisted away, her face hidden, her lips smashed against her husband's. Her arm was bare, one hand clutching her white purse. Behind his wire-rimmed glasses, Julius's eyes were shut. How did he embrace his wife wearing handcuffs? Did she slip inside the loop of his arms? They kissed as if they were alone in the world, as if no flashbulbs were popping, as if no one were shouting their names, as if they would never kiss again.

When my mother put up this photo, Dad said, "In front of the reporters! The warden and the guard went nuts. They stuck a table between them. A table! After that, new rules. No physical contact without a fence."

"How do you know that?" said Mom.

"The store's five minutes from the courts," said Dad. "Lawyers and cops come in."

The next photo showed the Rosenbergs separated by a fence, slumped inside a police van. The time for kisses was over. They didn't look at each other. The seasons had changed. Someone had brought Ethel a pretty velvet coat with a fur collar.

Beside this was her mug shot. At thirty-four, she looked like a perky teen dressed for a date. She wore a shiny white shirtwaist dress with cap sleeves and a pleated skirt, white sandals, white gloves with ruffled cuffs. Bright lipstick defined her Betty Boop lips. She had an Old World Jewish body: squat, no waist, wide hips. A studio portrait, except for the harsh light and the letter board: *FBI-NYC*. On the measuring stick, she reached five one. She'd been told not to move.

Look into the camera, don't blink, don't flinch. Whatever you do, don't smile.

In front of this photo were three more intimate ones. Two of Ethel at the beach, in an unflattering bathing suit. Rings of makeup made her eyes look sunken and feral. In one she was very young, beaming beside young Julius in snazzy black trunks. In the other she cradled a child in her lap.

It wasn't like looking at a photo of a woman in a bathing suit. Ethel wasn't pretty or sexy. She was Ethel, and she was dead.

In the last photo, cut from my mother's high school graduation yearbook, the same yearbook in which the photo on Mom's onyx ring appeared, Ethel held a modest bouquet: six roses. Beaming into the future. Always a smile for the neighbors, the little mouth with that big voice belting out "The Star-Spangled Banner." Didn't that prove she loved her country?

I couldn't tell Warren Landry that the vixen once lived upstairs from my mother, nor could I tell my mother about the book. It would be easy—necessary—to keep *The Vixen* a secret, though I would have to lie to the people I loved and respected most.

...

This was the height of the Cold War, the Red Scare. The world awaited the outbreak of nuclear conflict between the US and Russia. People behaved as if a real war were being fought around us, as if missiles were aimed at our living rooms. Sooner or later, the bomb would fall. Soviet agents were everywhere, masquerading as ordinary Americans until they were exposed, jailed or deported. The secret war played out in the beauty salon, the schoolroom, the church social, and the garage. Anyone could be accused. Anyone's life could be destroyed. Everyone was paranoid. Everyone was afraid.

Some of Ethel's relatives didn't attend her funeral. A few changed their names. The papers reported on the tragic struggle over who would adopt their two sons. Some relatives feared the consequences. Guilt by association was guilt.

Meanwhile, my own private war had broken out between my conscience and my ambition, my passivity and my wanting to do the right thing. I was being asked to edit a book of lies about a woman who could no longer defend herself, if she ever could. My family would have been horrified.

I wanted to keep my job. I wanted to be the hero who saved Landry, Landry and Bartlett from bankruptcy. I wanted to be promoted. I didn't want to take a stand. Most of all, I didn't want to be forced to make a decision.

Maybe I was panicking needlessly. Maybe *The Vixen* got better as it went along. Plenty of authors start out too strong, thinking the reader has to be grabbed and shaken into paying attention. Surely I could persuade the writer to tone down the beginning.

Lying in bed, in my parents' house, I planned my first conversation with Anya Partridge. Working it out had a lulling effect, but for the first time since college, I couldn't sleep. Neither fully awake nor tired, I read on:

As he strode into the courtroom for the arraignment, Jake Crain felt every eye on him. It wasn't just his chiseled features, his thick dark hair, the cut of his costly suit. People were angling to see what a legal genius looked like.

Crain was the state's star prosecutor. He had convicted the killer of the three schoolteachers, a millionaire embezzler, a copycat kidnapper who tried to re-create the Lindbergh baby case. He got them the maximum sentences. He was fearless and focused on making sure that these villains no longer endangered innocent American lives. But could he do his job when he so wanted to save—to take in his arms—the irresistible woman on trial?

Well, that wasn't *quite* so bad. Perhaps our hero, Jake, could be turned into a more compassionate soul, less volatile, less inclined to torment the Rosenbergs/Rosensteins and less stirred by an unhealthy attraction to Ethel/Esther.

This trial would be his greatest challenge. Esther Rosenstein had been charged with treason and conspiracy. It was a capital case. Crain could not allow the jury to be moved by this beautiful Mata Hari's two little sons, children she'd neglected as she seduced patriotic American males into helping her and her husband destroy our democratic system. President Eisenhower called Esther the unrepentant one. He'd said that she was stronger than the husband.

A fellow lawyer had warned Crain not to look directly at Esther. She was Circe: one look and he'd turn to stone—or, more likely, jelly. Men were powerless against her.

Circe? The writer must have meant Medusa. I'd make a note to correct that. I would tell Anya about the witches in folktales who could turn you to stone.

In my fantasy Anya was suitably impressed.

Crain ignored his colleague. That first time he'd seen Esther, in her cell, pressed against the bars, their eyes had locked, and they'd known that they were equally matched. Was that lawyer-speak for overwhelming passion? Jake would have to wait, be vigilant, stay professional, and find out.

I'd cut the word *overwhelming*. I sighed and turned the page.

Now he saw Esther, across the courtroom, behind the table at which she sat beside her lawyer, Joseph Frank.

Frank was a pissant that, with one flick of his fingers, Jake could spin out of the courthouse. Esther was the force he would need to contend with as he struggled to defend our way of life.

Esther stared at Jake with her lidded, smoky eyes. His eyes devoured her glossy hair, her white neck, the fur-collared velvet coat that strained to contain her breasts. He tried not to look at her like a man, but like a lawyer trying to understand why such a handsome specimen would commit capital treason.

I'd change *his eyes devoured* to *he saw*. I opened the manuscript at random and read an extremely peculiar scene in which Esther mumbles prayers before an altar, hidden in a kitchen cupboard, in which she keeps the pelt of a dead fox.

It was Esther's spirit creature, the magic object she consulted in uncertain times.

Enough. I let the manuscript drop. I fell asleep and dreamed yet another transparent dream: Our house was on fire. I was across town and couldn't find my way home. Someone was inside the house, but I didn't know who. Then my parents and I were inside the burning house, even as I watched the fire from a distance. Waking, I smelled smoke, but it was part of the dream, and I went back to sleep.

...

The next morning I woke up and knew I had to move out of my parents' apartment. I had to escape my mother's photos of Ethel. I couldn't work on *The Vixen* there. I couldn't *think* about the novel without picturing Ethel's sweet graduation portrait—and the photo of my mother on the flip side of her onyx ring. Everything seemed like a sign: Time to go.

I asked around at the office. The elevator operator knew someone whose cousin was renting out a studio apartment on East 29th Street and First Avenue, across from Bellevue Hospital. Across from the morgue. On the phone the cousin told me why I didn't want to live there. The apartment was old, noisy, dark. The neighborhood was hell. He didn't want to waste our time, taking me to see it. When I heard how much he was asking, I told him it sounded perfect.

All night I heard howling ambulances, even though my bedroom was at the back of the building, facing a brick wall. On the street there were screaming, sobbing people who'd come to the morgue to identify the bodies of loved ones. Despite the obvious drawbacks, I liked it there. I could afford it on my salary with minimal help from my parents. It was mine. It was home.

My parents were sad when I moved out, or so they said. They'd gotten used to my absence before. It was time for me to leave the nest, or so they told themselves. Now that I have grown children, I understand that such feelings can be mixed.

I loved them, but I needed to go. I had my own life in the city.

My apartment was a fifth-floor walk-up. I could hear the cockroaches scatter when I turned the key in the lock. My parents bought me a mattress, and I purchased some kitchen things from the Goodwill, enough to make coffee and toast. Back then you could still salvage decent furniture left on the sidewalk for the garbage trucks. The apartment was my refuge, my sanctuary. It was where I could hibernate and pore over Anya Partridge's novel and try to decide what to do.

After what seemed like a decent interval, I told Warren that I would work on the book. He seemed to think I'd already agreed, which, I supposed, I had.

I said that I would have more specific comments to make to him and the writer after I'd read it again. Meanwhile I persuaded myself that I could make it less awful. I could improve it. Another editor—one whose mother hadn't known Ethel—wouldn't have cared enough to bother.

Warren had told me we could alter the characters' names. *If* the writer agreed. I told myself that would help. I rehearsed how I would overcome Anya's hesitations and persuade her to make the changes I wanted.

Meanwhile I kept track of the slush pile. Every so often I'd find a book that was not all that much worse than *The Vixen*. Why was Anya Partridge's novel better than the books I rejected? I knew why: unlike *I, Barbarian* and *The Igloo Lover*, *The Vixen* was expected to make money. Warren had ticked off the reasons: it was timely, it was provocative, it was a page-turner, and it had just enough sex so that readers could be titillated without worrying that they might be reading—or, worse, *caught* reading—a dirty book.

CHAPTER 3

In the midst of my moral crisis, my uncle Madison Putnam called and invited me to lunch at his favorite French restaurant, Le Vieux Moulin, on East 53rd Street.

Like many people, I was afraid of Uncle Maddie. He could be snobbish, mean, and dismissive. My mother said he was that kind of guy: you felt as if he were poking you in the ribs, even when he was nowhere near you. My father—his brother—steered clear of Maddie at family celebrations. But it was hard to avoid him because from the minute he showed up, he'd start trailing us around, asking how long we thought the "festivities" would last and how soon he and Aunt Cheryl could get the hell out without hurting everyone's feelings and making the family hate him more than they already did. I didn't think our family hated him. I thought they wanted him to like them.

Even though I was scared of him, I was always disappointed and vaguely insulted when he left our family parties early. I wanted him there as a buffer between me and my father's boisterous relatives, the great-aunts who pinched my cheek till it hurt, the great-uncles who slipped back into Yiddish when they drank, the second cousins in their blue suits, the wives with scarlet nails, turquoise eyelids, tangerine hair, a flock of exotic parrots stuffed into sparkly dresses. I wanted to follow my uncle out of those wedding venues and banquet halls, not so much my actual uncle as what he represented, *who he was*. I wanted to accompany him back to the world he was rushing off to rejoin. It didn't occur to me that I was already in the process of leaving those jolly family parties, nor did I realize that once I left, I could never get back in. My relatives saw me differently. They seemed different when I saw them.

I had a lot to thank my uncle for. I believed he was on my side. He'd gotten me my job at Landry, Landry and Bartlett. His dazzling career as a critic and public intellectual had shown my parents that one could be rich, successful, and widely respected without becoming a doctor or lawyer.

Aunt Cheryl came from money. Years ago, they'd had a formal wedding at her parents' Sutton Place townhouse. Even so, we wondered: How did Uncle Maddie manage to live as lavishly as his wealthy friends and the famous writers he published? How did he afford his palatial Upper West Side apartment on his salary as the editor of a monthly journal, even with his lecture fees and the help of the magazine's donors? How did he summer in the Hamptons, support a succession of girlfriends, and pay for the costly home for the disabled, in Western Massachusetts, where my cousin Frank had lived since early childhood? The family never mentioned Frank, and I'd never met him.

I hadn't seen my uncle for more than a year before I went to work for Warren. Whatever Uncle Maddie did to get me my job hadn't required my input. There hadn't been an interview, or even an application. When I'd called to thank Uncle Maddie, our conversation was brief and polite.

He wasn't someone I felt I could ask for help. I didn't want him to think I was weak. But I welcomed his invitation to lunch. I was desperate for advice.

Forbidden by Warren to mention *The Vixen*, I had no one to ask: Was it ordinary for an editor to be obsessed by his author's photo? Was it normal to spend every minute dwelling on what I thought of as *my Anya Partridge problem*? Was it standard procedure to dream about "my" writer?

Even then, in that ignorant era when men were no better than Neanderthals, I knew it was wrong for an editor to masturbate over his author's picture. But wasn't that what Warren hoped? That the book-buying public would have dreams like mine? Wasn't that the purpose of Anya Partridge's portrait—to make everyone, male and female, long to crawl into that rumpled Chinese bed and give her a reason to put out that vampy cigar? Now, when I woke to the smell of smoke, I didn't think of burning houses but of Anya's cigarillo.

No wonder I had erotic dreams. I lost count of how many men Esther Rosenstein slept with, in *The Vixen*. Not that the act was described in detail—this was the 1950s—but there were recurring motifs. "Esther and the FBI man were finally alone. No one would ever know what they did during their 'clandestine' meeting." Or, "Esther stretched her supple body and lay back on the hotel bed as the Russian scientist opened the bottle of French champagne and double-locked the door."

Much of the novel was about the Rosensteins' crime, their love for the Soviet Union and hatred for the United States. But the heart of the book was the sexual tension between Esther and the attorney general, a flame ignited in Esther's cell and complicating the trial for everyone. Would their attraction compromise the government's "airtight" case against the Russian spy ring? Would Esther and the prosecutor steal a moment to uncork the champagne and double-lock the door? These questions were meant to hook the reader.

One dramatic subtheme was Esther's inability to be satisfied by her husband, Junius. "Even in the act of love with Junius, *in flagrante delicto*—or *flagrante* without the *delicto*—Esther found herself wondering if there were really no calories in an average-sized serving of Jell-O. As much as she enjoyed making love, she could never forget that the fate of the American Communist Party depended on her keeping her figure."

Those were some of the novel's funnier lines. But they were also depressing. Was Anya purposely being humorous? I had no one to ask.

Until then I'd thought of sex as something you did with your Radcliffe girlfriend in your dorm on Saturday night until visiting hours were over and you got dressed and walked her home along with all the other couples who'd been doing the same thing. It was fun, it felt good, you shared a jolt of pleasure. I didn't understand why lovers in books wrecked their lives just for the congenial warmth I felt for Marianna. My relationship with an author photo was already more passionate and obsessive than anything I had experienced with my flesh-and-blood girlfriend.

...

As I worked my way through Anya's novel, I noticed a page was missing.

The gap occurred in a crucial scene involving the torn box of Jell-O, the innocent children's dessert, the symbol of the American home that, ripped into pieces, identified one traitor to another.

Anya had changed things. It was no longer the spy and Esther's brother who recognized each other when the Jell-O box pieces matched up. Now it was a Russian agent and the Rosenbergs/Rosensteins themselves whose secret signal was the puzzle that spelled out J-e-l-l-O.

In the manuscript, page 114 ended like this:

Esther went from man to man and took the two halves of the Jell-O box. The spies were downing vodka shots, so at first they hardly noticed. But they could hardly ignore the way Esther held the box, slightly above her head, tilted toward her mouth, as if she were eating low-hanging fruit.

While her husband and the Russian agent watched, she licked off the leftover powder. There was no leftover powder. The cardboard fragments had been in the agent's pocket and the coffee can in Esther's cupboard. Still she flicked at the lint, the coffee grounds, the intimate detritus that these homemade espionage tools had gathered in their dark corners.

"Mmm," she said. "Amazing. Good to the very last drop."

There was no page 115.

Page 116 began with the Russian agent thanking the Rosensteins for their help in securing a lasting peace through the sharing of scientific information that rightfully belonged to the workers of the world.

I thought of Julia, my pregnant predecessor. I remembered her saying that sometimes writers omitted pages to catch the reader at the publishing house for not finishing their manuscript. I didn't think that Anya would do that, especially since her novel appeared to have come by a more direct route than over-the-transom. I still didn't know how it got to Warren. I'd asked him twice, but he'd evaded the question. It hadn't come through *my* office. I sensed that Anya Partridge wasn't the type to exchange advice with other suspicious writers on how to expose the lazy editor who lied about reading her work.

Anya, or someone, would find the lost page or re-create the missing scene. All I had to do was be patient and not tell anyone about *The Vixen*.

. . .

In the midst of every conversation, every casual chat at a party, I'd think: Can this seemingly honest guy be trusted? Can I tell this perfectly nice woman about *The Vixen*? Talking about it—to anyone—might relieve some of the pressure. I even considered therapy. There must have been a doctor willing to help me tackle the conflict between principle and ambition. But therapy was expensive. I couldn't afford a doctor *and* an apartment.

The only reason I considered confiding in my uncle was because he was my blood relative. He was the only person who knew Warren and my family. Otherwise I wouldn't have told him anything I didn't want the world to know. There were so many ways he could betray me at minimal risk to himself. My uncle, being the prick he was, might think it was funny. A game. The game of the plume of smoke rising from his nephew's head. So what if he ruined my life for the fun of serving up some gossip about a junior employee? Without incriminating my parents, without mentioning my mother's connection to Ethel, he could say I was a commie fellow traveler subverting Warren's patriotic efforts to fictionalize the crime of a convicted spy—and keep the firm afloat.

I decided to hope for the best and approach the subject obliquely. Uncle Maddie was an editor, and my problem with *The Vixen* was, after all, an editorial problem. He might enjoy playing the seasoned mentor, the avuncular sage. He'd drawn me into his sphere. Maybe something he said would resign me to the fact that my future hinged on a novel "proving" the Rosenbergs were guilty.

I prepared for our lunch as if for the job interview I'd never had. I practiced what I would say. When I'd called my mother to tell her I was meeting Uncle Maddie, she said, "Don't forget to thank him for your job. I read that they serve snails at that place he likes. Don't order them. Snails eat dirt."

I went to work as usual, but I didn't eat breakfast. Still afraid, after all this time, to brew a fresh pot of coffee at the office, I drank the dregs, and the scorched acidic brew made me queasy. I felt better by 12:30, in time to meet my uncle.

In fact I had recovered enough to be thrilled by the restaurant's smell of butter, wine, and garlic, the undertone of lilies, soap, men's cologne. Light bounced off the maître d's spectacles and his thinning spun-gold hair as he showed me to the bar, where Uncle Maddie was waiting.

My uncle was extremely fat. *A large man*, my parents said. Larger than life. Your uncle has *a presence*. From the back, his wide bottom overhung the bar stool like a mushroom cap on its stem.

Uncle Maddie moaned softly and grimaced as he climbed down from the stool.

"Simon! I'm sure I've told you the brilliant piece of advice I heard from Greta Garbo."

"No, I don't think so. Remind me."

"She said the trick to seeming young is not to groan when you get up. My dear, *dear* nephew." He gave me two hearty slaps on the shoulder, one for each *dear*.

Men no longer look like they did then. They don't wear hats. Their hair doesn't cap their heads in oily, marcelled ripples. When I try to remember my uncle's face, I picture Henry Kissinger with several more chins, twenty more pounds, and deeper bulldog furrows.

He waved at the bartender to have his drink carried over to our table, against the wall. The coral-pink wallpaper shone with an amber light, and the diners emitted a low masculine hum like the subway rumbling beneath us.

My uncle said, "You won't mind if I go around and take the wall side? Was it Kit Carson or Wild Bill Hickok who said, 'Never sit with your back to the door'? Half this room would probably enjoy seeing me get shot. Ha-ha."

He must have caught the look on my face.

"I assume you understand when someone is joking even if you don't *get* the joke."

Uncle Maddie's insults weren't personal, and I was relieved, not having to face the room. I was aware of being younger than everyone else and of how cheap my suit jacket was: my sad imitation of Warren. I imagined that everyone saw the gravy spot on my tie.

One consolation of age is that you no longer think that everyone is staring at you, probably because they aren't.

I could barely even look at my uncle, let alone follow what he was saying. Uncle Maddie tucked a napkin into his shirtfront before we even got menus. I wasn't going to do that, and I was relieved that he didn't seem to expect it.

"What did you drink?"

Did? The past tense confused me.

"Drink when?"

"In Cambridge," he said. "What was your poison? When you lived in Cambridge."

He couldn't bring himself to say *Harvard*. My mother said he resented my having gotten into the Ivy League. He'd gone to City College. I hadn't believed her, but now I wondered. It seemed impossible that a man like my uncle could envy someone like me, though years later I realized that there might have been plenty of reasons, starting with youth and good looks.

The honest answer to his question was caffeine: coffee and more coffee. I hardly drank alcohol. Marianna didn't drink. I'd drunk more at the literary parties I'd attended since I'd gone to work for Warren than in four years at college.

Despite his weight and age—still in his early fifties, he seemed ancient to me—Uncle Maddie was, my mother said, *a regular Don Juan*. Everyone knew he cheated on Aunt Cheryl with much younger women. It would disappoint him to know what a semimonastic life I'd led *in Cambridge*.

"At Harvard?" I said.

"Is *Harvard* no longer in Cambridge? Where the hell else would I mean?"

"A whiskey sour, please," I told the waiter. The only drink I knew.

Uncle Maddie waited until the waiter was out of earshot. "Please, Simon, no mixed drinks." He raised his glass of something golden, as if toasting me, but actually demonstrating the purity of whatever it was.

I had nothing to toast him with yet. He took a long, annoyed swallow.

"No cocktails please, unless you're queer? Are you queer?"

"No," I said. "I'm not."

"Don't get me wrong. It would be fine with me if you were. Maybe not the best thing for your career. But maybe not the worst. Depending. They take care of their own, like everyone."

"I like girls. I had a girlfriend at school." I sounded as if I was lying.

"So do I," said Uncle Maddie. "I mean, I like girls too. So that settles that. Now tell me one true or beautiful thing that you learned in college."

My drink appeared, and I took several gulps of the cloyingly sweet, burning liquid.

"Easy, big fella," my uncle said. "Pace yourself. What did those Harvard geniuses teach you?"

"Old Norse," I said.

My uncle shut his eyes. I studied the coarse white hairs striping his eyebrows, the brown splotches, like potato-peel scraps, stuck to both sides of his forehead.

"Old Norse. Now *that* will be useful in the modern world. Which isn't to say that I don't believe in a liberal education for its own sake."

I knew I was supposed to ask about my uncle's ideas on liberal education. Doubtless he'd written something on the subject that I could pretend to have read.

Instead I said, "Have you read *Njal's Saga*? It's great. I wrote my senior thesis about the chapter where Njal and his family are burned alive."

Why was I talking about myself? Why did I think he would care? If I'd wanted to impress him, it was a huge mistake. My uncle tilted his head. Beneath his heavy lids, his dark eyes glittered with a hard mean light.

"Your dear mother told me that. She's terribly proud of you. Well, good. Good for you. You would have been the smartest guy in the thirteenth century. I suppose you can always teach. Thank God Warren Landry is introducing you to reality."

Reality? Was *that* reality? Editing *The Vixen, the Patriot, and the Fanatic*? Being told what to do by Warren and insulted by my uncle? For four years I'd retreated into a vanished past in which the sneer on my uncle's face could start a feud that would cost the lives of generations.

I said, "I'm very grateful. Really. Thank you."

"Don't mention it," said my uncle. "By which I mean: Don't goddamn mention it, kiddo." By which he really meant: Mention it. Acknowledge my power, my influence.

The waiter delivered menus the size of the *New York Times*, bound in leather, the oxblood color of the folder that held Anya Partridge's novel. Inside was a list of foods, illegibly handwritten in faded brown ink, in French.

Escargot. Snails eat dirt. The sugared whiskey lurched up into the back of my throat.

Uncle Maddie said, "Do you need guidance? The *coquilles Saint-Jacques* are delicious."

Yes, I needed guidance. But not about seafood. "I was thinking of trying the escargots."

My uncle looked appalled by my tentative mini-rebellion. A protest against what? Against his guidance? A protest against my mother's advice, but he didn't know that. I was more surprised than he was that I was ordering snails: a pointless gesture that I already regretted.

"It's a free country," he said. "By all means try the snails, but they get old rather quickly. Anyhow, let me suggest the steak frites for the main. Not as . . . adventurous as escargot, but dependable."

"Sounds good." It sounded *very* good: more protein than I'd eaten in weeks.

"The usual, Mr. Putnam?" the waiter said.

"That's right. Steak frites medium rare. Hold the frites. Wait. No. My young nephew here might *enjoy* the frites."

"I would," I said. "Yes, thank you."

"Youth! Well, it's a trade-off. High metabolism, low finesse. Lots of vim and vigor but no experience and none of the social graces. Isn't that right, James?" my uncle asked the waiter.

"That's correct, Mr. Putnam."

Another scotch for Uncle Maddie, and we'd split a bottle of Bordeaux. When the waiter motioned at my empty cocktail glass, I nodded, and Uncle Maddie winced, but not at my ordering a second mixed drink. He was looking past me.

"Fascinating," he said. "Don't look now. Four o'clock. With that marvelous girl." He mentioned a writer so famous that even I knew his name. "That gourmet morsel is his daughter. He wants everyone to know that, but it's fine with him if strangers think that she's his latest squeeze."

My uncle knew many of the men in the room, and when they stopped by, he introduced me. His nephew, Simon, a recent Harvard graduate currently working for Warren Landry. If he resented my having gone to Harvard, that didn't stop him from boasting about it. Warren's name inspired responses too complex and various for me to interpret.

When he wasn't greeting his friends and acquaintances, my uncle gossiped about the last guy whose hand he'd just shaken. The poor slob's divorces, disappointing book sales, rivalries, drinking, mistresses, his abysmal behavior. Sometimes I recognized the names, sometimes I didn't, especially since he only used first names and assumed I knew who everyone was. I wasn't expected to speak, just to make gestures and sounds, chuckles of admiration, head-shakes of disapproval.

My uncle asked, "So how's the job? Is my friend Warren still running the place into the ground?"

"I like it. I—I *really* want to thank you."

"Honestly, I don't envy you. Try not to drown in the slush pile of wasted lives. You would not *believe* the unsolicited crap that comes in even at *our* humble journal. That Hollywood wit who said that writers were monkeys with typewriters got it wrong. Writers are monkeys with typewriters and strong opinions on subjects they know nothing about."

The snails were an ingenious delivery system for garlic, butter, and parsley. I liked how the individual ramekins let me track how far along I was in the eating process. The snails tasted like meaty mushrooms, neither delicious nor like dirt. I was glad they were chewy. It gave me something to do while my uncle forked up his tiny scallops, talking all the time.

It seemed there had been a party, and a writer whose mediocrity my uncle had exposed in a take-no-prisoners essay came after my uncle with a broken beer bottle, until the writer's wife dragged him away. The next day the writer called and apologized, wanting to stay friends and obviously hoping that my uncle would review his next book. Which was never going to happen.

Somewhere around the second glass of Bordeaux, on top of whiskey sours, I began having trouble following the conversation. Every so often my uncle's face swam out of focus, and his lips moved like those of a tropical fish, gulping air, gulping wine, gulping nothing.

I was glad to see the snail ramekin go, but daunted by the meat torpedo, smothered in skinny fries. I was hungry, but I hadn't counted on working so hard, sawing away at my food. My uncle was briefly silenced by the demands of cutting and chewing, but he swung back into his story, which now involved lawyers—

"Uncle Maddie, can I ask you something?"

"Ask me anything, Simon. My life is an open book. Ha-ha."

"Have you, with all your experience—" I hated how I sounded, pitiful and wheedling. I hardly recognized my voice.

"Oh, please," my uncle said. "Spare me."

"Have you discovered a secret for dealing with *difficult* writers?" I hoped he wouldn't ask if I meant anyone he knew. I couldn't mention Anya Partridge, not that he would recognize her name.

"What do you mean by *dealing*?"

"Have you ever persuaded a writer to change the entire point of an essay?" I tried not to think about *The Vixen* lest something show on my face. If necessary, I would pretend to be talking about Florence Durgin's poems. I would act as if that were my only book, as if I were asking my uncle how to make the gloomy poet rethink her mournful sonnets.

"More times than I can tell you, I've . . . well . . . I've gotten authors to chuck every word they've written and start from scratch. I mean *ditch* the whole goddamn thing. Tear it up into tiny pieces, toss it in someone else's wastebasket, then rewrite it top to toe with no guarantees from us. I could *tell* that the idea—the *germ*—was there. Inevitably the problem was faulty execution. Yes. Faulty execution."

Did I imagine that my uncle looked hard at me when he said *execution*. Twice. Why *wouldn't* he stare at my hand when it shot out, shaking my water glass, sloshing water onto the table?

"Sorry," I said.

"Don't worry." He slapped a napkin onto the wet spot and signaled for the waiter to bring him another napkin. "That's what comes of drinking cocktails. Always bad news. They soften the brain. Slow the reflexes. At least it was only water."

I said, "I'm afraid my author's problem goes deeper than faulty execution."

There. I'd said it. *Execution*. The planet still turned on its axis.

"Well, then," said my uncle. "Can I ask: Is your author by any chance a *she*?"

I nodded, realizing, too late, that two fried potatoes were sticking out of my mouth like fangs. "How did you know?"

"Instinct. Women, bless them, are *much* simpler creatures. One step closer to our cave-dwelling ancestors. I suggest making the writer—the *lady* writer—fall in love with you. *Madly* in love. She'll beg for your advice. She'll do anything to please you. She'll write an entirely different book if she thinks that's what you want. I could tell you about women whose names you'd recognize, tough babes but touchingly female, real women, as tender and vulnerable as any other—"

Anya's photo materialized before me. Despite my febrile dreams, it seemed unlikely that I would inspire her mad love, or that I could persuade her to change Esther from a nympho spy-seductress into an idealistic duped American housewife. And yet if my—to be brutally honest, *frog-like*—uncle had made so many women fall madly in love with him, it was obvious that I understood nothing about women. If Uncle Maddie could make them his slaves, sex had only a nominal relation to my companionable dorm-room affair with Marianna.

The alcohol had kicked in. There and then I decided that I would persuade Anya to see me. I would assure her that it would be easy to make the changes I wanted. To fix it, sentence by sentence; to turn Esther from a scheming traitor into an overly trusting wife and sister. I would put off asking for certain concessions: renaming the characters, for example.

I said, "I think my author is out of my league. Romantically." I'd already said more than I wanted. What if Uncle Maddie repeated this to Warren? They would know that I hadn't meant Florence. I doubted that Warren would tell my uncle about Anya and her novel. I wasn't sure that Warren liked or trusted my uncle, but Warren must have respected or feared him enough to agree to hire me.

"Leagues are for baseball. For Little League. There's no such thing as *leagues* where romance is concerned." My uncle looked insulted, as if I subscribed to some Darwinian ideas about natural selection that might inhibit his sex life. He wiped his mouth with his napkin. A judgment had been passed.

"Well! How *are* your dear mother and father?"

He was looking over my shoulder to see who he might know. He didn't care how my parents were. It was politeness, an afterthought. Lunch was over without my having gotten the answers I'd wanted. I remembered my original plan: to approach the problem obliquely. Hadn't I been oblique enough? It was worth one more try.

I said, "Mom's headaches have gotten worse since . . . I know this might sound strange, but she hasn't been herself since . . . " I let my voice trail off.

Mom hardly ever got off the couch. I visited them every Sunday, and though my parents and I tried to make one another laugh, I felt miserable when I left. On the subway to Manhattan, I dreaded the moment when the train descended into the tunnel, the moment when it seemed too late to get off and go back and spend another evening trying to make them happy. I told them about the slush pile, and we shared hearty but sympathetic laughs about the manuscripts I'd read that week: *The Count of Monte Christmas*, *The Laboratory Mice's Revenge*.

I never mentioned *The Vixen*.

Not even Uncle Maddie could avoid asking, "Your mother's gotten worse since *when*?"

"Since . . . well . . . actually . . . Mom was pretty upset about the Rosenberg execution."

I was taking a risk. At that time you didn't say those two words to someone who might have a different opinion of Julius and Ethel.

My uncle turned a pinkish purple of a violent intensity that I wouldn't see again in nature until my first desert sunset.

"Oh, the poor, poor Rosenberg martyrs! Murdered by the Feds. You know who wanted that couple dead? The Communists, that's who. So those stupid schmucks would live on forever as the People's heroes. Goddamn right, the Rosenbergs should have been saved from the chair and given life sentences for *stupidity*. The woman was an embarrassment. Have you read her letter to Eisenhower? Comparing herself to the six million Jews killed by the Nazis, to the Jews enslaved in Egypt, calling Eisenhower the Liberator, pimping out Moses, Christ, and Gandhi, blithering about how this great democracy is 'savagely destroying' a small unoffending Jewish family. A small unoffending Jewish family! Have you ever heard such bullshit? They were Soviet agents, liars who even lied to each other."

I didn't want to argue with my uncle. I didn't know what I'd say. I thought about my gentle father and his sweet, unfunny jokes. How could he and my uncle be siblings? I wondered about my paternal grandparents, dead before I was born, and about the thread that tied my dad to his successful bully of a brother and to Mort, the martyred parachute soldier, the uncle I never met.

"You know what the worst part was?" Maddie said.

The worst part of what? I'd lost track. I shook my head no.

"That fool Ethel and that idiot Julius, they *didn't* believe they were guilty. They didn't think they'd committed a crime. Those self-righteous Stalinist stooges. Oh, and do you know where this heroic couple lived? Knickerbocker Village! Roosevelt-era commie housing!"

Was he holding the Rosenbergs' *apartment* against them? My uncle was practically shouting. Diners at other tables must have been looking at us. I imagined that I could feel their eyes on my back. Many of them knew my uncle. Maybe he got this agitated at every lunch. He had to maintain his reputation as a curmudgeon, but also a fearless, incisive critic who could spot the hopelessly middlebrow and expose every flaw so that readers would never bother with a second-rate talent again.

"Imagine! These backwards *shtetl* Stalinist Jews *wanted* to live in public housing. Can you feature that? They want to live among the People."

My parents lived in a modest apartment. Uncle Maddie knew that. At least it wasn't public housing. *At least it wasn't public housing.* I wished I hadn't thought that. One lunch with Uncle Maddie had turned me into the kind of snob who judged people by the square footage of their homes. The minute lunch ended, I would have to turn back into a human being.

"They believed they were *helping* us by *selling* the bomb to the Soviet Union! To the Never-Never Land of freedom and justice for all. And who was their Peter Pan? Stalin! The murderer with more blood on his hands than Hitler!"

My uncle's voice rose on *Hitler*. The waiter glanced at our table.

"If it were up to these left-wing Puritans, there would be no beauty, no truth, no pleasure. You know that story about Lenin and Beethoven? Lenin said he couldn't listen to Beethoven anymore, since Beethoven makes you want to stroke people's heads. He couldn't listen to Beethoven because now he needed to *hit* people over the head. That's what the Rosenbergs wanted! To hit us over the head. Or nuke us. Which could happen now the Russians have the A-bomb, thanks to your friends the Rosenbergs. Bye-bye, Beethoven, pal."

"The Rosenbergs weren't my friends. But I don't think they should have gotten the chair—"

"Oh, don't you now? Look around. Imagine this place and all these nice people reduced to radioactive ash."

I was grateful for his permission to turn around. The nuclear holocaust hadn't happened. The restaurant was unchanged, except that, as I feared, people were staring at us, or trying not to.

"Oh! And did your parents tell you the Rosenbergs were killed because they were Jews?"

"I can't remember." In fact my mother had said as much when we'd watched the rabbi arrive at Sing Sing.

"You know who hated Jews? *Stalin.* Stalin murdered Jews by the truckload. Stalin liked nothing better. If Ethel and Julius were citizens of their beloved Soviet Socialist Republic, they would have been dead years ago, their two little boys would be digging latrines in Siberia. They'll tell you that the Soviets have solved the problems of poverty and hunger. Sure. If you murder half the population—fill those hungry mouths with stones and dirt—problem solved! Every Communist is a Trojan horse, a time bomb brainwashed to explode all over innocent patriotic Americans.

"You'll forgive the mixed metaphor, Simon, but you understand. The Rosenbergs were arrested in broad daylight. Their trial was conducted in public with journalists present. In Russia they would have been taken away under cover of darkness, thrown into prison and never heard from again. I suppose your parents would have been happy then."

"I don't think my parents would have been happy about that, Uncle Maddie. I really—"

"You realize I'm making a point." A brilliant idea was occurring to him. He was in a hurry to write it down. "Waiter! Check, please!" He searched his pockets for a pen.

The waiter delivered the bill in a sort of leather wallet. I watched my uncle count out twenties and slip them into the folder. I had never seen anyone pay that much for a meal. He scribbled his brilliant thoughts on the back of the receipt and stuffed it into his pocket.

"Let's do this again," he said.

Not until the waiter pulled away the table did I try to stand and realize how drunk I was. It would have been fine if I hadn't had to say goodbye to my uncle and stay on my feet. I sagged against the table. The waiter dropped the table and propped me up like a mourner at the entombment of Jesus. Uncle Maddie stepped back, raised both hands in the air, and let the waiter support me.

"Should I hail the young man a taxi?" said the waiter.

"Thank you," said Uncle Maddie. "But where should we have him delivered? My nephew is in no shape to go back to work. Perhaps he should go visit his parents who, I believe, live in Brooklyn."

Anger briefly cleared my head. He *believed* we lived in Brooklyn? Uncle Maddie had been to our apartment, and we had been—once, on Aunt Cheryl's fortieth birthday—to his Upper West Side palace.

"I have my own apartment now. On Twenty-Ninth and First."

"Big boy," my uncle said.

When the waiter was gone, my uncle said, "Regarding what you were asking, I have some useful advice."

I felt sober enough to concentrate. To listen and remember. Without my mentioning *The Vixen*, Uncle Maddie knew what I needed to hear. He was about to give me a nugget of publishing wisdom that would help me deal with my Anya Partridge problem.

Uncle Maddie cleared his throat. "Listen, son. Never drink cocktails. And you'll do very well."

And that was it. As I leaned forward to shake my uncle's hand, I slumped against him. He wrapped his thick arms around me. I was shocked by his size. Embracing him was like hugging a huge spongy tree. I drunkenly tried to interpret his hug. Was he just keeping me upright or was it affection? Mild affection, I decided, but affection nonetheless.

On my part, it was love. A boy's love for his uncle. The unreasonable love of blood for blood, of flesh for flesh. A young person's love for family, for history. For himself. I feared and disliked my uncle, but now I clung to him as if I were drowning instead of just drunk. He *knew* my parents. He'd known me as a child. The grandparents I never knew were Uncle Maddie's mom and dad. He must have felt something for us. For me. My father was his brother. However difficult and unpleasant, he was squarely on my side. My uncle. Dad's only living brother. Dear, dear Uncle Maddie.

CHAPTER 4

At that time I was deeply involved in love affairs with two different women, neither of whom, as far as I knew, was aware of my existence. The first was Anya Partridge, with whom my dream romance grew more heated with every night I put off deciding how to "fix" her book.

The second was with my coworker Elaine Geller, the firm's publicity director, a woman as pure-hearted and angelic as Anya was (in my fantasies) calculating and carnal. Unlike the fantasy Anya, Elaine was warm and thoughtful and kind. She knew the names of everyone's spouse. She remembered children's birthdays. My glacial fellow workers melted in her presence. She always seemed intensely aware of everyone in the room, sympathetic to whatever they might be going through, and she had a welcoming smile for the most socially awkward and least "important" employee—in other words, for me. Something about her made me want to be a better person, better than the guy having an unhealthy relationship with his writer's author photo.

In Professor Crowley's folktales, Elaine would have been the good sister and Anya the evil one, the white rose and the red rose, the blond and the raven-haired beauties. The fairy-tale Elaine would have been virginal, whereas the real Elaine was having a long, on-again, off-again romance with Warren Landry. Their relationship had outlasted his affairs with other women, amusing adventures that seemed to him as natural, as reflexive as breathing. No one told me this; no one confided in me after that first blast of gossip about my pregnant predecessor, Julia. But neither did anyone bother lowering their voices when I was close enough to overhear them at the water cooler and coffee maker. My colleagues talked as if I weren't there: an insult and an advantage.

No one had seen Elaine and Warren together outside the office except at breakfasts and lunches with agents and writers. But everyone noticed how they looked at each other at those meetings at which Warren refused to meet anyone else's eyes. Only lovers and close family members could gaze at each so steadily, with such openness and ease. We'd all seen Elaine leaning on Warren's arm at the office Christmas party. But by that point in the festivities, everyone needed a strong arm to lean on. I had no memory of whom I spoke to at the party, or of what I said, which is why I thought I might have mentioned "The Burning" to Warren. Afterwards, I would have wandered the city all night had not a helpful junkie couple pointed me toward home.

Elaine was small and blond, perky as a cheerleader, but not conceited in the way that I imagined cheerleaders were, not that I'd ever met a cheerleader. Everything about her was bubbly and forgiving. Again according to overheard gossip, she'd good-humoredly weathered the break that Warren took from their romance, long enough to impregnate my predecessor, Julia, who might also have been pregnant by her other lover, the biographer of Pancho Villa.

It said something about Warren, about Elaine, about our office culture, and about the era in which we lived that no one commented on the age difference between them. Elaine was probably thirty, but guessing her age would have been like asking, How old is Tinker Bell? She was an exemplary human being and also good at her job, an intelligent reader whom editors and journalists trusted, whose recommendation could persuade them to feature our books in their pages. She was often away from the office, shepherding foreign authors to interviews and lectures, soothing the anxious, distracting the homesick, charming the cranky.

Passing me in the hall, Elaine sang out, "Hi, Simon! How are ya?" her bright voice still lightly freckled with the Midwest. I never stopped being surprised and pleased that she remembered my name, especially when so few of my colleagues seemed to know who I was. If they thought about me at all, I imagined they assumed that I owed my job to nepotism (true), that I was unqualified (false), and that I would soon be fired (maybe yes, maybe no, depending on what happened with *The Vixen*). Once, over the communal coffeepot, a senior editor—speaking as if I weren't there—compared reading the slush pile to the futile labors of a heat-struck prospector panning for gold in a dry streambed. I smiled, but before I could amuse them with the latest rejected titles—*Love in Venice* and *Death Hates the Hangman*—they had gone back to their offices.

No one, as far as I knew, suspected that I'd been chosen for a sensitive assignment. I wondered how long it would be possible to keep *The Vixen* a secret.

Did Elaine know? Once she'd glanced into my office when I was working on *The Vixen* and held my gaze for an extra beat. Did I sense some understanding? She might have heard about *The Vixen* since she was intimate with Warren. I knew that people said things in bed that they would never say elsewhere, though my postcoital conversations with Marianna could have occurred, quite comfortably, in the Kirkland House dining room.

If things went as planned, Elaine would be in charge of making Anya's book the success that would save the company. She and Warren, Anya and I, the printer, and likely a few others would be co-conspirators, not in a crime so much as a sin, the sin of slandering the dead, the sin I happened to have written about in my college senior thesis.

I hadn't forgotten Ethel's letter to her lawyer. *You will see to it that our names are kept bright and unsullied by lies*. Each time I recalled Emanuel Bloch's voice breaking on the word *lies*, I thought of my mother, on the candy-striped couch, weeping for Ethel, her neighbor.

...

Around the corner from our office was a diner, George Jr.'s, where I often ate lunch after I moved out of my parents' apartment and my mother no longer channeled all her love into a dry chicken sandwich. At the diner, a dollar bought a bowl of New England clam chowder. If you asked for extra oyster crackers and crushed them into the soup, it made a paste that filled your stomach through the day and into the evening if there wasn't a party with free hors d'oeuvres.

Many of us ate at George Jr.'s, except the cleaners and the mail room guys who brought their lunch, and the lucky editors with expense accounts who frequented restaurants even more costly and fashionable than Uncle Maddie's Le Vieux Moulin. I longed to be taken, and to take others, to wherever Warren, and sometimes Elaine, disappeared at lunchtime.

To be seen at George Jr.'s was to admit that you weren't dining out on the company dime, and we staggered our lunch breaks to avoid running into a coworker. Only Warren enjoyed holding breakfast meetings in the diner's coveted window booths. He liked taking foreign authors to a place that seemed so American, so *ironic*. So Edward Hopper. Elaine often attended these meetings, and as I passed them on the street, I'd see her glowing in the diner window, in the orange morning light.

One afternoon I sat at George Jr.'s counter and pretended to scan the menu before I ordered the clam chowder. I looked up to see someone waving at me from the stool nearest the wall.

Elaine. The only person at Landry, Landry and Bartlett who would invite me to join her. Elaine pointed at the empty place beside her. I felt shaky, partly from hunger and partly because I was about to have lunch with Elaine. I was glad I hadn't ordered yet so I could change seats without further annoying the waiter and letting Elaine see that I was planning to eat glue. I would have to find another dish, something less cheap and disgusting.

I said, "Fancy meeting you here!" Had a man ever said a sillier thing to a woman? Oh, let the A-bomb fall now. Destroy the world if that's what it took to make Elaine forget what I'd just said. I was horrified by my selfish prayer. I didn't deserve to be sitting there with a pure, radiant soul. Elaine was not only attractive but also powerful at the firm, like a wholesome, sexy, warmhearted female Warren, if such a thing could be imagined. Every cell in my body felt desiccated, abraded by self-consciousness and discomfort. I wanted Elaine to see me not just as the lowliest editor in the company but as a former student of Folklore and Mythology, a graduate with high honors who had channeled his scholarly expertise into becoming the brightest rising star at the firm.

My clownish greeting hadn't dimmed Elaine's smile.

The waiter loomed up behind the counter. "Hey, fella, weren't you just sitting over there?"

"Guilty as charged. That was me."

"Really? I thought it was your twin brother." His offhand contempt sent me back to praying for world destruction.

Elaine saved me, saved the world. "George, this is Simon. Simon, George. I *made* Simon move over here and keep me company. He was too nice to say no."

Clearly, George adored Elaine. Everyone did. He shoved the menu at me and left.

"Friend of yours?" I asked. The wrong tone again! I was almost as nervous talking to Elaine as I'd been with Uncle Maddie. Once more my voice didn't sound like my voice, whatever *my voice* meant.

"Well, yes. I come here a lot." Only Elaine would admit that. Ev-

eryone wanted everyone else to think they were lunching at Le Pa-
villon. Elaine went to those lunches. She could afford to be honest.

A bowl of magnificent mac and cheese steamed on the counter before her. Of course Elaine would know the perfect thing to order.
After lunch, I would pick up her check. I would insist. My treat. Anything else would be ungentlemanly. So what if Elaine probably earned
ten times more than I did?

She said, "Have you tasted George's mac and cheese? It's the most
scrumptious thing in the world." I looked at the menu. Mac and
cheese: $2.50. If I had that and coffee, and paid for Elaine's lunch, I
would blow half my weekly food budget. What was money compared
to the charm of that one word, *scrumptious*? I could live dangerously,
on the edge, and if my money ran out, I could stuff myself at my parents' house for the price of a subway token.

For now, I could save a dollar and prove that I was my own man
by forgoing the mac and cheese and ordering the grilled cheese on
white. I preferred Swiss cheese, but even in those tiny details, one
hesitated to seem unpatriotic. American cheese? Yes, please. *American* cheese.

George took my order, shrugged, and returned too soon with two
slices of barely toasted bread enclosing a half-melted, canary-colored
slick—oily, hard, and doughy at once, a repulsive combination.

Elaine regarded my sandwich. Her delicate jaw shivered with concern. "Simon, you can ask George to toast it more. I'll ask. He won't
mind."

"That's okay. I like it this way."

"Do you want some of my mac and cheese? There's way more than
I can eat."

Elaine was offering me food from her plate. We'd hardly spoken
until now. Did I want our first real conversation to make her feel that
she had to feed me?

I said, "Mac and cheese takes me back to high school lunch. Back to prehistory." By equating school lunch with prehistory, I'd clumsily hoped to minimize the fact that Elaine was older than I was. Of course she hadn't gotten my meaning. I'd only embarrassed myself again. I took another bite, put the sandwich down, and stirred three sugars into my coffee.

Steaming under a buttery crust, Elaine's lunch was irresistible. She gestured at my coffee spoon, with which I awkwardly dug into her bowl and scooped up a few shells oozing tendrils of goo that stuck to my chin. I pawed at myself with a paper napkin. I wanted to weep with shame and pleasure.

"It's a strange time," Elaine said, in her melodic cigarette voice and at the clip of a taxi rattling over cobblestones. "Hard to know if we're moving from the dark to the light or vice versa. I like to think it's getting lighter, don't you? That's the Indiana in me. That's how I was raised."

The Brooklyn in me wasn't raised that way, but I wasn't going to say that. "Strange how?"

"Did you watch Edward R. Murrow rip into McCarthy on TV last week? *Finally* someone has the nerve to open his mouth!"

Was Elaine saying what I thought she was? People didn't criticize McCarthy unless they knew you *very* well.

I hadn't heard what Murrow had done. I'd stopped thinking about McCarthy, though my parents remained obsessed. He was still spreading his poison, destroying lives, putting our democracy at risk. I knew the threat was serious, but I'd worry about our endangered democracy after I decided what to do about Anya Partridge's novel.

Now Elaine was putting my dilemma in perspective. How could I have imagined that my trivial ethical problem with a lousy novel was a *crisis*? Senator McCarthy was terrorizing the country. Tragedies were playing out in Washington and throughout the world, and I'd been acting as if the world consisted of me, Anya Partridge, Anya's book, and Warren. Changing the novel wouldn't bring back the

Rosenbergs. I'd been thinking that it mattered because the book—my working on the book—was a betrayal. I was betraying a dead woman, betraying the truth, betraying my parents, betraying that part of myself—my integrity—that was still in the process of being born. Was I taking myself too seriously? I reminded myself: it mattered.

Elaine said, "We've been watching the hearings. It's all so gosh darned totalitarian."

Such is the power of sexual attraction that *gosh darned totalitarian* seemed like the most adorable phrase I'd ever heard. Such is the power of sexual attraction that all I could think was: *We? We've* been watching the hearings. It was painful to picture Warren and Elaine watching TV in bed.

"Meanwhile Eisenhower announces that we've had the H-bomb for two years." Elaine shook her head, thoughtfully closing her eyes long enough for me to wipe the grease off my chin. "For two years we've been testing weapons that make Hiroshima look like a playground quarrel. Setting them off in New Mexico, or some South Pacific atoll where the islanders are already having babies with fifteen toes. I'm sorry. I get obsessed. Listen to me, starting off this pleasant lunch with McCarthy and the H-bomb. We skipped the weather, the office gossip, not that I know any—and boom! Straight to Armageddon. You've hardly touched your sandwich. Are you sure it's okay?"

Elaine was right to apologize, though not for the reasons she thought. I had no problem with what she considered inappropriate lunch conversation. But her mention of McCarthy and the bomb had taken me back to the Rosenbergs, back to my parents' apartment, back to the *game* of the plume of smoke rising from Ethel's head.

The week before, at dinner, I'd told my parents that I'd heard some publishing gossip, probably false. Someone was writing a commercial novel based on the Rosenberg case. In the book, or so I'd heard, the Ethel character was definitely guilty of espionage—

My mother said, "Is the character *called* Ethel?"

"I've *heard* that the writer calls her Esther." How would I have heard *that*?

I held my breath until my mother said, "Anyone who would write a book like that will get his own private circle in hell. And his readers will be right there with him. He can autograph copies while demons stick them with blazing-hot pitchforks."

I said, "What makes you think the author is a man?"

"Because," said Mom. "A woman would never do that."

I'D MISSED WHAT Elaine just said. I tried to look as if I'd been having interesting thoughts. "What? Sorry. I got distracted."

"Bad boy. I said, 'Remind me what you're working on.'"

Elaine wouldn't have asked if she knew. Unless Warren had instructed her to test me, to see how well I kept a secret.

I should have said Florence's poetry. I said, "Actually, this . . . hard book." I shouldn't even have said that. But I wanted to know how much Elaine knew.

"Hard *how*?"

"Complicated."

"Another word for *hard*. I might as well tell you straight-out. I know about *The Vixen*."

How often had I longed to hear someone say that! But if Elaine knew, why had she asked me to remind her? *Was* she spying for Warren? If this was a test, I'd failed. But I was glad she knew that I was the person Warren had chosen to trust with this important and sensitive matter.

"You know about it?" I pushed aside my plate and leaned on the counter, studying Elaine as closely as I could without seeming creepy and intrusive. I saw nothing beyond her luminous surface, no tics, no contradictions, no tells hinting at a hidden agenda.

"Sure! I read the book." Elaine pretended to stick her finger down her throat and gag.

How sweet it was to laugh about this, and what a huge relief. "So you know."

"Didn't I just say that?" Elaine laughed again, then touched my arm to make sure I understood that she wasn't laughing *at* me. I felt as if my skin were burning inside my jacket, where she'd touched me. Her laughter suggested that my problem had a humorous side I'd missed. She would help me take myself less seriously and realize that our publishing *The Vixen* was funny. In a way.

Right then my love for Elaine deepened into something richer than an office crush. It was a special kind of love, born from gratitude and attraction. A sweet, saintly woman was helping me. The few minutes I'd spent in Elaine's company had shrunk my elephantine problem to the size of a mouse. A three-hundred-page mouse, but a mouse nonetheless. The smell of frying hamburger and the tangle of breakfast bacon had been magically alchemized into aphrodisiac incense.

I knew my worries would return as soon as I was alone, but I was thankful for this respite from trying to decide how to ask a woman I'd never met if she could tone down the sex scenes involving a mother of two who died in the electric chair. How to ask if she would *consider* changing the characters' names to something less like the real names of the people on whom they were based, consider changing the scenes in which they conspired to overthrow our democracy.

Elaine said, "I'm the only one who knows besides you and Warren. And the author, of course. So your secret is safe with me."

My secret was safe with her. *Safe.*

I said, "Have you met Anya Partridge?"

"No. She's supposed to be a recluse, or so Warren tells me. He's met her. I think he may have slept with her, but I can't make myself ask. He says she's crazily ambitious, that once the book comes out she'll be all over us, and we won't be able to get rid of her."

I had never heard anyone say, I think he may have slept with her, but I can't make myself ask. I had never heard anyone say anything that cool. But what shocked me more was the phrase *once the book comes out.*

The book. It made everything real. Since that first conversation with Warren, I'd half persuaded myself that *The Vixen* was a bad dream I'd forget when I woke up. *Once the book comes out.* Five words had put a stop to my wishful thinking.

George was spinning a milkshake. The whir of the machine made it difficult to hear. As a second milkshake followed the first, I decided to say something about how bad the novel was.

When the machine stopped, Elaine said, "*The Vixen* isn't *War and Peace*, that's for darn sure."

The Vixen isn't *War and Peace* was what Warren had said. In case I needed further proof that they were in this together. So what? Elaine had admitted as much. We laughed. I was grateful. I adored her. I trusted her. Or almost. I knew that Elaine was closer to Warren than she would ever be to me. But that seemed right. It was the natural order, like the planets' revolution around the sun. I wanted to say that if publishing *The Vixen* was supposed to shore up the firm's finances, couldn't we find another commercial novel that was less cheap, less mean-spirited and meretricious? A book that didn't portray my mother's childhood neighbor as a traitor and a slut. A book that didn't malign the newly dead whose children had survived them. I wanted to be honest. But I kept my mouth shut. Elaine didn't need to be involved any more than she already was.

Elaine said, "We need money. Warren thinks this book will make some." And then—as if she'd read my mind, "There are worse books out there, believe me."

"And better ones?"

"Maybe, but let's go with Warren on this. He thinks it's a sure thing. I keep telling him there are no sure things in publishing, but he insists. If it fails, he'll take the blame. He's always been good about that."

Take the blame for what? I wanted and didn't want to know why he'd apologized to Elaine.

"I understand," I said. And I did. I had to be careful—for everyone's sake. If I was going to complain about *The Vixen*, I'd have to take the literary and not the political route.

I said, "I've got all these awful sentences from the book stuck in my head . . . "

No one could resist Elaine's trilling, melodic laugh. "Like what?"

Weirdly, it felt like betraying Anya. Why was I protecting her? Did I already think of her as *my author*? Or was it because I'd looked at her photo and done the things we'd done in my dreams? Mocking Anya's work was my mini-revenge on her for writing the book that was weighing on my conscience and occupying my waking life.

"One sentence, Simon. Come on."

"Okay . . . Let me think." I didn't need to think. "'Ripping open the buttons of her green prison dress, Esther said, "Prosecute *this*. J'accuse, Inspector Javert."'"

Elaine giggled. "Dear God. We do know the book is going to need work. I assume that's why Warren picked you. He believes you can do it. He needs you to turn this into something we can publish without totally losing our credibility. And if you get it right, believe me, he'll notice." Her crystalline blue eyes stared unblinkingly into mine. I nodded. What had Warren semi-promised me? More desirable real estate at Landry, Landry and Bartlett.

"I wondered why he chose me." I would have loved to tell Elaine about my mother and Ethel, to hear her reassure me that history had nothing to do with my having been assigned this novel.

"It's obvious," Elaine said.

"Obvious how?"

"You want me to tell you how talented you are?" She smiled. Were we flirting? It crossed my mind. I dismissed it.

"No." But that was precisely what I wanted. I wanted to hear her say: Warren asked you to edit the book because he thinks you're a genius. Warren didn't pick you because you're the most dispensable, least threatening employee, the newest, the most likely to do what he says and not ask questions. The office drone with the fewest friends. The furthest out of the loop. The one whom no one speaks to. The one most likely to keep a secret. None of that was flattering. Maybe she *meant* the most talented, the most promising. Maybe that was what Warren had said.

"Warren tries not to tell me too much. He says women don't like to see men panic about money. He's from that generation. But I know he's worried. He's not sleeping. He's up reading at three a.m. We were fine when Preston was here, but now that he's in the loony bin—"

The loony bin? The nature of Preston Bartlett's illness was guarded like a state secret. Elaine had just said *loony bin*. So naturally, so lightly.

"Preston tried to strangle Warren. Two Christmases ago. At the office Christmas party. It was terrifying. They knocked down a wall of books. Everybody was screaming. Preston and Warren were yelling insults and curses, slurring their speech. We couldn't figure out what they were saying, which was probably just as well."

Elaine's voice dropped, so that I had to lean even closer. "Warren has never told a soul, not even me, what the fight was about. And poor Preston's in no shape to reminisce. Security was called, and they took him away in an ambulance. Preston's too rich for a police car, but not so rich they didn't shoot him up with something. He got very quiet. And from then on it's been the usual hospital nightmare: he wakes up, has some kind of a stroke, and no one notices till morning. Or so we've heard. The Bartletts don't sue. They're not that kind of family. No one, not even Preston, is worth seeing their names in the paper. Better let their son turn into a vegetable than have their society friends find out what happened."

Was Preston really a *vegetable*? When I'd seen him, in the office, he'd seemed perfectly lucid when he'd twice asked to see Warren. Elaine was there.

"That's terrible," I said.

"It is," said Elaine.

"I saw you being nice to him when he demanded to see Warren."

"Poor Preston," Elaine said.

I felt a warmth, a connection. This was our work, our present, our future, the fate we shared.

"Preston hasn't taken his money out of Landry, Landry and Bartlett, but most of it is going to pay for the luxury asylum where they've got him warehoused. Unless the firm has a big commercial success, we'll all be looking for jobs. Warren will be dragging around a little red wagonload of failed foreign novels. Is that what we want? Warren's a good guy, complicated but decent. He loves books. He loves literature and writers. A rare thing, I can tell you. He believes in publishing. He believes he was born to do this work. How many people can say that?"

I couldn't answer. I couldn't speak. I was silenced by the admiration in Elaine's voice. I willed George not to bring the check just yet.

"There's a lot Warren doesn't talk about. I've never met his wife. I know they have separate bedrooms and that she has a problem with weight. They have five sons. Five! They all play football. Warren always assumes I know which son he's talking about, even though he's never told me their birth order or even their names. Never shown me pictures. At first I thought this meant he didn't care about me, then I thought it meant he didn't care about them, and now I don't know what to think. Oh my God! What have I said?"

"Does he talk about what he did in the war?"

"Sometimes. Not much. He tells the same stories again and again."

Before I could ask which stories, Elaine went on. "He has screaming nightmares. Yelling and twitching. Terrifying. I guess there was
some damage. He was a little old for the draft. He volunteered. He
had a gift for intelligence work. He knew people from college. His
old-boy network."

Screaming nightmares. Elaine had heard them in the darkness.

"His old-boy network," I repeated.

"Look, Simon, I really love the firm. I respect the books we do.
I want it to survive. And as for *The Vixen, the Patriot, and the
Fanatic* . . . Warren thinks the title's great, but we're going to have to
discuss it."

Anya's novel was coming out. There would be meetings about the
title. Elaine would be at those meetings. I wasn't alone. She was on
my side.

Elaine said, "If it's any comfort, Warren has promised that this is
a one-time thing. He swears we're not going commercial. Or even
profitable, most likely. *The Vixen* could give us a year. Then it's back
to business as usual, a business in which Warren says he sees a great
future for you, Simon."

Did Warren really say that? Elaine was flattering me. I wanted
Warren's good opinion. I wanted this warmth to last.

"You can trust Warren," she said. "Tell him you want to make the
book better. That's why he gave it to you. He'll help. We both will.
And really, Simon, I'm sure we will all get to heaven if the worst sin
we ever commit is publishing one . . . imperfect novel. In the larger
scheme of things—"

Imperfect. The larger scheme of things. Why hadn't I seen it? Why
had I gotten stuck on a detail: one imperfect novel about a public double murder. Why had I let my mother's childhood friendship make
me think that this was more serious than it was?

Elaine said, "I'll help. We'll be working together, which will be
fun, won't it?"

Fun? A shiver ran down my spine.

"We can do this, Simon. Promise?"

"I promise."

Elaine toasted me with her last forkful of mac and cheese. I raised my water glass.

"Don't toast with water," said Elaine, "unless you want to be poor the rest of your life. Not that there's a real chance of that. Tell Warren you need to speak to him. He'll help you with Anya's novel. Don't have your talk in the office. Have a drink with him after work. And here's some friendly advice: Eat before you go. Line your stomach if you're going to try and keep up with Warren."

For someone who hardly drank, I was getting a lot of advice about drinking. Uncle Maddie had told me not to drink cocktails; Elaine was suggesting that I line my stomach. Did I seem like a boy pretending to be a man who could hold his liquor, at a time when that was essential to making one's way in the world?

We'd finished our food, or anyway, my ghastly sandwich had disappeared. The checks came. Elaine grabbed mine. When I tried to grab it back, along with hers, she said, "If you want to arm wrestle, we can. I've had lots of practice muscling down more determined check-grabbers than you, so I can guarantee I'll win. And I don't think you want that."

Arm wrestling Elaine might have been fun. But not there, not then.

"I'll put it on my account. Let's make Warren buy the young folks lunch while the company can still afford it." She stood and, checks in hand, headed toward the cash register. "This was great! Excuse me, I have a few errands to run. I'll see you back at the office."

My good mood faltered because my time with Elaine was coming to an end. But I liked the idea (*my* idea) that she didn't want to be seen with me returning to the office. As if we'd *been together*. Which we had, in a way. I chose to see Elaine's caution as a tribute to my power to make our coworkers gossip, or even make Warren jealous.

"Thank you, George," I called out as we left.

"See ya soon, Elaine," George said.

CHAPTER 5

Warren told me to meet him at the Cock and Bull, on 67th and Third. He said he loved the name of the tavern—his *local*—because it was such a *trenchant* comment on human nature. He said that if I was early, I should mention him to the bartender, who would take good care of me until he arrived.

I got there early. An elderly couple sat at the corner of the bar, leaning together over glasses of white wine and cooing like pigeons. The bartender gave me a long frosty stare. Was everyone here a regular? When I said that I was meeting Warren Landry, the bartender went from trying to stare me down to trying to figure out if I was someone he was supposed to know.

"Of course." He asked the lovebirds if they would mind moving over. The corner seats at the bar were reserved.

The old couple seemed marginally less insulted when he said the next round was on the house. I'd never known that bar stools could be reserved. It was first on the long list of things I was eager to learn, though I knew that Warren would never respect me if I acted like his overeager student.

I lowered my briefcase onto the floor, lightly kicking it every so often to make sure that it was still there. I didn't want Warren to see my cheap briefcase, but I wanted Anya's manuscript nearby. I was prepared to quote from it, chapter and verse, to show Warren how well I knew it. I had arguments for every change I thought the author should make. Well, not *every* change. That would have meant changing every word—and the entire basis of the novel. Hadn't my uncle said that you could get writers to start from scratch? If you could make the writer fall in love with you. That wasn't what Warren wanted to hear, nor what I wanted to tell him.

Behind the old-fashioned burnished wooden bar was a massive Surrealist painting of a bull brought to its knees, its rippling back bristling with picadors' lances, like frilled toothpicks in a giant bleeding hors d'oeuvre. Attacked, the bull twisted away from the rooster sinking its claws into its sinewy neck. Triumph flashed in the rooster's eyes.

"Max Ernst," said the bartender.

I bobbed my head to show that I knew who Max Ernst was.

"He used to live around the corner. He traded the painting for free drinks. Imagine how much top-drawer booze a masterpiece like that buys you. It almost broke the original owner, but it still brings in the tourists. So I say, Good for him. The artist."

I ordered an Irish coffee, hoping the caffeine might offset the whiskey. I needed to keep a clear head. I was so focused on the rooster slashing at the bull that I was startled when the bartender slid me a chipped coffee cup topped to the brim with whipped cream. Was he mocking me? Serving me a girl drink? I swallowed the cream as fast as I could, but not quickly enough. The last white flecks still mustached my upper lip just as Warren flew through the doorway like Superman come to save the day.

"Mr. Landry," the bartender said. "Excuse me, but you're letting in the cold."

"So I am," said Warren. "My apologies." He bowed, rolling his hand from his forehead.

The bartender chuckled obediently.

"Old boy! Great to see you!" said Warren, as if he and I hadn't passed each other in the hall, an hour ago, at the office. He waved at the painting over the bar. "Extraordinary, no? Isn't this place a hoot? How many establishments have names that describe what goes on there? Laundromats, I suppose. There's an EZ-Clean on Lexington that should really be called Not-So-EZ-Clean. Well! We're not here to talk about laundromats, are we?"

He tossed his exquisite camel coat and felt hat on a coat rack. "What's your poison?"

"Irish coffee. I wanted the caffeine—"

Warren regarded the greasy coffee with the same horror that my uncle had directed at my whiskey sour. What a crime it was, in those days, for a man to drink the wrong "poison."

"Last week I interviewed a young woman applying to be Elaine's assistant, which, believe me, Elaine needs. And do you know what the silly girl ordered? A tequila sunrise! Not a chance that a tequila sunrise drinker could work for Landry, Landry and Bartlett. No matter how big her breasts are."

I was supposed to smile, but I couldn't. A tequila sunrise sounded intriguing and possibly delicious, but I turned down the corners of my mouth, like Warren. I wondered if he talked to Elaine about a prospective employee's breast size, and how Elaine responded. Our receptionist, Violet, had enormous breasts. She was in her sixties and had been with the firm since it started.

"I knew these guys in Central America, they'd chase some seriously rugged mezcal with bootleg cough syrup and . . . well, that's for another time. We're still looking for someone to help Elaine. So get out the word. But perhaps you better warn the pretty girls that they might not get paid until we're on firmer fiscal footing. They should be prepared to extend their dependence on their trust funds or the parental allowance."

Trust funds. Parental allowance. Warren seemed to believe that Simon Putnam came from a class for whom such advantages were routine. What had Uncle Maddie told him? I gulped my coffee too quickly, and tears burned my eyes. I knew what *firmer fiscal footing* meant. *Firmer fiscal footing* meant *The Vixen*. When he'd dropped the manuscript on my desk, Warren had said it wasn't a bomb, but that was what it felt like now, ticking away under our feet.

"Well, at least an Irish coffee is in the right family. The whiskey family, twice removed. Bartender!" Didn't he know the bartender's name? The bartender knew his. The voice in which he said *bartender* was a voice from the Gilded Age, when the cook was named Cook. That time was gone, but not entirely. It was remarkable how that one word, *bartender*, could combine so much self-mocking irony and un-assailable privilege. "A double Glenfiddich, lots of rocks—and an-other for my young friend."

The bartender clinked down our glasses, and Warren slid him a fifty. A fifty! Did he mean to keep drinking all night? I needed to stay sober. I was on a mission. I would never have a better chance to ask Warren what I should do about Anya Partridge's novel. I needed to know what my limits were, how much of her book I could change, and whether I could meet her.

"Drink up. We're the last generation to stay pleasantly high all day. Warren Landry predicts: this is the final historical moment when inebriation is considered superior to sobriety. Down the hatch!"

Flattered that Warren saw me as a member of his generation, which must have signified something more essential than chronological age, I raised my glass and tried to look carefree and reckless, an effort sub-verted by the effort required to look carefree and reckless.

"*Skoal*," Warren said. "Cheers. *Salud! Cincin! L'chaim*. Five's the charm."

"Excuse me?"

"Never mind. Every day I wake up and think, Well, today's the day I quit drinking. And every night I go to bed and tell myself, To-morrow. You'll quit tomorrow. You're too young to know what I'm talking about. You young bucks still believe that you have endless tomorrows."

Young buck? Me? "I—I don't—"

"Sorry. I've had quite a day. I spent the morning pleading with our accountant to make the figures add up a different way. And then I spent the afternoon on the phone with our creditors, assuring them that those figures had added up the way I wanted. We do have a business manager, the venerable Mr. Healy. But if he knew how dire our situation is, the old geezer would have a stroke. I'm protecting our money guy! Can you beat that? You might wonder why I'm telling you this. But first . . . another round! Thank you!"

I knew why he was telling me this. Underneath his talk about money was *The Vixen, the Patriot, and the Fanatic*. Anya Partridge was our Joan of Arc, and I was her loyal Duke of Alençon.

"You know we have something in common," Warren said. "Our education, for starters."

"We both went to Harvard?" Why had I made that into a question?

"More than that, old boy. We had the same professor. I took Crowley's 'Mermaids and Talking Reindeer.' What a blast! The most fun I had in four years. I mean the most fun I had *in a classroom*, if you get my meaning. What a character the old boy was, especially in my day, when he was still gallivanting around with Sicilian witches and whatnot. I always thought of Crowley as the hero in the pith helmet in the Tarzan films who comes crashing through the jungle and rescues everyone from the dinosaurs or cannibals or whatever the problem is. The guy who goes into the Amazon and gets all the good drugs. Whoops. Was I not supposed to say that?"

"Crowley's revenge class," I said. We were speaking a private language: communicative, elitist.

"Ah, the good old days," Warren said. "Crowley was a friend of my great-aunt's. He came for lunch one Sunday. I was too young to know who he was, plus they hustled me out of the room when he starting telling a dirty story he'd heard from the Albanian sworn virgins. Of course I eavesdropped. Father meant me to. My old man was turning my sexual education over to Robertson Crowley and a coven of militant lesbians who lived by some medieval code of revenge. I still remember a story about what happened to some village idiot who vowed to fuck the first twenty virgins he met. Grisly. Grisly and depraved. And I was a child. A boy!"

"He didn't tell that story in class," I said.

"Well, he wouldn't have," said Warren. "Not even then. I was five years old, for Christ's sake. All I knew was that some guy was doing something dirty to someone else's daughter. At that point my father was doing something similar to our neighbor's wife. So Crowley's little folktale didn't go over all that well. He was never invited back. When I studied with him, I didn't remind him of our brief acquaintance. If he remembered, which I doubt, he didn't hold it against me. I loved his stories. And I think he had a lot to do with my becoming the person I am. With my choosing the life I've chosen."

So Warren and I *did* have something in common. I said, "He was a great teacher." I fought the impulse to add that Crowley's recommendation had failed to get me into graduate school. I didn't want to seem like a loser, to signal that working for Warren had been my second choice.

How did Warren know I'd taken Crowley's class? Had he seen my college transcript? I felt as if I'd been spied on, vetted. As if a secret had been ferreted out.

The dark bar had begun to seem vaguely sinister. Warren had said that *The Burning* was the author's preferred title—the title of my thesis. Had that been a coincidence too? How much did Warren know about me? He'd been a spy during the war. Why was I surprised by his ability to find out the details of someone's life? Specifically, *my* life, my college career, which hardly seemed worth investigating. How much did he know about my family? I tormented myself by imagining Warren and my parents in the same room. I imagined fleeing the room—and never seeing any of them again.

"But I'm sure you didn't suggest a drink to share nostalgic Harvard memories, Simon. What did you want to discuss?"

"I wanted to talk to you about Anya Partridge's novel."

"Of course! I should have known. Our little vixen who's going to shower us with gold. Did I ever tell you about that night I was in a hotel bar in Berlin, this was maybe in '42? I was undercover, pretending to be an arms dealer negotiating with the German high command. This gorgeous broad sits down beside me. She's practically begging me to take her upstairs. What else could a gentleman do? At breakfast the next morning she confessed that her husband was away at the front, and I knew I'd discovered the heart and soul of our campaign. We would convince the German soldiers that their wives were all madly fucking draft dodgers, bureaucrats, and foreign profiteers. The Germans would desert, go home, and murder the home-wrecking bastards. The one thing men fear more than losing a woman is losing her to another man. We fear that more than death. I assume you kids still learn about Helen of Troy, unless our educational system has deteriorated more than I thought. That, as you'll remember dear Professor Crowley saying, was the original *ur*-story of revenge. The heavy price and punishment for stealing the wrong woman."

I thought of the Icelandic sagas, of the tragic feuds started by women. Women were always shaming and nagging their relatives into avenging a death, a dirty look, a trivial insult. Was Warren warning me away from Elaine? Steal a woman—and it's war. I *wanted* to think that could be true, but I knew that I wasn't even remotely a threat.

"Do you know my favorite part of my war work?" Warren was saying. "I loved naming the missions. Operation Othello! The literary touch! That's why they wanted me on board. Times like that, I knew we would win. My God, to feel that *sure* again. That certainty of being guided, of being on the side of the angels. Operation St. Anthony's Fire. Obviously not a real plague, not even *we* would do that.

The rumor was enough. Fear works wonders, as you've doubtless noticed. It's a vital weapon in any arsenal, if used judiciously. Oh, the bedbugs! You wouldn't believe how easy it is to persuade vermin to move from one set of beds to another. Operation Vitus. Amazing how rapidly a few itchy bites can demoralize a population. We had an entomologist consultant from St. Louis. So . . . what's happening with *The Vixen?*"

"Right," I said. "*The Vixen.*" I'd practiced how I was going to begin, but now I couldn't remember. "Mr. Landry—"

"Warren. Please. How many times must I ask my team to call me Warren?"

My team? Was I on Warren's team? Calling him by his first name was the least I could do for a teammate. "Warren, I realize this novel is a special case, not what we usually publish." I drained my drink in one swallow because that was what men in the movies did for courage. "But I think the book could be better."

"Better is good," said Warren. "Better is optimum. Better is why we hired you."

The Vixen couldn't have been why they'd hired me. Anyway, better wasn't enough. I needed to know how far I could push Anya Partridge. "On the sentence level there's lots that could be done. And in a larger way . . . I feel she draws an awfully hard line about something that's never been clear."

"*A larger way.* Meaning . . . the politics? The Rosenberg case? Is that what you're saying? Please tell me that's not what you're saying."

"I guess that's what I'm saying." How had *that* slipped out?

"Jesus Christ help us," said Warren.

Why didn't Warren order more whiskey now that we really needed it? He turned toward me so that I had to lean back, regarding him from a perspective that turned the bull-and-rooster mural into a backdrop for the lecture that I sensed coming on.

"I don't know your true feelings about this subject." He caught himself mid-sneer and seemed to be listening to a voice—Elaine's?—reminding him that true feelings were nothing to be sneered at. "Unless you are suggesting tearing our vixen to pieces and publishing a pro-Rosenberg, pro-Moscow, pro-Communist, pro-atomic-spy novel. And if that's what you have in mind—"

"It's not." In fact, I'd been thinking of something halfway between Anya's novel and the book that Warren was describing.

"If that's what you're suggesting, then let me tell you that such a novel will never see the light of day. That would be the first problem, and the second would be that if such a book *were* to be published, we would lose our jobs, our business, and probably find ourselves—or anyway, you would find *yourself*—testifying before some hostile, functionally illiterate Senate committee. Then we would all go to jail or, best case, drive taxis and starve. And our authors would be left without a publisher. Is that how you envision our future . . . Mr. *Putnam*?" He pronounced my name as if he knew that Putnam wasn't my legitimate surname. Had Uncle Maddie told him? Uncle Maddie would never. It was his last name too.

"That's not what—"

"You can't be too careful these days. Perception is everything, and you can't be perceived as being soft on Communism, as having been tarred with Herr Marx's gluey brush. At the same time you can't be too anti-Russian since, if Communism falls, as it certainly will, Russia might be our next market." Warren chuckled. "In any case, something that *seems* anti-Communist—our *Vixen*, for example—is not so much anti-Communist as pro-American. Because here in the United States we are free to write anything we want. Do you see what I mean?"

Yes, I did. And I didn't. My doubts didn't stop me from nodding so vigorously I felt vaguely motion sick.

"Dissident Eastern Bloc authors don't get published in their home countries. We've put a few of these brave refugees on our list, but only after they'd gone safely into exile. One Czech writer in particular . . . well! Better let sleeping dogs lie. Americans who publish the hard Left don't get to publish anymore, except, I suppose, for those broadsides some commie street bum wants to sell you for a nickel. And those of us in the reasonable middle are getting screwed from both sides. I hate to ask, I don't want to ask, but to quote Senator You-Know-Who, Are you, or have you ever been, a member of the Communist Party?"

I longed to know where Warren's question fell on the continuum between serious and ironic. But Warren was unreadable, partly because I couldn't bring myself to look at his face long enough to read it.

"No!" I said, so loudly that the bartender said, "Is everything all right, gentlemen?"

"Yes. For the moment, good sir," said Warren. "Everything couldn't be better."

I said, "No, I am not. I'm not a Communist. That is *not* what I'm saying."

But what *was* I saying? My mother had known Ethel when they were girls. I didn't believe that Ethel and Julius should have been executed. I had promised myself to keep Ethel's name bright and unsullied by lies.

I said, "I mean the literary side of *The Vixen*. I have corrections and suggestions on almost every page. I'm not sure how I can do all of it in a memo, or even with marginal notes. We spoke about changing the names. If the writer and I could just have a brief talk . . . "

"The literary side of *The Vixen*? I assume that's a joke. But it's funny. I like you, Simon. Let's play out our little drama. I'll get in touch with Anya. I'm sure a phone call could be arranged."

Here was where the whiskey helped. This was what it was for. "I meant a brief talk *in person*."

"You're saying you want to *meet* Anya?" As Warren grinned at me, over his drink, the wrinkles around his eyes seemed calculated to the millimeter for maximum merriment and self-assurance.

Oh, why wasn't I in some library, reading about warriors who had been dead for so long that nothing could hurt them? It was so much harder protecting the newly dead, who didn't need my help any more than the Vikings did. I was protecting something else, something even more precious than the future of the two Rosenberg sons. But I couldn't have begun to explain. In the sagas, you only avenge your kinsmen. Not your country, not your neighbors, not your mother's childhood acquaintance. Ethel and I weren't related. But she had grown up alongside my mother. Mom could have *been* her, except that Mom wasn't a Communist, and she'd married Dad and had me.

Another glass appeared before me, and I drank it down. How quickly would it kick in? Not fast enough to make me sound less shaky and stiff.

"That would be the ideal, yes. Talking to the author would be the *best-case situation*." My voice rose and faltered on the knife edge of control.

Warren threw back his head and laughed. At what? At his confidence, his authority, his current level of contentment? Perhaps he was laughing at my fear, my confusion, my desire for an easy fix. My longing for the scenario in which we would end the Cold War, defeat McCarthy and Khrushchev, bring Ethel Rosenberg back from the dead, and never publish *The Vixen*.

"Excuse me for asking, Simon, I should know the answer, but have you ever in your young life actually *dealt* with a living writer?"

Warren knew I had. Florence Durgin had cried when I told her that Warren wanted to postpone her book. She said that her tears were not about her. She wanted her son to see the book. Maybe her book would turn him away from the dangerous path he'd chosen. Human kindness prevented me from asking why her son couldn't read it in manuscript.

"Authors have to be pampered," Warren said. "Like helpless puking babies. Fed on white bread soaked in milk. Metaphorically, that is. In actual fact, they love to eat, especially when someone else is paying. Needless to say, Anya Partridge is not Florence Durgin. Anya's brain needs to be stroked. One word—one unintentional misunderstanding—and it's game over. Simon, have you ever *seen* a deer in the headlights?"

"Yes," I lied. I could imagine what a deer in the headlights looked like. I had never been on a country road at night.

"Anyway, our little Anya makes Bambi look like Winston Churchill. Our Connecticut deer are domesticated compared to the wild Miss Partridge. With this woman, kid gloves might as well be sandpaper mittens."

Wild and rough was what I'd dreamed. I stared down into the shot glass that seemed to have emptied itself.

"Refill?" said Warren. "*Encore?*"

"No thanks," I said. "I've got more reading to do tonight. I'm trying to keep up with the mail."

"Any gold in the slush pile?"

"Middle-aged suburban adultery. The last novel I rejected was called *The Concupiscent Commuter: A Love Story.*"

Warren laughed: an obliging chuckle. "I get it. Bad imitation Cheever. Boring. Been there, done that. Adultery is one of those sins that's more fun to commit than to read about. Though probably there are others . . . Gluttony, sloth . . . what am I forgetting? Maybe every sin except murder . . . and even that . . . well, anyway. Don't look so shocked. I'm joking! All right, give me a few days. I think I can arrange a meeting with Anya. Let me work on it. Bartender! One last round!"

But that wasn't the last round. It was the last business round. The last professional round. Now it was almost as if we were friends, a younger friend, an older friend, one of whom worked for the other. Warren held forth on a range of subjects: Abraham Lincoln, the Founding Fathers, the First World War, the Russian science program.

Why the British working class had resisted the teaching of Charles Darwin. The early career of George Orwell.

I was happy to listen. Nothing more was required.

Warren had a peculiar tic. He would reach back under his shirt and touch the back of his neck. I'd never thought about it, but now, having heard Elaine's account of the disastrous Christmas party, I wondered if he was probing the place where his former partner grabbed him. What was Preston Bartlett's problem? Without knowing the details, I took Warren's side.

I *enjoyed* hearing Warren ramble. Nothing was being asked of me except to stay upright, nod my head, and not fall onto the bar. My last memory of the evening is of Warren bundling me into a cab and calling the driver Driver.

I recall him giving the driver money and my address. I wondered how he knew it. It must have been on some forms at work. How did he remember? I was grateful that he did, that he could deal with Driver for me.

He said, "Let's do this again sometime. Better yet, let's have a proper meal. Cheerio."

Then he scuttled off down the street, moving surprisingly fast for an older man who'd drunk all that whiskey.

CHAPTER 6

Anya Partridge's author portrait gave no clue as to the location of her dark, seductive opium den of a bedroom. I'd pictured a sanctuary carved out of a walk-up or a basement apartment, something down a few steps from the street on the fringes of Greenwich Village or a bombed-out corner of Chelsea. But the card that Warren gave me said *Elmwood* and listed an address on River Road in Shad Point, which, I learned, was forty miles north of Manhattan. Everything about the name, the location, and Anya's photo converged into the image of a stately Hudson River mansion, the house where Anya grew up, or where she was being kept in extravagant style by her lover, an ancient but still lusty robber baron.

I was touched by Warren's offer to lend me his car and his driver, Ned, for my meeting with "our author." Did Warren call Ned *Driver*? Warren called him Ned. I was grateful, yet I checked the gift for signs of a Trojan horse. Was Warren so insulated that he thought I needed an escort to venture beyond the edge of Manhattan? Or had he found an ingenious way of knowing how long I spent with Anya? Was he Anya's jealous lover? I doubted it, considering how casual he was with Elaine and the women he courted at the office, all of whom seemed above and beyond possessiveness and drama. Maybe Warren was making sure I was doing a good job, not screwing things up with a writer we needed to succeed.

Ned was waiting for me outside the office. It was a foggy, raw April day that reminded me of the unseasonably nasty weather at my college graduation. Ten months ago. My God. How could all that time have passed? What did I have to show for it except some scrawled notes on a bad novel in my briefcase? The pages of the scholarly book that I would never write flipped past me, too fast to read, and my unwritten study of the sagas snapped shut before I could make out the title.

I told myself not to despair, to enjoy the moment. Relax. I'd never ridden in the back of a Lincoln before.

The sensation of floating above the road took some getting used to. I'd had dreams of traveling in an airplane that stayed on the ground and navigated the streets instead of the air. In those dreams I was always relieved because road travel seemed safer than flying, but now I felt disoriented, gliding along without feeling the blacktop bumping beneath me.

Ned drove up the West Side Highway, then over a bridge that took us past bluff-side Tudor manors and along the Hudson through enchanted villages, past a ruined castle. Had we left the twentieth century? Had I rocketed into the past with Ned at the helm of our time machine? Ned didn't speak. He didn't want me to speak. His silence discouraged conversation.

We passed a massive complex of high walls and towers and fences, and I recognized Sing Sing from TV. Not the place so much as its cruel, bullying spirit.

Ned didn't talk, didn't turn, didn't twitch. I was on my own with the irony of passing the place where Ethel and Julius died, and where Anya's novel was set. Ned knew it was Sing Sing, but probably not about Anya's novel.

How chilly it was. How bleak the sky looked, how sticklike and straggly the trees, how black and knotty the branches, how pale and stunted the grass. I weighed every banal observation about the weather, considered whether or not to mention it to Ned, and decided against it.

Not long past the prison we turned into a driveway marked by a sign that said *Elmwood*. My dreams of Anya, the tough-girl sexy rebel novelist in her cold-water basement flat had not included the manicured road that curled through a grove of ancient elms. I'd been closer to the mark when I'd imagined her as the pampered mistress of a Hudson River robber baron.

Ned stopped to let some pedestrians cross, shuffling like buffaloes at a watering hole. Bundled-up attendants pushed bundled-up patients in wheelchairs. Every head, healthy and sick, drooped on every chest. The attendants were in white, while the patients wore identical ugly parrot-green wool caps, pulled down their foreheads against the damp and chill. It was nice that they had warm matching hats, like members of a sports team, but the color flattered no one. There were too many patients and caretakers for me to think I was seeing someone's elderly clan wheeled out for fresh air.

Elmwood was an institution.

I asked Ned, "Does Miss Partridge work here?"

Ned waited till the last inmate was safely across the road. Then he said, into the mirror, "She lives here."

Ned's tone said *mental illness*. What clue had I missed? After all those months "battling" the slush pile, I had yet to learn that lots of troubled people wrote books, masterpieces and trash, better and worse than Anya's. Warren had talked in meetings about the gifted poets he'd known at Harvard who'd thrown themselves into the Charles and wound up at some ritzy nuthouse in the Berkshires. The difference was that we weren't publishing the deranged fictions that passed through my office. We *were* publishing *The Vixen*, and Anya's problems, whatever they were, had become my own.

That Anya might be a patient explained certain aspects of her novel, her familiarity with the justice system and incarceration. I'd assumed she'd invented all that, read a few right-wing columnists, and mined the dank recesses of her imagination.

The faux-Gothic stone mansion was overheated, and I began to sweat even as I pushed open the massive faux-medieval door. Rivulets ran down my armpits as I asked to see Anya Partridge. A nurse in a white uniform sat behind the reception desk. Another nurse, in an equally crisp white uniform, sighed, then rose and, looking back over her shoulder at me with resignation and pity, led me down the hall. I thought of Ethel's Death House matron, that final kiss on the cheek, the prison guard telling the world how sad Ethel was and how much she loved her sons. I expected locks and keys, gates, alarms. But there were none.

I could have found Anya's room on my own, so strong was the smell of incense wafting out from beneath the door. The nurse knocked gently, then stepped back, less like someone with good manners than like someone disarming a bomb.

"She's expecting you," the nurse said.

Anya Partridge opened the door, and we shook hands in a steamy cloud of perfume and French tobacco. She looked just like her photograph, as did the carved, canopied bed behind her, which she appeared to have just left. I was at once unsurprised and shocked that she so closely resembled her author portrait. I'd spent so long staring at it, I felt as if I knew her. And for a few deranged moments I imagined that she knew what we'd done in my dreams. As if she'd been there with me.

Beneath the florals and smoke was a syrupy candy scent that I thought might be opium. I was afraid to inhale, though I knew that was silly.

"You must be Mr. Putnam."

"Please call me Simon," I said.

"Then you must call me Anya. Come into my parlor, said the spider to the fly."

My strangulated laugh was pure hysteria. I wished I could take it back. I felt helpless, unnerved. Anya had already taken control. How had I let that happen? Surely this wasn't how writers and editors customarily started their editorial meetings.

Made up like a '20s vamp, Anya was delicate and slight. Her kohl-rimmed eyes stared up into mine, longer and harder than I was used to. Her face was fox-like, pale and pointed, her straight black hair bobbed and shiny as enamel. Her valentine lips were painted scarlet, her rouged cheekbones so prominent that her pale skin suggested a flawless tent stretched across a frame.

As she stepped into the hall, I saw that her eyes were a startling violet, her pupils encircled by a midnight-blue corona. At the start of *Njal's Saga*, a man is warned that the woman he wants has the eyes of a thief. He ignores the warning, and it costs countless lives. Was I looking into a thief's eyes? In college I'd thought I knew what that meant, but now I had no idea. Anya was younger and more coltish than she'd been in my dreams. I smacked my briefcase against my shin, to remind myself why I was there.

I was there to meet "my" writer. I had come for a professional meeting and not for a tryst with a sex-mad nympho with whom I'd done crazy stuff, night after night. How did I even *know* about some of the things we'd done? In my dreams, they were Anya's ideas. I went along and enjoyed it. I had to forget the sex dreams and (if possible) the Rosenbergs and focus on the fact that I was here to begin a working partnership with a debut novelist.

Anya's forthright stare, along with the slow smile that spread across her face, made me think I'd seen her before, not just in my dreams or her author photo. After a while I realized that I was looking at Esther, Anya's heroine.

Esther Rosenstein's eyes were violet, her hair black, her bee-stung lips painted scarlet. Anya had written about herself, about the vixen she wanted to be. It would be tricky to persuade her to make substantive changes. She wouldn't want to see herself as a plump, trusting housewife bamboozled into committing a crime because her baby brother asked her to do some typing. Anya wouldn't happily cross out the passage in which Esther kisses the prison matron farewell, insistently thrusting her tongue between the astonished matron's lips.

"Please," Anya said. "Do come in."

Closing the door behind us, she glanced along the corridor. "Have you seen Van Gogh's painting of the hallway in that last asylum? Saint-Rémy or Arles, I forget. All the doors are shut. It's a picture of a suicide about to happen. The scariest painting ever."

"No," I said. "I haven't seen it. I didn't—"

I was surprised and impressed that Anya knew something I didn't. At the same time I felt guilty for being so superior and condescending that Anya's knowing about a painting had surprised and impressed me. She'd written a book, and I hadn't, even if her novel was worse than anything I would have written.

"I saw the painting in a book about Van Gogh," she said. "Look it up."

Anya wore a short black slip beneath a cropped white fur jacket and over a long, silky burnt-orange skirt. Its hem pooled over embroidered slippers that curved up like cobras ready to strike. Bride of Dracula meets Turkish whore meets Edith Piaf, the little sparrow.

"I'll look for it," I said. "Presently."

Presently? I sounded like the detective in a British murder mystery who crashes the family gathering and ruins everyone's fun.

Anya fell back on the bed and offered me the only chair.

"Just throw all that crap on the floor." I tried not to look at the tangle of silky garments I had to displace. She'd known I was coming. She could have straightened up. The satiny chaos had been left there on purpose so I could feel the coolness slip through my hands. The chair's ebony arms enclosed a pair of rough Moroccan pillows so stiff I had to wriggle around to scoop out a spot for my back.

"Would you like some tea?"

I nodded, wanting tea less than the time it might give me. I looked around at the wood-paneled room, its windows divided into diamonds of smudged leaded glass, every surface fringed and covered in paisley and brocade, a bedroom for Sarah Bernhardt or Oscar Wilde. Or Mata Hari, to whom Anya's novel had—many times—compared its heroine. It was like a stage set, the fantasy lair that a young woman with money and privilege might construct, a chamber in which to take drugs and seduce besotted young men. I thought disloyally of Marianna's convent-like bedroom at Radcliffe, with the little Buddha and the Hindu gods that stared at us so disapprovingly as we scurried under the covers.

In one corner of Anya's room was a handsome Mission-style writing desk. On it was a green glass vase holding a spray of pens and pencils, a stack of snowy typing paper, and a tall, old-fashioned black typewriter.

Ethel's typewriter had looked like that. I'd seen a photo in the paper. I imagined Ethel typing: a favor for her brother. I didn't want to think about Ethel in the presence of someone who had written three hundred pages of smut and lies about her.

I still hadn't found out how Warren acquired Anya's manuscript. I'd assumed she'd given it to him at one of those literary parties at which people were friendlier when they heard where you worked, gatherings where people were *very* friendly to Warren.

That Anya lived in an asylum suggested an alternate route of transmission. I recalled Warren warning me that other publishers might jump on *The Vixen*. Maybe Anya had connections. Maybe her parents knew an agent who had sent it to Warren and others. Pretty girls had an easier time getting men to do things. There was also the chance that Warren was right about how well her book would sell and about the possibility that our competitors would know that too.

Anya said, "Remind me. Did you say *yes* to tea? They put something in your food here. You're always waking up with strangers leaning in your face, asking if you feel anxious or depressed. Of course you feel anxious and depressed when every morning you're woken up by a different pervert in a white jacket. They do funny things with time. One minute it's yesterday, and suddenly it's tomorrow. Has that ever happened to you?"

"Yes. I mean yes, I'll have some tea. That would be . . . that would be . . . Thank you."

"I take that as a yes," Anya said.

I watched her glide across the room toward the hot plate. It felt wrong to notice how her ass shifted under her skirt. I was an animal. My author was making tea, and my hands were trembling with desire. She was my writer and not my dream lover. I had to be clear about that distinction.

Anya poured us tea, handed me my cup, and set hers on the night table, then kicked off her slippers and scrambled onto the edge of the bed, perching there with her legs crossed, her bare feet twisted up and resting on her thighs. I wondered if she'd seen the famous photograph of Colette, whom she resembled, sitting like that, but without Colette's penciled-on cat whiskers. Warren said she looked like Colette. I wondered if he'd told her that and inspired her to look *more* like Colette.

"So, Anya! Uh . . . How do you know Warren?" It seemed like a neutral question until I recalled Elaine saying that maybe they'd slept together. Elaine hadn't bothered asking.

I sipped the oddly salty tea.

"Lime-blossom tea," said Anya. "Very Proustian, no? It doesn't taste like you'd imagine."

Marianna had served me lime-blossom tea. This tasted nothing like that. I didn't think this was lime-blossom tea, but I wasn't going to contradict Anya. Yesterday Warren had stopped by my office and said, "I have two pieces of advice. One: Stand up for what you believe. Two: Pick your battles." Whether or not this was lime-blossom tea wasn't a battle I needed to win.

"That was Proust's dirty little secret. His precious tisane tastes like fish food. Another joke is that queer guys say that lime-blossom tea is an aphrodisiac. I don't believe that, do you? Unless maybe you're queer *and* a Proust fan. Are you?"

"No and yes, I mean yes, I read Proust, and no, I'm not queer."

How had we veered so far off the track?

Anya's novel. Anya's novel.

"Warren," I reminded her. "How did you two meet?" Shouldn't I have started off by praising her book? Why not begin with a few compliments, however insincere? Because her book had upset me, and I'd dug in my heels, though I knew it wasn't the best way to begin a productive working relationship.

"I've met Mr. Landry a few times. But the person I actually know is dear sweet Preston Bartlett. He was here when I arrived. This lovely girl used to come to visit him. She was pregnant. She worked at your firm . . . Anyhow, *someone* thought she should quit. Did you know her?"

"I met her once." I wasn't going to confess that I'd taken Julia's office.

"I thought she should quit the minute she got pregnant. I believe in prenatal influences, don't you? I read about this woman whose baby was born blind after she went to see a blind jazz pianist and he looked straight at her, or whatever blind people do when they seem to be looking at you. I don't know what evil spirits that poor girl might encounter in the publishing world. I know it's unscientific, but people have known this stuff for centuries before there *was* science, and now they're always proving that 'unscientific' things are true. Anyway, I think it's better to stay home so you can control what you see. If you don't watch TV."

"Do *you* watch TV?" I wondered if Anya had watched TV the day of the Rosenberg execution. Maybe it would have made her soften her harsh, unforgiving portrayal of Ethel.

"Sometimes constantly, sometimes never. I don't have a TV in my room here. But there is one in the dayroom, and it is *extremely* upsetting to watch soap operas with mental patients. The screaming, the yelling, the carrying on. They *feel more* than normal people.

"Anyway, I wasn't going to scare that poor pregnant girl with my silly superstitions. She was so kind to Preston. Practically his only visitor. I got to chatting with her in the family lounge. I heard she worked in publishing. I asked her all about it. *Picked her brain*, as they say. What a disgusting expression! So I decided to write a novel, and one thing led to another."

"You decided to write a novel?"

"I assume that's why you're here."

This was when I was supposed to tell Anya how much I admired her book, how happy I was to be working on it, how there were just a few minimal edits I hoped she would consider. This was when I should begin to find out how flexible she was, how amenable to change.

Instead, I said, "Was her name Julia?" I still cringed when I thought about Julia. I must have wanted to probe that tongue-in-sore-tooth pain. Or maybe I hoped that Anya might say something to make the memory less painful.

"Whose name?" Anya inspected her manicured fingernails, painted black.

"The pregnant woman who visited Preston."

"Julia, right. Something like that. You're not drinking your tea."

As it cooled, the tea had taken on a cat-box flavor, and for a second I thought I might gag. The hero drinks from the witch's cup, and forty years later he awakens, still in her cave. What had Crowley's attractive teaching assistants thought the second, the fifth, the tenth time they heard that story? That story and every story. His students were enchanted. We only heard the stories once.

"I liked her . . . I mean, Julia. No one here is anywhere *near* my age. You're the first one in a while. Even the nurses are ancient. I gave my novel to Julia, who gave it to someone else, and then, according to Preston, Julia got fired. I don't think it was because she gave them my novel. I *hope* not."

"Obviously not," I said. "On the contrary! So . . . Anya. When did you start writing?"

"I've written since I was a girl."

As she said this, Anya straightened her shoulders, pulled herself up to her full height, and seemed to be addressing a crowd. I was witnessing the live birth of a public author. That was what Warren wanted, and maybe he wanted me to be the first approving witness to that transformation. There was a reason for that author photo, the same reason why we were publishing a middlebrow novel by a writer who looked like Anya. We were saving our business by selling her. Selling a product. And selling the Rosenbergs, though no one said that. I would deal with that later. Today was just about meeting "my" writer.

"I wanted to write about a really strong, really powerful, really *important* modern woman. Someone who got famous because she had *ideas*."

"Ideas about what?" I was instantly sorry I'd asked, afraid I was about to hear Anya's take on the evils of Communism. And there was something awful about her use of the word *famous*.

"Ideas about personal freedom. About not acting out of altruism or sentiment or, worst of all, guilt. About a woman who has sex when *she* wants to, *with* whomever she wants to. Like what's-her-name in *The Fountainhead*. I didn't much care for the novel, but I did think Ayn Rand made some intelligent points. Have you read *Gone with the Wind*?"

"No." I could have said I did, but I was already telling so many lies. Lies of omission, but still. I could be truthful about one small thing. "I think my mother read it."

"Did she like it?"

"I don't know." Mom had been embarrassed when I found the novel on a shelf among the books she'd used for her classes. Oh, my poor parents! What had I done to make them ashamed of themselves, afraid of me, of my *Harvard education*? What could have made them feel inferior to a person whose career might hinge on his ability to charm the author of a mediocre novel?

"Scarlett O'Hara stole other women's boyfriends and treated men like dirt, and my God, she *had slaves*—and everybody loves her! I was looking for a strong woman like that. So I got interested in Ethel Rosenberg, and it was off to the races."

Ethel as Scarlett O'Hara? I couldn't begin to make sense of that. What struck me was that Anya saw Ethel/Esther as a heroine. Then why didn't Esther seem like one? Because she committed treason. She worked for the Russians. My thoughts chased one another and vanished, the way they sputtered and skipped at the edge of sleep. I should have asked Anya to think harder, to read more, to consider a more nuanced view of Ethel/Esther. But how could I begin?

Had Anya told Warren that her literary inspiration was *Gone with the Wind*? Even I knew how well that book sold.

"Preston's the only fun person in this place. And the bar for fun has been set pretty low. Mostly it's drooling old guys. Should I not have said that? Was that mean? I'm *so* glad you're here."

"Not at all. You can say what you want. Your secret's safe with me."

Who had said that? Elaine. I was quoting Elaine. It made me feel more solid and less anxious, as if Elaine were standing beside me. Not that I wanted Elaine there when I was alone with Anya.

"What secret?" Anya looked wary. What did she think I meant? What secret did *she* mean?

I said, "It's just an expression."

"Well, that's a relief. Preston says everybody's got secrets, and that some people think it's their mission to find out everyone else's. But Preston's crazy, or so they say and . . . "

Anya wound and unwound her limbs, in a practiced, balletic series of motions. Every gesture revealed her awareness of being watched, and of the helpless intensity with which I was watching. I wished I didn't find it sexy. Everything would have been simpler if I hadn't wanted to touch her neck, her breast, to know how it would feel to kiss her.

"Preston's obsessed with Mr. Landry. But everyone's obsessed with something. Or with someone. Am I right? Right now I'm obsessed with my novel."

"Well, I guess that makes two of us." How had I let *that* slip out?

"Really?"

"Sure. That's why I'm here." I smiled. Anya waited for more praise, but I couldn't.

"Preston's a very intense old guy. Get him talking about Warren, and he'll go on all day, saying all kinds of outrageous things—"

"For example?" I was almost whispering for fear of spooking Anya into silence. I wanted to hear what Warren's former partner said about him.

"Oh, I don't know. Standard-issue paranoid conspiracy stuff. I can't remember exactly. After a while, I tune Preston out. I have to, if I want to keep what shreds of sanity I have left. Mr. Landry came to visit me here to talk about my book, and they had to drug Preston half unconscious so he wouldn't make a scene. I don't know what they thought Preston would do. Run Mr. Landry down in his wheelchair?"

So much information so casually deployed, but what rose to the top was: when Mr. Landry came to visit. What did he and Anya talk about? How long did he stay? Warren was Anya's publisher. He had every right to see her. How could I be jealous? I'd known Anya all of twenty minutes, not counting the time in my dreams.

"I don't know why Preston goes into that office. I think he does it to scare people, to remind them the corpse is alive."

"He scared *me*," I said.

"Don't let him. The old guy's a sweetie. No one breathes around here until he's back safe from his little expeditions to the office. Once Preston told me he'd been rooting around in Warren Landry's desk to find some tax papers, and he'd found documents proving that Landry was involved in some really evil stuff."

"Evil?" I said. "How evil?" It sounded unlikely. Why would Warren leave papers like that in his desk for anyone to find?

Anya shrugged. "*Evil* means evil. I don't know. I stop listening and forget, and then Preston gets paranoid and says his room is bugged. Julia told me that Preston confronted Warren at an office party, and Warren shoved Preston up against a bookcase. I assume they were drunk. I mean, who *does* that at a Christmas party? Pass the eggnog, and by the way, I know your dirty deeds, pal. Once Preston said that during his first year out of college, he lived with an Amazon tribe that built a landing strip for a plane bringing back the dead. He said he'd heard a dog sing the Communist 'Internationale.' He said he'd seen a city carved in the eye of a needle. He said that starlings were coming to kill us. He said that honey bees speak different languages depending on where they live."

I said, "Anya, what are you doing here? I mean here, in this place."

I watched her decide what, and how much, to tell me.

"The usual story. Unsuitable boyfriend, parents with so much money they found a friendly judge they could bribe to rule that I needed to be protected from the world, or the world needed to be protected from me. Someone had to be protected from something. I assume Mother and Father will keep me here until my unsuitable boyfriend finds another rich girl. Did Warren tell you I was an acting student before they put me away? Not just a student. An actress. I was really good at it and now . . . I like to think of everything as a blessing in disguise. If I hadn't been here, I wouldn't have met Preston and Julia. It wouldn't have occurred to me to write a novel. It seemed like a fun way to pass the time until my parents saw the light. Would you think less of my book if I told you I wrote it in a few months?"

"No. Not at all. Maybe that's where we can start." I extracted some pages from my briefcase and passed them to Anya.

She said, "What the hell? Someone scribbled all over this. Was it you?"

"There's not so much . . . scribbling," I said. "Not really."

I took the literary, tentative route, measured and polite. I suggested that all writers occasionally find a word they like and maybe, just maybe, use it a bit too often.

"Like what?" said Anya. "Like what word?"

"Well . . . *strode*. Jake *strode* down the prison corridor. Esther *strode* along the hall. The judge *strode* out of the courtroom. That's an awful lot of striding." A mocking note had crept into my voice, and I heard it too late. I was annoyed with Anya for putting me through this. And for some reason her beauty made it even more annoying. Ultimately, there wasn't much I could do. As Warren explained, the book I would have liked her to write would never be published.

"How embarrassing," said Anya. "I *do* know other words. *Walked. Moved. Left. Rushed. Hurried.* Change anything you want. I don't care."

Anya didn't mean *change anything*. She wasn't giving up total control.

"Help me figure this out," she said. "How is this supposed to work?"

By *this* I assumed she meant the editing process.

"I work on your book for a while, we discuss some . . . changes, then I give it to you and you do some work on it, then we can decide how to . . . make the sentences better and—"

Anya said, "Do you mind if I smoke?"

"Of course. Please. It's your room."

Anya put the pages aside, sat back on her bed, and lit up one of her black cigarillos. In my dreams she smoked after sex. I awoke to the smell of burning. She pursed her lips and blew a stream of smoke up toward her forehead. I longed to reach out and straighten the bangs that her smoky breath had ruffled. It seemed so unfair that I couldn't touch someone with whom I'd been so intimate in my fantasies.

In a kittenish soprano, high above her ordinarily throaty voice, she said, "Could *you* just make the changes? Pretty please?"

"Sure." I still had no idea how much she'd be willing to change, or how I would suggest it.

"One thing," she said. "I'm a terrible speller. I'm very self-conscious about it. If a genie popped out of a bottle and said, You can change one thing about yourself, I'd say, Make me a spelling-bee champion! Please fix any spelling mistakes. I won't be embarrassed. I'm embarrassed enough already."

"I didn't notice one spelling error." If *only* the problem was spelling.

"I want my book to be perfect."

"So . . . do . . . I," I said slowly, as if she and I were taking a solemn vow.

After a silence, I said, "And then . . . well . . . there's something a little bigger, a sort of, well, *thematic* thing I wish that you would just . . . think about."

"I don't like the sound of *something a little bigger*. How big? And what do you mean by *thematic*?"

I hesitated, wanting to get this right, knowing I wouldn't. "Well . . . Esther's character. Her conscience. Does she have any second thoughts about having sex with all those men?" It seemed safer than asking if Esther had second thoughts about giving the secret of the A-bomb to the Russians.

"No," said Anya. "She does *not*. Do *men*? Do men ever have second thoughts about sex? Not in *my* experience." Anya's experience sounded so much wider than my own that I deferred to her greater wisdom. "I don't care about the *thematic* part. Please. Make the sentences better. That's not my highest priority. That's *your* job, right?"

"That is," I said. "But still that leaves us with one big question. About the real life—"

Anya leaned forward. "The real life of . . ."

"The real life of the Rosenbergs." I felt light-headed with anxiety. What was I afraid of? A debut novelist we were going to publish regardless of what I did or said? I imagined Warren shaking his head. Watch the novice editor screwing up his first real job.

"Wait a second," said Anya. "I'm hearing something I don't know if I like. Tell me you're not one of those deluded commie morons who think the Rosenbergs were innocent. That they were martyred heroes who went to their deaths because they were *innocent*. This is America! We don't execute innocent people. You must be thinking of Russia. That's what they do in the Soviet Union. All you have to do there is get on some powerful person's nerves. Some politburo fascist creep. One false move and it's off to the gulag, comrade."

Politburo? Gulag? I hated how surprised I was when Anya knew something I hadn't expected. It wasn't her fault that she was beautiful, that she'd written a less-than-great novel. That she hadn't gone to Harvard, where I'd learned to be a snob, and now I was going to have to unlearn it.

I should have suspected that Anya had ideas. I should have paid attention to what her novel was saying. After all, she'd written a book, for which she deserved some respect, though not as much as she would have if *The Vixen* were better. It was essential to think about this project in a positive way.

Meanwhile I'd missed some connection, come unstuck in the conversation. What had I said to make Anya squint at me with such undisguised irritation?

"What kind of *point* is *that* to make about a woman—I mean Ethel or Esther or whatever the hell we call her—with two little kids? I'm not seeing it that way. I don't want to. I think the real Ethel wanted to be rich and famous, or at least live in Russia. As if any sane human being would want to freeze her ass off in Moscow, waiting on line for one moldy potato! She wanted to be a heroine. I don't think she wanted to be dead. Maybe she chose death over divorce. I wouldn't blame her, which is why I made the husband impotent. I admire her. I mean my character. Not the real person. I mean Esther. Not Ethel. Maybe Esther *liked* those men. Maybe she *wanted* to sleep with them. A light went on when I thought: Why not put *her* in control? Why not let the poor thing *feel something*, have some fun, experience some sexual pleasure before they strap her down and throw the switch?"

Why? Because Ethel Rosenberg had been a real person, on the surface so like Anya's Esther Rosenstein that people would think she was writing about the real woman. The guilty one. If readers had been uncertain about Ethel's alleged crime, by the time they'd spent hundreds of pages inside her twisted commie psyche, they would know she was guilty of espionage and worse.

But Anya was "my" author, *The Vixen* "my" book. If I couldn't live with it, I would have to turn it into something that I *could* live with— or quit.

I said, "Your novel is so . . . persuasive and convincing . . . maybe a little . . . too . . . convincing."

"Well!" said Anya. "Finally! That's the first halfway nice thing you've said about my book since you got here. But why am I reminding *you* that *The Vixen* is a *novel*? It's *fiction*, okay? It's not a history book. To be honest, I hate history. I'm not saying she was innocent, I'm not saying she was guilty. I made up a *story* about a woman who likes power and sex, who likes to control men. A woman who wants to rule the world. Even if she doesn't always know what she wants or *why*. Which is Esther's downfall. What woman doesn't want power? That's another reason why my parents put me here. They hate the fact that I'm determined to be what I want, do what I want, sleep with whomever I want. I've written a story that every woman can identify with, and your boss is right when he says that readers will love it."

It was hard to admit: how badly I wanted to sleep with a woman who had just said she hated history, wanted power, and planned to sell herself to the highest bidder. I'd thought I had nothing to learn from Anya, but I'd been wrong. I was learning how desire can make you unrecognizable to yourself.

Anya leaned toward me. "Preston says that Warren is having money problems. His ship is sinking now that Preston's not keeping it afloat. Now that they can't soak Preston for what's left of his trust fund. As for my contract—I'm pretty sure your boss screwed me. Metaphorically. But I'm young, and when *The Vixen* does well, I'll be on my way. It'll be good for me, for Warren, for your company, for you. So do whatever it is you do, make the sentences better, but, as smart girls tell their hairdressers, don't cut too much—leave what I want, how I want it."

Anya flashed me a practiced smile, calibrated for maximum cuteness and to at once affirm and deny her having just compared my editing her book to my giving her a haircut. "Can we put off the work till later? Can we blow this clam shack and have a little fun?"

Clam shack? It took me a second to equate clam shack with asylum. "Can you just leave—?"

"I'm free as a bird. Until ten tonight, when I turn back into a pumpkin. Depending on why we inmates were sent here, this place is less like a lockup than like a slutty dorm at Sarah Lawrence. Unless you're suicidal or having hallucinations. Or like Preston, who, let loose, would probably kill Warren. They'd have to be very careful if Preston wasn't in a wheelchair."

"And *why* does Preston want to kill Warren?"

"Haven't we been through that?" She leaned as close to me as she could without falling off the bed. "I thought we were getting out of here and doing something fun."

"Sure . . . I guess so . . . why not . . . sure, fun . . . Where do you want to go?" I stammered and then stalled, stunned by how quickly a professional meeting had devolved into something more like an awkward first date.

"Anywhere. We have Ned, Mr. Landry's charioteer, at our command."

"You know Ned?" Anya had said that Warren was only here once, yet she knew Ned's name.

"Warren and I went out for coffee in Purchase. Ned drove. I have a memory for names."

Warren and I. Not *Mr. Landry*.

"Why don't we go to Coney Island?" I heard myself say, as if from a distance. I admired whoever made that brilliant suggestion. If Anya wanted excitement, we could ride the Cyclone. I knew the place. I was comfortable there. I could impress her.

Anya clapped her hands. Her bracelets tinkled. "Coney Island! What a fantastic idea!"

It was strange, my having been so quick to suggest a place that I had spent so much effort and time—years, really—pretending not to have come from. But Anya was eccentric. An artist. Different standards applied. In her eyes, my having grown up in an amusement park—well, *near* an amusement park—might have a certain sexy cachet. She would see that I was more than an annoying guy in a cheap suit come to nag her about her sentences and shame her about her spelling. All the people from whom I'd hidden my origins—my school friends, colleagues, literary party guests, Warren, even Elaine—seemed, compared to Anya, pallid, pretentious, judgmental. I felt absurdly grateful to Anya, who had done nothing to earn my gratitude besides writing a flawed novel and thinking that Coney Island sounded exciting.

"I've never been there," said Anya.

"That's impossible," I said.

"Impossible? More things in heaven and earth than you ever dreamed of, Horatio, blah blah blah."

Our little vixen was quoting Shakespeare! A reader of *Hamlet*, Ayn Rand, and *Gone with the Wind*. Everyone was a tangle of contradictions—including me, it seemed. I longed to reach out and stroke the delicate face of the author of a book that had already tested my integrity, destroyed my peace of mind, and might yet ruin my career.

Apparently, the business part of our meeting was ending, and I still had no clue as to who "my author" was. Nothing about her fit into any category I knew.

I realized that I was nervous about going out in the world with Anya, and I looked around her room, searching for a way to delay our exit, even by a few minutes. What other reason did I have for asking, "One thing before we go. Can you do me a favor? Would you mind typing something for me on your typewriter?" I liked how this sounded—confident, cavalier—more like a literary man with a professional interest in how manuscripts are produced than an awkward, anxious kid about to venture into the unknown with a beautiful and intimidating young woman.

"Why?"

"I love old typewriters." That much was true. My ancient Underwood had been my mother's. I used it all through college and brought it back home when I returned.

"What should I type?"

"I don't know. The title page of your novel."

"That is so editor-y," Anya said. "But sure. It was Father's typewriter. He gave it to me when he got a new one. As soon as I get money for my book, this one's headed straight to the Smithsonian. Father says we could get a tax break, not that I pay taxes. But I expect to, soon."

"If the book does well—"

"My point exactly," Anya said. "Warren and I agree on that, and I trust him, don't you?" She rolled in a sheet of paper and typed slowly, with obvious difficulty. Hitting the stiff round keys required focus and effort. At last Anya gave me the page.

The Vickson, the Patriot, and the Fanatic
  A Novel by
  Anya Partridge

The Vickson? Anya wasn't joking about her spelling problem.

"Thank you." I said. "Will you sign it?"

I could tell she loved being asked. "Sure. I guess. But why?"

"As a promise about our long and successful working relationship."

That was how I would play this. Sleek, debonair, a little phony. I would imitate Warren—though, I feared, without Warren's charisma.

"Can I borrow your pen?"

Why hadn't I brought something more elegant than a cheap ballpoint? Anya didn't seem to notice as she grabbed the pen and signed her name with the flourish of a signatory to the Declaration of Independence. I slipped the paper into the blood-colored folder.

"I love that you carry my book with you. I hope you're carrying it close to your heart. Or close to wherever."

Of course I had her book. That was why I'd come. I chose to ignore her *close to wherever.*

"I don't want to lose it. Coney Island is an easy place to forget what you brought with you."

"Don't worry," she said. "We can leave it with Ned. Ned will guard it with his life."

Anya swirled a long cloak around her shoulders, wrapping herself in the folds of a garment that seemed all wrong, showy in a place where you might prefer to be invisible, likely to get snagged on a carnival ride. But the cape was dramatic and very attractive. Anya's pretty face popped out of it like a flower.

"Wait. I need to get Foxy. My lucky charm. I can't leave without it. It wards off the evil eye."

Maybe she did belong in a minimum-security asylum.

Hanging from a hook on the wall was an animal pelt. I averted my eyes as if from the sight of a living creature being skinned. When I did look, it was disturbing, not the stole so much as the enraptured, hypnotized way in which Anya wound it around her neck. It was like watching a love scene between a witch and her familiar. I thought of Esther's hocus-pocus with the animal pelt. More evidence that Anya was writing about herself. It would be hard to persuade her to cut Esther's fur fetish.

In those days, you often saw fur stoles made from the pelt of a fox or weasel with its head, tail, and claws still attached. Even when you were accustomed to it, the eyes and claws were a shock. No one would wear something like that now. They'd be afraid to leave the house. Even then, it was a statement about fashion and cruelty, a misguided mash-up of glamour, sex, and death.

With the fox draped around her neck, Anya vamped toward me half ironically and gave me a long look, so cartoonishly seductive that even I, who knew next to nothing about sex, felt pretty sure that eventually we would have it.

Giddy with desire, I still recognized a bad idea, though according to Uncle Maddie, plenty of men in our business mixed work and romance. One of the reasons I hesitated, or *told* myself that I hesitated, was that Anya's heroine, Esther Rosenstein, had the ability to conquer any man she wanted. The erotic spell she cast on Russians and Americans, spies and FBI men, her attempts to seduce the district attorney— that was the engine that drove Anya's novel. Unless I was careful, life would imitate art. Or maybe I was flattering myself to imagine that a woman like Anya would want to use me to get what she wanted, whether it be a book deal or a sketch of the A-bomb detonator.

Esther, the character, wore a fur stole when she was going after a man—and she prayed to it when she wasn't. That was where Esther got her nickname and the title of the novel.

"The vixen," I said to Anya.

"You're a clever one, aren't you? Simon, meet the vixen."

"Good to meet you," I said idiotically to the dreadful fur thing around her neck. Its shiny black button eyes stared at me. Anya bounced her shoulder blade and made the creature nod.

"Now can I ask *you* a favor?"

"Ask away," I said.

"Can you help me zip up my boots?" Anya sat down on the edge of the bed, pulled on two knee-high forest green suede boots, and turned up her palms, beseechingly, over the challenge of the zippers. Was *this* normal editor-author behavior? What was *normal*? Who zipped Anya's boots when I wasn't here? Who was here when I wasn't?

I knelt. Anya opened her legs. Her thighs were bare, firm, the color of cream. I caught a glimpse of black lace before I made myself stop looking. I wanted to weep like a child. I felt like a client kneeling before a dominatrix in a German Expressionist drawing. There I was between Anya's legs, thinking about Weimar art. I needed *not to be there*. What if my parents saw me? What would they think of the son for whom they'd sacrificed so much? How would they feel about this noble profession, this job that Mom had pressured my uncle to arrange? What would they conclude about this obvious waste of my education?

The boots were so tight that I had to gently compress Anya's calf to ease the zipper up, but she could have done it without me.

"There you go," I said.

"Thanks," Anya said. "Look. You're shivering. Poor baby. Dress up warm."

ANYA SIGNED OUT in the ledger on the reception desk, and the two nurses chimed, "Have a nice time, Miss Partridge." It seemed awfully casual for a patient leaving an asylum, and again I wondered what kind of place this was. Nothing made sense, but I wasn't going to ask questions and risk my chances of going to Coney Island with Anya.

The heavy door slammed behind us. We exploded into the gray day that seemed so much brighter than it had earlier. Anya ran ahead. I had to speed-walk to keep up. It was still misty and cold. In the soft wet light the gardens looked like I imagined England.

I said, "How long since you've gone outside?"

"I don't know. I told you. Time gets strange around here."

Ned was waiting for us in the driveway. Anya scrambled into the car. Unlike me, she seemed used to riding in luxury sedans. She slouched against the back seat. It might have seemed like harmless fun, daring but innocent, two kids playing hooky from school. But zipping her boots had changed that.

"Ned, do we have any champagne on board?"

"Not today, Miss Partridge," said Ned.

"Too bad," said Anya. "Warren never stocks anything good." *Never?* Anya said he'd visited once. How did she know that Warren never stocked champagne, and why did she need it now? Maybe she wanted to celebrate. Maybe she just liked it.

"What's on *your* mind, Mr. Editor? Why the tragic frown?"

I said, "I'm not frowning. I'm thinking."

"I bet you think too much."

I didn't want Anya thinking she knew how much—or what—I thought. Ned's presence made me self-conscious. I concentrated on the back of his neck just to focus on something. Then I looked out the window, where the landscape had magically turned green, though the sky was still gray. Half-open blossoms hung like yellow rags from the forsythia.

After a while Anya said, "I thought I'd be able to go home for Easter. But that's not going to happen. Easter's my favorite holiday. I like resurrection. Who doesn't? I don't mean zombies. I mean rising from the dead to save the human race. Not to eat human brains. How strange that we're having this conversation. Because look!"

We were passing a vast cemetery.

Anya said, "It's so crowded in there, the dead must be standing up."

I laughed even as I sensed that she'd heard that somewhere and had probably said it before.

It was a Jewish cemetery. Were my grandparents there? I knew they were in one of those massive graveyards just outside the city. Did my parents visit their parents' graves? I didn't even know that. I prayed for my grandparents to help me, though why would they? They'd never met me. I missed them suddenly, painfully. Was it possible to miss someone you never knew?

Where was Ethel buried? Her gravestone would be unveiled in June. Who would attend the ceremony meant to mark the year of mourning? Anya's novel had resurrected the Rosenbergs, not brought them back to life so much as dragged them from their graves. *You will see to it that our names are kept bright and unsullied by lies. The Vixen* had turned the Rosenbergs into Soviet sex zombies.

"I wonder where the Rosenbergs are buried." I knew that I shouldn't be saying that even before I reached the end of the sentence.

Anya shot me a quick, dark look.

"How should I know?" She stared out her window and didn't look at me when she said, "Easter. The bunny, the egg hunt. It's the only holiday not about death. The dead turkey, the dead presidents. Even our birthdays are about our death, if you see it that way—"

"Not Christmas," I said. "That's a birth. And Easter *is* about death. A crucifixion, to be exact." I sounded like a professor or, worse, a Sunday school teacher. Why couldn't I stop lecturing and have a normal conversation?

"Christmas has other problems. Must you *always* have the last word?"

"I don't, I mean, I—"

"I always go to St. Patrick's for Easter. They have the best choir and incense from actual *Bethlehem*. Sometimes you see celebrities. Once I saw Joan Crawford looking a million years old, in a pink Easter bonnet like a flying saucer landed on her head."

"What does your family do for Easter?"

"We argue," Anya said. "We drink and argue and get in the car and slam the door and drive off."

The back of Ned's shoulders revealed nothing but his concentration on the highway and the vehicles streaming by.

It was a long drive to the far edge of Brooklyn. But the excitement of being with Anya made the time go quickly. When the traffic stalled on the parkways, Ned displayed his encyclopedic knowledge of the backstreets of Yonkers and Flatbush. I welcomed every delay. I needed time to figure out what to do once we got to Coney Island. Should I take the lead and be the experienced man in charge—or should I defer to Anya? What would *you* like to do?

Anya was still rattling on about life holidays and death holidays, and I was no closer to solving my Anya problem than before. The foxy little novelist who'd done such crazy stuff in my dreams had turned out to be a wacky ambitious girl who didn't much care about whether the Rosenbergs sold the bomb to the Russians. She didn't care about literature or publishing. She didn't care about art. She cared about fame and money, about how her book would sell. She cared about being a bad girl, about having fun and breaking the rules, whatever she thought the rules were. Warren's May Day deadline was approaching, and it seemed unlikely that I would be able to make it.

Anya was right about one thing: the freewheeling spicy drama of the sexy spy and her international lovers was a livelier story than the mournful tale of the Communist stooge, good mom, and loyal housewife. Readers would prefer it. It would make them feel safer. The problem was: Anya's version was a lie. But so what? As Anya said, it was a *novel*. It wasn't *supposed* to be true.

So many things didn't add up. Where had Anya come from? What had she done before? A rich girl with fantasies of becoming an actress who'd scared or enraged her parents so much that they'd sent her . . . where? What kind of sanitarium lets its residents decorate their rooms like opium dens and breeze out whenever they want? And how had she gotten in contact with Warren?

Ned picked up speed on Ocean Parkway. I said, "Anya, where are you from?"

Anya hesitated. "If you start from where we were today and drive due east and a little north and don't stop until it gets so white bread and pastel and boring you feel like you're suffocating, that's where I come from. I don't think my parents noticed I was alive until I started bringing home scary boyfriends. They would never have let me go to Coney Island. They never approved of anything fun."

"I grew up in Coney Island." Even as I said it, I knew that it was a sentence I'd never said before, not even to Marianna, who believed I'd come from Manhattan. A sentence I'd never thought I'd say. Saying it made me feel closer to Anya than I'd felt to anyone since I'd left my parents' apartment. I reminded myself I'd just met her. But I'd stared at her photo. I'd dreamed about her, night after night.

Anya's bracelets clinked as she clapped her hands. "That's fantastic! What a fabulous place to be young! It must have been like growing up in freakshow Oz."

"Not exactly," I said. But it was. Coney Island was cooler than the suburb where Anya grew up, or the Darien mansion where I pictured Warren living. I had loved it, as a child, and then I had forgotten. Last summer, after graduation. I'd gone there every day, but I'd forgotten that too. I was grateful to Anya for having reconciled me to the truth.

It took me several trippy heartbeats to trace the tightness in my chest to the fact that we would be so near my parents' apartment, and I wasn't going to see them. I certainly wasn't going to bring Anya home. Hi, Mom, hi, Dad, meet the author of the sleazy novel about Ethel! Anya, meet Dad and Mom, Ethel's childhood friend.

My mother still had migraines, but they seemed to be improving. The Army-McCarthy hearings had begun, and when Dad came home, they watched them. The good guys appeared to be winning. McCarthy had said that the army was "soft on Communism," and the army had gone after him.

My mother believed that McCarthy's goose was cooked. My father was less certain. I tried not to see a connection between the hearings and Mom's headaches subsiding. Thinking that her pain had peaked with Ethel's execution and was improving now that the senator's power was waning would have made me hate McCarthy even more. It was one thing to endanger American democracy, but something else—something *personal*—to cause my mother pain.

Visiting them was nicer than it had been in a while. And yet I didn't go as often as I should, as often as I sensed they wanted. I was leading my life. They were proud, forbearing, respectful, but also, I knew, sad. They would have been sadder if they'd known what I was doing with Anya, sadder still if they found out that I'd been so near them and hadn't stopped by.

BY THE TIME Anya and I got to Coney Island, it was after three. The sea was a mean glassy gray, and the waves that licked the sand beside the road were bullying and insistent. The smell of sea salt was sharp and strong. The streets were half deserted. The season hadn't begun. I'd feared the amusement park might be shuttered, but a few rides and food stands were open for anyone crazy enough to be here on such a cold day.

Ned pulled over and stopped. I was anxious, here in the place I knew best. Being there with Anya had turned me into an outsider. Well, fine. Fear was part of the fun. You were supposed to feel jittery when you got to Coney Island.

I put my briefcase on the car floor.

Anya said, "Relax. I told you. Ned will take care of it."

Maybe some part of me *wanted* the manuscript stolen. There was a chance, a tiny chance, that it was the only copy. Then my problem would be solved by the thief, who would be crushed to open a stolen briefcase full of used typing paper.

"I'll be waiting," Ned said. "Come back when you want. Button up. It's cold. Have fun."

THE FOG MADE everything private. Mist swirled around us like a storm in a snow globe. The shooting galleries and food stands lit up and went dark as we passed. Warming their hands over trash can fires, the carnival barkers were silent, and the ticket takers seemed like ghosts waiting for the dead to ride the Wild Mouse. The world was waiting, stilled. The signs and marquees blurred and faded like a vintage postcard of an amusement park, a Japanese print of fog and clouds from which the Parachute Jump rose where Mount Fuji should have been.

Anya held my hand in a girlish, playful grip. Maybe I'd overreacted when she'd asked me to zip her boots. I blamed my dreams for my misunderstanding, for my assuming too much. I blamed her author photo. She'd asked a simple favor. It had meant nothing more.

Walking in the crisp sea wind restored our innocence, in a way, and the salt air repaired us. I felt as if we were teenagers, about to fall into a dream of love. As we walked along Neptune Avenue, I forgot everything except Anya's small, chilly hand in mine. And then I'd think: Boots. Zippers. *The Vixen.*

"Oh, look," Anya said. "Can we go on that?"

Of course she meant the Parachute Jump. I knew by the lift of her chin. There had been several accidents in recent years. Everyone knew it was dangerous. How ironic to be killed on the one ride my father begged me to avoid. I imagined my parents and Anya's parents brought together by grief. At least Anya and I wouldn't be there, mortified by the awkwardness of our families meeting, even or especially under those tragic circumstances.

"We'll freeze up there!" My voice sounded high and metallic. "Let's stay closer to the ground."

Anya pulled the hood of her cape over her head. My fingertips were numb. My jacket was too thin. When I'd left my apartment, I hadn't planned on winding up so near the ocean. "There's plenty to do without that."

I was grateful that she didn't insist we ride the Parachute Jump. Maybe she was eccentric, even daffy at times, but she wasn't willful or stubborn. She'd sensed my reluctance to go on the Parachute Jump, and the ease with which she'd let it go hinted at a natural sensitivity and kindness. I felt a surge of affection for the young writer who just wanted to see her novel in print. My job was to help her.

As we passed the game stalls, only some of which were open, the carnies glared at our leisure, our privilege, our youth, at something they might have mistaken for love. What would the cotton candy spinner think if she knew the truth? What was the truth? Maybe she could have told me.

The pavement was cracked and buckled. Anya made tripping and stumbling look like a dance step, but still she grabbed my elbow for balance. I longed to be suspended in time, in Coney Island forever, about to have fun, free from under the shadow of Warren, unburdened by Anya's novel. To stay like that, with Anya's hand, just like that, on my arm.

"Should we go on a ride?" Anya said. "Or eat something first? I'm starving."

"If we're going to go on the big rides," I said, "we should ride first and eat after."

"Brilliant point," Anya said.

Already we'd developed a rapport, sharing advice on how not to get sick. In Anya's novel, Esther vomits when the Feds knock on her door.

We passed the Tunnel of Love, its boats bobbing on a fetid ditch. From across the street we smelled mildew.

"Let's skip that one," Anya said. It wasn't funny, but we laughed, relieving the tension somewhat. "Have you read *Death in Venice*?"

I nodded. Thomas Mann. Shakespeare. Margaret Mitchell. Ayn Rand. Van Gogh. Anya's tastes were eclectic. Was she *trying* to confuse me? She was just being her own unique self. I'd never met anyone like her. Certainly not at Harvard.

"Bingo!" said Anya. "*Death in Venice* is my all-time favorite story. Mr. Editor College Graduate comes from a better class of guy than the ones I usually date."

Was I supposed to feel flattered? Did she think we were *dating*? *Were* we? By now she was so excited, looking around, I couldn't be the stodgy fun-spoiling pedant asking why she was drawn to the story of the dying baron stuck in plague-ridden Venice because of his passion for a beautiful boy. A passion for the wrong person. Or the right person. Was Anya warning me . . . or was it simply her favorite book?

The Wild Mouse, the Bobsled, the Thunder Train, the Whirl-a-Whirl, the Rocket Launch, the Tilt-a-Whirl, the Twister, the Bone-Shaker, the Sky Chaser, the Cannon Coaster, the Rough Rider, the Widowmaker, the Spine Cracker. Anya read the name of each ride aloud, and each one spiked her glee.

"What do *you* like to do here, Simon?"

What did I like? I liked hearing her say my name.

"Personally, I like the Cyclone."

"Wow. I didn't see you as a Cyclone kind of guy."

"That does it," I said. "Let's go for the hard stuff."

I would never again be so proud of being a "regular," not at the most iconic roadside diner or the trendiest restaurant or the most beautiful bookstore. I was thrilled that they knew me by name at a vintage roller coaster with a sketchy safety record.

Barb was taking the tickets, Angus working the switches.

"Simon," said Angus. "How goes it?"

"Come here often?" Anya doubled over laughing. A laugh so free it might have made Barb and Angus assume we were lovers. Wrong! We were an editor and writer riding the Cyclone instead of working. But maybe we were working, building a mutual trust that might help me persuade her to change her novel into something I could live with—and that no one would publish.

Anya said, "Can we ride in the front car?"

"That's what I usually do." I always stayed in the middle. The last car was supposed to be the scariest. I wasn't going to tell her. We were the only two passengers. What if Barb and Angus forgot us and quit for the day and left us at the top? But the smile that Anya gave Angus as he helped her into the car and pulled down the safety bar ensured that he would wait around.

After the first precipitous drop Anya put her arms around my waist.

"Hold on tight, girl!" Was that my voice? What had I said? Anya bent forward to feel the wind in her face.

When we plummeted a second time, Anya yelled into my ear, "This is how I imagine childbirth. Wave after wave of pain."

Anya didn't flinch, no matter how fast and far we fell. Faster than I remembered. The wheels had never rattled so loudly. Could Angus have ramped up the speed? Anya sat with her hands on the safety bar, like a puppy waiting to be taken for a walk, as we climbed and fell so fast that I thought the scaffolding would collapse, or our heads would fly off, or we would vault into space.

We smiled at each other as the ride slowed. Anya had tears in her eyes. We'd been through something. Angus lifted the safety bar, and Anya missed a step as she climbed out of the car. Angus leapt forward to steady her, but I beat him to it.

Anya whispered in my ear, "I want my book to sell a zillion copies." Her face was flushed, like a child's.

"So do I." Breathlessness made our voices sound heartfelt.

As we drifted away from the roller coaster, I felt scared. A delayed reaction—to what? I kept thinking of executions, of blindfolded men lined up against a wall. Where were the Rosenberg boys now? What would I do about Anya's novel?

Maybe this was simpler than I thought. I could work with the standard disclaimer at the front of works of fiction: "Any resemblance between the characters and real people, living or dead, is accidental, etc." We could run that in bold type. So it would be understood. After all, as Anya said, it was *fiction.*

"Can we go on the Cyclone again?"

"Let's give it a minute," I said. "Let our internal organs go back to where they're used to being."

"Good," she said. "I'm starving."

"Hot dogs? French fries?" I suggested Nathan's Famous.

"That's one thing I hate about men," she said. "They always try to tell you what to eat. I don't want to go to Nathan's. Let's try some place smaller and simpler and not so *famous.*"

I wasn't hungry, though I hadn't eaten all day. I hung back as Anya went from stand to stand. She kept vanishing into the fog, long enough for me to worry. Had she left me standing there? Would Ned and the car be waiting? What would become of Anya's book? What if I never saw her again?

Interrogating the vendors, her voice piped through the mist. "What's the least salty and most filling and delicious thing you have?" Finally she reappeared. How glad I was to see her! She led me to a falafel stand that must have met her specifications.

The falafel guy said, "I told her it's all good. Maybe try the rice pudding."

I paid for a bucket of rice pudding and a wooden spoon. Anya ate as we walked.

"Let's go on a dark ride." She'd finished most of the pudding. She offered me the rest. It was painfully sweet. The raisins tasted astringent. I ate as much as I could. Anya stuck her cold sticky hand in my pocket, and I wrapped my hand around hers.

The Spook-A-Rama, Thrill-O-Matic, the House of Horrors, the House of Madness, the House of Laffs, Devil's Pit, the Devil's Playground, the Den of Lost Souls, the Viper Nest, Angry Ghosts, Ghost Castle, the Haunted House, the Mummy's Tomb, the House of the Living Dead. Anya marched up to the booths and asked the ticket takers how long the ride lasted and how they would rate the experience for scariness on a scale from one to ten. I expected them all to say ten, but no one had ever asked them that before. Maybe it was the novelty that moved them to tell the truth. Five, one said. Six and a half.

I knew what was going to happen. I felt as if I were watching her renting us a hotel room. Or maybe I was misreading her. Maybe we'd have a couple of laughs, skip a couple of heartbeats, and stagger back out into the light.

At last she chose the Terror Tomb. The guy who took tickets wore a black top hat. He took our quarters and pointed at a car designed to look like a giant teacup.

Anya said, "The ride lasts twenty-five minutes. He says that for scariness it's an eleven."

The guy instructed us to lower the safety bar. Without looking to see if we had, he pulled a lever, and we bumped into the darkness. We heard shrieks. A light flashed in our eyes, stamping an image on the blackness, a shimmering bright blue sphere that lasted alarmingly long. When I could see again, I flinched as a decomposing corpse swayed toward us, so close that, if it had been real, we could have smelled rotting flesh. At the last moment it swung back, and we chugged past it down the track.

After a few minutes Anya put her hand on my thigh. Then she took my hand and put it under her skirt.

"Watch out." She pushed back the safety bar. She undid our clothes and climbed, facing me, onto my lap. Her mouth tasted of cinnamon and sweet rice.

Anya whispered in my ear, "Don't move. Let them do the work."

I heard a bloodcurdling scream, and the tunnel lit up, then went dark again. I closed my eyes and gave myself over to the pleasure.

Anya threw back her head and moaned at the same time as a ghost moaned, which made us laugh. Then we started again.

The skeletons swooping at us just missing us, added to the excitement. Briefly illuminated by a red light pulsing around a corpse that dangled from a gallows, we came our brains out. First Anya shouted, a guttural caw, down low in her throat. Seconds later I pulled out and heard myself make a noise I'd never made, a sound I'd never heard before. It was my voice, but I wasn't me.

Then I was. I was myself again, back in my body, on an amusement park ride, too stunned to pull up my pants.

NOW THAT WE are more relaxed about sex, at least in what we are willing to *say*, now that people boast about having sex in airplane bathrooms, I might be less surprised than I was that afternoon in the Terror Tomb, straddled by a young woman I'd known for less than a day. We were doing it in the dark but still more or less in public, in a teacup chugging past ghosts jumping out of cupboards, past cardboard genies rising from bottles, pirates slashing their swords at us, revenants clanking their chains. Probably I would still be shocked. Maybe anyone would. Especially a young person who'd only had tentative, semi-platonic sex in a college dorm room and had started the day expecting to edit a novel.

We straightened our clothes and tidied ourselves. Anya returned to the seat beside me and rested her head on my shoulder for the rest of the ride, as we swiveled and bumped past howling werewolves and coffin lids creaking open.

Our teacup spun one last time and came to a gradual stop.

"Well," Anya said. "That was something."

"Something," I agreed. "That was . . . something."

We stepped out of the teacup into a corridor. At the far end was a fun house mirror. As Anya and I approached, hand in hand, she shrank into a doll version of herself, while I too got shorter, but also wider. My bottom swelled and I waddled like a giant duck or a circus clown with his trousers full of balloons. Why should I feel humiliated? It was just a distorting mirror. Why did I think that I was seeing a future in which I'd be punished for what we'd just done? No one would have suspected. Not even I could believe it, except that my fly was half zipped, and I was still feeling a scatter of pleasant aftershocks.

"Don't worry," Anya said sweetly, pointing at the mirror. "We look nothing like that couple."

That was the last thing she said as we walked back toward Ned's car, not touching. We went up onto the boardwalk. Anya gazed out at the leaden sea. I was afraid she regretted the sex, that she'd acted out of some compulsion, and now we'd have to move past that toward a more conventional working relationship.

Now I recalled the passage I'd tried to remember when I came here the night of the Rosenberg execution. It was from Chekhov's "The Lady with the Pet Dog." His hero, Gurov, sits on the esplanade and watches the sea and thinks that everything is beautiful except what we do when we forget our humanity, our human dignity, and our higher purpose.

That night, in June, I'd watched a lurid sunset. This afternoon was a monotone brooding gray, but beautiful nonetheless. Would those garish pinks and purples have distracted me from the painful awareness of Anya beside me, her hip pressed against mine? Nothing could have distracted me. Nothing existed beyond that contact.

Anya and I said nothing. I couldn't tell if our silence was comfortable or uneasy, if I should end it or keep quiet. Perhaps we were simply calming down, slowing our heartbeats, preparing to keep Ned from suspecting that anything unusual had occurred. Unless it wasn't unusual. Maybe Ned dealt with crazier stuff every day. Maybe he was thankful when his passengers didn't have sex *in* the car. Maybe Anya did this on a regular basis. So? I had no rights to her. I was editing her novel.

Had Warren slept with Anya? I couldn't let myself wonder. Elaine said she hadn't bothered asking. I'd thought Elaine was too cool to ask, but maybe she didn't want to know.

I wanted to see Elaine. I wanted to talk to her. I wanted to tell her how confused I was, though I couldn't explain why. I imagined running into her on the street after Ned took Anya home. We could go for a drink. I would edit out the last part of my meeting with Anya. I hoped Elaine would never find out. She'd be disappointed. It would show her what I really was, an animal, a male pig dressed up as a bright young editor. But maybe I was misreading her. I was misreading our times. Uncle Maddie would have felt no guilt, and Warren wouldn't have pushed Anya away. Maybe he already hadn't. Whether Warren did or not, Elaine wouldn't have loved him less.

I wanted Elaine to tell me that everything would be all right. She was the only one I would believe, not Warren, not my parents. I was wasting my precious time with Anya, thinking about Elaine.

Ned was where he'd promised. He opened the door for Anya, and as she slipped into the back seat, I waited on the sidewalk. Leaning into Ned's window, I said it would be easier for them if Ned headed straight onto the parkway to drive Anya back. I could take the subway. I'd be at my apartment in no time, and they'd avoid the city traffic. If I'd looked at Anya, she would know that I couldn't bear to leave her. I was ripping off the Band-Aid.

Ned said, "Are you sure?"

"I'm positive," I said.

Anya said, "That would be great."

I was hurt that she could let me go without even a collegial kiss. But we were aware of Ned watching. "Thank you, Simon. Thanks for a fun day. See you soon. I'll do the work we agreed on."

We hadn't agreed on any work. Was Anya saying that for Ned's benefit, or did she think we had?

"No," I said. "Thank *you*. Thank you for everything."

Anya said, "I'm looking forward to working with you."

Ned said, "Don't forget your briefcase, sir."

"Jesus Christ. Thank you," I said.

I waited till Ned's car was out of sight, till the receding speck that was me disappeared in his mirror. Then I left—not toward the subway, but toward my parents' apartment.

My parents were so glad to see me that I felt guilty for not going there more often. It would have hurt them to know I was afraid that the rickety armature of my life might still collapse and drop me onto their candy-striped sofa in front of the TV.

So there I was again, with my family, having just had sex in a Coney Island dark ride with the author of a lurid novel about Ethel Rosenberg, a novel I feared would exist long after McCarthy was dead and forgotten. My parents didn't know. They never would. But there was one moment when I feared that my mother had read my mind.

"You know, Simon, this week I remembered the oddest thing. You know that Ethel wanted to be an actress. I recalled this god-awful drama they staged in a settlement house. She played the sister of a man who was executed. He didn't want his family to suffer, so he refused to give his real name. Is that wild or not? I mean, how life imitates art. *Bad* art."

"It's wild," I said. "You're right."

...

After my mother and father fell asleep, I went to my room and, against my better judgment, took Anya's manuscript out of my briefcase. I opened it at random, and the sentences I read didn't seem nearly as bad as I remembered. I told myself not to let sex cloud my editorial judgment.

With that, it all came rushing back. Anya's hands gripping my shoulders, her head thrown back so far that all I could see, in the pulsing red light, was the underside of her chin. I could still feel her hips under my hands, her skin against mine. All I wanted, all I would ever want, was to be with her again.

I wanted to stay awake and think about Anya more, but I fell asleep. I dreamed of Vikings, crowded on the deck, shouting: Pillage and burn!

CHAPTER 7

Only the elderly and the stylish young person with an interest in antique equipment will understand how a typewriter's quirks were its fingerprints. Detective stories used to turn on the half-filled circle in the lowercase *g* exposing the author of the ransom demand or the blackmail threat. At Alger Hiss's 1950 trial for espionage, State Department documents copied for transmission to the Soviet Union were traced to Hiss's typewriter and used as evidence against him.

The page on which Anya typed the title of her novel hadn't been done on the same machine as her manuscript. The ancient Remington hit the page so hard that its thick letters bulged on the other side. The manuscript was from a newer model. The typeface was thinner, more streamlined, but the middle prong of the capital *E* was broken. It appeared often, in *Esther*. The small *j* was crooked, the lowercase *i* had lost its dot, the upper lobe of the capital *B* was solid black.

Anya said that Warren gave her book to a typist, who mostly just corrected the spelling. Anya claimed not to know the typist's name. I was not about to ask Warren.

On the afternoon after our trip to the Terror Tomb, Warren stopped by my office. He closed the door and leaned against it.

"Well, old boy? How did it go?"

I'd been expecting this moment, dreading it, and I'd worked out my reply.

"Fine. I think Miss Partridge will be easy to work with."

I imagined that Warren knew every detail of my day with Anya. But why should I have thought that? It was just paranoia. Warren was opaque to me. The expression on his face, at once sly and abstracted, could have meant any number of things, none of which I could read.

AFTER THAT I noticed that Warren was popping in to see me less often. Maybe it should have bothered me to think that he had lost interest, but I was relieved. At least he wasn't reminding me of the approaching deadline. A few times he did ask casually—or faux casually—after *The Vixen*. Only Warren could project infinite patience and cranky impatience canceling each other out.

One afternoon Warren asked if "we" would be expecting *The Vixen* soon.

I said, "Anya Partridge and I have been meeting."

Warren raised his chin and his eyebrows, a theatrical show of patrician interest.

I said, "She's easier to work with than we expected. In fact she has some ideas, she wants quite a bit of input. So it's taking a little longer—"

"Don't tarry," Warren said. "Let's not wait until the dinner is cold."

"Anya's book will reheat it," I said, mortified by how clumsily I'd latched onto his metaphor. "I'll get you the revisions as soon as I possibly can."

"Sooner," said Warren, half out the door. "Sooner than you possibly can."

"That's what I meant," I said.

I should have left it at that. But some unruly spirit in me insisted on being heard. "You didn't mention that *our* author lives in an asylum."

I hoped that Warren hadn't noticed the ironic stress that had accidentally landed on *our*. But Warren noticed everything.

He closed his eyes and shook his head in gentlemanly exaspera-
tion. "*Asylum* is a little strong, don't you think? I'd say *country club
with nurses*. And even if it was a lockdown psycho ward, why would
that be a problem? You're new to this game and can't be expected
to remember the giant success of Mary Jane Ward's *The Snake Pit*.
Perhaps you saw the film with Olivia de Havilland. You can imagine how that boosted sales, and that other book . . . *A Mind That
Found Itself* has been in print since the Neanderthal era. In the book
biz, mental illness will never go out of style. Anyway, you needn't
worry. In many ways, our author is the sanest person you'll ever
meet. Certainly compared to most other writers. Asylum? I think
not."

"Maybe not *asylum*," I said.

"Maybe not," said Warren.

...

Every night I rewrote part of Anya's novel. It was like writing a par-
allel novel, in collaboration with Anya, a shadow novel that fit like a
slipcover over the original. I wrote in notebooks and I typed up pages
on my college typewriter, retrieved from my parents.

In my version, Esther/Ethel still had plenty of love affairs but didn't
spy for the Russians. I gave her a passionate sex life, nothing wrong
with that, but I toned things down. Arms yes, lips and tongues yes,
breasts once, but that was as far as it went. Rewriting these scenes,
I replayed some of what happened in the Terror Tomb. Flashes of
it, but not all. What I remembered was enough. Changing words
and rearranging paragraphs provided some of the thrill of physical
contact.

In my revision—as in life, I thought—Esther/Ethel's guilt was
more of an open question. My version represented the compromises
I was willing to make. I was trying to keep Ethel's name bright, to

create something that wouldn't make me so ashamed if someone—
let's say Mom—traced the book to me. The thought of my mother
finding out made my work seem reprehensible and pointless, and yet I
labored on. Rewriting seemed more productive than worrying.

Meanwhile, at the office, I kept up my alternately vigilant and lax
assault on the Herculean stacks of submissions. If *The Vixen* were a
secret mission, the slush pile was my cover. I liked thinking about it
that way. As if Warren had recruited me into a pretend game of secret
agent.

Out in the world were witnesses who could testify that I had spent
my time at Landry, Landry and Bartlett reading and returning books
to the writers who loved them more than I ever could. These strangers had evidence, letters I typed and signed. I was no longer hurt by
the memory of the senior editor comparing me to a heat-addled prospector panning for gold in the desert.

When I proposed my edits to Anya, I was surprised by how readily
she agreed. I was vain enough to wonder if Uncle Maddie was right:
if she'd fallen a little in love with me and was willing to revise her
book in any way I suggested. But I didn't believe that, and I didn't
push my luck. I still hadn't proposed that she change the characters'
names.

Inspired by what I'd learned about Ethel from my mother, I suggested that Anya, who frequently reminded me that she'd studied
acting and still wanted to be an actress, write a scene in which Esther
performs in a play about an execution. I don't know why I suggested
it except to break up the monotony of the narrative: Sex, espionage,
more sex, fighting with Junius, seducing the prosecutor, more espionage, more sex, more seduction. Death.

"Wouldn't that be corny?" Anya said.

"No," I said. "It could be great."

"I guess she must have been a pretty good actress to convince everybody that she was a regular housewife and not a Russian spy." For

a moment Anya seemed excited, imagining what she could do with what she'd learned in acting class. But almost at once, her shoulders slumped.

"I can't," she said.

"Why not?"

"Because it wouldn't add anything. It would just slow down the book." No matter what I said, no matter how sensibly I argued, I was unable to persuade Anya to humanize Esther by adding a section about her sad acting career. Maybe Anya, who'd wanted to be an actress herself, found it too painful—too close—to have her heroine fail that way. I decided to be more careful, more circumspect in how I tried to implement my agenda.

. . .

After that first visit to the sanitarium and our trip to Coney Island, Anya and I met in public places that she chose: cafés, coffee shops, hotel lobbies. I liked thinking that I was one of the few young editors who tucked a packet of condoms into his briefcase along with his author's manuscript, but I knew that Uncle Maddie would say that I was flattering myself, that it happened all the time.

Anya agreed to my suggestions, my minor deletions and additions. Often she didn't seem to be listening. Possibly she was distracted, as I was, by the fact that, after our "professional" conversation, we would leave the cafeteria or coffee shop or bar and find a secluded spot, also mapped out in advance and determined by Anya—the women's bathroom in the Plaza Hotel, the stairway of a parking garage, a quiet corner of Washington Square Park, a corridor on the Staten Island Ferry—and have quick thrilling sex, which she orchestrated as well.

My sexual experience was limited to my college affair with Marianna, with whom everything was so friendly and sweetly awkward that I never wondered who was in charge. But now that Anya was in control, it was at once relaxing and exciting to do what she wanted. It reminded me of the dreams I'd had before I met her, but my dreams had never taken place in the unlikely places we went.

Sometimes, in the heat of passion, when looking into Anya's face seemed more intense than I could bear, I turned away and found myself staring into the eyes of the fox pelt. It was unsettling, but highly charged. The dead fox seemed like the visible symbol of our stealthy romance. I didn't care if what we were doing was right or wrong. Sex with Anya was a gift, a series of gifts, though I might have preferred to get those gifts in bed. I fantasized being in Anya's comfortable Chinese bed, though I assumed the sanitarium had rules. At night I lay on my lumpy mattress and imagined caressing her.

Not long ago I read about a Hollywood movie star whose favorite place for sex was the back seat of an open, chauffeur-driven Cadillac convertible speeding north on the 110 freeway. If Anya were young now, she might be doing that. It's not what I chose to do later, after I fell in love with the woman who would become my wife and discovered how little I needed the risk. Or whatever Anya needed, and I needed because I wanted her.

I can't pretend I didn't like it. I can't pretend I've forgotten.

Every week or so, Anya would call and arrange to meet "to work on my book." *Work on my book* was like that phrase in Proust, *faire les cattleyas*, Swann's code words for making love to Odette.

Lying awake, I wondered: What if someone at the office found out? Either I'd be fired or gossiped about and secretly admired—or all those things at once. Did Warren know? Often, when Anya specified some distant meeting spot, I mentioned it to Warren, who said, "Why the hell does that crazy girl want to meet *there*?" But then he'd offer me his car, along with Ned, who picked Anya up and drove her to meet me. I chose to think this meant that Warren sanctioned our unusual working method.

Ned drove us back from wherever we'd met and dropped me off in Manhattan on the way to Shad Point. It was during those rides that I learned what little I knew about Anya.

She'd been born in New Haven. Her father was a railroad executive. Her mother gave cooking and ballroom dance classes (for fun, not for the money) to her Greenwich neighbors. Anya's older brother was a lawyer on Cape Cod. He used to beat her up when they were kids. That was where her problems came from, though she never specified what those problems were. She'd gone to a Catholic school for rich girls where she'd got into so much trouble that she was remanded into the supervision of her parents in some complex agreement with the court. She didn't say what the trouble was. She'd desperately wanted to be an actress, but her family wouldn't allow it. She'd taken a class with Lee Strasberg, who'd said that she had talent. She wanted to play Desdemona, the Duchess of Malfi, Hedda Gabler, Cordelia. She wanted to play Lady Macbeth, though she knew that the role was supposed to bring bad luck.

We could have sex against the garbage cans in back of the 21 Club, but I couldn't ask her anything that she didn't volunteer to tell me. Was she in treatment at Elmwood? I didn't know, and what if she was? Therapy was a fad then. Everyone was being analyzed, if they could afford it. People joked about analysis. They boasted and complained about the cost, and gossiped about their therapists. But you didn't confide your secrets, not even to your friends, in the easy offhand way that strangers do now.

Another thing we didn't discuss were the "ideas" in Anya's novel. Whenever I tried to get beyond the sentence-by-sentence critique, things went badly. Once Anya boasted that she didn't have a patriotic bone in her body. I was the one who thought it was *bad* to be a Russian spy, whereas Anya didn't care. I recalled the vehemence with which, at our first meeting, Anya told me that innocent people were never executed in America. What *did* Anya believe? I was less and less sure. Maybe she didn't know, either. She believed that Ethel/ Esther was brave, highly sexed, and misguided. She insisted that the real Ethel would have approved of how she was portrayed in *The Vixen*. I picked my battles and didn't argue.

Once, in a pizza spot in Queens, I said, "Are you really saying it was okay to give the atom bomb to the Russians? Not that I'm saying Ethel did, but I mean, *if* she did? And if so, was it okay for the government to kill her?"

Anya daintily wrangled a cord of cheese that had slipped off her slice. "I thought you were the one who thought she was innocent."

Did I think that? "I don't know. But I don't think that anyone should be murdered for instructional purposes."

"Obviously!" said Anya. "Anyhow, there *was* no secret. The Russians already had the bomb."

Hadn't someone else said that? Was it Elaine? Or had Elaine said that we already had the hydrogen bomb? "Why didn't you put *that* in the book?"

"It would have ruined the story. Anyway, who cares? After Hiroshima, no one's going to drop another atomic bomb. It was just too awful. I don't care if our leaders carry on like bull moose rutting in the forest."

"How can you be so sure?"

"I just am. Self-confidence is the bronze medal for surviving my screwed-up childhood. If I wasn't reasonably sure of myself, how could a mental patient write a three-hundred-page novel?"

"Mental patients write bestsellers all the time." I still hadn't read Florence Durgin's first book, but I'd read every word of *The Snake Pit*. Did that make me an authority on the literature of mental illness? I hated how I sounded: pompous, above it all.

"That's the plan," Anya said. "Bestseller is the plan. That's what this is about. Surely you realize that, Simon."

I didn't answer. I didn't move. I sat there recalling my uncle's disdain when I'd used the word *league* about romance. I still believed that Anya was out of my league, without knowing what that meant.

My knowledge of romantic love came entirely from books. My feelings for Anya were familiar from fiction, if not from life. I thought about her constantly when I wasn't with her. Her name was the last word I thought at night and the first word in the morning. At every moment I wondered what she was doing. I had long conversations with her in my head. Where had I read about the lover who couldn't wait to leave his beloved so he could be alone and think about her? I counted the hours till I saw her again, and I fought the impulse to cross off, on my desk calendar, the days until our next meeting.

I imagined telling her secrets that no one else knew. I'd tell her my life story, not that it was worth telling. But I hoped she'd think it was sweet. When I was a little boy, I fell in love with the hydrangea bush in front of the house across the street. I cried until my mother asked if I could have one of the blue flowers, big and round as softballs. Then I cried because the flower seemed lonely without the others. I cried again when the flower turned brown and my mother threw it out. Did I want Anya to see me as a weepy, flower-loving little boy? Did I want her to see herself as the flower I adored? I wanted her to think about me, anywhere, anyway, anytime.

I wanted to tell her what college had been like, how much I'd loved the library. I wanted to tell her about the Icelandic sagas, though all the stories that came to mind featured destructive, treacherous women. There was so much she didn't know about me. What I cared about, who my parents were, my secret hopes and fears. What flavor of ice cream I liked. She knew I'd grown up in Coney Island, that I worked for Warren, that I was editing her novel, that I would do whatever she wanted, whatever she dared me to do. I just wanted to be with her, to look at her, to be near her. Was this love? It wasn't what I'd felt for my college girlfriend, or what she'd felt for me.

Working on Anya's novel was like immersing myself in her psyche.

I wanted to go deeper. I had to keep reminding myself why her book was a problem. I questioned my reasons for trying to turn *The Vixen* from something cheap into something with insight and style. Was I vain to think I could do that? Was I doing it out of respect for Ethel's memory, to help Warren and the firm, or because I was in love with Anya? Did I think that improving the novel might somehow improve *her*? That was the *real* vanity, the unforgivable sin: the pride of thinking I knew what an improved Anya might look like. I have no excuse except that I was young, confused, afraid of what might happen next. Just getting through the day felt like memorizing poetry in a foreign language, outside, in a hailstorm.

I tried to think of a precedent. Romeo and Juliet? Forbidden love, there was that. But our relatives weren't killing one another in sword fights, and Shakespeare's lovers weren't having sex in public bathrooms.

...

A hundred pages or so into my—or, as I wanted to think of it, *our*—work on Anya's novel, Anya asked if we could meet in Gregorio's, a dark café in Greenwich Village.

By then I had grown accustomed to and *fond of* our "routine": minimal small talk, perfunctory book talk, agreement, agreement, then risky semipublic sex. By then I knew to search my surroundings, in this case the café, for the spot Anya had in mind for the final aspect of our "work." I looked, or tried to see, through the haze of smoke and darkness, past the scatter of beatniks in black, hunched over chessboards or paperback books. The room was so underpopulated, we could have been alone. We could have had sex—subtle, discreet, all the more exciting—in the café, and no one would have noticed.

Anya was waiting for me at a table, cradling a half-empty cup of espresso. I ordered the same. The caffeine made my hands shake. They were shaking already. The waiter didn't look at us, though we must have made a striking couple. I wondered if Anya had warned him or even paid him to let us do whatever she was planning.

I felt high from the caffeine and the promise of sex. Something about the paradoxical privacy of that public space made me relaxed—and bold. I decided to take a risk I'd been wanting to take and dreading.

I put the manuscript on the table.

I said, "Anya, I've been working hard on this, and we've been discussing your book. But now I need you to look over what we've done and give it some serious thought."

"Serious thought isn't my strong suit." Anya gave her fox pelt a tender pat on the head.

"*I'm* serious," I said. "Serious enough for both of us." Someone was talking: not me. An editor was speaking editor-speak. That professional drone was the only voice in which I could say what had to be said.

"Read what I've written in the margins, look at the words I've crossed out. If you want to restore or add or change anything, just do it, and we can go forward from there. Take your time. Take as long as you want. Well, maybe not as long as you want. Warren's going to be asking for the finished manuscript."

I couldn't read Anya's expression, but it certainly wasn't happy. I was sorry I'd said anything. This had been a mistake. Maybe I could fix it.

Anya twined her legs around mine underneath the table. "I don't need to look at it. I trust you. Do whatever you want."

Were we talking about sex or editing? This wasn't how writers were supposed to act, but Anya wasn't any writer. She was also an actress, as she'd often reminded me.

"Please." How could one word convey such wheedling desperation? If Anya didn't work with me now, maybe she never would. I'd be the only one making a few cosmetic improvements while still preserving the heart of this three-hundred-page crime against truth. I needed to feel that she was on board. Otherwise I alone would be beautifying the lie that Anya wrote and that Warren intended to publish. But such was the power of sex that every time we met, this lie, this crime, this potential crime, seemed more like a misdemeanor. This was how far I had fallen: I'd begun to find something intriguing, exciting, even admirable about the fact that Anya had written a book, even a book like *The Vixen*.

Without picking up the manuscript, Anya flipped through the pages. "You've written all over it so much I can't even read it."

"Then just look at it." I was pleading again. "Make whatever changes you want." Why did I care? *The Vixen was* improving, incrementally, with (despite what I'd told Warren) minimal input from Anya. I wanted *something* about this to seem real. I wanted to feel that this was how a real editor worked with a real writer. "Go ahead. Take the folder home. I mean . . . to you know . . . where you live."

I'd said the wrong thing again, but Anya didn't seem bothered. She was already annoyed at having been made to touch her book. She grimaced as she stuffed the pages into the blood-colored folder, which she pressed against her chest, then freed the head of her fox stole from under the cardboard so it stared at me, guarding the burden I'd put on its mistress. Its beady eyes had always seemed plaintive before, but now they seemed hostile, defiant. I half expected the pelt to hiss.

I waited for this part of our meeting to end, waited for Anya to tell me when and where to meet her now. I felt like I did on the roller coaster: exhilarated, giddy, braced for rescue or disaster.

Anya tucked the folder under her arm. "Well, then. I guess I'd better go get to work." As she stood and turned, the fox head bounced off the back of her black jacket appliquéd with a sequined parrot.

"Nice jacket," I mumbled.

Anya said, "Can you get this?" She meant the coffees, the bill.

"Of course." I was the editor. This was business.

She smiled sadly, a stagy sadness. Acting-school regret. Her shrug said, What can you do? Her shrug said, You should have known. I had no idea what her shrug said. I opened my mouth, but nothing came out.

She turned and left the café.

I finished my coffee, drank my water. I was disappointed, angry, shockingly close to tears. I waited till I was sure that Anya was gone. Where the hell was the waiter? I left more money on the table than two espressos could have cost.

...

A week passed, then another. I had made a fatal mistake. I would never see Anya again. This was heartbreak. This was what love songs were about, the sonnets, stories, and novels, though not the sagas so much. The women who leave Viking men are more trouble than they're worth, and when the Viking men leave women, the women curse them with magic spells that keep the men from having sex with anyone ever again. Everywhere men were grieving over women, women grieving over men. Only now did I understand what lovers mourned and suffered.

This was a whole new kind of pain, an anguish I'd read about but never felt. How strange to discover an emotion that the average teenager probably experiences long before high school graduation.

Getting out of bed took effort. How heroic of the lovelorn to shower and brush their teeth. I spent the weekend with my parents, who kept asking what was wrong. I answered "Nothing!" more harshly than I intended. My mother urged me to take a walk, but I didn't want to. Anya had ruined the Cyclone for me.

"*Now* we're worried," said Mom.

It required massive restraint not to waylay Warren in the hall and ask if he'd heard from Anya. The only thing that stopped me was the fear of making everything worse. There was nothing to do but wait.

. . .

Two weeks after I gave Anya her manuscript with my corrections, she called me at the office. When I heard her voice, I felt short of breath, and I faked a cough to hide it.

"Are you sick?" asked Anya.

She cared how I was! "Frog in my throat."

"Gribbet," Anya said.

I was too nervous to laugh.

She said, "Can we meet Tuesday afternoon?"

"Yes. Of course. I mean sure."

"Let's say two? Do you know where B. Altman's is?"

Everyone did. It was one of the majestic Fifth Avenue department stores that still existed then. An image flashed in front of me: sex in a dressing room.

"Are you still there?" Anya asked.

"Yes! I'm here!"

"Let's meet in the restaurant on the eighth floor."

"Great. That would be great."

"I have the manuscript."

"Even better," I said.

. . .

I'd never been to the department store. It wasn't the sort of place my parents went. What would they have bought there? It would have shamed my mother to wander around and not know where anything was.

I chose to think that Anya's choice of a meeting place was a good sign. It was where lady shoppers met for lunch, a civilized venue in which a genteel editor and writer could politely discuss her work. Maybe we wouldn't have sex afterwards. I could forgo the sex in exchange for the assurance that she and I were still working together. Or anyway, so I told myself, even as I hoped that work and sex could amicably coexist.

I was unprepared for the soaring magnificence of B. Altman's main floor, the lofty skylight, the caracol staircase, the arched walkways spiraling into the atrium that resembled the Tower of Pisa, only indoors and not leaning. The oxygen had been replaced by the heady perfumes that stylish young women playfully sprayed at me as I rambled through this Taj Mahal of commerce.

I was the only male on the elevator, except for the uniformed attendant. He called out, "Eighth floor, Charleston Gardens," and that was when I discovered that the restaurant was a reproduction of an antebellum plantation. Stately white columns bordered the faux front porch. A windowed portico ran along one wall. The tall trees and flowering vines of a painted garden spilled over a trompe l'oeil brick wall. All around us were artificial palms, hanging clumps of faux Spanish moss.

Charleston Gardens. I should have known. Even then, when historical sensitivity was even duller than it is today, I knew that the theme was grotesque. The waitstaff was clothed in toothpaste green. The waitresses wore pleated hats, like inverted paper cups. Even the younger waiters seemed stooped and shambling. Did none of the women nibbling crustless sandwiches and sipping iced tea notice that they were lunching in a replica of a prison? Would they have been so eager to meet their friends in a re-creation of the Soviet gulag or the commandant's garden at Auschwitz?

Anya sat at a table in the center of the restaurant. She was dressed in pink, with lace at her collar and cuffs, and her fox fur seemed at home in this pre–Civil War paradise. I knew that she meant me to think of *Gone with the Wind*, of how she'd conflated Ethel Rosenberg and Scarlett O'Hara.

Anya spotted me from across the room. Her smile was an invitation and a challenge. I assumed that she was savvy enough to suspect that the décor might test the sort of person who thought that Ethel shouldn't have been executed. Life was cheaper in places like the one that this re-created. Anyone who had a problem with that should probably stay up North.

Anya rose and kissed my cheek in a neutral, sisterly way. The oxblood folder sat like a stain on the pure white tablecloth.

She said, "I used to come here with my mother. Isn't it a hoot? They do the most wonderful chicken salad with grapes."

She moved the oxblood folder onto the floor by her chair.

The waitress called us *ma'am* and *sir*. We ordered chicken salad. And two iced teas.

"Sweetened?"

"That would be lovely," said Anya. I thought I heard, in her voice, a trace of a Southern accent. Well, sure. She was an actress. An actress and a writer.

I stared down at the table. Anya didn't seem to want to talk. After a while, a hand slid a plate between my frozen gaze and the snowy cloth.

"Thank you." I smiled frantically at the elderly waitress, who didn't smile back.

Dreading the cost, I contemplated the mayonnaise-beige scoop of expensive meat, studded with bubble-like grapes, neatly cupped in a cradle of iceberg lettuce. I picked up the heavy silver fork and managed to transfer a few gluey chicken cubes to my mouth.

"How do you like it?" Anya said.

"Delicious." I hated myself.

"Told you so," Anya said. "I love this place. It's so totally wicked. It's my people's version of Coney Island. The Terror Tomb for Connecticut WASPs."

The Terror Tomb! How I longed to be back there, on the dark ride, in that (comparatively) carefree time. How harmless those monsters and pirates seemed compared to the fluted plantation columns and the hairy Spanish moss.

Anya watched until I finished the chicken salad. Then we had coffee, served in china cups along with iced petit fours so sweet they made my teeth ache.

Only then, when the table was cleared except for our water glasses, did Anya reach down and hand me the folder.

I was eager to see what she'd done. I felt as if her having worked on our project would justify our being in this dreadful place and make up for the time I'd wasted waiting for her to call. Anya's response to my edits would vindicate me for having broken every rule of professionalism and propriety. Though hadn't my uncle implied that sex streamlined the editorial process? Why was I thinking of Uncle Maddie? It was *so unhelpful*. Perhaps because I was hoping that Anya would fall in love with me, even though I suspected that the opposite had occurred.

I didn't open the folder until Anya nodded. "Go ahead."

I leafed through the first chapter. Then I looked over every page until I was sure.

Anya had done nothing. My queries had gone unanswered. My annotations and edits were exactly as I'd given them to her. Unchanged, untouched, and, for all I knew, unread.

"I like what you've done," said Anya. No apologies, no explanation. Could she have forgotten what I'd asked her to do? Her stare was pure provocation. She hadn't forgotten. She'd meant to do nothing.

I slid the manuscript back in the folder. There was no point stating the obvious. I waited for Anya to speak.

She said, "The furniture department is on the fifth floor. At the very back of the floor is a little model home with a little model bedroom behind a little model door that no one ever opens."

I would do all the work I had to—and more. Just give me more of this, one more chance, one more hour with Anya. I would never again ask her to do anything more than meet me in the places she'd scoped out in advance.

She stood up and left in a swirl of pink. I paid the outrageous check and waited a few minutes. The oxblood folder rattled in my hand.

The model home was where she said it would be, in a dimly lit, under trafficked corner of the furniture department, near the freight elevators. Nothing about the structure made sense, its dollhouse scale, its attempt to look like a seaside cottage, its improbably weather-beaten siding. Was it meant to be aspirational? No sane adult would want to live here. Maybe a solitary, eccentric child, but that wasn't whom it was designed for. I imagined it as the work of some frustrated artist turned window dresser, a project that got its creator fired and continued to exist only because the store didn't need the space.

I opened the door and walked through a miniature living room, occupied almost entirely by a striped couch. I tried not to think about my mother. Past the shoebox-sized kitchen was a room painted robin's-egg blue, with a hooked rug on the floor, a double bed with flowered sheets and hospital rails.

Anya lay on the bed. As soon as she saw me, she hiked up her pink Southern-lady dress.

"Come here," she said, and I did.

The bed was narrow—but spacious compared to a spinning teacup in the Terror Tomb. Compared to the bathroom stalls and parking garages, this was wildly luxurious, though the sex was, as always, rushed and hot and quick.

Afterwards I sat on the edge of the bed, in the freakish dollhouse. I wished that this was our bed, our real house, the home where I lived with Anya.

My briefcase lay on the floor beside the bed. The problem of *The Vixen* hadn't gone away.

Anya straightened her clothes, kissed me, and left. Flung over her shoulder, the fox's head watched me follow her out of the funny little house.

Years later, when I heard that the department store was closing, and before the building was repurposed as a university graduate center, I went to look for the model house. Of course it no longer existed, and I wondered if I'd dreamed it along with all those other dreams of Anya.

CHAPTER 8

A confession: I still had a crush on Elaine, which confused me, because lovers in literature were purely devoted to one beloved at a time. Tristan didn't love Isolde *and* the publicist in his office.

Elaine maintained the exact same degree of friendliness and kindness as before. But at moments I sensed she wanted something more than a cheerful workplace acquaintance. Best case, wishful thinking. Worst case, more vanity, youth, and self-delusion. Anya had made her desires unmistakably clear, but my limited experience had left me still uncertain about what women wanted. This was the 1950s. Ozzie and Harriet, Lucy and Ricky, and my parents slept in separate beds.

The good sister, the bad sister. The Madonna, the whore. Wouldn't any decent human being prefer angelic Elaine to a dark ride through the Terror Tomb? My puppy love for Elaine made me think that my affair with Anya was missing something more intimate, tender, and romantic than discussing a trashy book with a woman who wasn't listening, followed by sex in a stairwell. The pain I'd felt when Anya had briefly stopped speaking to me had made me think I understood love, but my complex feelings about Elaine made me realize I understood nothing.

In the halls, over the coffee maker, I was edgy around Elaine, more so when I sensed (or told myself) that she was nervous too. I wanted her to find me attractive. I wished that I were more like Warren, more powerful and distinguished, Protestant and rich. I just wanted to be near Elaine, to stand beside her, to bask in her vibrant, comforting aura. Elaine was the only person I could have talked to about *The Vixen*, but I didn't know how to begin. I half wanted to believe that the truth about Anya might make Elaine jealous, but I didn't want my affair with "my writer" known around the office. I didn't want anything about *The Vixen* known around the office. Not that Elaine would have told. I assumed she'd also promised Warren to keep *The Vixen* a secret. She never asked me about the book. I never brought it up.

I respected the fact that Elaine was too busy for me, too involved in her work. *Our* work. I loved how smart she was, how freely she spoke up at meetings, how intently everyone listened, how good she was at her job. I wanted to be like her, but I knew that I would never be that comfortable, that at home in the world. I would never be the person who remembered birthdays, spouses' names, who could charm the vainest, most homesick and cranky foreign writers.

If Elaine admired me, it would mean that I was admirable. I wanted her to respect me, which was different from not wanting Anya to think that I was inhibited and dull. When I tried to sort out my feelings about the two women, I couldn't fail to notice how much those feelings turned on what I imagined they felt about *me*. My love for Elaine seemed so much *healthier* than my desire for Anya, whom I was still meeting "to work on her novel."

Even without Anya's input, *The Vixen* was getting marginally less awful. Still I held off proposing the major changes I wanted. Warren had made it clear that the book I had in mind—with complex characters and moral ambiguity, spun from the raw material of the Rosenberg case—would never be published. I told myself: Have patience. Think small. Word choice and variations in tone can make all the difference. What I had in mind was something that would surprise and please Warren, what he wanted—only better.

Anya seemed increasingly bored by our project, though she nodded dutifully when I suggested this or that. Suggestion. Nod. Suggestion.

Nod. For all the drama of her self-presentation and her sex life, she was so even-tempered I wondered if she was being drugged at the place she lived. That was how I thought of it. Not an asylum or sanitarium. A *place*. The place where she lived.

I was still ashamed of my connection with *The Vixen*. Would Mom hear about it when it was published and it became the success that Warren hoped it would be? My mother had stopped going to our local public library, and Warren was too cheap to advertise in any of the newspapers my parents read. If Mom heard about it, she'd know that it was my company, but I would insist that it wasn't my book, and she would believe me. She wouldn't think that I should have quit in protest. I didn't want to lie to my parents, but I told myself that I was saving them from needless pain and unhappiness.

Uncle Maddie and Warren had promised that I would learn on the job. Editing *The Vixen* was certainly an on-the-job education. I imagined that I was catching on, and that, at least for the moment, I had a difficult situation more or less under control.

...

One afternoon, Anya showed up for our meeting in an obviously foul mood. Her eyes were hidden behind dark glasses. We were sitting in a diner, in a window booth, along the West Side Highway. Car mirrors flashed by like fireballs. Anya kept her glasses on inside.

Glowering and sighing, she lit one cigarillo from another. "Look at this place. It's what you'd get if Edward Hopper and William Burroughs went into business and opened a greasy spoon."

"Burroughs? You've read *Junkie*?" I'd thought the book was an industry secret. Written under a pseudonym, the cheap paperback novel about heroin addiction was passed around like contraband at literary parties. It still surprised me when Anya knew something that I thought was beyond her. No wonder she was angry. My condescension was a mistake. She was a reader and, I'd come to think, an intelligent person who pretended to be daffier than she was. She wasn't really a mental patient, I'd decided, but a hapless imprisoned daughter.

Anya shrugged. Not charmed. Not amused. Not interested, really. "Order something. Go ahead. This one's on me. The first check from your boss came in. Half of my pathetic advance."

I didn't know how much we'd paid for Anya's novel, but I couldn't admit that, this far along in the process. Whom could I ask? Not Anya. Elaine might wonder how I'd let this slip by me. Could I pretend to have forgotten? Remind me, Elaine: How much did we spend on *The Vixen, the Patriot, and the Fanatic*?

"Anya, are you feeling okay? Is something wrong? You seem . . . "

"I'm fabulous." Anya frowned.

After that we were silent. No pleasantries, no small talk. None of the chatty neutral foreplay before I slid the manuscript out of my briefcase.

At the next table was a young couple, both skinny, both half asleep.

"Coffee?" A plump, middle-aged waitress materialized, smiling. Someone's mother, I thought. My own mother would still love me and forgive me, no matter what happened with Anya, even if Warren fired me and I had to move back home. My poor mother! Worry about Mom's illness should have put Anya's bad mood in perspective. But it just made everything worse.

"Nothing for me," said Anya.

"And for you, sir? Coffee?"

I pretended to consider it. I was performing for the waitress, who must have thought we were . . . what? A young couple breaking up. She'd seen plenty of that. The girl behind her dark glasses, the boy at a total loss. I ordered coffee and apple pie. I didn't want coffee; I didn't want pie. I wanted to seem normal. Apple pie was normal.

Anya said, "Can you please bring the check with his coffee and pie?"

This was not a good sign. The waitress and I knew it.

I put the manuscript on the table, first making sure that the surface was clean and dry. Professional, professional. This was a working meeting over coffee and apple pie.

I said, "Let's talk about *The Vixen*."

Anya's smile was kittenish and mean, and she kicked me under the table, hard enough so that it stung. I wished I could see her eyes. How many things could a nasty kick mean? I didn't know, with Anya. Elaine would never do that. Elaine would never hurt me.

"How about let's *not talk*," she said. "How about let's just drink our coffee and not talk. I'm tired. I had a rough night."

A rough night? Had Anya been with someone in her Chinese bed?

"Rough how?"

Anya's glasses weren't dark enough to conceal her withering look.

"Bad dreams," she said.

Good news. I wasn't jealous of Anya's dreams. I'd so often dreamed about Anya.

"Tell me I wasn't in them. Unless I was rescuing you."

"Actually, you *were* in my dream."

"Doing what?"

"Just what you're doing now. Being a nightmare." She laughed.

"A nightmare?" I hoped I didn't look as blindsided as I felt.

The waitress brought my coffee. A few drops splashed into the saucer. She eyed the manuscript. "Kids, you might want to move that."

The waitress had called us *kids*.

"Definitely," said Anya. "Let's put it away."

"Sure. Okay. For now." I put the manuscript in my briefcase and took a sip of the bitter diner coffee. I didn't trust myself to reach for the pitcher and add cream.

I said, "I know I've been asking a lot." In fact, ever since Anya had refused to work on the book, I hadn't asked anything. But it seemed like the right thing to say. Maybe it was her mood, the glasses. Maybe

I wanted a response. "Warren is on my case. Or about to be. We do have a deadline, you know."

"When?" Anya seemed mildly interested. What had happened to the young woman so fiercely invested in her future bestseller? That person had been gone for a while, but I'd chosen not to notice. Anya had stopped playing the part and hadn't yet found another. Maybe I was the one who had changed. I'd gotten more interested in her as a lover and less interested in her as a writer of a novel with serious problems. That was a mistake. Maybe everything would have been different if she'd written a better book: another thought I regretted.

"Warren says we need to go to press. Soon."

"Thank Jesus Christ you can smoke in here." Anya lit up from the butt still smoldering in the ashtray. I knew it would annoy her if I stubbed it out, but I couldn't help it. Anya curled her lip. Every move I made, every word I said, inspired a tiny twitch of annoyance and humiliation. I needed to leave, but I couldn't. I had to fix this; then I could go. I couldn't leave her in this mood, not that I knew what her mood was, nor what had caused it.

"Maybe we can talk about one . . . small detail. Would you *consider* losing the scene where Esther's seducing the Russian agent until she decides he's too ugly?"

In the scene the agent lectures Esther about how looks don't matter in the Soviet Union. Only party loyalty matters. Then he threatens to shoot her, and it turns her on. They lock the bedroom door and pop a bottle of French champagne.

"That scene doesn't really advance the plot, and she slept with another Russian agent just forty pages before—"

Why had I focused on that scene? I'd felt I had to say something.

"But they don't have sex," Anya said.

"Who doesn't?"

"Esther and the agent. Sorry. Did I miss something?"

"I think we're *supposed* to think they did."

"Oh, are we?" Anya said. "You should know. I honestly don't remember."

"Yes, I think we are. *Something* happens when they lock the door and open the champagne. They're not watching TV."

I smiled, but Anya didn't. "I'm not sure it's a good idea, having our heroine get excited when a man threatens to shoot her."

I was right, but I sounded like a stiff.

"My heroine," said Anya. "Not *our* heroine. Mine. Let's leave it for now, okay?"

"Okay. Can I ask you a favor? Can you take off your glasses?"

I expected her to refuse, but she didn't. Her right eye was ringed with a dark purple bruise. I looked around for the waitress. I glanced at the couple behind us. I didn't want them to think I was the one who—

Anya noticed and despised me for worrying about strangers before I worried about her. She stared at me, defiant.

I said, "Who did that to you?"

"I did."

"Seriously?" Was she going to tell me she walked into a door? No wonder she'd had a rough night. No wonder she couldn't sleep. No wonder she was in a bad mood.

Anya twisted a corner of her napkin, dipped it in her water glass, and scrubbed the bruise from around her eye. The purple eye makeup smeared and vanished and reappeared on the napkin. Her eye was perfectly normal. Unbruised. She must have painted on the bruise with eyeliner and shadow.

"A theater trick. Makeup 101. They teach you that in drama school."

"Jesus, Anya. Why would you do something like that?"

"For your reaction. You should have seen your face!" She fake laughed. I thought of Warren's range of fake laughs. What had I done to turn her against me?

In the long silence that fell, I thought of my dead uncle Mort, in the moment before that last jump out of the airplane. I thought of the sickening sensation of falling on the Cyclone, and the hope that the falling will stop. This was the moment before that, when the decision is out of your hands. You might as well do it, hang on or jump.

Say it, I thought. Just say it. See what happens next.

"A page is missing from the manuscript. You probably have it somewhere." I'd wanted to say this so often, but I hadn't dared until now. The fake black eye, the moody hostility. It had gotten to me. There was that. But I also wanted to know.

Anya looked out the window.

I said, "Maybe it's with an earlier copy. Look around. You'll find it. It's the middle of the Jell-O box scene, so it's important."

"Right." Anya turned and glared at me. "The Jell-O box scene. Important. I have no idea what the hell you're talking about, Simon." Her tone had the snap of patience breaking, the clipped diction of someone who has put up with a bad joke long enough.

I said. "You don't know *what?*"

"Right," she said. "The Jell-O box scene. I was kidding. You *do* get that it was a joke?"

Throughout this whole conversation, she'd wanted to hurt me, and she had, again and again. She'd made me feel stupid, ashamed. It was counterintuitive, that shame could be liberating. But by that point, if nothing I said could make things any worse, the good news, if you could call it that, was that I could say anything. I had nothing, or almost nothing, to lose, and I felt reckless and stupidly free.

"Listen." I drew out the *listen*, to give myself a moment. "Would you consider changing your characters' names? To something less like Ethel and Julius. It might confuse the reader who might not know if she—or he—is reading fiction or nonfiction, a novel or biography or—"

Anya's look was cagey. What was I trying to pull?

"I was just asking—"

Anya said, "What are you not *getting*, Simon? You *know* that I didn't write that book. You knew that from day one."

It took me a while to be sure I'd heard what I heard, and then a longer while to realize I had no idea what it meant. Was this another trick, like the fake black eye, equally unfunny? I tried to speak several times before I said, "*Are* you joking?"

"I'm dead serious," Anya said.

And this time I knew she was.

"If you didn't write it, who did?"

"I don't know. I don't care. I just know it wasn't me. I had an acting job to do, and I did it. I was hired to play a writer. A novelist living in a mental asylum. Warren prepped me and gave me some notes. I decorated my room and came up with the character, which Warren liked, especially when I added some stuff that he told me about, from the book. So you'd think it was about me. That I'd put myself in the novel."

Outside the window, a truck rolled by. On its side was a painting of two pigs, on their hind legs, dancing.

Often, when something shocking occurs, we think: I knew. I knew from the start. All the missed signals from the past flash like ambulance lights. Anya's detachment, her spaciness. It all made sense. Unless she *did* write the novel and was playing with me, this time giving me the metaphorical black eye. Another bit of drama to keep things interesting. To get a reaction. I knew she cared about making money and being famous more than she cared about her book, but it had never once occurred to me that she didn't write it. Who pretends to write a book and lets someone edit it without telling that person the truth?

She said, "Honestly, Simon. I couldn't finish reading the goddamn thing. What a piece of garbage! How could you think I could write that trash? I'm a *Death in Venice* fan, remember? I assumed you knew, that you'd kind of figured it out—and we were just playing along. Having fun."

My heart fluttered and stopped, fluttered and stopped. I pressed my chest to calm it. I looked at the couple behind us, nodding out

over their coffee. No one was paying attention to us, or to how I must
have looked, like a man just learning an active earthquake fault runs
underneath his house.

"Are you all right?" said Anya. "You *did* know, didn't you?"

"Sure, I'm fine," I lied. "And no, I didn't know."

"Bad Warren. Bad, bad Warren. I'm an actress, not a writer. You
must have figured out that I'm an actress *playing* a writer."

"Excuse me for assuming you wrote the novel that has your name
on it. Nothing that's happened, not one word that you or Warren said,
would have made me think otherwise." This was not the moment for
grouchy resentment, but that was how I sounded.

"No need to get all up in a twist. I did a good job, didn't I? Regardless
of what my parents or anyone thinks, I can actually *act*. Am I right?"

Had all of this been playacting? Not the sex, please not that. But
what a brilliant distraction the sex had been, a distraction from any
natural curiosity, from any questions I might have asked. Was nothing about Anya real? The asylum, the Chinese bed. Why wasn't
Anya contrite? Apologetic for lying to me and to how many others?
What had brought on her sullen mood? And why was she telling me
this now? Was it because I'd suggested she think about changing one
scene? Just *consider* it, I'd said. Or was it because I'd asked about the
missing page?

If Anya didn't write the novel, who did? Warren seemed the most
likely suspect. I could imagine him after hours, drinking whiskey,
having fun. What if everyone but me was in on the joke? Who was
everyone, anyway? Did Elaine know? Of course Warren couldn't admit he'd written a book like *The Vixen*. It wouldn't have been funny.
It would have damaged the firm's reputation.

"Can we talk about this the next time?" Anya said. "I told you. I
had a rough night. I'm having trouble concentrating."

Anya leaned across the table and grabbed my wrist and looked at
me, hard. Her laugh was sharp, wicked, mocking.

"You should have seen your reaction, Simon! Your expression!" She widened her eyes, overacting astonishment. Or was she imitating me? "I *really* got you that time."

What a relief! I forced a sad little chuckle. But also . . . what a weird joke. Why had Anya said that? She'd made me doubt something I'd taken for granted. She'd meant to unnerve me. But why? And what if she *didn't* write *The Vixen*? I still really wanted to believe that she had. It would make everything so much . . . simpler. I needed to calm down. I needed to believe that Anya wrote the novel, that she'd been joking when she'd said she hadn't. We'd talk about it the next time. My questions would be answered. I could handle the uncertainty. Somehow I would get through the time until I found out the truth.

Anya said, "I'll explain. It's not like I said. I don't know why I said that. Meanwhile . . . I have an idea for right now. I'm going down in the basement. Follow me in three minutes."

She put a five-dollar bill on the table and pointed toward a stairwell and was gone before I could ask her, What are we doing? I knew what we were doing. It was the only way to make things right.

The basement was damp, but I liked the wet-plaster smell. It was like a crypt beneath a church, or one of those wine caves that maintain the same temperature year-round. Giant boxes and tin cans were stacked against the walls. There were cabinets, shelves, sacks of this and that, a wooden storage chest on which Anya sat, swinging her legs.

That was how we did it. With her sitting on the chest and me standing. The chest was the perfect height. She guided me between her legs. She'd found this place for us. The idea of her having looked for it—of her thinking about us doing this here—added to the excitement.

From the moment she touched me, I forgot—*forgot*—her saying she didn't write *The Vixen*. How could I have remembered when nothing existed beyond the pleasure of being with her. That was part of it too, the way it disappeared the world.

Only when we were finished did I recall that something was wrong. Then I remembered what it was. What was true, and what was a lie? It would have been rude, even cruel, to ask Anya just then, to segue directly from sex into interrogation. I'd wait until the next time. I'd ask again about the missing page. We'd have an honest conversation.

Later I regretted not insisting that she explain. We should have talked more, and more freely. Why couldn't I have asked about the place where she lived? Was it an asylum or a sanitarium . . . or what? Was I afraid of offending her? Of hurting her feelings? Of turning her against me? I'd learned not to push Anya on subjects she chose to avoid. She would go silent and drift away and leave as soon as she could.

After we had sex in the cellar of the diner, she kissed me, which she'd never done. It crossed my mind that she was kissing me good-bye. I told myself I was being paranoid and sentimental.

Of all the failures of nerve in my life, this one rankles the most: the fact that I didn't ask, didn't insist that Anya explain, that she tell me what she knew. I assumed I would find out. I assumed I would see her again. I would figure out how to ask her.

I said I wanted to walk home. I couldn't face a car ride with Anya, with Ned up front and my unanswered questions thickening the air. I wanted to be alone. Once more I wanted to leave her so I could think about her, but it wasn't fun anymore. I was anxious and sad.

"Fine," said Anya. "It's nice out."

It wasn't nice at all. A fog of car exhaust hung over the West Side Highway. The pollution made my eyes sting. My misery must have been so obvious that a little boy gave me a seat on the train. Maybe I was getting old. Maybe Anya had aged me.

Alone in my apartment, my thoughts battled opposing thoughts, then surrendered to new invasions. I wondered if Anya was lying, or if she was—as Warren would say—*having me on*. Certainly she was capable of it. I didn't know *what* she was capable of. I didn't know her. Who could imagine that you could read and reread someone's novel, go to Coney Island with that person, have risky sex in many unlikely places, and remain a stranger?

Maybe she hadn't written *The Vixen*. She'd often seemed to forget essential plot points. When her attention lapsed, I'd assumed it was because (as Warren reminded me) some writers hate even the most minimal criticisms or suggestions. Anya wanted to be a commercial success, but she didn't have what I imagined as a writer's pride, the tender care and concern for her book's future. I thought of the two different typewriters, of the way she'd spelled *Vickson*. She said a typist fixed her errors. Maybe there were no errors to fix. Maybe she didn't write it.

Many of Crowley's tales were about shape-shifting beasts: women who turned out to be foxes, warriors masquerading as ghosts. I thought about Melusine, the wife in the French fairy tale who—when her husband breaks his promise not to spy on her in her bath—turns out to be a dragon. Only now did I understand that those stories were lessons about how little we know about one another. If you can't tell what species a creature is, or if it's alive or dead, how could you possibly know if your lover wrote a potential bestseller?

That night I couldn't sleep. I lay awake, imagining conversations I would never have, heart-to-heart talks that shifted from confrontation to disbelief to confession, penance—and, ultimately, forgiveness. Laughter! I should have let Anya give me a ride home from the diner. Maybe something else would have happened. Maybe everything would have turned out differently.

Once more there was no one to tell. Warren? Elaine? I could hear the pitch of Elaine's voice rising on each question. *Now* you find out that your writer isn't the writer? That she's posing. That she's a fake. If she didn't write it, who did? What took you so long, Simon? If it wasn't Anya, who was it? Elaine would be right to ask—unless she knew the answer. How humiliating it would be to watch her trying to make me feel less embarrassed and bewildered. I wondered if Warren had set me up, the new guy, to be the stooge, the sacrifice that bled out on the altar of someone's bizarro plan. But what *was* the bizarro plan? And whose plan was it?

...

I went home. I skipped dinner. I opened *The Vixen*, but set the manuscript aside after a few sentences. I tried to read a new translation of *Egil's Saga*, but it put me to sleep.

I woke up drenched with sweat. My mother used to say that everything looked brighter in the morning. But that morning everything looked gloomier than it had the night before.

Maybe Anya had simply gotten bored with me and my requests for tiny changes. Now Warren would have to deal with a writer so unhappy with her editor that she denied writing the book. How often did *that* happen? No wonder she'd seemed out of sorts. She lived in a sanitarium! How much criticism had I expected her fragile ego to absorb? I should have kept things professional, been more honest about who had the power. But who *did* have the power? Anya. Always Anya.

Warren would never forgive me for panicking. For not being able to take a joke. This was not a matter of life and death. This was a novel that may or may not have been written by its putative author. The world wasn't ending. The A-bomb wasn't falling. Everything would work out.

But what would happen when the Rosenberg boys went to junior high, presumably under assumed names, and someone discovered their identity, and some smut-peddling bully slipped them a copy of *The Vixen*? There was their beloved dead mother having kinky sex with Russian agents. It would be my fault—mine and Warren's. No wonder Anya wanted to distance herself from this misbegotten project. I would have to live with it, no matter who wrote it.

Working for Warren was my job, my only job. My first and, for all

I knew, my last. My so-called career hung in the balance. If I tried to stop the inevitable, I would wreck my future. I'd been admitted, on a trial basis, to a charmed circle of angels, to the starry heaven over which Warren presided, and I feared being cast back into the outer darkness of Coney Island.

I called the sanitarium, and a nurse told me that Anya wasn't taking calls.

"Is she there?"

"Not at the moment," the nurse said. Then she hung up the phone. I called back, but no one answered. I imagined the phone ringing and ringing, echoing down the ghostly hall.

...

Not since my first day at work, when I'd tried on every piece of clothing I owned, was I so nervous about going to the office. I decided to get there early. I imagined the designer, the copyeditor, the colleagues who had barely bothered to learn my name now taking one look at me and assuming the worst: My departure, my doom was imminent. My professional death warrant had been signed.

If the only reason to publish *The Vixen* was to make money, then it hardly mattered whether Anya had written it or not. But the doubt she created had instantly depleted whatever minimal confidence I'd gained since coming to work for Warren. Why would Warren continue to employ an editor so incompetent that he didn't even know if his author wrote the book?

As far as I knew, only Anya, Warren, Elaine, and I knew that *The Vixen* existed. As far as I knew. Was I the laughing stock of literary New York? If Uncle Maddie found out, he would think it was funny. Ego, pure ego, had deceived me into thinking that I'd been chosen for an important job. But why would Warren and Elaine waste the company's precious time and money on such a complicated joke?

Walking toward my cubicle, I heard someone typing, like snow-flakes tapping a window. I followed the sound down the hall. I was ready to confess everything to the early-bird typist. We had solitude in common. Solitude and insomnia. Sleeplessness and loneliness seemed like character recommendations. Trust this fellow sufferer. You are not alone.

The sound was coming from Elaine's office. Elaine! The person I most wanted to see. The one I most needed to talk to. The woman—one of the women—I loved.

Elaine's door was open. She glanced up and gave me a smile so warm that all my fears seemed to melt away. Or *almost* all my fears.

Even at that ungodly hour, Elaine looked lit from within by the milky light of human kindness.

"Hi, Elaine. What are you doing?" What did it *look* like she was doing?

"Writing a press release for Warren's baby." I must have looked startled. "France's brilliant New Wave novel," she explained. "Hey, Simon, are you okay?"

How tactful and gentle her question was, when she could just have said, You look awful!

"Rough night."

Rough night. That's what Anya had said. I didn't think Elaine was wondering, as I had with Anya, if *rough night* meant sex with someone else.

"It happens. Would you like some tea?"

She filled a heavy orange mug with steaming liquid. Even her choice of teacup—the sturdy honest ceramic versus Anya's translucent china—seemed like evidence of superior virtue. So why was I long-ing for Anya? For the same reason that the hero chooses the seductive evil sister, for the same reason why those stories always end badly.

The tea smelled of dead flowers and earth. I took a sip, then forced another. I'd never thought of Elaine as the type who would drink something so repellent. It was more Anya's style. How little I knew about either of them. How little they'd let me know.

"Thanks," I said. "This helps. Nothing like hot tea." Could I have said anything more banal? I was conscious, as I often was when I spoke to Anya and Warren, that I didn't sound like myself. I heard myself mimicking Warren in his jolly mode accepting a cup of tea. I'd forgotten who "myself" was. How would he have sounded?

"What's the matter, Simon? Tell me. We have"—she checked her watch—"a good half hour before the daily hell breaks loose."

I blinked back mortifying tears. This was the woman I should be with. Sooner or later, Elaine would realize that I could give her so much more than Warren, so much that Warren lacked: loyalty, fidelity, youth . . . I stopped short of comparing my body with his. It would have felt like violating a biblical prohibition.

I said, "Elaine, have you ever had an author stop taking your calls?"

I'd called Anya again last night, but Anya hadn't called back. I'd called twice more. I'd left messages with the nurses.

"More times than I can count. Especially with the foreign ones. Oddly, it's often the Germans. To them an appointment is something that *might* happen tomorrow."

"Have you ever had an author actually . . . *disappear*?"

"Florence Durgin!" said Elaine. "Oh no! We've been concerned about her ever since we signed her first book. Has something happened to Florence? I told Warren it was a mistake to postpone her book—"

"Nothing's wrong with Florence. She's fine." I didn't know that. I hadn't heard from her since I told her that her poems were being bumped off this season's list. The first chance I got, I would call Florence and invite her to lunch.

"Then . . . who . . . ?"

"It's Anya." How sweet it felt to say that, to let my anxiety overpower my fear that Elaine would find out what Anya and I had been doing. Maybe I no longer cared. Elaine would forgive me. She must have forgiven Warren so much. Nothing human was beyond her compassion and understanding.

I said, "Anya Partridge won't answer my calls."

Already I had a sense—a premonition—that Anya would never call back. In the sagas people *know* when their loved ones have died in battle. They know long before the corpses are sent home or abandoned in the field to be eaten by crows.

Elaine said, "Anya was always a recluse. Or anyway so she said. You do know she's an actress. She loves playing the adorable little Shakespeare-quoting oddball."

How did Elaine know that Anya quoted Shakespeare? She'd said she never met her. Probably Warren told her. Everything had an explanation.

Was it possible that Anya was telling the truth and Elaine was lying? What if Anya *didn't* write *The Vixen* and Elaine knew that? The thought crossed my mind, lightly and not long enough to do any lasting damage.

She said, "I'd assumed Warren warned you about her being a hermit. Frankly we were all surprised when she agreed to meet with you."

All surprised? We were *all surprised?* *All* was more than two. Who else knew about this?

"Warren sent your photo to her. That must have done the trick." Elaine smiled.

Elaine was telling me I was handsome, that my photo had changed Anya's mind, but I was too panicky to feel flattered. I'd waited, for so long, for any sign that Elaine *saw* me, let alone noticed what I looked like.

I couldn't remember anyone taking my photograph at the office. What had they sent Anya? In my Harvard yearbook photo, I looked startled, as we all were, when the photographer said "Look at my hand" and we saw he was missing two fingers. A veteran. A war photographer, maybe. In the photo, I looked like I was thinking of my father and the Japanese corpses.

Maybe someone had taken my photo at the office Christmas party I barely remembered.

"Listen." I was whispering. "Elaine. The last time I saw Anya, she claimed she didn't write *The Vixen*."

Elaine did a goofy double take that would have seemed less charming had her lovely face been possible to disfigure. "Of course Anya wrote it!" She laughed. "Who else would churn out that crap? The poor captive princess in the tower. The diva literary genius—in her own mind. Trust me, Simon. She wrote it."

Elaine's blue eyes were wide and innocent. The mask of sincerity. Where had *that* thought come from? Forced to decide who was telling the truth, I made the obvious choice. The more I doubted Anya, the more I needed to believe Elaine. I couldn't begin to think that both of them might be lying. I trusted Elaine. I did.

"Anya thinks she's written a masterpiece. She's probably annoyed at you for asking her to change a word. She *really* wants her photo on that jacket. I won't be able to get rid of her once we start doing publicity."

Why was Elaine so critical of Anya, who, if she wrote or even pretended to have written *The Vixen*, was doing our firm a favor? Maybe it was about Warren. Maybe Elaine *was* jealous. Or maybe she suspected that I had . . . a crush on Anya. I wanted *that* to make her jealous.

"I'm already going to publicist hell for saying any of this. I'm supposed to be discreet. Upbeat. That's my job. Just sometimes it gets wearing."

Elaine was confiding in me about the stresses of her job, and all I could think was that she was competing with Anya. I thought of Anya straddling me in the dark ride, Anya moaning and purring like a cat in the restaurant cellar. I was a terrible person. I couldn't look at Elaine. I turned toward the door to see what the noise was: the babble of supplicants in the hall, all wanting something from Elaine.

"Don't worry," Elaine said. "It's your first real experience with writers—not counting Florence, who on the scale of things is low-maintenance. Be prepared. You're the scout leader, the pet trainer, the spouse, the shrink, the servant, the boss. You're the dad. Anya needs you. She'll be back on board, boasting about the book, asking Warren for an advance on the next one. This is a business transaction. Her awful book will rescue the firm"—Elaine knocked on her wooden bookshelf—"and we'll make money. Just keep doing whatever you're doing. Be patient and try not to worry."

It didn't matter how much Elaine knew. She had my best interests at heart. I loved Elaine. I loved her. My little fling with Anya would end, and then Elaine and I . . .

"Thank you, thank you, thank you, Elaine." She was my dream human being. So beautiful, so thoughtful, so capable of comforting me with just a few kind words. Thank God she existed.

I went back to my office and dialed Anya's number.

One of the nurses answered. "Let me try and reach her," she said. Silence. Silence.

"She's not answering. Would you like to leave a message?"

"Could you tell her Simon called. I'm just checking to see if she's okay. You know what? Don't bother. Thank you. I'll call back."

Moments later, the spirit on the staircase said, loud and clear, Can you please tell Miss Partridge that her editor called?

Why hadn't I said that?

. . .

After three days with no word from Anya and three more sleepless nights, a letter arrived in my office. It had accidentally (I assumed) slipped between two manuscripts. Normally I might have chucked the envelopes onto the growing pile, but something guided me to look between the submissions, where I found the letter.

Anya lived in the world, or partly in the world. She was a functioning human being. She wasn't stupid. I knew this, and yet I was amazed that she'd put an actual postage stamp on an actual envelope and sent it to my actual address at the firm. I'd underestimated her again. That was why I'd lost her.

My name was spelled wrong. *Simon Putnum.*

Inside was one page, a few lines typed on the vintage machine I'd seen in her room. I recognized the heavy punch of the keys, the blurred defective letters.

> Dear Simon,
>
> I didn't want to have to do this. I wanted to avoid it, I thought everyone was having fun, it was like theater or a play or a joke, a great acting roll for me, or a giant adventure, and then it got so serious, and then I found out some other things, and then I had a talk with Warren, and then you had to go tell Elaine. I'm going someplace, maybe Korfu. See you when I get back. Take care of the Vickson for me. I came to love her, sort of like you'd love a cute adopted baby.
>
> Please don't try to come look for me. Promise. It's not safe.
>
> Love, and I mean that,
> Anya

Vickson. Korfu. What kind of person was I? The woman I loved had disappeared, and I was critiquing her spelling.

Love, and I mean that. She meant that. Maybe Anya loved me. Maybe she *had* loved me. Maybe that was why she'd written me a note. Maybe I'd meant something to her. Maybe she'd started to fall

in love with me, though she hadn't planned it. Maybe she'd taken a
risk. Maybe her health—her mental health—wasn't strong enough.
Maybe I would never know what happened. Maybe she didn't write
the book. Maybe she'd been forced to pretend she had. Maybe Warren
or someone had something on her. Maybe he was blackmailing her.
Maybe he knew her parents. Maybe they were all in this together.
What had she meant by *It's not safe*?

I needed to see her and tell her that we could figure it out. We could
help each other. We'd started off on the wrong foot. What would have
been the right foot? Something less reckless, more professional, *anything* besides sex on a dark ride. I would tell her that her novel was
great. The best I'd ever read. Her letter was just a gesture. A dramatic
gesture—theatrical, like everything about her. People made gestures
all the time. But what if Anya was in trouble, and I didn't help? What
if I'd been too preoccupied by my own selfish concerns to recognize
a soul in pain, a woman in danger? I would never forgive myself.

I decided to go find her.

CHAPTER 9

I found the letter in the afternoon, too late for me to leave. The next morning I called in sick. It was true, or almost true. I was exhausted. I'd hardly slept.

I asked the clerk at the Port Authority bus terminal how to get to River Road in Shad Point. He unfolded a map and turned it around, then turned it around again. A bigger bus, a smaller bus, then a taxi. If there were no taxis, a very long walk. I bought a round-trip ticket.

The driver took a different route from either of the ones Ned had taken. I was relieved when I realized we weren't going to pass Sing Sing.

As the suburbs thinned and the pretty countryside streamed by, I felt a rush of independence. I hadn't asked Warren's permission. I wasn't using his driver. I was on my own. Just as Maxwell Perkins tracked down Hemingway, just as legendary editors had always succeeded in flushing great writers out of their burrows, I would find Anya. So what if Anya wasn't a great writer? Some compromise could still be brokered between trash and treasure. Everything would be clear again. Her book would be back on track, and if that's what it took to make her happy, she and I would continue having sex in basements and funhouse rides.

The fruit trees were in feathery bloom, the white apples and pink cherries. Every blossom was a message: I was a week past Warren's May Day deadline.

I took the big bus, then waited for the smaller bus. I was sure it would never arrive. I would be stranded here forever. Behind the bus stop was a forest from which came unnerving rustles and cries. Alien territory. I was a city person, and the forest knew it. Somewhere an owl hooted. Weren't owls nocturnal? Professor Crowley told us a story about a man who heard an owl call his name and knew he was going to die. Whatever *this* owl was saying, at least it wasn't *Simon*.

I almost wept when the bus arrived. I thanked the driver so profusely that he turned and watched me until he must have decided I wasn't a threat to him or the (two) other passengers.

I got off where the agent in Port Authority had told me. Being the only person to get off a bus in the middle of nowhere is unnerving. There were no taxis, no pay phones. The country road was deserted. I started walking. Only rarely did I have to move over for a car. I might have tried to hitchhike, but that scared me more than walking.

Dandelions speckled the emerald grass. An improbably red cardinal perched on a branch to watch me pass. Somehow I had forgotten the beauty of the world. I remembered spring mornings, walking to Crowley's lectures. How sharp and green the air had smelled, how much it felt like the country but with neatly mown lawns and well-kept paths lit by the auras of golden students.

I'd been blind to everything but *The Vixen* and its author.

Just when I'd started looking for a rock or tree stump to rest on, I spotted the Elmwood sign. I walked up the manicured driveway, past the magisterial oaks. The distance from the road to the house was much longer on foot. No attendants, no wheelchairs. Maybe it was lunchtime or rest time or therapy time. I leaned into the heavy, faux-medieval door and nearly stumbled into the hall.

Anya would be there. Everything would be solved. We would get past this rough patch. We would have a future in which to improve her book or not—and decide what we meant to each other. I was excited to be there. I would overlook what happened the last time I saw her. We would start over, from where we were, before she made that pointless joke about not having written *The Vixen*.

Had the nurse at the reception desk looked so anxious before? A second nurse joined the first, and when I asked to see Miss Partridge, they exchanged glances. Perhaps that was why there were two of them, so they could cooperate without speaking.

The older one said, "Miss Partridge has been discharged."

Discharged? I felt dizzy. I needed water. I thought about Mom and her dizzy spells. Why hadn't I been a better son? But I was a good son. It was no one's fault that I'd had to grow up and leave home. I was so far from Coney Island. I had risen and fallen and risen and fallen.

"Do you think you could let me into Anya's room?"

Again the nurses looked at each other.

I said, "She asked me to look for something she needed. Something . . . with sentimental value . . . she left behind."

That made no sense. If she didn't tell me she'd been discharged, how could she have asked me to retrieve something she'd forgotten? Nurses were trained to think logically, but something about me—or Anya or both of us—scrambled their scientific training.

One of them pointed down the hall. "The door's unlocked. No one's there."

Even so, I knocked softly and eased open the door as if I might disturb Anya napping—or writing.

The flocked bordello wallpaper had been ripped down and hung in strips. There were dents in the walls. A pitted wooden floor, dust balls in the corners. A bare bulb hung on a cord. No canopied bed, no glowing red lights, no rumpled sheets, no Persian rugs.

I jumped when I sensed that someone—a nurse—had come up behind me.

"Our guests often strip their rooms when they leave. For some reason they need to obliterate every home comfort we encourage them to create. As if they're erasing their time here. I've seen them paint over walls they've smeared with . . . well, never mind! And those are the patients we *help*. The ones who get out. Often we find their possessions in the dumpster down the road. I've furnished my house with their discards, and it's a lovely house indeed. They toss away magnificent things. Unhappy memories, I guess. Who can blame them? I'm not supposed to be telling you this."

"I won't tell. I promise. Do you think you could please leave me alone for a moment?"

"Of course. I don't think we have anyone else checking in today."

She closed the door behind her. I sank down onto the dusty floor. I wanted to curl up and weep. I'd lost the love of my life. I would never see Anya again.

Had I not been sitting on the floor, I would never have spotted something under a radiator across the room. At first I mistook it for a mouse. I yelled and jumped up. I was glad no one saw me.

It was Anya's fur stole, the pelt with its head and claws. Anya would never have abandoned her totem. I wanted to think that she'd known I would try to find her, that she'd left it to send me a message. We were connected. She knew me. When she asked me, in her note, to please not come look for her, she'd known that I would.

But she couldn't have been sure. And she'd loved that fur stole. Maybe she'd lost it in a struggle. Maybe a kidnapper kicked it under the radiator. Most likely she wasn't thinking of me when they took her away. Who were *they*? Were *they* violent? Was Anya in some kind of danger?

I extracted the fox from its hiding place, avoiding the eyes that had looked into mine at so many intimate moments. I put the stole under my jacket. The claws scratched me through my shirt. I welcomed the pain. Anya didn't want me to forget.

Back in the front hall, I asked the nurses if Anya had left a forwarding address. The one in charge said, "You understand we can't give out that information. Many of our clients are public figures."

What difference should it make whether a mental patient was famous? I knew what difference it made. I said, "Of course. I understand. Thank you."

I'd almost reached the door when I turned. "Do you think it would be possible for me to visit Preston Bartlett?"

I didn't know why I said that, why I thought of it then, why I hadn't thought of it earlier. Something or someone was speaking through me. Please let that someone be Anya.

Another long look passed between them. Nurse More-in-Charge said, "That might be lovely. Preston used to get visitors, but he doesn't anymore, and human contact is so important. He'll miss Anya terribly. They became great friends. We often see unpredictable things. Unexpected connections forged. The heart wants what the heart wants. Sometimes the heart wants friendship. Someone to talk to. What did you say your name was? Should I say you're a friend of Anya's?"

"Simon. Simon Putnam. Can you please tell Mr. Bartlett that I'm an editor at Landry, Landry and Bartlett? Wait. No. Just say I'm a friend of Anya's." The nurse took off down the corridor lined with shut doors that, just as Anya had said, looked like Van Gogh's asylum.

I would never again meet anyone so original, so intriguing. Oh, Anya! Where had you gone?

CHAPTER 10

The victim enters the pitch-dark room. Hello-o? Is anyone here? A faint sound, the creak of chair legs, the sudden glint of the blade. The metallic voice of the killer, the flash of the knife, the blood. It's the meat and potatoes of horror films, a foolproof jolt to the limbic brain.

No one answered when I knocked, so I eased open the door. Some counterintuitive impulse made me close it behind me, losing the light from the hall. If Anya's room was a jungle hothouse, all opium and musk, Preston's room was glacial, suffused with the sweet antiseptic perfume of rubbing alcohol masking something less sparkling clean. Blobs of pale multicolored light jiggled and pulsed in the dark, and a dusty glow seeped in through the single window shrouded in black.

I had never before and would never again feel the hair on my forearms rise the way it's said to, in the presence of the uncanny. I remember thinking that I had left the land of the living and entered the antechamber where the newly dead wait for further direction.

From the depths of the gloom, a quavering voice said, "Who the fuck are you?"

The light that flashed on was sudden and blinding, though—as my eyes adjusted—I saw that it wasn't all that bright, and that it came from a small, old-fashioned hurricane lamp on a desk.

Preston Bartlett sat in his wheelchair, facing the window. I recognized him at once, though from the back he looked more like a buzzard than a man: the ornithological rake of his shoulders, the wing-like elbows jutting over the arms of his chair, the dry unruly crest sprouting from his domed head. In one of Crowley's revenge tales, a miserly landowner is reincarnated as a vulture, subsisting on the scraps thrown away by the villagers whom he almost starved when he was a human being. Those stories were coming back to me lately, more often and more clearly. I found it consoling to think that my experience was part of a pattern, ancient narratives of lying and heart-break not unique to me.

I felt, as I had with Anya, that I'd left my century and wandered into a time that never existed. Maybe Elmwood catered to patients with delusions of having been born into the wrong era. How foolish I'd been to assume that Anya would always call me, that she would always be there when I wanted to see her, or at least when she wanted to see me so we could "work on her book." I heard myself utter a cry of despair. That was my real voice escaping at this highly embarrass-ing moment.

Preston wheeled around and regarded me with blistering irrita-tion. I'd seen him in the office, asking to see Warren, but up close he looked more forceful. Intimidating, even. An old buzzard maybe, but a hungry one eyeing its dinner.

"Close the goddamn door," he said. "And quit that goddamn sob-bing."

"It's already closed." I'd made a noise. I wouldn't have called it sobbing.

He motioned for me to sit on the ottoman near his feet, then kicked it as far away as he could. It was awkward, lowering myself onto a seat that my host had just punted. The ottoman had landed on its side, and I had to right it.

"Come closer." He scooped the air toward him. I moved the otto-man nearer to where it was before he'd kicked it.

Sitting at his feet like a disciple, staring up into his dried-apricot face, I found it hard to believe that Warren and Preston were college classmates. Preston could have been Warren's father near the end of a long hard life. Sunk deep in their sockets, his eyes were ringed with indigo. He stared at me with the fixity of a madman, a part he clearly enjoyed, from his tufted scalp down to his bony fingers clenching a silver-topped cane. His posture was aggressive and defensive at once, as if, like a toddler with sharp scissors, he feared that someone would take away his cane. He pounded the cane on the floor. I slid as far away as I could without falling off the ottoman. His piercing gaze and glassy eyes made him look gaga, but only a genius of sanity and Machiavellian cunning could have made me feel so cornered and so at a disadvantage.

Preston turned up the lamp a notch, and I saw that his face was more canine than avian, an elongated dog's head on a rachitic bird's body. As my eyes adjusted, I took in more of the room, its institutional awfulness unspoiled by any attempt to make it homey. A desk, a lamp, a bed. It reminded me of my office, which made me feel marginally less jittery.

I said, "I'm Simon Putnam. I—"

"I know who you are. You work at my former firm. Why do I say *former*, when I hold a controlling interest, as you doubtless know? Where my name is still on the door, behind the reception desk, and most importantly on the spines of the increasingly inferior books we publish."

I bristled at that *inferior*. Then I remembered: *The Vixen*.

"What do you do there, Mr. Putnam, if that *is* your real name? Fetch coffee? Empty wastebaskets? Draw on the floor with colored chalk? Or do you work in reception? I hear it's become fashionable to hire attractive young men for positions that used to be filled entirely on the basis of breast size."

Thanks to Warren, I was used to men talking that way about women's breasts. It still made me uncomfortable, but less than it might have if Warren hadn't made a point of not hiring the tequila sunrise drinker regardless of her breast size. Mom would have been disappointed in me for going along with the joke, for not finding a firm, polite, but manly way to say that this was insulting to women.

"Simon," I said. "Call me Simon."

"Fine. Simon it is."

"I'm a junior assistant editor."

"I don't expect you get paid."

"Modestly. Very modestly." I chuckled. Preston's face stayed blank.

"If this social call is about money, if that bastard Warren has sent you to wring one more dime out of me, forget it. They charge thousands of dollars in this place so I can have fresh pineapple with my dinner. What do you think fresh pineapple costs, were one to buy it in a shop?"

"I don't know that much about pineapple," I said lamely. "Mr. Bartlett, I promise this isn't about money. I'm not even here on business. I'm a friend of Anya's. I mean, not a *friend* exactly."

"You're her friend, but not her friend. Then what are you *exactly*?"

"I'm her editor."

"I see. I assume you're working on her so-called bestseller. Her lurid fantasy about the Rosenbergs. What a grotesque idea."

So Preston knew the story, or some of it. Not the details of my relationship with Anya, I hoped. Would anyone, even Anya, tell this ailing elderly gentleman that she'd had sex with her editor in the Terror Tomb? I was encouraged to hear that Preston believed that Anya had written the novel.

"I was wondering if you knew where Anya went."

"Be careful. Very careful. You don't know who's listening. Dollars to doughnuts they've got this deathtrap wheelchair bugged."

"Who has?"

"Don't play innocent," he said. "So you're the selfish son of a bitch who broke Anya's heart?"

"No. I mean, no, I don't think so." I hated feeling flattered by the suggestion that I might have broken Anya's heart and gratified by the image of myself as a selfish son of a bitch. How could I have broken her heart when she had broken mine? What pleased me was the implication that I'd meant something to her, that she'd seen me as more than just a guy who droned on about a book she did or didn't write, a guy she had sex with in semipublic places. The fox scratching me under my jacket was momentarily exciting.

I had *The Vixen* in my briefcase, in the hopes that I might find Anya. But now I was alone with the problem of the novel—and Warren's deadline. The exciting part of my job had vanished along with Anya, leaving only the question of what to do now. Warren and Elaine would track Anya down, the novel would come out, and I would be fired for getting my author spirited off to Greece, if that was where she'd gone. Warren should have known that it was risky to award a book contract to a bright, unstable young actress in a mental institution. But *The Snake Pit* made a fortune. A beautiful mad-as-a-hatter author wasn't an automatic no.

Preston said, "I'm pretty sure you're the guy she talked about. Though honestly, to look at you, I'm beginning to wonder if Anya was as intelligent as she pretended." His wide, slack mouth froze into a rictus half-smile. "I'm joking. Some men came and took Anya away. Last night. Or maybe the night before that. Or the one before that. They do strange things to time, in this place."

Anya had said something similar. The memory shouldn't have lifted my spirits, but the thought of her did.

"They threw her possessions in a moving van. She was crying. All us lunatics watched from the front door. They didn't care. Who would believe a gaggle of mental patients, if we even knew what we were seeing? I assumed her parents hired the goon squad. She was gone in one night. Something convinced them to spirit her out of here. I heard she went to Corfu."

"Corfu?" That was what Anya had said in her letter, though she'd spelled it wrong. I deserved what I was getting for being the kind of snob who, under the circumstances, would critique his beloved's spelling. I needed to feel superior. It was all I had.

"Greece. You do know where Corfu is, don't you? One never knows what young people know these days. God help me. I sound like Warren."

He did. I tried to imagine them discussing books or business. Preston must have been a different person. I wondered about their falling-out, their fight, about why Preston wound up here and ceded control to Warren. If I was patient, lucky, or clever enough, Preston might explain.

His room was musty, airless. Cloying. I felt like a deep-sea diver watching the dial on his oxygen tank sink dangerously low.

"How long do you think you have?" he said.

"How long do I have?" Was I in danger? Was there some threat to my well-being, my life, of which I was unaware? Anya's defection had so upset me, anything seemed possible.

"Unlike me, *you* have a lifetime, young man. I mean: How long do you think the company has before Warren runs it into the ground? Which at this point may not be a bad thing."

I felt the stirring of pride I hadn't known I possessed. Wasn't that the point of publishing *The Vixen*? So the firm *wouldn't* go under? *That* was why I was here. Anya was a footnote. *The Vixen* could still be fixed. The gods of literature and even Mom would have to understand.

"I think that Warren believes *The Vixen* will make money. Enough to float us until he can bring out a French novel he thinks will sell— and steer us into the black." I was conscious of speaking in the plural, as if I were a partner in our shipwreck of a publishing company. The *Titanic* sailed through my mind, tipped sideways, and disappeared.

"You believed Warren? And what were *you* supposed to do? Pray for a publishing miracle?"

"I hadn't thought about it," I said, though I'd thought about little else since Warren dropped the manuscript on my desk.

"No one thinks about anything until they find themselves institutionalized, with plenty of time to think. Let me get this straight." Preston jackknifed so far forward I worried he might tip out of his wheelchair. Grim scenarios ran through my mind, all involving my calling the nurses who knew I shouldn't be there. The only reason they'd let me visit Preston was so I'd briefly keep the old buzzard out of their hair.

"You think this is Warren Landry's plan: Every semiliterate housewife from Bar Harbor to Santa Barbara is going to rush out to pay full price for a hardcover book that will do for the Rosenbergs what Scarlett O'Hara did for the Civil War? And the pennies these women spend will sustain the business without massive infusions of cash from me?"

Scarlett O'Hara. How extensively had Preston discussed *The Vixen* with Anya?

"I did," I stammered. "I mean I think . . . I thought . . . I . . . "

"Is that where you thought the money would come from? Salvation, rescue, paid for, dollar by hard-earned dollar, by American readers starved for a thriller about a nympho Soviet spy. And *that's* why you believe that Warren is publishing this book?"

"Yes, I guess I do. No?"

"Bullshit," Preston said.

I knew I should have been horrified, but I felt hopeful. Maybe I could have an honest conversation about *The Vixen, the Patriot, and the Fanatic* with a certified madman.

I said, "Can I tell you a secret, Mr. Bartlett? Will you promise not to tell?"

Preston's shrug was as good as a promise.

"Anya claimed that she didn't write the book."

Preston said, "Who cares who wrote the goddamn book? The only thing that matters is who wants it published."

"And who is that?"

"Young man! I'm astonished! Are you mentally defective? Surely even in your brief sheltered naive life you've heard of the CIA!"

CHAPTER 11

By now many readers will have figured out what took me so long to realize in those more trusting and innocent times, namely that the Central Intelligence Agency was covertly masterminding the publication of *The Vixen, the Patriot, and the Fanatic*.

Since then, we have learned how many cultural products and events—literary magazines, art exhibitions, concert tours, and so forth—were founded and mined for "soft power." This was the so-called "cultural cold war," when literature, music, and art were deployed to fight the spread of Communism by glorifying the American way of life, our intellectual superiority and unfettered freedom of expression. The traveling show of Jackson Pollock and other American artists, orchestras and theater groups on international tours, journals like *Encounter* and the *Paris Review* would, it was hoped, convince our allies, our enemies, and the undecided masses that America was a paradise and that Americans, if not all angels, were squarely on the side of liberty and justice.

I could tell that Preston loved wising me up, educating me. "Some genius at the Agency must have decided that a lurid bestseller was the best way to persuade all those misguided ninnies upset by the Rosenberg execution. If world opinion disapproved, why not show the world how treason looked from the inside, from the traitors' evil commie perspective?"

"Have you read *The Vixen*?"

Preston grimaced. "A chapter or two. As much as a sentient being could stand."

"Did Anya know who was funding her book?" I almost didn't want to know, but I needed to find out how deep the conspiracy went.

"If she did, she truly was a marvelous little actress. She seemed to *believe* in her awful novel. But I never asked her directly. These days, I often think, the less we know, the better."

I struggled to keep from slipping off Preston's ottoman as I tried to decide how credible or delusional he was. We were, after all, in a madhouse. A luxury asylum, but an asylum nonetheless. I knew that the disturbed often imagined being spied on.

Even the sanest of us had reason to be paranoid at that time. Washington was in the grip of men who believed that our country was overrun with Russian agents masquerading as loyal American citizens. But it was one thing to know that such men existed and another to listen to an old man making outrageous accusations about a boss I admired and respected and longed to emulate.

Preston ranted on, listing Warren's crimes against humanity, some more unlikely than others, but none of them—given what I knew of Warren—entirely beyond belief.

"Another inspired scheme: Attach incendiary devices to starlings and send them to blow up the parliaments of Europe—terrorist attacks from the sky that we could blame on the far left—and install puppet dictators. But the birds exploded in the agents' hands, resulting in painful third-degree burns and bloody, feathered ceilings."

"Really?" was all I could say. "Can that be true?"

"I swear it on what's left of my life. Not much collateral, I admit, so you'll have to take my word. I swear on what's left of my shrinking patrimony after I pay the bills here. Did Warren tell you he'd planned to spread a rumor that the bubonic plague was sweeping Eastern Europe? Supposedly the disease had been preserved by mad monks in the Caucasus, and now the Russians had set it loose to subdue the restive Eastern Bloc nations. They alone had the antidote, the cure, and if the Czechs and Poles and Hungarians didn't get in line . . . well, you can imagine.

"The success of these operations never mattered to Warren. He just liked planning them. He didn't care about the results. He gave two shits about consequences. He only cared about means."

I recalled Warren saying something like that. I forgot the context. But I remembered the phrase: *two shits about consequences*.

...

Narrative turns on those moments: The shock of finding out, the quickened heartbeat when the truth rips the mask off a lie. The friend who is our enemy, the confidant revealed as a spy. The faithless lover, the demon bride. The maniac faking sanity. The deceptively innocent murderer. We enjoy these surprises. We demand them. They delight the child inside us, the child who wants to hear a story that turns in a startling direction.

In life, it's less of a pleasure. There's none of the bubbly satisfaction of finding out who committed the crime. An opaque curtain drops over the past, obscuring whatever we thought we knew. Hearing Preston rant about my boss, I felt no exhilaration. No *So that's it! I always suspected*. I felt unhappy and confused by Preston's allegations. It was important not to panic. I rejoined the conversation, having missed a few of Warren's sins.

"Oh, and that cult of Holy Saint Somebody who lived in the wilderness and ate bugs. Some left-wing Greek Orthodox priest was plotting to sell the saint's bones to a dealer in Manhattan and funnel the proceeds to the KGB. An elaborate money-laundering scheme stinking of frankincense and myrrh. Warren blew it wide open."

"Really? I can't imagine." But I could imagine, all too well, the younger Warren thinking this sounded like *fun*, a ballsy creative adventure.

"Stop saying *really*. It's real." Preston transferred his cane to his left hand and held up his right, two fingers hooked forward. "Scout's honor."

Again he sounded like Warren. Was he imitating him or speaking in the voice of their common background?

"Do you know Warren's favorite thing? *Naming* covert programs, assassinations, and coups. According to Warren, the Agency has on its payroll some highly educated, wickedly humorous fellows who always get his literary jokes. Operation Garden Snake. Operation Steppenwolf, not one of his proudest moments. How unfortunate that the research subject decided to throw himself from a fifteenth-story hotel window. How inept of the Agency not to book the guy on a lower floor. Sometimes Warren made up the name first and *then* the operation. Operation Ahab. What reader of *Moby-Dick* would go on that mission? Five hundred soldiers parachuted into Rumania. When they disappeared without a trace, five hundred more were dropped."

Was my uncle Mort among them? All that remained of him was our familial fear of the Parachute Jump and a framed photograph of a guy who looked like a younger, thinner Dad. No wonder Uncle Maddie hated Communists. Could Warren have been responsible for my uncle's death?

I reminded myself that Preston wasn't testifying under oath. He was raving in a darkened room in a mental asylum.

"These guys are trained to keep secrets. Take the bullet. Eat the cyanide. Torture them fucking senseless, they won't talk. But not my man Warren. After three martinis, he's Mr. Blah Blah Blah. Señor Boca Grande. He'll tell you everything he knows, plus a lot he doesn't know, plus a lot he wishes he knew. And no one cares. Someone up there likes him. He keeps his spymaster status. He retrieves some floating turd from a writer's toilet, gives it a sexy title, and offers it to the government as a propaganda bomb. *The Vixen, the Patriot, and the Fanatic*. By the gorgeous, gifted debut novelist Anya Partridge. Seriously? Are you kidding? It's the CIA's three-hundred-page wet dream."

"Can you prove this? Any of this?"

"Why should I? I don't have to. Either Warren is lying, or I'm lying, or everybody's lying. You're probably lying about *something*. You wouldn't be human if you weren't. So you're just going to have to work this out on your own."

"I can't."

"What was that?"

"Sorry. I was talking to myself."

"You've come to the right place for that, ha-ha."

Preston laughed like the madman he was. I laughed like a maniac too. My eyeballs jittered in their sockets. I thought of Lucy, terrified that Ricky was plotting to kill her.

Logic required an effort that I was willing to make. "I can't believe the Agency would retain a guy who can't keep his mouth shut when he drinks."

"Oh, really? End-stage alcoholism is the number one job qualification on a prospective agent's CV. You've heard of the two-martini lunch? How about the six-martini lunch—and then it's back to spreading democracy around the world."

I was shocked, less by what Preston was saying than by how sane he sounded.

"Do you know what Warren wanted to call his mind-control project? Operation Svengali. Too bad that the suits in Washington decided it was too obvious. What's the point of a secret name if everyone knows what it means? What a brain! If Warren wasn't in publishing, he could rule the world!"

Was Preston mocking or admiring? It was hard to tell. Politics and morality were so thickly mixed with animosity and grievance, betrayal and personal loss. What if they'd locked up the wrong guy, and it was Warren who should have been hospitalized, not Preston? Was there anything Warren *hadn't* done when he wasn't busy running one of the country's most distinguished publishing houses? Or was Preston out of his mind?

Preston seemed to have lost all fear that his wheelchair might be bugged. "There was this Malaysian writer whom Warren promised to publish. He lured him to a hotel bar in Singapore where the guy was arrested by the secret police. An Iranian journalist left a New York book party with Warren and hasn't been heard from since. And that sexy Czech novel with that idiotic title . . . *The Smile of Disillusion*?"

I hadn't read the book, but I'd seen it in a display case at the office.

"Warren published it against its author's will. The writer begged him not to bring it out in the West. His freedom, his family, his life would be in danger. Warren told him not to be a pussy. Sure enough, the book comes out, sells five copies. The writer's fired from his university job and has to work as a window cleaner. Know what Warren said? 'Why the hell did the guy give me the book if he didn't want it published?' That's your Mr. Good Guy! That's your lover of world literature! That's your . . . Mr. CIA Agent! Even that unfortunate woman, that sub-sub-minor poet who adopted the Japanese kid with the messed-up face—"

"Florence Durgin." Just saying her name felt like testifying to the truth of what Preston was alleging.

"Poor thing. She knew about some dirty deal in postwar Japan. Some covert yakuza business. The Japanese kid told her a secret that the Agency didn't want known. Florence threatened to go public. Warren agreed to print two volumes of iambic pentameter teardrops and snot that no one will ever read."

"I wouldn't say *no one*." I was insulted on Florence's behalf. Her first book hadn't sold outstandingly well, but it had done better than expected.

"Okay, you're right. No one but the typesetter. And maybe the editor. Maybe. A deal was struck. No wonder she's a disaster. Warren didn't bother hiding what he wanted from her."

"Which was?"

"Her silence. We printed a couple hundred copies and wrote it off as a tax deduction. It's one of the cheaper prices that's ever been paid for silence. Bargain basement, really."

My impression was that Warren had edited Florence's first book. Preston didn't seem to know that I was working on her new collection. Probably no one thought it worth mentioning.

I said, "Her second book hasn't come out yet."

"It will. Eventually. Trust me."

Did I trust him? So much he'd said seemed far-fetched, yet so much else seemed plausible.

"Warren's most catastrophic fuckup involved some unfortunate Albanians."

"Albanians?"

"You know where Albania is, don't you, son?"

Albania was one of Professor Crowley's special places. He'd spent years in High Albania, transcribing the fireside tales of the sworn virgins. One of the stories popped into my head. Scorned by a famous beauty, a man takes his revenge by serving the beauty a fruit that makes horns grow all over her face. Strangely, the memory, or maybe just the momentary distraction, soothed me.

"Eighty-seven Albanians. All dead." Preston slashed a bony finger across his throat.

"All dead," I repeated.

"Eighty-seven dead Albanians. Is that not clear? Warren assembled a ragtag band of anti-Soviet resistance fighters. Women who fought with the partisans. Tough broads who dressed like men. He'd heard about them in some college class, and he'd gone there to find them."

"In what class?" I asked, though I knew.

"Who the hell cares what class?" Preston said. "Warren told them they had reinforcements all over Eastern Europe. Lie number one. He promised that American soldiers would back them up if the going got rough. *Big* lie number two.

"Pursued by Soviet agents, the Albanians holed up in a barn outside Berat. Safe in Athens, Warren tried to wire for help, but the wire service was down, so he went out for dinner. A marvelous little ouzeri, is how that bastard tells the story.

"The Soviets torched the barn, killing all the partisans trapped inside. And because the project died before it was officially born, Warren named it posthumously. The Burning."

The room had grown cold. Colder than before.

"The Burning," I said.

"The Burning," said Preston.

"That was the title of my thesis, my senior year at college."

"Coincidence." Preston shrugged. "'The' and 'burning.' Two common words."

"And, according to Warren, *The Burning* was *The Vixen*'s original title."

"Not so coincidental. I assume that Warren knew about your paper. He has an appetite for pointless trivia and elaborate private jokes that put people on edge."

Elaborate private jokes. The image of Anya and her fake black eye flashed past me—and vanished.

"Except for his friends in the Agency, or so he claims, no one thinks his jokes are funny, not even the girls he's fucking. Anya, Elaine, that poor sweet Julia who used to come and see me before Warren tired of her and . . . How did I get off on that?"

"Before Warren tired of her and *what*?"

Preston said, "How should I know? Why are you even asking?"

I was paralyzed. Mute. How much did Warren know about me? There was so little to know. I looked up at the ceiling, the corners hairy with spiderwebs. Searching for . . . what? Microphones, cameras? I was as bad as McCarthy seeing commies under every bed. This way paranoia lay. That way led to the truth. The directional sign had spun around and kept turning and turning.

Let this all be a madman's fantasy, and my life could go on like before. I was a fool to have visited Preston, to have come here in search of Anya. I should have coped with her disappearance without shredding the fragile calm of a mental patient. If what Preston said about Warren was even partly true, how could I continue working for him? And if Preston was lying, shouldn't Warren know what his partner was saying about him? I wondered if Preston told Anya what he was telling me, if her knowing what he'd said about Warren had something to do with her disappearance.

"Is that why you and Warren had that fight? At the office Christmas party?"

"God, no. I already knew all that stuff. I'd decided to make my peace with it. Warren is a charismatic guy, in case you haven't noticed. Not just capable but brilliant. His taste in books is stellar. His instinct is razor-sharp. People want to be around him. People want him to like and respect them."

I nodded, against my will. That was what *I'd* wanted.

"It was thrilling at the beginning, when Warren and I were working to publish the best books by the best writers on the planet. Then everything changed, and I watched it change. I watched it slip out of my control. There was nothing I could do. No way to stop it. It was only when he invited his loutish, incompetent, wicked, *deeply stupid* spy-boy buddies to more or less run the company that we'd worked so hard to build—that's when I drew the line. I didn't believe we should be working for *them*. I hadn't planned on that line running through a bookcase that turned out *not* to be fixed to the wall.

"Cheap bookcase. Low-wattage bulbs. With all the CIA interest in the books Warren publishes, you'd think they'd spring for new carpet or decent lighting, let alone salaries and rent. But in my experience you don't go into the espionage business unless you're a bit of a sadist, and that sadistic need for control trickles all the way down the food chain. Some bigger fish than Warren must have enjoyed watching him sweat as soon as my rivers of money began to dry up. The Agency could float the firm, but someone wants to make Warren suffer. And of course he's made a few costly mistakes for which they might want to make him pay. So you do see how *The Vixen* fits into the larger scheme, doubling as cash cow and propaganda bonanza?"

Preston couldn't have sounded saner. Maybe he wasn't demented. My view of him had shifted back and forth from incarcerated lunatic to silenced truth-teller.

"Meanwhile they brought me here and subjected me to . . . medical treatments."

"That's torture!"

Preston shrugged. "The drugs are excellent. Tip-top. Pharmaceutical grade. The staff enjoy their work. Nice women, one and all. The electroshock was unpleasant. I miss the coffee maker at work, the books, the secretaries, but—"

"Electroshock? Someone needs to be told!"

"I would strongly advise you not to. I suggest you not tell anyone that we had this conversation. They don't like people talking. Anyway, I'm not complaining. I feel quite pacified. At peace. I was never going to win my fight to keep the spies out of the firm.

"Life is simpler here. I can stay high as a kite! I always have someone to take me out when the walls start closing in. I like being wheeled into my former office like some crippled show pony—it's better than working there, knowing what I know. It's only when something disturbs my peace of mind and reminds me . . . "

There it was. I knew it. I'd disturbed Preston's peace of mind. I'd reminded him of what he'd lost. Sorry, sorry, sorry. And all because of a woman. The Vikings got that one right.

"You can do whatever you want with this information. It no longer matters to me. Monks meditate in mountain huts for years looking for the peace of mind I've found here. No sitting on the cold, cold ground in the Himalayan snow for this geriatric lone-wolf Buddha. If I were you, I'd act as if all this never happened."

Preston didn't sound like a man who'd found peace of mind but like a man whose heart had been broken. It wasn't my place to tell him that and perhaps undo whatever good the medical staff had done.

"Thank you," I said. "I need to think."

"That sounds like a plan. I assume you can show yourself out. It's very simple. You open that door and leave. You'll forgive me if I don't go along to chat up the on-duty nurses. The instant you walk out, they will inform the authorities that you were here and for how long. Someone will transcribe the conversation that my wheelchair has transmitted, and the document will go into the files they are compiling against us."

Preston's paranoia was reassuring. The needle that had been tipping between belief and disbelief tipped back toward the conclusion that he was mad.

My hand was on the doorknob when I said, "One more thing . . . if you see Anya, could you please tell her to get in touch? No matter where she is, no matter—"

"I don't think I'll see Anya again," Preston said. "I don't think you will, either."

Preston spun his wheelchair around. His time with me was over.

. . .

I don't remember if I thanked him or said goodbye. I remember thanking the nurses at the front desk, the younger and the older one, kindly and kindlier, both white, blond, dressed in white, as if they'd been dusted with flour, waiting to be fried. I watched the nurses change and change again from sweet-tempered health professionals to snarling prison guards. *Could* they have been listening to a transmission from Preston's wheelchair? They were nurses, not spies. I'd caught Preston's illness. If Warren intended to sow a plague, so did his former partner.

I felt weirdly compelled to prove that I was a visitor and not a potential escapee or inmate. Of course I was upset. But even later in life, whenever I was introduced to psychiatrists, therapists, even survivors of breakdowns, I'd watch myself working to convince them that I was sane, like a drunk driver walking the white line for the police.

I said, "Someone might want to check on Mr. Bartlett."

"We do check on him," she said. "Every hour. Not when he has visitors. We trust them. Should we not?"

"Of course," I said. "You should. Could you tell me the best way to get back to the city."

"Would you like us to call you a cab?"

I saw myself hustled into an unmarked car. I could almost feel the rough hand pushing down my head, shoving me into the back seat.

"No thanks," I said. "That's all right."

I must have walked to the station. I must have taken the train to the city. I must have made my way back to my apartment. I must have heard the roaches welcoming me home.

Though it was still afternoon, I fell asleep and had violent, chaotic dreams that I forgot upon awakening.

I called in sick, the second day in a row. A terrible flu, etcetera. I didn't want to infect the office. As if anyone cared. I couldn't face my colleagues. Was Elaine part of this too? Was she involved in whatever plot Warren had contrived? Was I wrong to tell Elaine that Anya denied writing the novel? Is that why Anya was taken away?

I showered and dressed. I sat on the edge of my bed. I let time pass. I tried to steady my heart rate, my breathing. I considered calling my parents. I thought about calling a doctor.

Then I found my address book and telephoned Florence Durgin.

CHAPTER 12

invited Florence to lunch. I was sorry I had no news to report about the publication of *Autumn Light*, but I thought it might be *quite lovely* to have a chat over *a proper meal*. I had never in my life said *quite lovely* or *a proper meal*. I was finally turning into Warren just when I least wanted to become him. I said that since Florence's book was forthcoming, though not on this season's list, she might want to make a few changes. I would have said anything to persuade her to see me, even though I sensed that Florence wouldn't require much persuasion.

In the silence during which Florence pretended to consult her schedule, I reminded myself to be compassionate, generous, and patient, even as I lied about why I wanted to see her.

We were in luck. She'd had a last-minute cancellation. We arranged to meet the next day, at Amir's Turkish Café, on Lexington and 27th. It was near my apartment, and I thought I might be able to afford it. I could tell she was disappointed that I hadn't suggested one of the midtown spots where famous writers and publishers met for legendary lunches. Her ingratitude wouldn't have annoyed me so intensely if I also didn't wish we were going to a fancier place. Sharing this jealous resentment inspired a low-boiling fury that made me insist—to Florence and to myself—that Amir's was *better* than wherever the Warrens, the Elaines, and the Uncle Maddies of the world were eating lunch.

"It's a fun place. Lots of young publishing people go there," I said through gritted teeth.

After we hung up, I took the train to Brooklyn and spent the rest of the day and night with my parents. Visiting them seemed like the most useful, virtuous, penitential thing I could do.

But my visit helped no one. My mother's migraines had come raging back, more painful, erratic, and debilitating. The doctors had changed her prescription, but the new medication made her sleepy and forgetful, and she refused to take it. I felt guilty for being relieved that my mother's health prevented my parents from noticing how distraught I must have looked. We ate dinner in front of the TV: the 1946 David Lean film of *Great Expectations*. I couldn't watch the scenes in Miss Havisham's ruined bridal chamber. I thought of Anya; I thought of Preston. I had to look away.

How could I sleep in my boyhood room when I had begun to suspect that I might have been working for the enemy of everything my family believed in, of every ideal we shared? Surrounded by liars, I'd become one. Never, not under torture, would I tell my parents that I was editing a long filthy lie about Ethel, concocted and funded by her enemies, if not by her actual killers, then by others as cruel and deranged. Without agreeing, I'd become the CIA's most ignorant, underpaid, low-ranking employee. So low-ranking that I hadn't even been told that I was working for them.

I was yet another innocent dupe whom no one would believe.

I woke up exhausted. My mother was stretched on the couch, under an ice pack. For the first time I could remember, she didn't offer to cook me breakfast. She flinched when I hugged her goodbye. I was sorry for feeling relieved to leave, to escape into the light.

My father and I took the train into Manhattan. How peaceful, how normal: dad and son going to work in the morning. I should have taken the job in his sporting goods store. I might still need it, if they'd hire me.

Even our trip to work was a lie. I was lying to Dad about going to the office. I went home and changed my clothes and lay on my bed and closed my eyes until it was time to go meet Florence Durgin.

...

I was terrified of Florence, the way you can only be scared of someone who exhibits all the qualities that you most fear in yourself. Florence's watery indecisiveness—was that my fatal flaw? Was that why I couldn't decide what to do about *The Vixen*? Why I couldn't act on what Preston had told me about Warren? Should I confront Warren? Denounce him and quit the firm? Find myself called to testify before a Senate committee? Or should I do nothing and hope for the best?

The restaurant was empty except for Florence, who must have begun to suspect that I'd lied about its popularity with the bright young literary crowd. Maybe she'd started to wonder what else I was lying about. Or maybe I was the only one who was thinking about lying.

Alone in that sea of tables, Florence looked like someone stranded on a desert island, not a new arrival but a reconciled exile. From the doorway I watched her alternate between anxious perusal of the menu and quick anxious glances toward the door. I was half afraid to make eye contact and half afraid to catch her off guard.

On every wall was a rug woven with an image of a white mosque against a cloud-flecked scarlet sky. Above the carpets were gleaming swords, below them filigreed tables, samovars, hookahs, kilim-covered banquettes. Amir's—where I'd never been, but only passed—was decorated like a sultan's antechamber, and Florence looked as uncomfortable as she would have been in the sultan's harem.

On this warm afternoon, she wore a mouse-colored cloth coat and a matching hat, a felt helmet pulled tightly over her curls. She seemed weighed down by gravity and at the same time unmoored, floating inside a private bubble of obligation and sadness. She half smiled when she saw me, then half rose, then decided against doing either. We shook hands, our limp protracted handshake mercifully interrupted by a waiter in a tasseled fez and a graying moustache.

He asked what we wanted to drink. They had some excellent Turkish wines.

"I don't think so." Florence took off her hat and placed it on the chair beside her, then patted down the curls that sprang free. "It's awfully early in the day."

I said, "Do you have anything stronger?"

The waiter grinned. "Raki. Turkish whiskey."

"A double for each of us. And keep them coming, will you?" *Keep them coming* was another phrase, like *a proper meal*, that I'd never once uttered before. But wasn't that how editors were *supposed* to talk? For all I knew, Warren was saying those very words at one of the stylish midtown spots where Florence wished we were. Make that a double—and keep them coming. If I got Florence a little drunk, a little loosened up, I might persuade her to tell me what I wanted to know.

Earlier I'd watched her studying the menu, but now that a decision was required, she shrank from it as if from a list of tortures. Maybe I only thought about torture because I'd been thinking about Warren and wondering if torture was involved in his covert actions. *If* what Preston said was true.

The waiter brought two shot glasses, ruby red flecked with gold. He filled them with clear liquid.

"Down the hatch," I said.

I drank mine, as did Florence. We coughed. Already I felt that mysterious sense of well-being.

"My goodness! The Turkish liquor must be *terrifically* strong. I feel quite tipsy already."

"Have another," I suggested.

"Are you . . . having another?"

"Yes, indeed I am."

"I'm afraid to," said Florence. "I don't know what—"

"Don't be afraid," I said.

The waiter seemed proud of us, the older woman and the younger man, partying in the middle of the day. His approval was heartening. I knocked back another raki, hoping it wasn't expensive and that I would be able to pay the check, even or especially if I was drunk. The alcohol gave me courage and at the same time fear, helping me with one hand, threatening with the other.

When Florence asked what to order, if I had any suggestions—she assumed I'd been there before—I steered her away from the expensive roast lamb and swordfish pilaf, toward the cheaper stuffed grape leaves, the salads and dips.

I said, "The portions are huge here. If we split two appetizers, it should fill us up."

For all I knew, the portions were tiny, and I dreaded the awkwardness of splitting anything with Florence. But even that seemed better than a bill I couldn't pay.

"Another raki," I said. "Florence? Join me?"

"Why not?" said Florence. "There's nothing else on my schedule for the rest of the day."

Since coming to work for Warren, I'd been drinking with experienced drinkers, men with a high tolerance who held their liquor better than I did. But now Florence had taken on my role, and I had become her Warren, her Uncle Maddie, lowering her defenses with every sip.

"So! Florence!" I said, before the food arrived to sober her up. "Tell me how you came to write that marvelous first book." My enthusiasm sounded so false I wondered how anyone could be fooled, even Florence. Only later, when I became a writer, did I discover how susceptible writers are to praise, no matter how blatantly hollow.

Florence stared into the middle distance. I had made a mistake. Tell me, Quasimodo, how did you get that hump? Tell me, Captain Ahab, how did you lose that leg? Tell me, Mr. Rochester, when did you go blind?

She said, "I assume you know about Junchi."

I knew that Florence's first book was a suite of poems about the pain and glory of adopting a boy badly disfigured in the bombing of Nagasaki.

"I knew it would be a challenge, adopting a fourteen-year-old with burn scars on half his face and not one word of English. But I'd wanted a child for so long, and the adoption agencies were so obdurate in their refusal to allow a *mature* single woman to adopt. I'm certain that many less qualified, less stable, and less loving young couples were given as many babies as they wanted."

"Surely not *as many* babies as they wanted."

"Oh yes, it's true," insisted Florence. "As many and more. I always used to see stories about adoptive families of twelve. Heroic, everyone calls them. But I'd say just plain greedy."

I hoped that Florence didn't get argumentative when she drank. So many people did. Though my college experience with drinking was limited, I'd caught up—caught on—at the literary parties.

"I'd left my name with agencies where my plight fell on deaf ears. And then one day I got a call from one of the more elite organizations, saying they had a child with a painful history. A child? Painful history? Junchi was no longer a *child*, and *painful history* was quite a euphemism for the atomic bombing of Nagasaki. I didn't hesitate for a moment." Florence downed the last of her raki. "You can't imagine what it's like to have so much love and no one to give it to."

"You're right, Florence. I can't imagine." The love that Florence was talking about was nothing like what I'd felt for Anya. Maybe it resembled what my parents felt for me, but their love was more relaxed, since they'd had me from birth and never had to beg to raise me.

"Just the thought of adopting Junchi made me feel like my heart was expanding. But the reality was hard. I don't have to tell you—it's the second poem in my book—how I had to school myself to touch that scarred flesh with unconditional love, to lay my palm on that rutted cheek as if it were smooth or just afflicted with ordinary teen-age acne. As I wrote in the poem. I'm quoting myself."

I felt a little like I often did, reading unsolicited manuscripts. Si-multaneously compassionate and irritated for the involuntary swell of pity.

How could I not have read Florence's first book? Something al-ways kept me from getting past the dedication: *"To Junchi. And to those who helped. You know who you are."* After what Preston said, I saw Florence's reticence about her mentors' names in a different light.

I'd been so preoccupied with *The Vixen*, I'd lost focus on anything else. I'd begun averting my eyes from the torrent of manuscripts flood-ing my office. And Florence's need to make small irritating changes in her new book had hardened my heart. I couldn't let myself *think* that, not if I wanted our conversation to go well.

The saintly waiter brought the taramosalata and the tzatziki, each divided into two separate portions with a basket of pita bread. I was grateful that I wouldn't have to dip my bread into the same plate as Florence. That, and the raki, relaxed me.

I said, "This is a wonderful place!"

"It is," said Florence. "Who would have thought?"

"So tell me more about Junchi." I was hoping to work my way around to confirming or disproving what Preston said about why her poems were published.

Florence sighed. "I don't think anyone really expected Junchi to learn English. A few people involved in the adoption knew about his circumstances, who his parents were and where he'd come from. But they couldn't imagine that a boy with so many strikes against him would ever be able to tell me what he'd been through."

"And what *had* he been through?" I modulated my voice to sound interested, not interrogative. Even so, Florence ignored my question.

"It took a while. First we had the problem of trust. And then there were language and cultural barriers. The words for *criminal* and *threat* and *blackmail* are tricky to translate from one language—one culture—to another."

"What?" I'd managed to drop my bread into a bowl of yogurt. "Criminal? Threat? Blackmail?"

"It took years for the story to emerge, and frankly some details are still unclear."

"Should we have a drop more raki?"

"I think I've had enough," she said. "I'm boring you, I can tell. Oh, I've drunk too much."

"Not at all." I refilled her glass from the bottle that had appeared, as if by magic, on the table. Only now did I notice that she was still wearing her coat. She caught me looking, unbuttoned it, and shrugged it onto her chair back, revealing a similarly mouse-colored shirtwaist dress of dimpled cotton.

"Junchi's father was a notorious gangster, a war criminal and profiteer. Some kind of a double agent. He made a fortune during the war and was directly and indirectly responsible for many, many deaths. Near the end of the war the father insisted the boy go stay with his maternal parents . . . in Nagasaki. Where he'd be safe."

Florence shuddered and shook her head. I reflexively mimicked her gesture.

"Both his grandparents were killed in the bombing. It was a miracle he survived. He has no memory of the burning city, the trauma. You've heard of selective amnesia. By then Junchi's father had been installed, with US government help, at the very highest level of Japanese government."

"What do you mean, *with US government help?*"

Florence looked around stagily, leaned forward and whispered, "C-I-A." She said each letter like a word. I concentrated on keeping my face blank, to conceal the strain of hearing what I knew and didn't want to believe. "Maybe it was still the OSS. I'm not sure about the dates when they switched over or what they called themselves when.

But I know what happened and who did it. The same bad men working under different names and in new disguises."

"How do you know?"

"I'm not a fool," said Florence. "Regardless of what you may think—"

"Florence, I don't . . . I never—"

"I figured out the truth. I pieced it together with the help of a pen pal who works in the adoption agency in Japan. Junchi's father had become even more powerful. Respectable. Squeaky clean. My pen pal was brave to tell me. She'd taken a liking to Junchi. Someone let something slip about who was supporting Junchi's father, who had installed him in office. And it was us, our intelligence agency, working undercover, unsuspected by anyone except one brave woman at a Tokyo adoption bureau—"

So there it was.

"What a brave woman!" I parroted.

"Junchi remembers feeling unwelcome at his dad's house after his mother died days after the war ended and his father remarried. It's a common story. But history and Junchi's scars gave it a special twist. His stepmother convinced his dad to put him up for adoption. At that time, in Japan, burn scars were a mark of shame. No one wanted to be reminded of the defeat they'd suffered. Remember the Hiroshima maidens? Ostracized for being disfigured, they came here to be treated by our plastic surgeons. Free of charge, I think. It was all so noble and generous of us that everyone forgot we dropped the darn bomb on them in the first place."

I nodded. I had some memory of that. I didn't want Florence to know that I was stuck on the story about her son's father being a gangster backed by the CIA. The part of the story that matched Preston's.

That was how Florence's book had come to Warren's attention. Likely it was also behind the decision to palm the boy off on a sentimental American lady and make the gangster's new wife happy.

"As I said, it took time. First for Junchi to trust me, then for him to learn English, then more for him to tell me about the past. I hated how he had been treated, as a bargaining chip. This wonderful boy was part of a package deal. I hate to imagine what else was in the package."

"Meaning?"

"Murder."

"Murder? Who was murdered?"

I'd gotten unsubtle. But it was too late to unsay it.

Florence put her finger to her lips. "Anyone who knew too much. Anyone who stood in the way. It's a miracle my friend in the adoption agency survived, and that no one came after *me*."

I said, "That must have been awful for you."

"*Awful* isn't the word. If I may disagree with my *editor* about a word choice." She smiled at me, coquettishly. My mouth ached from smiling back. "It was how I got Junchi, so I was grateful. But the thought of what he'd suffered and who installed his dad at the top . . . I felt as if someone ought to apologize, not to me but to him. And the American taxpayer!"

Florence's voice had risen. I was glad the place was empty.

"I poured my heart out in my poems. Along with my feelings about my son and his injury and the war. But I couldn't live with what I knew. I went to see my congressman and told him about Junchi and his father."

So there we were. Florence and Preston agreed about why her book was published. I blinked away the touching image of Florence, in her mouse-colored coat and hat, waiting, her hands in mouse-paw gloves, folded in her lap, on a bench in the chilly hall of the Capitol Building.

"My . . . Oh, dear, I'm feeling a bit . . . fizzy. In the brain."

"Enjoy it," I said, too brusquely. "So what did your congressman do?"

"At first he didn't know what I was talking about. I assumed he'd be grateful. But once he understood, he didn't look happy. I'd dropped a problem in his lap. He invited me to lunch at a *very* swank steak house in Georgetown."

Swank. The way she said it made it clear that Florence wanted me to know: she hadn't forgiven my failure to take her someplace *swank*. It was maddening. I hadn't chosen Amir's to make her feel worse about herself. After all this raki, I'd have to eat at my parents' house until my next paycheck.

"My congressman asked lots of questions about my background. I had nothing much to say. Mother and Father left me enough to live simply. In fact my representative only wanted to talk about Junchi. He kept saying how brave I was."

"And you were," I said. "You are brave. Very brave." I couldn't stop saying *brave*, perhaps because I was frightened. What had happened to Anya? What would happen to me?

"Thank you, Simon. If I may call you Simon?"

"Of course." What had she called me until then?

"I explained that I'd tried my hand at some sonnets about my life with Junchi. Amazing! What a coincidence! The congressman loved poetry! Oh . . . and . . . he hoped I wouldn't repeat what I'd told him about Junchi's background. Not to anyone. Was there anything he could do for me? I said nothing could make me happier than seeing my poems in print. He'd see what he could do. I didn't feel wildly hopeful. But that same week Warren Landry called. He wanted to look at my poems, and then he called back and said he wanted to publish them. With a few changes. Improvements. You know how brilliant Warren is. I don't have to tell you."

"What kind of changes did Warren suggest?" I wondered what the poems were like before Warren's edit.

Florence dipped her pita into the tzatziki and slipped it expertly into her mouth. "Simon, you've stopped eating. I can't possibly finish all this marvelous food by myself."

Obediently, I tore off some bread and dipped it in the sauce. The dill and mint were delicious, the yogurt slightly off.

"Warren was adamant about removing every mention of Junchi's father. He said that politics and history made the poems seem shrill. *Shrill* was the last thing I wanted. I took those poems out. I had a metaphor about arms, about military armaments versus putting my loving *arms* around my son, but Warren cut that too. He said it would limit my readership. Controversy would keep my readers from being purely heartened by my sacrifice. If Warren didn't like a metaphor, I was happy to lose it."

An edge had come into Florence's voice. She was making sure I understood that she was comparing me negatively to Warren. Why wasn't *I* line-editing her book?

I wondered why he and the others bothered placating Florence. Who would believe a dippy middle-aged woman poet in a mouse-colored coat? Something about her must have scared them. It certainly scared me. In any case they had her now. Her son had gotten into trouble. She wouldn't want that known. If I mentioned it, our amiable lunch would be over. I wished that being with Florence didn't make me miss Anya so intensely, that being with a lonely person didn't make me feel so alone.

Florence said, "The rest is in the poems. I was amazed my book did well. I think it touched a nerve in people who want to believe that something good came out of the war. I guess we don't like remembering we dropped the bomb. Of course we had to do it to save millions of American lives."

Why was I thinking of Ethel? Because the reporters had said that she and Julius had endangered millions of lives. Eisenhower said it, and so did the judge who sentenced them to death. Saving and losing millions of lives. Be careful when you hear that.

I said, "I'm glad you're pleased with how we're publishing you." I hoped I sounded like an editor. I thought I sounded like a jerk.

"Am I glad that you're publishing me? I'm just glad they haven't *killed* me."

Was Florence joking? I couldn't tell. I hadn't taken her for a joker. *Who* was going to kill her? Instinct told me: You don't want to know. I knew too much already.

I let a silence pass, waited a beat, then laughed, and Florence laughed too. Ha-ha. Florence had been kidding about someone wanting to kill her.

In a novel like *The Vixen*, that would be when the hero asks, Florence, do you think you might ever want to tell someone that your book was funded by the Central Intelligence Agency? Why exactly do you think they want to keep you quiet about your son's gangster–CIA puppet father?

But this was not a novel, and I was not its hero.

I said, "Your poems are wonderful! It's an honor to work with you, Florence. I can't wait for your book to come out."

CHAPTER 13

It was hard to stay hopeful, and yet I continued to hope that the evidence piling up against Warren would turn out to be a misunderstanding. If not a simple misunderstanding, then a complicated one. Warren would prove that he was what I'd thought: A privileged, powerful, confident guy who loved literature and wanted to publish good books. Books from foreign countries. But even that phrase, *foreign countries*, suggested something sinister and more complicated after Preston's accusations.

Florence had corroborated Preston's story. Warren and his cohorts bought Florence's bargain-basement silence. Why would poetry featuring a Japanese gangster with covert ties to the US arouse the attention of a politician who arranged to publish the book with targeted excisions? It was hardly the wildest thing that Preston told me. I wondered if Warren gave the operation one of his arty names. Operation Icarus.

I kept telling myself that the truth about Warren and *The Vixen* couldn't be what it seemed. My memory of Preston was already blurring and receding. Nothing was proven. The meaning of Florence's story depended on how (and if) you connected the dots between a yakuza and a suite of sonnets about a foreign adoption. For all I knew, Florence was as paranoid as Preston. I was still defending Warren, against all evidence and common sense, still telling myself that everything depended on the conclusions one drew from gossip and rumors.

The problem was still *The Vixen*. Whatever Warren had or hadn't done in the past, *The Vixen* remained all too current and real. Of all the things that Preston said, the one that stuck in my mind—the one that seemed most probable—was that *someone* saw the novel as three hundred pages of pure propaganda.

Had I sensed that from the start? If so, I'd repressed it and clung to the official story: the project was all about money. How ironic that greed had become the best-case option, less loathsome than an effort to influence world opinion with cheap commercial fiction. Or was I just too undefended, susceptible to Warren, to Preston, to Anya, to anyone who told me what to think?

...

Once we know that something turned out all right, that we navigated a rough patch more or less intact, it becomes harder to pity our younger self or remember the grief and confusion, the dread of the disaster that didn't happen, the panic of the deer frozen in the headlights of the car that stopped in time. Now I see my situation for what it was, but at that time it was everything. My past, my future, my work, my love. My entire life.

It all seemed so serious, perilous, and tragic. As if my mortal soul were in danger. Every small step forward might be a leap into the abyss. I believed my life would never change, that everything was final. In a way, a *bad* way, I *had* turned into Warren. Like my boss and his CIA buddies, I believed that *The Vixen* could convince the world that the Rosenbergs were guilty. I feared that millions might read it and accept its view of Ethel or Esther, or whatever the novel called her.

I believed that it was my moral duty to prevent *The Vixen* from seeing the light of day, at least in its present form. I owed it to Ethel's memory. I owed it to my mother. And I needed to find out what happened to Anya. Who wrote the book if she didn't? *Was* it a CIA plot?

If I threatened to expose Warren's ties to the CIA and he fired me, he'd find someone else to edit the book, which would appear as is. While I, having stood on principle, would have ruined my life. I would be unemployed. Unemployable. After I was investigated by the appropriate committee, my name would go on a list. Dad would have to beg the sporting goods store to hire me part-time.

All night the numbers on my watch glowered at me in the dark. Hours pretended to be minutes. At least, not sleeping, I didn't dream. My waking dreams were nightmares. Night after night I saw Warren's thin lips unleashing a volley of insults. I saw his face swell into the giant mask through which you entered the Terror Tomb. I heard Anya whispering in my ear, Don't move. Let them do the work. Who did she mean by *them*? The demons, the pirates, the ghosts? The poky little teacup rumbling over the track? Their voices were like tunes I couldn't get out of my head. What tormented me most was: I would never see Anya again. I would never find her.

Just a week before, I might have figured out how to ask Elaine about Preston and Anya. But after getting Anya's note, after talking to Preston and Florence, I didn't trust anyone. I couldn't tell if I was being paranoid or sensible, and not knowing scared me.

The only solution was to talk to Warren. It would require all my courage, but how else would I know if Preston was telling the truth? In the sagas, wise men give advice about how to find something out, on the sly. The bird and animal gods say: Go here, pretend you're this person, ask for that person, say this, then say that. But how could I interrogate a trained spy, if that was what Warren was, and make it seem like conversation? Produce your half of the Jell-O box and see if the stranger's half matches.

Florence's explanation of how her poems came to be published neither convicted nor exonerated Warren, but it did echo Preston. I needed to meet with Warren, to hear what he said, to find a way, however circumspect, to find out what really happened.

In any case, I had a good reason for needing to see him. Our author had disappeared! That must be the *definition* of what an editor needs to tell his boss.

In private.

...

I'd only been to Warren's office once before, when he'd welcomed me, my first day at work. The décor was British gentleman's club circa 1930. Dark wooden bookcases, deep red carpeting, subtle lighting, portraits of hunting dogs at attention, waiting for the bugle's call to terrorize a perfectly innocent fox.

A vixen.

That first time, I'd wondered if all those leather-bound books were real. Dry-mouthed and on edge, I imagined that some were hollowed out to conceal Warren's premium liquor bottles. This time the books suggested dead drops for espionage exchanges, hiding places for guns, and the painted dogs seemed poised to hunt down a fugitive slave or secret Jew.

At one point Warren had casually mentioned that he hoped to place *The Vixen* at American libraries all over the world. Though I'd been uneasy about the prospect of an international readership for Anya's novel, the library program had sounded worthy and pragmatic: spreading the products of American literary culture. But now the idea of the American libraries seemed less wholesome, more nefarious. Propaganda 101. The Rosenbergs' crime would be freely available to read in, even borrow from, friendly libraries worldwide.

How did one find out if somebody worked for the CIA? Agents were trained to conceal their mission. I was not a spy or a detective. I was a student of literature, a graduate in Folklore and Mythology!

"My dear boy." Warren half rose from his desk and waved me into a club chair. "What is so important that you needed to talk to me *asap*, as you so charmingly told my secretary. Wait. Don't tell me. Is this about Anya leaving for Corfu?"

"Corfu?" That was what Preston had said. What Anya wrote in her letter.

"Corfu. With her understandably concerned parents. The child is brilliant, but she has periods of, let's say, extreme behavior. As soon as her parents sense an *episode* coming on, they send her to that rest home where you met her. And if that fails, they spirit her out of the country to lie around on some delightful Mediterranean beach until she's feeling better."

"When *what* fails?"

"Her time in the . . . facility."

"Do you know what made them think she was about to have an *episode?*" I tried to give the word the same stress as Warren, though I couldn't tell if his tone was serious or ironic. It was the kind of question I would never normally ask, but my fears for Anya's safety made me braver than normal.

"Ah yes," said Warren. "The episodes. I believe there have been several. Some have lasted for quite a while. According to her poor parents, they begin with a rather dramatic uptick in the lies, the drug use, and the acting out."

"The lies? The drug use?" I feared that I already knew about the acting out.

"Yes, I'm afraid. Diet pills are hardly the handmaidens of truth. Our vixen would make the most outrageous claims about what she had and hadn't done."

Had Anya lied about not writing the book? It was almost a relief. At least it made things simpler. Only then did I realize that Warren was talking about her in the past tense.

"Is she all right? Are you sure? Why wasn't I told she was leaving?" I tried to make it sound like a series of questions and not accusations.

"Someone would have informed you. Sooner or later. We all have a lot on our plates, Simon. The world does not revolve around you. Your *Vixen* is not the only book on our list."

So, it had become *my Vixen*. "And what now? What about Anya?"

"Don't worry. Let's assume she'll be back as soon as someone wants to interview or photograph her. No one held a gun to her head to make her pose for that author portrait. Anyway, I'd be off to Corfu too if someone offered me a free trip. Wouldn't you? Let's just keep our fingers crossed that she's back in time for publication. If not . . . Well, we're fortunate to have that author portrait."

I filled my lungs with air, exhaled, and inhaled again.

I said, "The last time I saw Anya, she told me she didn't write *The Vixen*."

Warren laughed. "My point exactly. Mental instability is hardly a rare thing in writers, as you're about to find out."

As I was about to find out? Meaning . . . if I stayed in publishing? Apparently, he wasn't firing me. But did I want this job? Did I want to be the lowest-ranking, most underinformed agent of the CIA? I hated admitting, even to myself, that I preferred working for Warren and his evil associates to helping my father at the sporting goods store. That was how corrupt I was, how shallow. I wanted an interesting life more than I wanted to do what was right.

"Insanity comes with the territory!" Warren was practically crowing. "Anya wrote the blessed book. Scout's honor. Trust me. Do what you've been doing and then leave the goddamn novel alone and let it do whatever *it's* going to do. I assume it's what Anya wrote only . . . a bit . . . smoother. I'll take a quick look, if you want. Or not. Give it a light edit. Or not. Just ask me. Or not. I appreciate the work you're putting in, Simon. We can basically print what I gave you all those months ago. I trust that by now you've made the novel into something no less commercial but more in line with something we might actually publish. Finish what you're doing, and then we'll just go ahead and put this sucker into production."

"That's great," I said. "That would be great."

Warren picked up some papers from his desk. Time to leave.

Was it Freud who said that the most trenchant insights occur when a session is ending? Journalists say they get the best material after they turn off the tape recorder.

I said, "I went out to that . . . sanitarium to look for Anya, and I had a sort of conversation with your former partner. Preston."

"Thank you. Did you say *Preston*? I do know my former partner's name. And what sort of conversation is a *sort of conversation*?"

I winced. "I meant conversation. We had a conversation."

"Hilarious," Warren said. "You really are the wittiest young man."

"Preston is quite a character," I said.

Warren did a stagy double take, then cackled. Part rooster, part lifetime smoker. "Okay. Hang on. I get it now. The emergency. Your tone. The bullshit about Anya. So Preston treated you to one of his rants about my crimes against humanity, and you want to know if it's true. Am I a CIA superspy?"

I must have nodded.

"Well, let's have a little liquid help with this top secret question." As Warren stood and crossed the room, I was briefly transfixed by the costly beauty of his fawn-colored suit. I would never have a suit like that. How shameful that, with so much at stake, I was suffering over fashion.

Warren extracted a whiskey bottle from a scooped-out faux book. The pleasure of seeing my old fantasy confirmed was momentary, at best. He was the boss. He could keep a full bar on his desk if he wanted. But he liked the theater, the Prohibition-era drama. He filled two shot glasses so high that whiskey splashed my hand when I took it. I wiped my hand on my pants, which I hated for being so obviously cheaper than Warren's.

"Cheers," he said.

"Cheers," I said.

We poured the whiskey down our throats. Everything depended on my not coughing.

He said, "So you want to know if I attached incendiary devices to starlings and dosed research subjects with psychedelic drugs and watched them jump out hotel windows. You want to know if I staged coups in Central America, overthrew legitimately elected governments, started civil wars, installed dictators. If I am responsible for the deaths of I-forget-how-many Albanians—"

"Eighty-seven," I said, despite myself. "Eighty-seven Albanians."

"My God. Old Preston really got to you, didn't he? Well, okay. I'll admit it about the Albanians. It haunts me still." Warren grinned. "Imagining those Albanian broads in their last . . . Well! I take the blame for that, unless some journalist or senator gets nosy after all these years. In which case I have no idea what you're talking about. Anyway, I'm kidding. You realize that, don't you, Simon? I suppose I'm not busy enough—spying, ordering executions, overthrowing governments, spreading lies, *and* running the greatest literary publishing house in New York, if not the entire *world*. I suppose I have endless free time in which to publish propaganda disguised as fiction written to justify US policy and the flawlessly transparent trial and execution of two Russian spies?"

So much for the stealth inquisition. Warren knew everything Preston said and more. I chose to find it reassuring. A guilty man would never lay out the charges against him like that. He'd made it sound like the fantasy that it probably was.

Warren said, "You want to know one great thing about being American as opposed to, let's say, Russian? One of the *many* great things about living where we live, one of the *blessings*, is that *I don't fucking have to tell you if I did those things or not*. This is *not* a fucking show trial. No one's forcing me to confess. I don't have to say, Yes, old boy, I did this. No, dear fellow, I didn't do that. I don't have to tell you if I am a literary publisher or a secret agent. Unless you're deposing me under oath, which means nothing, either. Any bottom-feeder can take the Fifth. One thing McCarthy got right: taking the Fifth doesn't mean you're innocent. 'I invoke my privilege under the Fifth Amendment and decline to answer that question.'" Warren's face contorted in savage mimicry of a noncooperating witness.

"I have my constitutionally guaranteed God-given individual right to keep my dirty little secrets, and you have your constitutionally guaranteed God-given individual right to keep yours. And fuck you if you don't like it. *Is* that a good thing or not?" Warren's tone had grown increasingly hectoring. I grabbed the chair arms to steady my hands.

"I guess it's a good thing?" I said. "I mean, I know——"

"Wrong! It's good *and* bad. Want to know a story your friend Preston probably didn't tell you?"

"Sure." What else could I say?

"Okay then. This was right after the war, when everything was fresh and clean and just brimming with meaning and . . . *purpose*. I had a dream assignment, working with the squad that tracked down looted Old Master paintings and restored them to their rightful owners. You know about that, I assume."

I nodded.

"And I assume you also know that tired philosophy-classroom chestnut: The museum is on fire. An old lady is in the gallery, and you have to choose which to save, the Rembrandt or the old lady. Your average high school sophomore can chew on that forever while their teachers take a well-deserved nap.

"Well, I got to have it both ways, and the building wasn't even burning. The old widow *had* the Rembrandt. Her husband was a celebrity Nazi who amassed a ton of stolen art. I held a gun to the ancient relict's head and asked where the painting was, and she told me. I returned it to the nice Jewish family who'd fled to Shanghai, where I happened to have business, so it worked out. I hand-delivered the painting. I saved the old lady *and* the Rembrandt. Who wouldn't want that on his résumé? Everything I've done for the government has been like that—like saving the Rembrandt and the old lady."

I said, "But nothing was burning."

"What?"

"The museum wasn't burning, the old lady wasn't burning, the painting wasn't burning, nothing was burning—"

"Six million of your people were burning. Or had recently burned. Have I gotten the figures wrong? And how do we measure the deaths of eighty-seven Albanians against that statistic?"

It was unfair. It was wicked. Warren was using the Holocaust to win an argument. To make a point. But I didn't object. I didn't have the strength. Six million versus eighty-seven. I'd depleted my reserves of courage when I'd asked about Anya.

I couldn't meet Warren's watery blue eyes, which, before I looked away, seemed to express consummate understanding and mockery of anyone weak enough to need understanding.

"Please don't tell me you're one of those idiots who object on principle to our intelligence community. What we do to protect *you*. Don't tell me you're one of those *infants* who believe that the Soviet Union is going to let us live our peaceful, productive, blissfully capitalist American lives, and everyone will play nice and share the wealth and the natural resources? Each according to his needs. You do know what's been going on in Russia? The Doctors' Plot and the show trials and more slaughter than Hitler's wildest dreams. The mass imprisonments and disappearances and the gulag and the massacre of the Polish people and starvation and—"

I said, "I'm not a Communist. I'm certainly not a Stalinist. Far from it, actually, sir."

Sir? Who says *sir?* A soldier. *Scout's honor.*

"So we agree. Where we differ is in how we view our *personal responsibility* for preserving our cherished American freedoms. It's not your fault that your generation takes everything for granted. It's been handed to you on a platter. Whereas my generation knows that you have to fight for it, fight with your lives, and we're *still* fighting. We're like sharks. If we stop fighting, we die."

"Moving," I said. "If sharks stop moving, they die. Supposedly."

"You're a clever one, aren't you. Let's not quibble about details. You young men will never see what we saw. And once you've seen the horror, you can't unsee it. You boys will never know how quickly and easily brutality can take over."

I saw the photo of my father and the dead Japanese soldiers.

"I'm surprised that no one at Harvard approached you about working for us. Though since your friends the Rosenbergs spoiled things for everyone, things have changed. They're casting a smaller net."

"Approached me how? Who is *us*?" The first question was real. I knew the answer to the second.

Warren refilled our glasses. "To Harvard. *In vino veritas*." He downed his whiskey, and I did the same.

"*Us* is the big boys installed at our dear alma mater. Quite a few Agency guys were on the faculty. In senior positions. Academics at the top of their game can do a lot of lucrative consulting. In my day the Agency recruited everyone with decent grades, that is, everyone from certain family *backgrounds*, regardless of how well they'd done in school. Really, who cares about grades? The vetting depended on what sort of people you came from. Old New England families and Midwestern aristocracy—they siphoned off those gene pools first.

"If that wasn't who you were, they might ask a few more questions. If they decided to interview you at all. Your mother's friendship with Ethel Rosenberg would have surfaced rather early in a background check. Come on. Don't act so surprised. Girlish astonishment is not an attractive look on a full-grown man."

No one knew about Mom and Ethel.

I said, "They weren't actually friends. They lived in the same building."

"Close enough," said Warren.

"How do you know?"

"A little birdie told me. I'm sure you wouldn't want me to blow the little birdie's cover."

As far as I knew, Uncle Maddie was the only person except for my parents who might have known. For a split second I almost laughed at the thought of someone referring to my enormous uncle as a little birdie. I could almost imagine Maddie revealing Mom's connection to Ethel as one of his sour, gossipy jokes. But that would have meant bringing the Rosenbergs literally too close to home. Anyway, superspy Warren must have had many ways of uncovering secrets without extorting them from my curmudgeonly uncle.

"Here's an interesting fact. A chapter in my story, a footnote to yours. Want to know who recruited me?" Warren tipped back his head and shut his eyes. "God help us. You know we could both go to jail for even having this conversation."

Mr. Big Mouth, Preston had called him. Señor Boca Grande.

"Or maybe we don't go to jail. We wind up in the nuthouse with Preston. There are some things we've sworn to take to our graves. But I say, hey, let's celebrate our Viking heroes as their longboats head into the sunset. Every foot soldier, every *lumpen* draftee, gets thanked for his service. But the brave guys who work in secret also deserve our gratitude and respect. Yes or no?"

"I guess so," I said.

"Maybe the reason I'm even minimally surprised that you weren't tapped is that I was recruited by your old friend Robertson Crowley."

Robertson Crowley. Of course. That afternoon when I'd waited to see Crowley, when I'd watched my classmates emerge, one by one, from his office, I'd been right about him spending so much longer with other students, younger versions of Warren but some women too. It was an uncomfortable memory, a fleeting impression I didn't want confirmed. Robertson Crowley. The travels. The explorations. The stories. The acolytes and disciples.

Warren put his fingers to his temples. "Let me recall how they put it, those old guys. They'd say, 'Would you like to work for our government in a *really interesting way?*'"

I said, "Professor Crowley wasn't my friend."

"Just yanking your chain, old boy. It's a figure of speech. Certainly you didn't imagine that Crowley's teaching salary or his anemic book sales or his modest inheritance was paying for all that adventure travel and research? Do you know what it costs to buy a reindeer-hide tent in Lapland? To feed the great-grandchildren of the Sicilian witches before they'll say one word? To bribe the Albanian lesbians not to kick your ass? Not cheap, even then. The one thing Karl Marx got right was: Follow the money. Which in Crowley's case led straight to Capitol Hill. He needed a supplemental income. Of course that was in their glory days, before they tightened the budget, or learned to use money to control anyone whose leash they enjoyed yanking. A hardworking literary publisher, for example.

"But it was never about the travel and research opportunities . . . or the financial support. Crowley believed in the mission, as I always have. As I do. He and I believe in keeping order and peace in the world. Is there anything *wrong* with that? Is that mad? Tell me, dear boy, do you believe that's *un-American?*"

"But why Sicily? Albania? Lapland? Crowley wasn't working in Moscow."

"Do you imagine that our beloved professor chose the places he did because he wanted to hear a whopping fabulous fairy tale about a feral baby and a werewolf? How many stories do we need about princes turning into frogs? The stories went into his books and his teaching. But those countries were chosen *for* him because they were strategic. Our people had questions about their people, local government, a military buildup, information more *crucial* than a haunting by somebody's dead girlfriend's restless ghost. Not that he didn't bring back some great yarns. But they were . . . gravy, you could say. His quote-unquote *research* in Albania laid the groundwork for me when I went there later. You young men will never see what we saw, the wholesale murder and suffering that totalitarianism can inflict. And you will never have our resolve, our determination to keep it from happening here."

At what cost? I thought. You were a murderer too. But I said nothing. It would have made Warren think less of me, if that was still possible.

"Revenge. Dear old Crowley meant every word he said about the sweetness of revenge. If there was one thing Crowley loved, it was making the bad guys pay. And pay dearly. If you were plotting against America and Crowley found out, God help you."

I didn't want to know what *pay dearly* meant. I didn't want to know what Robertson Crowley did. I should have listened to his lectures more closely. Revenge wasn't just a plot turn for him, not just a story line. It was a moral imperative. A logical plan of action. Permission for mass murder. I'd understood nothing about those Viking sagas. I never asked myself why human beings *wanted* stories about repaying murder with murder, about why a kinsman's death must be repaid in blood.

Warren let a moment pass, long enough to make it clear that he was in charge of the silence.

"No wonder he loved Albanians. Those crazy bastards live for revenge. Their law code is based on it. I'm still looking over my shoulder for that Albanian pretending to be an Italian waiter who's been searching for me all this time. Or some ancient dead lesbian's widow. You're not working for them, are you, Simon?"

Had Warren lost his mind? I was definitely not working for the Albanian sworn virgins.

"Joking," Warren said. "At the end of his class, as you doubtless remember, we were supposed to go to him for advice. I was flattered when he closed the door, proud when he asked if I'd thought about serving my country in a *very interesting* way. It couldn't have been less hush-hush or more straightforward. Later, of course, I understood that these end-of-semester conferences were mostly about recruitment. Though not, as it happened, yours."

Warren turned his palms up. Look. He had nothing to hide.

"And that was it?" I said. "You went to work for the government. And publishing has been a . . . sideline? A front?"

"I've never thought of it like that. With such a *crude* formulation. What is the front, what is the back? What is the middle? What *tedious* vulgar distinctions." He walked over to the bookcase, and when he turned around to face me, he seemed to have grown taller, younger, more vital.

"Guess," he said. "Take a guess. What single achievement in my long career am I most proud of?" He hooked his thumbs under his lapels.

I tried to think of a writer he'd published and championed, a Pulitzer Prize winner, a Nobel laureate. None came to mind. The company's list circled my memory, swirled, and vanished like water down a drain.

"I don't know, I can't—"

"Then let me tell you. I loved the details."

"The details?"

"I mean, when they'd ask *me* to supply a missing—a necessary— detail. You do know what a detail is, don't you, Simon?"

"Yes. Of course."

"Yes, of course, *what*?" Warren sounded increasingly prosecutorial as he prepared to list his accomplishments. "When we hear *detail*, we think small, but I'm talking large. Historically large. *Monumentally* large. The missing piece, the story within a story that makes the whole thing seem credible. *Real*. I'm the go-to guy for that. The detail. The guy with the piece of evidence everyone can relate to, the plot point everyone can comprehend, except that people think—oh so wrongly!—that no one could make it up. Well, guess what? You *can*. Because I'm the guy who does it. I'm the lucky guy who pulls the chicken that lays the golden eggs out of his ass. I invent the chickens *and* the eggs."

"What do you mean?"

"What am I not making clear? All right, let's take an example you might understand. The Rosenbergs' magic Jell-O box. One of the big guys came to me and said, 'Warren, old boy, we need you to make up a secret signal. Some commie hocus-pocus by which Ethel's brother and the Russian agent will recognize each other. Something a little . . . you know . . . special. Memorable. Something everyone will believe.' I said I'd think about it.

"Well, it just so happened that my wife was having digestive problems. All she could eat was Jell-O. Do you have any idea what it's like to live with a morbidly obese woman consuming obscene amounts of Jell-O?"

I wished Warren hadn't said that. It seemed like the worst thing he'd said so far, though I knew it wasn't. At least he didn't expect an answer. He'd half forgotten my presence. He knew that someone was in the room, but not necessarily me. I felt sorry for Warren's wife, married to a man who talked about her that way. A more compassionate person might also have felt sorry for Warren, the victim of his own bad choices, going home every evening to a woman he didn't love, to sons whose names he hardly knew. He was so unlike my loving parents, telling strangers about my Harvard education, my full scholarship, my bright future.

"There were Jell-O boxes all over our kitchen. I had to throw them away. Every night I came home from work and disposed of cardboard containers. Sure, I was annoyed. I was taking my irritation out on an empty package, ripping it up into tiny pieces, when I thought: Got it. Secret signal. Fit the pieces together. Espionage 101."

"That was you?" I said. "You made that up? You invented the Rosenberg Jell-O box?"

"Come on," said Warren. "*If* you think the Jell-O box was a lie, *if* you think it was all an invention, then the only logical conclusion, the only *obvious* conclusion, is that *someone* had to make it up. Someone like yours truly. If God is in the details, what does that say about me?"

"You're joking." I knew he wasn't. I wished he were.

"I've risen in the Agency. Higher, if not to so high they can't still yank my chain about money. And how did I rise? The only way. By hard work. By being good at my job. Of course, before this . . . Jell-O thing, I'd had other major successes. Are successes really successes if no one knows about them? If a tree falls in the forest . . . ? I seem to have gotten off topic."

"What successes?"

"Well! How polite of you to ask." He paused, deciding, or pretending to decide, between multiple options. "I suppose my biggest personal triumph was Alger Hiss's pumpkin. I invented that too. Grew the whole big orange squash from a teensy pumpkin seed. Need I walk you through that history?"

"That's okay. I know it."

I knew the case all too well. I'd been in high school when Alger Hiss, a lawyer and Justice Department official, was tried for espionage. One key piece of evidence was the jack-o'-lantern in which Hiss was alleged to have hidden rolls of microfilm of classified documents that he was giving the Russians.

"Once again I can thank my family, my long-suffering wife and sons. One of my sons was carving a pumpkin, and I thought, Wouldn't that be a terrific dead drop? So when they came to me about the Hiss case, it took no time to come up with the *detail* they needed to make the evidence *pop*."

On *pop*, an alcohol-laced spray misted the air between us. Had Warren been drinking before I came in?

"But that's lying." Why not say it? Why not stop pretending to be the person Warren wanted me to be? Pretending to be Warren.

"A lie?" He rubbed his chin, mock-thinking. "Maybe. A fiction, I'd rather say. Anyway, so what? Hiss and the Rosenbergs were guilty. So what if there was no Jell-O box? No pumpkin. Details, as I said. The reason I can tell you all this is that no one will believe you. You think you're learning on the job? Well, learn *this*. I work with writers, men of enormous talent, creativity, and imagination. But *my* creativity is what gets things done. Whose words *matter*? Who is the one with an imagination deployed in the service of something higher than putting pretty words on a page? Who is the great writer? The real artist. Not my writers. *Me*. I'm the one whose details *matter*."

I stared at him with a fixity that made his face slip out of focus. Was I supposed to ask why he did what he did? He'd already told me. Should I ask: How could you live with yourself? What would that accomplish besides making me feel braver and less complicit than I was?

"So now *you're* the guy who knows it all. The brilliant young detective. But what are you going to do with all that knowledge, Simon? Go to the press? The government? They already know. Besides, it isn't your job. It isn't your business. Your job is to bring a novel in on time. Your job is to have *The Vixen* on my desk, all buffed and shiny, a juicy delectable little piggy ready to go to market. Can you do that?"

I nodded.

"Good. Because look what just came in."

He handed me a mock-up cover.

The Vixen, the Patriot, and the Fanatic
 A Novel by Anya Partridge

The fat purple typeface dripped shiny purple droplets down a lurid orange page. In the upper right quadrant was a beautiful blond woman in a long tight dress with a mermaid tail sewn from the American flag. In one hand she held a leash. At the end of the leash was a large red fox. I thought of Anya's pelt in a cardboard box in my room, under a burrow of papers and books.

"It's . . . amazing." I'd always thought I'd be more courageous if I was put to the test. But I'd pictured a Viking test, a standard-issue challenge to one's bravery and resolve. I'd never pictured a test like this. I'd lacked the imagination. However bad I'd thought *The Vixen* was—the cover made everything worse.

Warren grinned. Did he really like this cover? Did he think it was funny? Irresistibly commercial? Could we publish something so radically different from the sober elegant jackets for which the house was known? We never used images, just a background of some deep color and an elegant white type to communicate our seriousness and high ideals.

"Glad you like it," said Warren. "Glad you like the cover as much as we do."

He laughed, then abruptly stopped laughing. "You didn't really think we'd publish something this . . . slutty. We were just winding you up, a bit. Seeing how you'd react. Sorry if our little joke didn't strike your funny bone. This is the actual cover."

He handed me another mock-up. No image. Just type, against an off-white background. Larger type than we usually used, but that was the only concession. *The Vixen* was in red letters, *The Patriot* in type patterned with the Stars and Stripes, *The Fanatic* in bold, hard black-and-white letters that looked part Communist, part Nazi.

"What do you think? Is it too much? A little loud for us, right?"

I couldn't answer because my eyes had misted with tears as I tried to understand why Warren would have gone to all the trouble creating the fake cover. Why would he do that to me? He couldn't have done it alone. More people must be in on this. More than I suspected. But who? Who were they, and how much did they know? It must have meant telling others the secret in order to design the phony cover as another test of my courage and dignity, another test I failed. I failed again to persuade myself that being the butt of a practical joke was a sign of acceptance, like hazing, a harsh initiation into Warren's club.

"Good. Then we're understood. You've missed our May Day deadline. I want the finished manuscript by . . . let's see. Two weeks from today. On my desk. At the latest! Or send it straight to copyediting. I assume that will work for you."

"I'll make it work," I said.

I was about to leave when Warren held up one finger.

"You know," he said, "I do think it was a pity that Crowley didn't recruit you. Despite the family security concerns, you would have been good at the job. You're intelligent and sensible. Reasonable. Even . . . *malleable*, when necessary. You know that it's often a wise idea to listen to people who know more than you do. And to do what they tell you. That's why I thought you'd be a good choice for this, spinning Anya's straw into gold for my political friends."

Malleable meant spineless. Is that what Warren thought of me? Was it true?

"Malleable?" I needed to hear how it sounded.

"Do you want me to spell it out? In all the time I've known you, Simon, I have never heard you say one word that you didn't vet for my approval. You've wanted me to like you, as if we were ever going to be friends. Even over drinks, even drunk, you didn't have the balls to say what you really thought. What is the point of drinking, old boy, if we can't have our . . . disagreements? Anya walked all over you, as I knew she would."

I needed to ask him what he meant, but I seemed to have forgotten how to speak. Warren paused a moment, to let the dust of the ruined city settle.

"How did I get distracted? Right. We were talking about recruitment and family security concerns . . . so let me ask you about your family's sympathies. Tell me: How do your people vote?"

It was none of his business, but I said, "They voted for Roosevelt. They're Roosevelt Democrats."

"Ah, Franklin," said Warren. "Dear homely Eleanor. I'm sure you know that funny story about their fishing expedition." He waited.

I shook my head no.

"Well, apparently the Roosevelts were fishing off the coast of Long Island, and someone in their party caught a fish. Eleanor asked the captain what kind of fish it was. 'A jewfish,' the captain said. Eleanor said, 'Oh, dear, I was hoping we'd left the Jews behind in New York.'"

Warren's imitation of Eleanor's wobbly voice was perfect. The voice that had brought my parents such comfort and reassurance now aimed its nasty bigotry at us. And Warren thought it was funny.

My enduring shame is that I didn't tell Warren Landry to go to hell, or punch him in the nose, or make some other pointless dramatic gesture. My enduring shame is that I promised to get the manuscript in on time. And I thanked him.

"Thank you, Mr. Landry."

"Warren," he said. "How many times must I remind you . . . ?"

"Warren."

I left his office door open.

"Please close the door," he called after me, but I didn't: my small, pitiful act of rebellion.

. . .

After my meeting with Warren, the world looked different, streaked with filth and at the same time washed clean, stripped of the grimy veil behind which filth had hidden. The elevator was crowded with strangers, all either plotting or being plotted against. Wind whistled up the elevator shaft. I felt the wind blow through me.

Crowley! That beatific old man who'd learned so many obscure languages and customs, whom so many strangers trusted, to whom people told the magical stories they'd handed down for generations.

The old fraud had been a snoop, a covert op dispatching coded reports about troop movements and fortifications. Maybe he was saving some lives, probably ending others.

I couldn't risk lunch at George Jr.'s. I couldn't face Elaine or anyone from work. I walked the extra block to Nedick's and sat at the counter and ordered an orangeade and three hot dogs: suicide food. My drink was the color of an atomic blast. I took a sip, more from curiosity then thirst. Flecks of fake pulp stuck in my throat. The hot dog spit fat in my mouth. I longed to be back on the boardwalk, eating hot dogs, mourning Ethel on that sad Friday night when she died. Before everything that happened since.

A kindly waitress, name tag Kate, asked, "Is everything okay?" Nothing was okay. Everything was *not okay*. But thank you, no, I'm fine. The ground had given way beneath me. Everything was a lie. I should have stayed in the thirteenth century. The Icelandic lords had spies who attended feasts at their enemies' homes and reported back. But those murders and revenges were so personal, modest, domestic. There was bloodshed and death, but *so little* death, *so little* blood compared to what Warren had likely shed. I no longer doubted what *The Vixen* was meant to accomplish or what I'd been asked to do. I knew how I must have looked to Warren. How much of myself I'd lost. The question was how I could find and reclaim it.

...

I left Nedick's and returned to the office.

On my desk was a slip of pink paper, torn from a pad and printed with *While you were out*. It was the form that the receptionist, Violet, used to notify my colleagues about missed phone calls. No one ever called me at work. Could it have been Anya?

Despite everything I still wanted to see her. I wanted the old lies back.

The message said, *Your father phoned. Meet him at Mount Sinai Hospital. Room 1401.*

Elaine stopped me on my way out. She must have been there when the call came in. She knew everything. She cared.

She said, "Simon, if there's anything I can do . . . " Tears shone in her eyes, magnifying their beauty.

"Thank you," I said. I wished she'd met my parents. I wished she could go to the hospital with me. I wished she knew more about me. I wished I could tell her I loved her.

. . .

I could have learned to live with the memory of my mother lying under the blanket in her thin hospital gown and ID bracelet, of my father facing the door, spread-kneed, perched on the edge of her bed. I could have learned to ward off the onslaught of grief when I remembered the harsh, flickering light behind my mother's head, the indigo shadows beyond its reach, the stark composition of two figures. My mother's head was shaved and wrapped in the kind of thin mesh netting they put on expensive melons and tubs of ricotta. What were Mom and Dad doing in a Caravaggio? A Rembrandt?

More painful memories would come later, scenes from my parents' last days. And yet that vision—Mom, Dad, the rumpled hospital bed, her washed-thin white shroud flecked with tiny blue stars—has stayed with me. It was my first early warning, the opening sentence of the sad book already being written.

My mother had her eyes closed. She didn't hug or kiss me, but she knew I was there. She smiled. She knew that a smile was required. I felt she'd already left our world and risen out of reach. I wanted to hold on and keep her from floating further away.

I leaned down toward her.

"Don't kiss me, honey," she said. "I'm surgical-quality sterile germ-free. They'd have to start from scratch." That didn't sound scientific, but I wasn't about to correct her.

I thought about Orpheus trying to rescue Eurydice from the underworld. Did I know any stories about grown children bringing a parent back from the dead? Aeneas carried his father on his back, but the father was alive. Demeter went to the underworld to rescue Persephone, but Persephone was her daughter. The rescue story I longed for would have violated the natural order. Crowley hadn't told us any stories like that. The dead returned for vengeance but not for mother love. I could still hear Crowley's voice in my head, but I couldn't see him. The brave explorer drinking psychotropic home brew with the sworn virgins had turned into a seedy mole, slinking from doorway to doorway in some state socialist slum, leaving coded messages in a keyhole in Palermo.

"They drugged her," said Dad.

My mother said, "I'm still here. Don't talk about me like I'm not." She sounded more annoyed than anything, which was a comfort, as she meant it to be.

Dad said, "Can I explain our situation to Simon? Simon, what can I tell you?" He was talking to me like a child, but I didn't mind. Love and fear were inventing a new language that we understood, even if we'd just learned it.

There had been new tests, more tests, different tests based on earlier tests. Images and numbers. My mother's migraines weren't migraines. There was a growth in her brain. The doctors wouldn't know what was going on until they went in there and looked.

In there meaning *in my mother's head*? Went *in* and looked? This was not the time for Mr. Harvard Graduate to judge the word choice of the doctor who would soon have my mother's brain, my mother's life, in his hands.

Mom said, "These doctors act so modern. They know all the latest research. But if you ask me, we're stuck in George Washington's times, bloodletting and sticking on leeches."

My father said, "They're trying to help."

Mom said, "I must be dying if you're telling me not to criticize."

I expected jokes, attempts at jokes, from my nervous dad. I wanted to hear Mom groan and tell him to lay off the humor, though she loved and appreciated his need to lighten things up. But we'd been changed beyond recognition. Would my father ever be funny again? It depended on what happened now. I had never contemplated two such different futures.

Two men in pale green scrubs and shower caps wheeled a gurney into the room. Dad and I scrambled out of their way. One attendant suggested that Mom remove her ring—the one with *1931* in tiny diamonds on the onyx that flipped to show her high school picture—and leave it with hubby.

Hubby. The word made us flinch.

"For medical reasons?" asked Mom. "Is my hand going to swell?"

"Probably not," said the attendant. "It's a legal thing. If it's stolen, the hospital will be liable, and we'll all feel bad—"

"No one's going to steal it," said Mom. "I'll chance it. It's the least of the risks I'm taking here, don't you think, guys?"

No one was willing to rank-order the risks my mother was taking. They let her keep the ring. It was her protection, like Anya's fox pelt. The thought of Anya seemed unlucky under the circumstances. I'd been trying not to think that the attendants' uniforms were the same green as the uniforms of the waitstaff in the department store restaurant where I went with Anya.

Dad put his arm around me. I tried not to cry. I didn't cry.

One of the attendants patted my father's shoulder; another thumped my back. Reassurance, encouragement. How many shoulders had they patted, how many backs had they thumped that day? Why couldn't I be grateful? Because they were taking my mother away. I shut my eyes as they wheeled her out. I was praying and praying.

Dad took me down to the cafeteria. We each took our own tray. We were separated on the food line by a young resident who couldn't wait another second for his cracked, iridescent sheet of roast beef in pale greasy juice. At the register Dad and I discovered that we'd each ordered a large side of mashed potatoes with gravy and three pats of butter. It was the first time we'd laughed all day. Dad insisted on paying for us both. It hadn't occurred to me to offer.

He said that Mom had been in pain, but she was going to feel better. Then we ate our potatoes. After that we sat in the family waiting room on the neurology floor.

A minute passed, or an hour.

Dad said, "No atheists in *this* foxhole."

I said, "Did they say that in the war?"

"Not where I was," said Dad.

It was strange that he'd mentioned atheists, because I couldn't stop praying. Let my mother be okay and I would do anything. I wouldn't hesitate, I'd never waver, I'd do the right thing about *The Vixen*. I would see to it that Ethel's name remained bright and unsullied by lies. I would be brave and honest. I'd be the kind of person my mother would be proud of.

I remembered a line from Rilke: "Shorter are the prayers in bed but more heartfelt." It was from one of my favorite poems, "The Lay of the Love and Death of Cornet Christopher Rilke," a prose poem about a knight who falls in love and sleeps with a beautiful woman the night before he is killed in battle. When I'd read it in college, I'd felt it was written just for me: so medieval, so modern. In the waiting room, I thought, Rilke wrote the poem to rescue me from this place, at this moment.

"Shorter are the prayers in bed but more heartfelt." The line was beautiful, but untrue. Long or short, in this place or that, all prayers are heartfelt. Everyone in the waiting room was praying nonstop as they dozed or chatted or looked at their watches.

I closed my eyes. I faked sleep.

Dad said, "Are you okay?" He was rooting through a pile of ragged magazines. Had his arms gotten skinnier in the past days, or had I only now noticed?

"I'm fine," I said. "I'm resting. Close *your* eyes a minute."

My father said, "I'm keeping your mother alive. You can do what you want."

Keeping Mom alive meant *Time* and *Newsweek*, *Good Housekeeping*. Dad didn't care. He turned pages. I'd been so unhappy when I lived with them. Now I wanted those months back. I hadn't known enough, hadn't been wise enough to love that time in my life.

My father was doing a crossword puzzle when I fell asleep.

"SIMON." DAD ONLY had to say it once.

I opened my eyes to see a nurse who seemed to be saying that Dr. Albert was just getting out of surgery and would come in to see us.

I asked, "How did it go?"

The nurse said, "The doctor will explain everything." She wasn't allowed to tell us.

"Please." I couldn't help myself.

"She'll be fine," said the nurse.

When she left, my father said, "Do you think she was telling the truth?"

I thought she was. I hoped she was. I didn't trust myself to answer.

Dr. Albert's salt-and-pepper beard was trim, his wire-rimmed glasses shiny, his hands and his green scrubs too immaculately clean for someone just getting out of surgery. It was thoughtful of him to have changed so he wasn't covered in Mom's blood.

He said, "Well, that was a piece of cake."

His bedside manner was just this side of clinically insane. Opening up my mother's skull had been *a piece of cake*? Maybe he was nervous or had problems communicating. But charm and tact don't matter as much when you have good news. No one says *a piece of cake* when a patient died on the table. Or if the prognosis was dire. He was communicating perfectly well. He was eloquent, in fact.

"Piece of cake for *you* maybe," said my father.

"Obviously." The doctor laughed. "For me. Your wife—your mother—will be fine. The small meningioma, that is to say the *growth*, that was causing"—he looked at Mom's chart—"Mrs. Putnam's headaches turned out to have been benign and easily excised."

Growth. Meningioma. Mom's pain had had nothing to do with the Rosenbergs or McCarthy. That's what the doctor would have said if I'd asked.

Dad said, "This is my son. Simon. A Harvard graduate. He's in publishing now. He's an editor."

"What house?" asked the doctor.

"Landry, Landry and Bartlett." After my meeting with Warren, just saying it would have been uncomfortable if my relief about Mom hadn't made everything else seem unimportant.

"I didn't mean what *publishing* house. What *Harvard* house?"

"Kirkland." The home of the public school wonks.

He shrugged. "Eliot," he said, though I hadn't asked—and I could have guessed. Eliot House was where the prep school students lived, the guys who would go on to be Upper East Side neurosurgeons. The arty rich guys, like Warren, favored Adams House. The surgeon's asking me which house I'd been in, and his telling me he'd lived in Eliot, was a comradely backslap and a put-down, both at once.

"What did you major in?"

"English."

No way I was going to say Folklore and Mythology and watch a brain surgeon's response. But it wouldn't have mattered. Dr. Albert didn't care.

He said, "I'm quite a reader. When I get two minutes." He held up both hands and rotated them, miming a surgical pre-op scrub and how busy he was. I stared at the thick, hairy fingers that had just been inside my mother's skull.

He said, "I've been wanting to read that new book, that bestseller . . . *The Roosevelt Family of Sagamore Hill.*"

Jewfish, I thought. *Jewfish.*

The doctor was waiting for a response.

I said, "I'll send you a copy," though we hadn't published it. The doctor would forget our conversation as soon as it was over.

"That would be great," he said. "Very kind of you."

A self-involved phony had saved my mother. Yet still I wanted to kneel. I wanted to weep. I wanted to kiss his hands and hug him.

The nurse urged Dad and me to go home and rest. She would watch over Mom.

My father took a cab all the way from Mount Sinai to Coney Island, an unheard-of expense. He dropped me off at my apartment. Did he want me to come home with him and stay overnight? He wanted to be alone. We both did. And yet we clung to each other as I got out of the cab.

I hadn't forgotten my prayers, my promise to do the right thing. All I had to do was carry it out. One step after another.

Ten days later my mother came home, already feeling much better.

devoted every moment to rewriting *The Vixen*. I worked on it at the office and through most of the night, at my apartment. I used the version I'd edited with Anya, but I went further to turn it—word by word, sentence by sentence—into something halfway decent.

When my intervention came to light, *The Vixen* would never be released, though it would be a much better book than the one Warren had entrusted to me. The novel wouldn't say that Esther was guilty. It wouldn't insist that she was innocent. The reader would mourn her death even though no one knew for sure exactly how much she knew, or what she'd done.

I worked in a fever of exhilaration and purpose. I was taking revenge. Not on Anya, not so much on Warren, but on the lying and pain, the grief and death that men like McCarthy—and Warren and Crowley—had caused.

It was the sweetest kind of revenge: wholesome, direct, guilt-free. A revenge without violence, without corpses or blood. A plot was being foiled, justice was being served, without injury or death. No real harm was being done except to Landry, Landry and Bartlett, which had never been what it seemed, or what I'd been led to believe. There was a slim chance that Warren would report me to the authorities whom he pretended to scorn and fear, but I didn't think he would. He'd want the whole thing to go away. Never to have happened.

I made minimal edits to the first ten pages, so that someone—for example, Warren—skimming the book for a quick read wouldn't be alarmed. I had to keep the characters' names, Esther and Junius, though I longed to change them. Anyway, it wouldn't matter if the book never appeared in print.

Around page eleven, I started making substantive fixes, eliminating the trashiness and the clichés, making Esther more complex: a woman who knew what her husband believed but not what he did. In my version Esther lived by the highest ideals. She was a loyal American. She believed in justice for all. She hardly understood the crimes she was accused of. She'd wanted to be an opera singer and wound up housebound with two boys, knowing that her life would never be better than it was, but that most people had it worse. That was what she thought about when Junius lectured her about Communism, speeches I had to keep short for fear of alienating the reader. She thought about the contradiction between her love of comfort and her desire that everyone in the world could be as comfortable as she was. She'd never lost the hope of someday singing on stage. Sometimes she heard Puccini arias in her head. Writing that, I thought about how I'd wanted to study medieval Icelandic: about my wanting that still.

With each line I wrote and rewrote, I felt as if I was keeping a promise to my mother, a promise I'd never actually made. I'd promised whatever I'd prayed to when she was in surgery. God, love, science. The god of something. I'd promised to do the right thing. Prayers in extremis can be quickly forgotten. But my heartfelt vow stayed with me.

I tightened pages and trimmed scenes. I added an episode in which the Rosensteins' lawyer tells them that the state has, as its most damning evidence, the Jell-O box they'd allegedly used as a signal. My character Esther says, "I always hated Jell-O. It was bad for the kids. But Junius, with his sweet tooth, insisted on having it in the house. As it's turned out, Jell-O *was* very bad for us—*fatal*. It was my husband's fault, though I loved him and I love him still."

In my novel, Esther tells the prison matron at Sing Sing, "Who would have believed that I would be going to the electric chair because my husband liked a gelatin dessert? A monster must have invented the story about the torn Jell-O box. The match-up with the Russian never happened. Not in my kitchen, not in my sister-in-law's kitchen. Nowhere. It never happened. It was evil to say that it did."

I hated knowing that the Jell-O box was Warren's invention. Obviously I left out the passage in which Esther licks the Jell-O powder while the spy and her husband watch. The missing page was still lost, but I rewrote it.

I was making this scene up partly from scratch, since the original page was still missing. But no matter what I would have liked, I couldn't leave out the Jell-O. It was part of history now, though as Anya (oh, Anya!) said, a novel wasn't history. Whatever I did, the Jell-O found its way onto the page. I wrote a scene in which Esther dreamed she went to the supermarket, and there was nothing on the shelves but boxes and boxes of Jell-O.

This was the first time I felt as if a piece of fiction were *writing itself*, the first time I experienced that sense of being guided, the freedom *of no longer being myself*, a glimmer of those moments of grace that I was lucky to enjoy from time to time, later, in my life as a writer. Perhaps, like love, those flashes of freedom and inspiration might have seemed less precious if they weren't so rare, so unexpected, and, like love, so impossible to fake or will into existence.

On weekends I went to the library to read old newspapers and microfilm. Making Esther my point-of-view character with necessarily limited knowledge gave me the freedom not to know—not to say— exactly what happened. The author and the reader could only know as much as she did. She'd done some typing. She and her husband were Communists. She loved her children. And after her conviction, she knew that she was going to die. I felt something like the pleasure I'd imagined when I'd thought that Warren might have a great book for me to edit. Later I'd feel a deeper joy, writing the book I'd imagined, but for now this was fine with me. It beat paralysis and despair.

One problem with the original version of *The Vixen* was that the reader was supposed to celebrate Esther's death. She'd slept with way too many men, neglected her kids, and betrayed our country. I made her death a tragedy and turned her fictive romance with the district attorney into a doomed love affair. I made her love her husband no matter what he'd done—or not. No matter what *she'd* done. Everything I'd learned in college, in life, it all went into *The Vixen*. As the book improved, so did my mood.

As long as I was writing, I felt almost . . . optimistic. Maybe it was the experience of losing myself—and forgetting my problems. I wasn't worried. I wasn't afraid. I was happy, writing.

Revising *The Vixen*, line by line, was how I became a writer. It showed me what I could do, what I wanted to do. Rewriting *The Vixen* was, for me, like taking the first mild seductive dose of a drug to which I became addicted. Writers start out in many different and peculiar ways: as reporters, factory workers, cops, secretaries, teachers, mental patients.

But it's always seemed to me that the way I started writing was one of the strangest.

I would be lying if I said that I never thought, This will show Warren how *malleable* I am. Even many years later, I'd catch myself thinking, This will show Warren, and I'd have to remind myself that Warren Landry was dead.

. . .

Now I had three versions of the novel. The original, the one that I'd created "in collaboration" with Anya, and this new one, drastically altered, the novel I might have written if I'd wanted to write a novel like *The Vixen, the Patriot, and the Fanatic*. Which I never would have wanted. I never would have written anything like that, but improving it had become an obligation. My assignment to myself. It was work I believed I *had* to do, as good a reason to write as any.

At the office, I kept the manuscript in the drawer to which Julia had given me the key. I'd read a few lines, then lock up the pages. I don't know why I acted as if someone might steal the novel, or as if it might detonate in the hands of an innocent office cleaner. Maybe I feared that Warren might sneak in and read it when I stepped out for lunch.

Fixing its broken sentences, its overwritten paragraphs, its corny, euphemized sex scenes all made me think of Anya. What a terrible writer! If indeed she wrote it. Warren had told me more than he should, but he'd still insisted that Anya was the author.

One afternoon, I slid the manuscript into the drawer and, thinking of a sentence I wanted to add, instantly took it out again. Or tried to.

Something stuck. The drawer wouldn't open. I reached behind the stack of pages and felt a sheet of paper wedged in the runner. I gently pried it loose, smoothed it out.

I'd found the missing page.

The previous page ended with the Russian agent and Junius Rosenstein watching Esther lick the Jell-O box. Esther told them that the Jell-O was good to the very last drop as Agent Gusev struggled not to imagine what else her pretty pink tongue had touched. The government never claimed that this scene took place in their kitchen—it was alleged to have happened at Ethel's brother's house, in New Mexico. But Anya (or whoever) must have thought it worked better this way, and I had to admit that she (or whoever) was right.

The novel resumed on the page I held now.

Comrade Gusev knew that he would do anything—anything. He would betray his country or blow up the planet to lick the powdered Jell-O off the tip of Esther's tongue. So history turned on this kitchen

drama that this irresistible spy enacted with the simplest prop: a box
of strawberry dessert.

It was Warren's Jell-O box. Now it belonged to the world. It was the detail that everyone knew. But it was Warren's creation.

Under interrogation Agent Gusev told the attorney general about the
Jell-O. The patriotic lawyer asked him how he could have done the
evil he did, how he could have made the world more dangerous, ex-
posed every man, woman, and child to the threat of nuclear annihi-
lation.

When Gusev told the prosecutor about the Jell-O box, the lawyer
was infected with the fatal desire to watch Esther Rosenstein pleasure
an empty box of Jell-O. So you could say that the Jell-O box did
seal the Rosensteins' doom, not only because it was the Communist
spies' secret signal, but because it promised the kind of pleasure that
no man could resist.

There was another paragraph, but I couldn't go on. I wished the page had never resurfaced. I certainly hadn't needed it to continue my revision.

But the content mattered less than *where* I'd found it—and the typeface.

This wasn't the thick blurry alphabet produced by Anya's vintage typewriter. The streamlined type, the tiny flaws in the letters, were identical to those in the version I'd gotten from Warren. Julia was the only one who would have opened and closed these drawers in the months before I got here. Julia must have typed it. Julia had put the manuscript in the drawer. Maybe she'd locked it up, as I did. I needed to see her, to talk to her, to ask her what she knew.

Could she have written *The Vixen*? I hadn't thought to suspect her. I knew so little about her. I'd only met her that once, and what

I'd thought and remembered was: She was very pretty. Lovely and haunted and angry. I'd sensed there was something she wanted to tell me.

I went out to the reception desk and told Violet that I had found a ring in my desk. In Julia's former desk. I was pretty sure it was gold. I assumed it was Julia's. I wanted to return it.

Violet asked, Was it valuable? I said I didn't think so. She waited for me to show her the ring, but she could hardly insist. She offered to mail it to Julia. She could insure it and (don't tell Mr. Landry) charge it to the firm.

"I want to return it myself. I want to tell her I'm sorry for . . . I don't know. Taking her job."

Violet looked as if I'd just appeared, as if she'd never seen me before. She said, "I always thought that girl got screwed. She calls here every so often. Looking for copyediting work, poor thing. That baby's probably four, five months old."

She wrote Julia's phone number on one of the pink slips—*While you were out*—on which she recorded telephone messages like the one that said to meet Dad at the hospital. It made me superstitious, but also determined. It reminded me of my hospital waiting room prayers.

"Give Julia my best, okay?" Violet said. "Give the baby a kiss for me."

"I will," I said. "I promise."

As I waited for Julia to answer the phone, my panic should have been a sign that something more was at stake, something beyond the likelihood that she had written or typed *The Vixen*. As the phone rang and rang, I thought: Everything is lost. I reminded myself that if no one answered, I could always call again later.

I was about to hang up when a woman said, "What." Not a question, not a hello.

If a heart could turn over, mine did. A baby yowled in the background.

I said, "Should I call back later?"

Julia said, "How can I answer that if I don't know who the fuck you are?"

"Simon Putnam." I didn't want to say, The guy who took your job. "You showed me around your office . . . "

"Oh, right. Are you still working for *Warren*?" She gave his name a funny stress that I didn't know what to make of. One rumor was that she'd had Warren's child. The baby wailed again.

"Yes," I said. "I'm there. Here. For now." Why did I say *for now*?

I was ready to spill my private torment, then and there, on the phone, over the shrieks of the baby. It took all my self-control not to blurt out everything that had happened since I inherited Julia's office.

No one was better qualified to understand and help me. Julia knew Warren, Preston, Elaine. She and Anya had met in the lounge when Julia visited Preston. For all I knew she'd written *The Vixen* and recruited Anya to play the writer. Robertson Crowley recruited Warren. And Warren had recruited me, even if I hadn't known it.

I wanted Julia to admire the depth of the crisis of conscience I'd been having since *The Vixen* landed on my desk. Once I'd wanted to tell Elaine, tell a therapist, tell total strangers. My urge to confess had grown stronger now that I knew why I had been ordered to keep the book a secret.

I said, "Violet sends her regards." How insipid! *Violet sends her regards.*

"Violet sends her regards?"

Another protest from the baby explained Julia's impatience with a guy who had taken her office and was calling to waste her time.

I said, "Violet told me you do copyediting. I might have some work for you."

"Fiction?" she said. "Nonfiction?" Already her tone had warmed, more like someone wanting a job than someone wanting to end a conversation.

"Fiction," I said.

"Can you mail it to me, or messenger . . . "

I explained that it was sensitive. A rush job. We'd pay more. When had I gained the authority to use the Warren-esque *we*? "I could deliver it myself."

She hesitated, then said, "I assume it can wait till tomorrow?"

"Of course."

"Fine," she said. "Wednesday. Let's say two. That's usually Evan's nap time. So it's possible, not likely but possible, that we could actually talk."

CHAPTER 15

A warm morning, early June. On my way to Julia's, I sweated through my shirt before I reached the subway. Yet I refused to loosen my tie or unbutton my jacket, to shed any part of my uniform, my mismatched suit of armor.

I tried not to worry obsessively. Having met Julia once, I felt that, like Anya and Elaine, she was—in the phrase that maddened my uncle—*out of my league*. The little I knew about her made me think less of myself. That she had a child made me feel that I wasn't an adult. Her living in Harlem impressed me more than it should have. My vague anxieties barely masked my preemptive guilt about involving a single mother in something that might get her in trouble, when she likely had enough trouble of her own.

I took the wrong train to the wrong stop. I got out on the west side when I should have been east. I walked through two parks, past a synagogue, three churches, under a railroad embankment. There was a hint of a breeze, a cool rustling of silvery leaves. I might have enjoyed the walk had I not been in hell.

The address Julia gave me didn't exist. I wandered up and down Madison between 134th and 135th, from the just-too-high number to the just-too-low number, as if the right place would materialize the next time I walked by. Two old men playing cards on their stoop, kids playing stickball in the street watched me pass and return. I tried not to project the misery and frustration of a man come all this way to see a woman who has given him a fake address.

Finally an elderly woman in a jacket with gold buttons and a hat swaddled in navy tulle directed me down a narrow alley between two apartment buildings.

I emerged into a courtyard. In the middle was a wooden cottage that seemed to have been airlifted from some family farm and dropped in East Harlem. Or maybe the owners of the house held their ground while the midsized buildings went up around them. However it got there, the cottage seemed ghostly, like Brigadoon or Atlantis, a mirage that would vanish when I left and be gone when I returned. When I returned? When would *that* be? I was already planning a next time. Next time I would know how to get here.

Inside, a baby was crying. Loudly. The sound rang up the fire escape, into every window, behind every shivering curtain.

Julia answered the door holding a chubby baby just old enough to ride her hip. Clearly, it wasn't nap time. The baby was naked, red-faced. Neither of them looked glad to see me. Fat tears wobbled in the baby's eyes, but he'd stopped crying. My arrival had shocked him into forgetting whatever he'd wanted or didn't want. I was *not* going to give him a kiss from Violet.

That day at the office Julia had worn a little black dress that made a bold statement about the pregnant belly beneath it. Since then she'd adopted a more downtown boho style, rolled jeans, striped T-shirt, the espadrilles of a Venetian gondolier or a Paris newsboy. Her hair was cut short, in a boyish tangle. I longed to put my hand over her free hand, the hand not holding the baby, the hand with which she was distractedly rubbing her forehead.

She looked as if she couldn't wait for me to drop off the manuscript and leave, as if she had no more time for me than she'd had that day in the office. Her impatience only added to the attraction I'd felt when I met her. It was as if I'd hardly thought about other women—not Anya, not Elaine—since then. But I was thinking about them now, so that wasn't true.

Julia was prettier than I remembered, yet something about her seem faded and blurred. It was a look I would come to recognize in the faces of new mothers, expected to glow with maternity but who seem pale and drained, ravaged by sleepless terror about a helpless creature they hardly knew before they became responsible for its survival. Preoccupied by my own insecurities, I could still intuit Julia's fear: that the world had moved on without her, that motherhood was exile, that she'd begun to feel like an abandoned child with a child of her own. Though her situation was very different from mine, she reminded me of how I'd felt when I'd been cast down from academia and landed in front of my parents' TV.

I couldn't look at Julia for long. It was even harder to look directly at the baby.

The dark-haired, dark-skinned baby was definitely not Warren's. I'd heard that Julia had an affair with the Mexican author of a book about Pancho Villa. Later I would learn that the biographer was paying Julia's rent and lived with his wife and two sons a few blocks away.

I couldn't have said if the baby was pretty or homely, dreamy or alert. All I saw was the infant mirror of my own fear. I was terrified of the baby, afraid that he would judge and despise me because of some character flaw invisible to adults. I worried that Julia might hand the baby to me, offer to let me hold him. I would drop him, or squeeze too hard, and he would cry even louder. I wanted the baby to like me. But why would he welcome a strange man competing for his mother's attention?

Julia and her baby gave me the same blank stare. I thought I should probably smile at the baby. I started, then stopped. My smile would be false, and the baby would know that.

I'd brought *The Vixen* with me. I took the manuscript out of my briefcase, an awkward maneuver made clumsier by the fact that I was still standing in the doorway, aware of the mother and child watching.

I waved the pages like a peace flag. A flag of surrender. Julia and the baby regarded me with eerily similar scorn. Was contempt in a baby's emotional range? It seemed so, with baby Evan.

"Oh, right," said Julia. "You. Come in."

Her house was one large room, with a bed on one side, a simple kitchen on the other. The place smelled faintly of baby shit, boiled milk, laundry soap, and cigarettes—perfumes that, it now turned out, I loved above all others.

Still holding the baby, Julia sat down at the rickety kitchen table and motioned for me to join her. She popped one breast out of her T-shirt and attached the baby to her nipple, something we've grown accustomed to seeing, but that startled me then.

"Yow." Julia eased the baby away from her. "Don't bite."

Julia gave him her breast again, but now he didn't want it. They grappled gently. The baby howled. Julia shrugged. She was used to whatever this was. Reattaching himself to her nipple, the baby flashed me a look of triumph that would forever affect the way I saw the Madonna and Child. I saw, in the infant Jesus, the competitive pride of being closer to his mother than anyone else would ever be.

I tried to hand Julia the manuscript. She shook her head. Then she shrugged again and took it, struggling to hold three hundred pages with one hand and a nursing baby with the other.

I said, "Do you think—"

I didn't know what I planned to say next, which was just as well. "Think?" said Julia. "I haven't had a thought for months."

The baby had stopped nursing. Julia eased the baby off her breast, and he began to yell again. She put him over her shoulder and gently rubbed his back in small circles, which only seemed to make him angrier.

Julia said, "He doesn't like company. Not that we have any, ever."

So it *was* me making the baby cry. How could I calm him? By leaving. The one thing I couldn't do.

The manuscript lay on the table between us. Julia glanced at the title page and said, "*The Vixen?* You're fucking kidding me. Oh, please, dear God. Not this again. The proverbial bad penny."

"So you've seen this before?" Of course she had. I'd found the page in her desk.

"I typed the goddamn thing," she said.

"You didn't write it, did you?" It was a risky question, but I had to know.

"Jesus. You've *really* got to be kidding. What do you think I am?"

I believed her. I believed that she hadn't written *The Vixen*. Something in her tone, something in her expression, convinced me. I believed her, and I was relieved. Even if it meant that my questions about *The Vixen*'s origins might go unanswered, I was glad that she wasn't the answer.

She pressed the baby to her chest and turned the first pages with her free hand.

"Sorry. I can't even look at it. I'm desperate for money, but I can't do this."

"Why not?" I needed to hear her say it.

"Why? Because it's filth. A disgusting piece of shit. Two people died, two little boys lost their parents, and now Warren's publishing a trashy novel about executing a sex-crazed commie spy? I knew that this was in the works, but I never believed that Warren would do it. Oh, he's a real fanatic. He thinks he's a patriot, but he's just an egomaniac. He lives in his own country. Population: one."

Nothing had made me happier in the months that had passed since Warren first dropped the folder on my desk.

"I changed it," I said. "I rewrote it. It's different from what you typed. Go ahead. Please. Start reading around page ten."

Lost in milky ecstasy, the baby allowed his mother to skim a few pages.

Then Julia said, "What *is* this?"

I TOLD JULIA everything, far more than I should have, more than she wanted or needed to know. I told her about watching the Rosenberg execution on TV, about my mother having known Ethel, about what my parents said on the night Ethel died. I told her about Uncle Madison, about our lunch, how he'd gotten me the job. *Her* job. I told her about meeting Anya, about the Terror Tomb and our strange affair and Anya's disappearance and my going in search of her and my talk with Preston.

I told Julia everything except that I already loved her. Later we would look back and, like all lovers, hardly believe there was a time when we didn't know each other well enough to say the most important things.

I shouldn't have told her about the sex with Anya. That was a mistake. I realized that even as I said it. I would pay for it later. I only hoped I would get the chance. But I was determined to be honest, and my half-crazed monologue was, for me, a sacrament of confession. The soul baring of a confused young man, about to be unemployed and broke, wanting to be forgiven and maybe even admired by an unemployed broke single mother.

I watched Julia for a reaction, but her face stayed blank. She didn't speak. She never asked me to explain or elaborate. Meanwhile I had the sensation of speaking in my own voice, with a fluency I'd never had with Warren or Uncle Maddie, not with Anya or even Elaine.

After a while the baby fell asleep. Julia eased him into his crib, then returned to the table, poured us each a coffee cup full of red wine that I gulped in a few grateful swallows.

She said, "I typed the novel because he asked me. Just like poor Ethel, I guess. How bizarre, that *typing* can get you in so much trouble. Warren and I . . . I'd rather not talk about me and Warren."

That was fine with me. I didn't want to hear it.

I said, "Warren wants *The Vixen* to be the Rosenberg story read round the world. The slutty spy-witch who our government had to burn at the stake to keep from destroying the human race."

"I know that," Julia said.

"But my version is different. And once they figure out what it is, no one's going to let it get out into the world."

"Why are you bothering?" Julia said.

"Because I have to. It's something I have to do." I couldn't tell her about my prayers during my mother's surgery. It would have seemed like a pathetically obvious bid for her sympathy.

"And what do you want from me?"

"I want you to copyedit my version."

"But why do you need me? If it's not going to be published—"

"Because it's *become* my book, my novel . . . My protest. I want it to be right."

That wasn't true, and Julia knew it.

The truth was: I *didn't* need her. She could give the manuscript back to me, exactly as it was, and it would make no difference. Her input wasn't required. Warren didn't care if the book had inconsistencies and accidental repetitions. Typos and grammatical slips wouldn't bother the CIA.

I didn't need a copyeditor. I wanted an ally. A co-conspirator. I didn't want to do this alone. I wanted her in this with me. I wanted to do it together. Lying to her was a bad way to begin, but telling the truth was beyond me. It was inexcusable to drag her into my protest, my low-key revenge, my barely visible act of resistance.

Julia and I can thank my selfishness, my cowardice, and my lies for everything that followed, for our happy life together. I have long ago been forgiven.

Eventually I forgave myself, always more of a challenge.

Julia rested her elbows on the table. In the dusty light, without saying much, we contemplated a plot to dominate world opinion through commercial romance fiction.

She said, "As if it's a sure thing that the whole world will read a lousy novel. All this would almost be funny if Ethel and Julius weren't dead."

"Plus eighty-seven Albanians," I said. "And who knows how many more, thanks to Warren and his pals."

"Okay," she said. "We're on. Let's do this for the eighty-seven Albanians. And for the who knows how many more."

I loved how my words sounded in her voice. Already I saw change in Julia, a gentle lightening, a gradual turn, as if the sun were edging back into her visual field. Something larger seemed possible, beyond this room, this house, her child. I didn't know why she wanted to do the right thing for Ethel. I could only speculate about why she wanted to do the wrong thing for Warren. Or why she wanted to help me. All I knew was I wanted her help. Her agreeing was a sign.

She smiled like someone waking from a restful nap. I said, "I took out the scene where Esther licks the Jell-O box."

Julia burst out laughing. Her laugh was throaty and free, sweeter than Anya's, more heartfelt than Elaine's. She said, "Good to the very last drop."

"The very last drop," I said.

We laughed together. No one but Julia and I would have gotten the joke. Not even Anya, oh, Anya. There were so many reasons why I could have never joked about her book, around her, even if I'd wanted. It was nice to be able to laugh. No one except Julia knew *The Vixen* as well as I did and shared my vision for its future, which was to say: no future at all. Elaine and I had laughed about the book. But we couldn't now.

I heard my voice, my real voice, catch as I asked, "Do you know who wrote it?"

Julia said, "Didn't Warren tell you?"

"He insisted Anya did. But she—"

"I was in the office when they wrote it."

They was more than one person. *They* was more than Anya. More than Warren. I braced myself to hear that Anya and Warren wrote it together so they could laugh at my efforts to improve something that was just the way they wanted.

"The three of them."

"Three?"

"Warren, Elaine, and your uncle."

"My uncle? My uncle Madison Putnam?"

Julia looked at me.

I'd suspected Warren. I'd steeled myself to hear his name. But my uncle and Elaine?

It took a while to sink in.

I didn't know which defection, which . . . *betrayal*, hurt me more. In the sagas, the worst crime is to betray a blood relation. Uncle Maddie was my father's only living brother. My family. My blood. My father's brother. The man I'd wanted to follow out of those long loud family weddings. The uncle who was on my side, who not only helped me find a job but also got my parents to let me follow in his dinosaur footsteps. That lunch, that pillowy hug, his warm forgiving fatness. How safe I'd felt falling into him, not even embarrassed to be so young and drunk. The cushiony flesh of my flesh. And all that time he was mocking me, ranting about the Rosenbergs while he and Warren and Elaine were conspiring to torment me in ways that only he—knowing my mother, knowing me—could have devised and carried out. I remembered something he said that day, calling the Rosenbergs' apartment *Roosevelt-era commie housing*. Only now did I recall that in *The Vixen*, Esther complains to the district attorney, "Our apartment is practically public housing." It was Uncle Maddie's line, but I hadn't made the connection. Sometimes you don't see something unless you're looking for it. It shocked me that Uncle Maddie was speaking to me through the novel. It was too painful to wonder what Elaine had contributed to the book. I'd felt safe and hopeful with her. I'd thought she believed in me.

"Uncle Maddie, Warren, and Elaine? Madison Putnam? The three of them wrote *The Vixen?* They were in on it together?"

Julia put a consoling hand over mine. Uncle Maddie, Warren, and Elaine. It made for a confusing dynamic, the pleasure of Julia's touch versus the pain of having been betrayed by my uncle, my boss, and the colleague with whom I'd thought I was in love.

No wonder Elaine had giggled when she asked if I could remember the novel's worst lines. For all I knew, she wrote them. She—or Maddie or Warren or all three—they'd *meant* those sentences to be bad. And the idiotic sucker, the naive fool worked so hard to improve them. Those lines were funny, but I was funnier. It was like a schoolyard bully's prank, except that the playground was the United States, the Red Scare, the Cold War.

I was wrong to have loved Elaine. Foolish to have trusted her. She was never on my side. She was like one of those duplicitous women in the Icelandic sagas, the women with the thieves' eyes, but unlike their hapless Viking victims, I had never been warned.

Even knowing that, I missed her, or maybe I missed the idea of her. Thinking of her had been like traveling to a relaxing holiday spot that was now off-limits, forever. It was almost worse, losing someone who had never been mine. It was more embarrassing than losing a love, which was tragic. A chill seeped into the warm space that Elaine used to occupy in my thoughts.

Maybe my uncle and Elaine weren't the ones who decided to involve me. Maybe that was Warren's idea. That was still awful, but not *as* awful, not such a *personal* betrayal. I'd never imagined that Warren Landry loved me. I'd thought or wanted to think that Elaine and my uncle might.

Julia's baby began to cry. I felt that he was crying *for* me, taking on my burden, shedding the tears I couldn't cry in front of his mother. Julia lifted him out of his crib and rocked him till he fell back asleep. Then she returned to the table.

"They started writing *The Vixen* after the Rosenbergs died, just when it was becoming clear that many people were angry about the execution. There were all those demonstrations, in London and Madrid, Stockholm and West Berlin. After some protestors were killed in Paris, I remember Warren saying that the world needed to be reminded that we Americans were the good guys. The guys in the white hats."

"And?"

"And what? They took turns writing chapters. They were having so much fun, it only took them a few months."

Anya had said the book was written quickly. That, at least, was true.

"They met in Warren's office after everyone went home and drank gallons of whiskey and read aloud what they'd written. Every Thursday evening."

I pictured Warren's office. The fox-hunting dogs on the walls. I wondered if they had subconsciously inspired *The Vixen*'s coauthors.

"You could hear them all the way down the hall. The two men bellowing like bulls and Elaine's annoying girly giggle."

I'd always liked Elaine's laugh, but now I understood what Julia meant. Looking back, I saw Elaine's geisha-like aspects, her ability to give people—Warren, me, writers, editors, lunch counter waiters—what they wanted. I hated seeing our relationship as a calculated seduction. Had Warren instructed Elaine to charm me, or had she volunteered?

Later, I would think back over every moment I'd spent with Elaine and tried to decide how much of what she did and said was sincere. What about that lunch at George Jr.'s, when she'd started off by praising Edward R. Murrow for shaming McCarthy on TV? Did she think I wanted to hear that? Warren didn't like McCarthy, either.

Julia said, "I'd never seen Warren have more fun than when he was writing that book. He never had that much fun with me. Those evenings they met to work on *The Vixen*, Warren asked me to stay late. And the next day he'd ask me to type the pages. Keep it a deep dark secret. I knew what they were doing. I wasn't paid extra, but there was some vague promise I'd be rewarded when the company ship came in. I shouldn't have done it. I needed the job. I guess that's what they all say. I needed the job."

"I've certainly said it." A horrifying little laugh escaped from between my lightly clenched teeth.

At the sound of my voice, the baby started up again, this time gasping for air between howls. Was he turning a pale blue? It was dramatic and frightening, but Julia wasn't alarmed. She picked him up and rocked him. Her soothing him was like a magic trick. I tried to look less impressed than I was. Julia had no interest in my reaction, which impressed me even more. Neither of us moved until we heard the baby's soft regular snuffling.

Julia said, "Anya didn't write one word, though I'm sure she read it. Or some of it. She read it to help her play the author of that book. You do realize that she's smarter than she pretends."

I was afraid to look at Julia. I didn't want her to see what I was feeling, not that I knew what that was. The floor beneath me felt gelatinous. I held onto the table.

Everyone was acting. Everyone was lying.

Anya had read the book. I knew it, just as I'd known she was smart. Perhaps her forgetting certain plot points was acting, theater, her way of signaling what she couldn't say. Maybe she'd tried to save me. Maybe she'd begged me to save her. I'd been too self-involved to notice.

I'd assumed that Anya gave the fur fetish to her heroine, Esther, because she herself had that quirk. I assumed it was an autobiographical detail, borrowed from life. That was partly why I'd never questioned the fact that she'd written the novel.

I'd had it all wrong. I'd had it backwards. The fur piece was *already* in the manuscript that Anya was given to read and pretend she'd written. That was where she *got* the idea. Her adopting the fur piece was the sort of thing an actor might do to prepare for a part, in this case the part of Anya Partridge, the beautiful, half-mad author of *The Vixen*.

Now I knew why she'd left the pelt under the radiator. Why not? It was never a good-luck charm. It was a theater prop. I'd thought that it would be hard to make Anya change the details that were aspects of herself, but they were *never* aspects of Anya, or whoever she was. They were details in a novel that she read and pretended to have written.

Warren loved details. They were his contribution to history, the visible signs of his greatness. Once he'd discovered Anya, he'd probably tweaked the novel so that Esther resembled her putative author: the violet eyes, the black hair, the bee-stung scarlet lips.

Julia said, "I met Anya in the lounge when I went to visit Preston. I was the one who found her for Warren. That part is my fault. I take full blame. I was the pimp. The procurer. They needed someone to play the writer. Anya wanted to be an actress. Maybe she *is* an actress. Maybe she's really gifted."

Oh, she was gifted all right. A hugely gifted actress. I never doubted her for a moment, except once, when she told me the truth. Maybe the role of Anya-the-writer would turn out to be the juiciest and most challenging part of her life. It was extreme experimental theater, played out in real life, with her overdone bedroom as a set and the city as her stage.

Julia said, "I knew she'd be perfect. A smart little rich girl whose parents stashed her in a rest home to get her away from a bad boyfriend and a shitload of diet pills. The boyfriend's dad was a doctor. They'd stolen Dad's prescription blanks."

Diet pills? Was Anya taking them? Her flighty affect made more sense now, though until then the only use I'd known for diet pills was to stay up all night to study for an exam.

Julia had deceived me too. Another lie of omission, the kind I'd told so often. By the time I took over her office, I'd known she was hiding something. Why should she tell me what Warren was planning? She was leaving. She'd been fired. I was taking her job. Why not let me suffer a little? And why should she—alone in that crowd—have been truthful?

We were all lying, leaving things out, deceiving one another.

"Anya gave me her headshot. She'd been trying to get acting jobs. Warren saw the photo on my desk and said, 'Aha, the little vixen author of our little *Vixen*.' That was how Anya became our writer. Their writer. *Your* writer." Julia's face clouded over. I could tell she was looking for something unkind to say about Anya. She couldn't help it, no more than I could help being flattered that she cared enough to compete with the woman with whom she sensed I'd been enthralled. It was one of those moments, at the start of love, when you are trying to say the unsayable without having to say it.

"She and Warren met several times to work out the part she'd play for the world. And first, I suppose, the role she'd try out on you."

So that was what I'd been to Anya: a long, leisurely rehearsal. The thought was so painful that I couldn't look at Julia. I stared down at my hands. I'd already told Julia too much about Anya. I didn't want her to read the rest in my face.

"Anya loves playing to the camera," Julia said. "Her being so pretty is a plus. And they need her. What would people say if a distinguished publisher, a vicious public intellectual, and respected literary publicist admitted to writing *The Vixen, the Patriot, and the Fanatic*? They need a front, a beard, a pseudonym, an alter ego to hide behind." I was relieved to hear Julia speak of Anya in the present tense. But Julia wouldn't know what had happened to her. Where Anya was, or even if she was alive.

After a silence, I said, "And *why* did they want to publish *The Vixen*?"

"Come on," said Julia. "Seriously?"

"For the money?" Preston had told me the truth. Warren admitted it. But part of me still clung to the bearable lie. The story about the money.

"Not even you believe that. The money was never going to come from readers. It was always covert government funding."

I hadn't wanted to believe Preston. But I'd known he was right.

"It was always about Warren wanting to show his pals at the Agency that he wasn't getting older, losing it, that he was still a force to be reckoned with, still a source of the smart, creative schemes that no one else would think of."

Julia's voice had grown louder. Hush! I thought. The baby!

"I see." And I did.

I finally saw what everything and everyone had been trying to tell me all along.

"Why me? Why did they give the book to me?"

"That was your uncle Madison's idea. He thought it was hilarious. Side-splitting. He laughed so hard I was afraid he'd have a seizure. No one else thought it was *that* funny. But he couldn't explain. What did you *do* to that guy? Because your uncle laughing like that—it's not a pretty sight."

It was all too easy to imagine what Uncle Maddie could have held against me. I was young; I was good-looking. I'd gone to an Ivy League college. I came from a family that reminded him of where he'd come from.

"Did you know they were going to give me the book when I came to work there?"

"I'm sorry," Julia said. "I'm really sorry. Warren gave me a thousand dollars as severance pay. Hush money. We both knew he was buying my silence. I was pregnant, Simon. I had no savings. I needed the money. I figured you could handle it, see through it, work your way out of it. I assumed you'd know what to do. I mean . . . Warren said you'd gone to Harvard."

As if Harvard had taught me what to do when my uncle, my boss, and a woman I thought I loved asked me—as a joke—to work on what turned out to be a piece of lying propaganda. I shut my eyes to contain the rain of tiny stars inside my eyelids, the stars that cartoon characters see when they're hit on the head.

Uncle Maddie had tricked me, set me up to act the lead in a comedy that he and Warren and Elaine scripted. All that avuncular advice, those appeals to family feeling, all that *make the writer fall in love with you*. It was all part of the joke he was playing on the fool, the dupe, the patsy. His nephew. At our lunch, he'd known about *The Vixen*. His rant about the Rosenbergs was the one sincere moment in that entire conversation. The food, the gossip, the mock-professional advice was more of his famous so-called humor. *My dear, dear nephew*, those hearty slaps on the shoulder.

Maybe he'd thought it was funny to send me, the child of parents who believed that the Rosenbergs shouldn't have been executed, to work on a project that "proved" that Ethel was guilty. Or maybe it had nothing to do with me. Maybe it was all about my uncle. About the dirt he'd dished at lunch about every man whose hand he shook. And now I was one of them, subject to something crueler than gossip and slander because our connection went deeper than a lunchtime acquaintance.

Julia's hand still cradled mine. I was in pain again. I wanted Julia to *see* that I was in pain, which lessened the pain. My desire for her sympathy was an analgesic.

"That's why I gave you the key to the drawer," she said. "I knew they'd give you *The Vixen* sooner or later. I don't know why it took them so long."

I thought, but didn't say: My uncle wanted it, but they needed to see if I would do what Warren told me.

Years would pass before I could bring myself to tell Julia that Warren had called me: *malleable*.

Julia said, "I thought you might want to lock it up. I used to."

How could she know that I'd do that? She knew me. She'd understood me from the moment we met. Julia had given me the key. Maybe she would have warned me if I'd asked, but I didn't know what to ask. But she was looking out for me, even when I'd thought she hated me simply for existing. That we'd both locked up *The Vixen* suggested a likeness, a connection strong enough to compensate for the fact that she should have warned me. Was there enough trust between us now for . . . what? I wanted to believe there was. I believed there was. Julia wasn't Anya or Elaine. She was the only one who wasn't acting.

I wanted to touch her arm. Just touch it.

She said, "I hardly know your uncle. He tried to grab my ass once when he was drunk, but I gave him a look, and he stopped. That was all it took. Warren, on the other hand, is a sadist. Not sexually. But in every other way."

I tried to keep my face neutral.

"Though maybe Warren and your uncle are both sadistic. In different ways. I don't know. I lost touch with the office and the whole situation. I thought about you sometimes—"

She'd thought about me. She'd thought about me. So what if she'd thought about a poor stupid dupe, a sad little pawn in a game played by the dupe's boss, his uncle, and the CIA?

"Warren is *not* a good person."

"So it turns out," I said. The Jell-O box. The pumpkin. The fake *Vixen* cover. The jewfish.

I was just winding you up.

Julia could have said more, but she didn't. I was encouraged by her lack of desire to talk about Warren. In my naive opinion that meant she'd never loved him. I still wanted to talk about Anya, though not to Julia, not anymore. I knew so little about love that the compulsion to talk about it seemed like proof of its existence.

Julia said, "Warren's a bloodhound. There's nothing he can't find out. When he figured out who Evan's father was, which I tried to keep secret, you know what that shithead said? 'Dear Julia, don't tell me you're ruining your life for a *biographer of Pancho Villa?* We didn't want to publish that infantile boy-on-boy love letter to some fucking *bandito.* But the boys in Washington decided, Let's show the world how much we love our Central American *hermanos.'*"

She'd gotten Warren's inflections, his tone.

"You sound just like him," I said. I thought of Warren imitating Eleanor Roosevelt and the McCarthy hearing witness taking the Fifth Amendment.

"Thanks. I guess. I honestly don't know where he and Elaine and your uncle got the idea of writing *The Vixen.* Cases of whiskey, maybe. Warren figured out that *The Vixen* could be leveraged into a guaranteed circulation, international sales, government money to do what he thought was the right thing, politically speaking, if not exactly at the highest level of art. He and your uncle agreed about the politics, about the Rosenbergs, and about not wanting to be exposed as the coauthors of a trashy novel. They had something on each other. *The Vixen* was their secret. It brought them closer, you could say."

Closer than either of them was to me. I hated the thought of them talking about me. Talking and probably laughing.

I was glad that Julia seemed unaware of what this was costing me. Or maybe she just had a lot to say. Maybe a dam had broken. I remembered how, in her office, I'd thought she was holding back. At least I'd been right about one thing.

"Having Preston sent away was wrong, but Warren got sick of Preston nagging him about principles. Right and wrong!"

Preston, the medicated vulture so paranoid he thought his wheelchair was plotting against him. He was right to be suspicious. He'd learned his sad, disappointing lessons. Maybe if I'd been more mistrustful, *smarter,* maybe if I'd had the nerve to approach Preston when he'd visited the office and asked to see the real boss, by which he didn't mean Warren, maybe if I'd asked what he meant, none of this would have happened.

And I might never have met Julia. Was this all working out for the best?

"Preston was right, but he was wasting his breath. And he couldn't help himself. It broke Preston's heart when he found out where Warren was taking the company. Straight into the arms of the spy boys. There was nothing Preston could do. Making Warren stop seeing himself as a secret agent would have been like telling him to grow a new brain."

And you had an affair with him? The voice in my head thundered like the Sunday pulpit voice of Jonathan Edwards. If I let it preach, I would lose her. Elaine was lost. Anya was lost. I'd never really had them. I would probably lose Julia. Maybe I was wrong again to think that she was on my side.

"Warren underestimated how much he needed Preston's money. How much money he needed. Warren's a practical guy, but only until he regresses into a spoiled twelve-year-old rich boy. I guess he was insulted because the Agency could have made his money problems go away. But they liked watching him dangle. Just like Warren and your uncle Maddie liked watching you . . . squirm."

I was grateful that she wasn't including Elaine in the rapt audience for my misery.

"These guys know where power comes from, they know how to keep it. It's not all that personal, Simon."

I thought about my uncle and Warren chortling about my ludicrously earnest college thesis. "The Burning." I'd told my uncle at lunch. My mother boasted about it. My uncle must have told Warren. He'd said that *The Burning* was Anya's original title. Then there were the dead Albanian partisans, so much like the massacre in *Njal's Saga.* Everything looped back on itself, dense as a bramble thicket in a fairy tale. I couldn't see my way through. Maybe Warren had read my thesis, for a laugh. Robertson Crowley had recruited him even as Crowley worked his side job, transcribing folktales and teaching. Those classes were his cover, just as publishing was Warren's. A crude formulation, according to Warren. And not even true. He loved books. That part I believed. And he loved being the boss.

A siren dopplered by, obliterating the silence in which I imagined I could hear Warren, Uncle Maddie, and Elaine laughing their heads off at my not getting their joke. I had no sense of humor. It was a fun experiment with a practical side, thanks to Uncle Maddie's nastiness, thanks to Warren's business skills and Cold War connections. Thanks to their deepest political beliefs. And Elaine? Warren asked her. Even if she'd had doubts, she'd thought it might be fun. She was flattered to be asked to conspire with two powerful men: literary lights. I'd flattered myself that she had feelings for me, if only just kindness and pity. I didn't blame her as much as I blamed Uncle Maddie. She wasn't a relative. And yet it was more *shaming* to be betrayed by a beautiful woman than by a fat middle-aged man.

It took all my courage to say, "You typed it. You found Anya for them. You helped them. You helped them lie." If Julia never spoke to me again, I would have said what had to be said.

"I had a job. I'm not proud of it. I thought that nothing would actually happen. I thought they'd lose interest and quit writing. A typing job, I thought. I was an English major. I don't have many skills. If Ethel gets a pass for typing, I should get one too."

I said, "That's not funny."

"I know," said Julia. "I'm sorry."

We laughed. It was wrong to laugh, but it felt good to laugh with her at something that wasn't funny. I thought of my father's unfunny jokes. My mother and father would like her.

"I was pregnant. Desperate for money. I would have typed *Mein Kampf* if Hitler paid enough."

"Really?" I tried not to look shocked—an unattractive look, said

Warren. Despite everything I was still hearing his advice on how to be a man, or at least look like one. "You know I'm Jewish, right?"

It felt a little like telling Anya I'd come from Coney Island, but more serious and important. I was startled by the ease with which I'd disclosed something that I'd never exactly concealed—but never volunteered, either. I trusted Julia. I loved her. I wanted her to know everything about me. It was a declaration, to Julia and myself. I wasn't Warren and never would be. I felt a flicker of regret and then enormous relief.

"I do," she said. "I do know. I assumed . . . because of your uncle."

"You knew that Madison Putnam is Jewish?" Uncle Maddie had done an excellent job of playing a descendant of the Puritan Putnams.

"I always thought your uncle was like a child who thinks that if he closes his eyes, no one can see him. I'm sorry about the Hitler remark. I make stupid jokes when I'm nervous."

I'd never heard a woman say that. I'd thought that using humor to stave off anxiety was something only men did, that only my father did for our little family.

"I would never have typed *Mein Kampf*. What do you think I am? *The Vixen* was just so boring. Even by bad-book standards. I could hardly stand to type it. I assumed no one would read it if it ever *did* come out. It makes *Gone with the Wind* look like, I don't know, *Macbeth*."

Julia's mentioning *Gone with the Wind* made me want to tell her about meeting Anya in Charleston Gardens, but I didn't want to think about that lunch, or that model home.

A silence fell over the baby's sweet rhythmic wheeze. I felt bizarrely content. I wanted to stay here forever. I dreaded the thought of leaving. I could deal with anything if I could just be with Julia and the baby. One more day, one more hour, one more minute with them. Then I could return to the world in which three people I'd trusted—some more, some less—had conspired against me.

She said, "My parents are divorced. I wasn't going to do that to a kid. But now I've done worse."

"Evan looks like he's doing fine." *Was* it fine for a baby to cry so much? It seemed like the right thing to say. Julia made me want to be kind. Already a better self was emerging from the arid chrysalis that had admired Crowley—and Warren.

"I never hear anyone say Evan's name. Except his dad, who comes around every so often, and the pediatrician when I take Evan in for checkups."

Wasn't it premature for me to be jealous of the baby's father? Had Julia loved him? Did she still? I'd been reflexively jealous of Elaine and Warren, of Anya and Warren. All that was a mistake.

"Whenever someone calls him Evan, I have the strange feeling he's already grown up and left me. I'm filled with dread. I'm with him every minute, and it drives me crazy, but I want to cry when I think about what a short time I'll have until he's on his own and gone."

I saw my parents' sad faces every time I left their apartment.

I said, "You've got decades before that happens."

On the table was a half-dried splotch of orange goo.

"Baby carrots," Julia said.

What was funny about baby carrots? Nothing. It didn't matter. I was so happy to be here, laughing at nothing with Julia.

I said, "Will you copyedit it?"

"I already did," said Julia.

"No," I said. "This version. Just give it a once-over—it doesn't need much. I looked it over myself."

We both knew it didn't need anything. If the book was never going to come out, what did comma placement matter? How patiently Anya had submitted to those tedious corrections of something she hadn't written. I shouldn't have thought about Anya. I didn't know why I was.

I wanted encouragement. Courage. I wanted someone who knew what I was doing and thought it was right. Someone who would stand by me. It was selfish, implicating Julia in a scheme that could backfire, badly. I have no excuse except that I was young and wanted so much to be with her.

"We'll get this to the printer. You've worked for them, so no one will think twice if we pay you, higher than the normal rate because it's a rush job."

"Don't tell Warren you hired me. He'll get suspicious."

"I won't." Another level of agreement had been reached between us. Agreement or conspiracy, we were in it together.

"You think they're really going to publish this? Warren's signed off on it?"

"Warren will sign off on something. But not this, exactly. Trust me."

This was how espionage must feel. False reassurances, fake confidence, the pretense of expertise. If one mission failed, you lied and moved on. There was no reason for Julia to trust me. But she liked hearing me ask her to try.

The baby whimpered in his sleep.

"You'd better go," she said. "When do you want this done?"

"The sooner, the better," I said.

In the doorway, we hugged goodbye. Our contact was brief and neutral, but in those days it was less common for acquaintances to embrace. A hug meant more then, and I was encouraged.

Riding the subway downtown, I felt lighter, as if by leaving the manuscript with Julia I'd shed such a heavy burden that I kept checking my pockets for my wallet and keys.

I WENT DIRECTLY to my parents' house. Everyone who was important to me, everyone but my mother and father, had lied to me and betrayed me. And in the space of one day I had fallen deeply in love with Julia, the only person I knew—besides Mom and Dad—who hadn't plotted against me. Julia had failed to warn me, there was that, but I understood.

Around my parents, I had to act as if nothing were wrong. It was better to pretend to be strong, better than falling apart. I couldn't risk saying anything that might lead to the subject of Uncle Maddie— Dad's brother—and his role in this. Nor could I hint that I was giving up the life that my mother had lobbied so hard for me to live.

It turned out to be a good night, lucky and historic.

The ninth of June 1954.

The night McCarthy began to fall.

McCarthy had gone after a low-level army defense employee, a devout church lady whose crime against our democracy was not knowing how to cancel her dead husband's free subscription to the *Communist Daily Worker*. McCarthy had persecuted a Jewish dentist from Queens just because he went to college with Julius and knew Ethel.

Then McCarthy made a fatal mistake: he insulted a brigadier general. He should have left the army alone.

In the spring of 1954, the government investigated McCarthy on charges that he and Roy Cohn had tried to obtain special privileges— no kitchen duty, custom-made boots, a free pass to leave the base whenever he wanted—for Cohn's friend David Schine, who had been drafted into the army after going on a whirlwind luxury tour with Cohn, investigating Communism abroad.

On that night, the ninth of June, they replayed the hearings about Schine's custom-made boots. My mother said, "Getting comfortable shoes for your boyfriend is a million times better than ruining innocent lives. The boots were the least terrible thing they did."

Dad said, "People don't like the rich getting special shoes."

"That's what the Communists say *they* don't like," my mother said. "And *they* give rich people the fanciest shoes plus fur coats and limousines, and they send everyone else to Siberia."

During commercials my mother brought plates of food from the kitchen: chicken, potatoes, pastries, cookies, coffee. Could she tempt us? Yes, she could. Her feeling better tempted us. Making up for lost time, she ate everything. If this kept up, she'd be back in her class-room in the fall.

"Listen," said my father. "They're kicking McCarthy's ass."

"They're yelling about points of order," said Mom. "They've been doing that all day. Point of order! Point of order!"

McCarthy was up to his usual bullying tricks, insisting a rumor is proof, this time targeting Fred Fisher, a young lawyer working for Joseph Welch, the special counsel for the army.

My parents and I watched Joseph Welch play the country attorney out of a '30s Hollywood movie, an older, craggier Jimmy Stewart, or Henry Fonda as the young Abe Lincoln. A folksy, plainspoken trial lawyer who'd taken the train down from Boston, a hick in a tweed jacket and a bow tie. He said he'd think up some questions to ask the witnesses. And if he didn't like the answers, well, then, gosh, he'd ask another question.

He was the spirit of American democracy going after McCarthy. Why didn't McCarthy see? Why didn't McCarthy know that America was waiting for the slipup that would let the country lawyer go in for the kill?

My mother shook her head as McCarthy spoke about how this young man, this Fred Fisher, belonged to the legal arm of the Communist Party. Then he called Joe Welch an actor who played for a laugh and was blind to the danger posed by the Communist menace.

My mother said, "He's got that part right. Welch is an actor who acts like he's not acting."

Before today, the word *actor* would have made me think of Anya. Actually, it still did, and still hurt, but not as much as it would have if I hadn't spent the day with Julia.

Dad said, "McCarthy should have watched more Jimmy Stewart films."

Welch said, "May I have your attention?" but McCarthy kept talking.

Welch repeated, "May I have your attention?"

McCarthy said he could listen with one ear and talk—

"I want you to listen with both."

Joseph Welch sounded like a calm but firm preschool teacher.

And there it was. Something happened. The power had started to shift.

Welch defended Fred Fisher. The "legal arm of the Communist Party" turned out to be the Lawyers Guild. Welch announced that Fred Fisher was now the secretary of the Newton, Massachusetts, Young Republicans Club.

"Another éclair, Simon?" my mother said.

"No thanks," I said. "One is enough."

"You can't really refrigerate them. And then you get food poisoning."

"Please," my father said. "Both of you. Please."

Welch said he'd underestimated McCarthy's recklessness and cruelty. *Recklessness* and *cruelty*, the most obvious words. So why had no one said them in public till now?

"Here it comes," said my mother.

Welch said, "Have you no sense of decency, sir, at long last? Have you left no sense of decency?"

Decency. The magic word that broke the spell of the wizard's enchantment. We were by no means out of the woods, but we could glimpse the bright clearing.

"Finally, someone says it! It's over," said Dad. "Simon, spend the night with us. Let's celebrate."

"It's not over," said Mom.

"Maybe," said Dad. "But it's ending."

My father opened a bottle of warm champagne that exploded all over the furniture. We were too happy to bother wiping it up. I couldn't let myself notice that it was cheap champagne, nor remember how annoyed Anya was because Warren hadn't stocked champagne in his car.

I was ready to go to bed, to close my eyes and think about Julia.

My parents and I toasted Joe Welch, the United States, democracy, freedom. With each toast, the champagne tasted better. How dear and kind my parents were! How selflessly they loved me, how intensely they hoped for the best for me and asked nothing in return.

Could I bring Julia to meet them? It might be tricky. She had a child. I was getting ahead of myself, but that was where I wanted to be.

"To home," I said. "To family. To . . . work."

My parents raised their glasses.

"I'm sleepy," I said. "It's been a long day."

"A long good day," said Mom.

A long good day. She was right.

"Good night," I said.

"Sleep tight," said Mom.

"Good night, sweet prince," said Dad.

...

A few days later, I picked up the manuscript from Julia's. I didn't stay long. I didn't have to. I needed to be on my way—but only to prove to myself that I could resist the desire to stay forever. Julia knew what I was doing and why. She was on my side. She wanted me to stay. She knew I would come back. The most casual look, the most "accidental" touch, was freighted with meaning and promise.

She said, "Technically, is this sabotage? Treason? Not that I care. Not that I'd tell you not to do it. I'd just like to know. Actually, I *do* care. I don't want to go to jail. I have a child."

"You won't." I was sorry for promising something I didn't know for a fact. Baby Evan was napping. I apologized, in my head.

Julia grinned and encircled my wrists with her fingers, like handcuffs. I blinked to dislodge the image of the handcuffed Julius embracing Ethel.

I liked the idea of Julia and me as brave Resistance fighters. It was sexy, starting off as an outlaw couple, the Bonnie and Clyde of commercial-fiction sabotage. It would have felt like being kids again, two teenagers falling in love, but the presence of baby Evan reminded us that we were grown-ups and that our actions had consequences.

The word *consequences* reminded me of Warren. I worried he might have poisoned certain words for me, forever.

...

I left the lightly edited manuscript on Warren's desk. It was close to what he'd given me, with enough small changes to make him think I'd done something. I carefully placed the note I'd typed, on top of the title page:

Here you go. Crossed every t, dotted every i. The Vixen is locked and loaded and ready to go out and bewitch the world.

Warren would notice that *locked and loaded* suggested a gun, which didn't go with *bewitch*. A gun would be ready to shoot the world, not enchant it. Fine. Let Warren disapprove of my mixed metaphor, be distracted by my word choice. A while ago, it would have been unthinkable to let Warren doubt my command of the language.

In the note I added that I was sending it to the printer.

In fact I sent the printer my own heavily altered version, with a few small corrections from Julia. I didn't tell Warren that.

Warren sent me a note, via office mail. *Bravo! Last-minute kudos for finally pushing out the baby.*

I filed an invoice that said: *Copyediting $100.* Could it be paid in cash? If the finance office asked why, I'd invent a story about the copyeditor's tricky divorce and sticky tax situation. But no one asked. Less paperwork to fill out. An envelope with two fifty-dollar bills appeared on my desk.

The printer called to give me the date when the proofs would be ready. I asked if we could skip the galley-proof stage, since the novel had been so meticulously edited. He said it was unusual, but he didn't see why not. Less work for him. Just so everyone understood: if typos and mistakes crept in at the end, it wouldn't be his fault.

I told him not to worry.

...

I expected to get caught the first day that *The Vixen, the Patriot, and the Fanatic* appeared as a hardbound book. The official pub date was still three weeks away. A mail room guy brought five advance copies to me and, I assumed, to Warren. More copies must have gone to Elaine. I skimmed through it. Word for word, it was what I wrote. My version of *The Vixen*.

I still wanted to think well of Elaine. I wanted to believe she hadn't meant to hurt me. My view of her hadn't darkened enough to include malice. I still couldn't have stood that. If not malice, then . . . severely misguided humor. In which case she might enjoy the story of *The Vixen* taking yet another turn. This time the joke would be on Warren. I wondered if she knew that I knew. If she knew *how much* I knew. I imagined her worrying about what she would say to me, whether she would apologize. I was curious, but I avoided her. It required quick turns down corridors, hasty trips to the men's room, but I managed not to run into her at the office.

And yet I was never for one moment unaware of where she was. Along the mazelike corridors, behind closed office doors, I tracked her from my desk. I thought about her so much that, in a way, we were closer than we'd been when we were friendly, when I let my crush on her obscure who she was and where her loyalties lay. I imagined different scenarios: She begged my forgiveness. She laughed at me. She denied having misled me or having done anything wrong. Only one of these things could happen, and if we actually met, one of them—perhaps the worst—would turn from fantasy into fact. It was easier not to see her, to let my doubts and grief remain foggy and abstracted instead of fixed in memory: sharp, permanent, and cruel.

I willed Elaine not to read *The Vixen* until Warren saw it. I wanted him to read it first, to come to it without having been warned. I wanted him to be horrified—and worried about how his Agency friends would react.

Writers are often asked about their readers, asked whom they write for, whom they imagine as their ideal audience. But writers only rarely picture someone actively reading their book. Maybe they do when they first send out a manuscript, or when a book is newborn, its fate uncertain. But after a while that fantasy—a stranger, a chair, a light, their book—feels too personal, too intrusive, too much like really seeing yourself through a stranger's eyes.

And yet I loved imagining Warren reading *The Vixen, the Patriot, and the Fanatic*. I loved wondering on what page he would finally figure out that something was terribly wrong. That the book shared only its characters' names and the first ten pages with whatever witchy toxin he and Elaine and my uncle Maddie had brewed at those whiskey-soaked weekly meetings.

Not just words and sentences, but the novel's entire substance had been changed.

I liked to picture Warren making this discovery in various settings. On the commuter train going home, in his office at the end of a day, at the bar in the Cock and Bull, at his kitchen table late at night.

I imagined him reaching a certain point in the book and yelling, *What the fuck is this?* The thought made me smile. It was among the reasons I'd bothered. For the pleasure of imagining this, though not for the pain that was sure to follow.

I waited for the ominous knock on my door, or for the door to fly open. How slowly time passes when you're expecting trouble. But none of the dreaded outcomes occurred. Elaine must have been busy.

Warren wasn't paying attention. That was unusual for him, fortunate for me. He must have been focused on something else. Neither of them seemed to have read *The Vixen* beyond the first few pages. Quite possibly they hadn't even opened the book.

An anonymous reader "in government" was the first to alert Warren that *The Vixen, the Patriot, and the Fanatic* had "severe problems." The wheels of power are said to turn slowly, but it took less than a week for the US Information Agency to cancel its order to stock American libraries abroad.

Warren called me into his office and shouted, as I'd known he would. Having imagined this scene so many times made it marginally easier, though I couldn't have known how often he would call me *pathetic, stupid,* and *idiotic.* What *stupid* fool, what *pathetic, idiotic* moron, would do such a thing, and why? I kept saying that I didn't know, but I did.

I knew why I'd done it.

I'd done it for Ethel. For my mother. For the jewfish. For the eighty-seven dead Albanians who finally had their revenge, however mild and bloodless.

"If it comes to that," Warren said, "which I hope it won't, our firm has top-drawer lawyers to whom you will not have access. You, Mr. Putnam, will have a public defender. One week out of community college law school, this loser will be the only thing standing between you and serious jail time."

"What would be the charge?"

"Theft. Treason. Child abuse. Breaking and entering. You name it. A Senate committee decides to investigate how a book so full of bullshit could possibly be published. Published by *us*!"

He paused. He wanted me to know he was deciding my fate. He wanted me to know he'd decided.

"If the worst *doesn't* happen, you can thank my political connections. I'll help you, but only so I won't have to think about you rotting away in jail just because you're *stupid*. I should let you get what you deserve, but it's easier to save your retarded ass. Easier for me."

He kept repeating himself, losing track and starting over again. I wondered if he was entirely well. I felt sorrier for him than I should have. I'd meant to cause him trouble but not to do him physical harm. I hadn't imagined that I could.

"Now get the hell out of here."

I thanked Warren for hiring me, for how much I'd learned on the job. I said I meant it. I did.

He said, "Fuck you, Simon whatever-your-name-is."

Even after everything, I was hurt that he would say that. That was probably why I said, "*You* wrote *The Vixen*. You and Elaine and Uncle Maddie."

"*Now* I'm insulted," he said. "*Now* I'm cut to the quick. For you to suggest that I and your uncle and Elaine could squeeze out that piece of shit. I have no idea who wrote it if it wasn't your insane girlfriend Anya. Or whoever wrote it for *her*. She wouldn't be the first pretty girl to make up a crazy story and sell it to a guy who thought her photo was hot. A guy who admired her tits. In this case me. And you. She played us. We were your girlfriend's marks."

Warren didn't blink, not once. He was a practiced liar. How could I have wanted to be like him? He was right: I was stupid.

I said, "I don't think that's fair to Anya. I don't believe that's what happened. And she's not—she never was—my girlfriend."

"That's not what I heard." Warren's tone was insinuating. "Fair to Anya? You're hopeless. We should never have hired an embryo like you to do an adult's job. I assume that you wrote this . . . malodorous commie excrement that we sent to the printer. That *you* sent to the printer. And that has now appeared between hard covers. Of course it will have to be pulped. We'll have to ask for your advance copies back. You'll be lucky if the government doesn't go after you. Plenty of guys in Washington will be mightily pissed."

"What happened to Anya?" I asked.

"How would I know? She'd not *my* girlfriend. Last I heard, she'd gone to Corfu."

I said, "What if I go public about what *The Vixen* was intended to do and who was paying for it?"

"Oh, is that a *threat*? That's rich! That's precious! I'm trembling. What will happen? No one will believe you. They'll think you're the crazy commie you are. A commie spy like your friends the Rosenbergs. And now you have to the count of five to get out of my office. One . . . two . . . "

"Don't bother counting," I said. "I'm gone. I guess Florence Durgin will need a new editor."

"Nice of you to think of her, but Florence is fucked forever. For which she can thank you." I could hear Warren shout through the door as I closed it behind me.

There were earlier versions of the manuscript of *The Vixen*, one of which Warren possessed. He could still have arranged to publish that. But by then, the heart, the energy, and the fire had gone out of the project. No one wanted to touch it. None of *The Vixen*'s three authors wanted to go public. No one else would think that their work—their joke—was righteous or useful or funny.

CHAPTER 16

That was my last day at Landry, Landry and Bartlett. Nothing was said about unemployment compensation or severance pay. No goodbye party, no after-work drinks, none of the tearful celebrations that mark a worker's retirement, a cop's final day on the force.

I left without saying goodbye to Elaine. Our avoiding each other, not saying goodbye, communicated more than anything we could have said. It was like a conversation. After all the talks we'd had in my thoughts, why bother in real life? Neither of us really wanted to hear what the other had to say.

I bought a bottle of French champagne, way more expensive than I could afford. I took it to Julia's little house, along with the hundred-dollar copyediting fee. We drank the entire bottle. I was loose but not too tipsy to hold baby Evan. Maybe just tipsy enough. I let him play with my sunglasses. He hummed. Julia wiped the baby spit off my glasses after she took them away from him. That made him cry, but I was getting used to it. His tears no longer scared me.

By the end of that day, I felt strong and proud, almost good enough for Julia. Sabotaging *The Vixen* had been a modest gesture of conscience. In the scheme of things, not much. It wasn't as if we'd conspired to overthrow a dictator. Though it hadn't been entirely risk-free. Our protest could have gone wrong. I felt we'd averted disaster, steered the *Titanic* past the iceberg.

I wasn't the person whom Ethel had charged with keeping her name unsullied by lies, but I'd done my best. Maybe I hadn't reacted quickly or decisively enough, but I'd come through. My parents would be proud if they heard what I'd done. But I hoped they never would. My mother would know I'd done it partly for her, but I'd rather she didn't know. She would hate the fact that her brother-in-law wrote something like that about Ethel. She'd never much liked Uncle Maddie, but still.

Every trial of the spirit I put myself through, every sentence I wrote and rewrote, seemed, in retrospect, necessary. I should have said no when I first read *The Vixen*. But I wouldn't have found my vocation. I wouldn't have found Julia.

. . .

There were rumors and counter-rumors, rumors contradicting earlier rumors, but eventually I found out what happened at the firm after I was let go.

It came as a surprise to many people that Landry, Landry and Bartlett had a board of directors, and that this mysterious board had the power to fire Warren. Word about the "problem" with *The Vixen* had filtered down from the anonymous reader "in government." The mysterious head of the mysterious board called Warren into his office and told him how disappointed they were. The board remembered the day, not long ago, when Warren signed off on every word he published, when he was on top of his game. The simplest oversight would have saved the firm the cost of the thousand copies of leftist propaganda that now had to be pulped.

Robertson Crowley was on the board of directors, as was Preston Bartlett, ex officio. Neither of them attended the meeting at which Warren was officially censured.

I was ordered to return the advance copies of *The Vixen* to avoid some harsh but unspecified penalty. But I was able to save two bound copies that I have, on my desk, as I write this.

...

For a long time afterward I waited for the two Feds in suits to show up at my door and flash their badges. In my daydreams I faced a committee of senators convened to ruin my life.

But that didn't happen. Maybe no one noticed. Maybe no one cared if *The Vixen* was published. Maybe everyone had moved on.

Six months after I left the firm, Landry, Landry and Bartlett closed. The office was shuttered, publication ceased, the employees dispersed. I wondered what happened to Elaine, but I never saw her again. When I reentered that world from the other side, as a writer, I kept expecting to run into her, but I never did. Something always kept me from questioning people she might have known, asking if they knew where she was.

Nothing was said about the writers under contract to Warren, and no one mentioned poor Florence Durgin and her son. From time to time, I'd look in bookshops for her second volume of poems. But it seems never to have appeared, which is something I deeply regret.

There were formal dinners, panels, and programs celebrating the firm's achievements. Of course I wasn't invited, nor could I bring myself to attend the forum, open to the public and chaired by Warren: Landry, Landry and Bartlett: The Glory Years.

After a decent interval, Warren Landry was tapped to head a small conservative family foundation based in Georgetown.

...

Julia and I got married. I adopted Evan, whose father got tenure at the University of Cincinnati and was fine with the adoption. We agreed that Evan's father would get him at Christmas and for a month every summer.

Julia's parents had misgivings about her marrying a Jew, even one named Putnam. My parents said that marrying a woman with a child would never work out. They were wrong, all wrong, and when our happiness proved too obvious to ignore, our families were reconciled. My parents adored Julia. Her parents tolerated me. The in-laws chipped in to help us buy a house in Nyack.

The house was tiny, but we loved it. It had a large backyard. When every last leaf fell from the trees in winter, we could see the bright consoling ribbon of the Hudson.

...

The only problem was that, once again, I was out of work and didn't know what to do next, though this limbo seemed less frightening than the purgatory of my parents' apartment. Apparently Uncle Maddie had told the publishing world that I had personally torpedoed a project so costly and important that it was largely responsible for the failure of Landry, Landry and Bartlett. His refusal to explain what that project was made the gossip even juicier and more damning.

I believed that I had been contaminated, early on, by my association with Robertson Crowley, whose secret life turned out to have been an open secret. He was the last person who should have written my recommendation for the liberal admissions committee at the University of Chicago. True or not, I believed that academia was forever beyond my reach. Or maybe I didn't want that life, and I blamed its inaccessibility on forces outside myself.

I never spoke to Uncle Maddie again, and he never attempted to get in touch. I avoided the boisterous family gatherings I thought he might attend. My parents told me that he stopped attending them too. I wanted to think that he was afraid of running into me. When I resumed going to the weddings and parties, I enjoyed them less than before. I felt that I'd been tarnished by my contact with people like Warren and Uncle Maddie, that just knowing them had walled me off from the people I'd known in childhood, from a way of life I truly valued only when I'd lost it. It was as if that part of my family was a language I'd forgotten how to speak.

I'd wanted to separate myself from them. Be careful what you wish for.

When my uncle was gone from my life, I discovered I didn't miss him, so maybe I'd only loved the person I imagined he was, and, more shamingly, the ways in which I imagined he could help me.

I told my parents that Uncle Maddie was partly why I'd been fired, which in some sense was true. But when they asked for details, I claimed to have signed an agreement not to tell. When they persisted, I said that Maddie had given one of Warren's big books a career-ending review, and Warren took it out on me. I'm not sure they believed me, but they let the matter drop.

I think my mother was relieved to not even have to *consider* begging my uncle to arrange a second chance for me at another publisher. I never knew how my father felt about the possibility that his brother was responsible for my misfortune. It wasn't a question I could ask. I think Dad was secretly glad to have more evidence against a successful sibling who, my father believed but never said, was a defective human being whose moral compass had been broken by too many pretty girls and too much rich food.

I'm a forgiving person who doesn't hold grudges, a quality that's been helpful in our long and happy marriage. But I never forgave Uncle Maddie, who, near the end of his life, wrote a book about all the dear friends to whom he'd stopped speaking because they were crypto-Communists.

I read about his death in the papers. After some uncertainty, I decided to skip his memorial service in the Cathedral of St. John the Divine. A reporter who attended noted that most of the brightest stars in Madison Putnam's literary firmament had long ago ceased to shine. The paper named my cousin Frank as Madison Putnam's sole survivor.

...

There was a shortage of teachers in the Nyack public school system. Julia aced the test and was hired. She loved teaching third grade, which endeared her to my mother, who returned to her own classroom for a few years before she retired.

Julia and my parents approved of my staying home to take care of Evan and, three years later, of baby Aurelia. I knew it was temporary. I enjoyed it. The phrase *stay-at-home-dad* hadn't been invented. There was no need for it. This was the 1950s. The playground mothers saw me as the human equivalent of a feral cat that had to be closely watched.

When I looked back, it seemed strange that I'd begun to panic about my future within days of my college graduation. Because now, weeks and months were passing, and that was fine with me. I read. I took care of the children, the house. Sooner or later I would go back to work. I hoped I'd find work I enjoyed.

As I hung out the laundry and cooked dinner and walked the kids to school, I sometimes thought about *The Vixen*. Out of all my time working for Warren, I kept focusing on one moment. I can't pretend that I forgot about Anya and the dark ride. But more often I returned to that afternoon when Warren first gave me the manuscript of *The Vixen, the Patriot, and the Fanatic*.

How I'd hoped the blood-colored folder contained something other than what it did. I'd so wanted to find a novel about the Vikings, reasonably well written, a book that could make the reader care about men and women, heroes and villains, who led such romantic lives and who had been dead for so long, if they'd ever existed. I imagined a Viking novel populated with complicated characters whom we would feel we *knew*, though they lived at a different time and according to different rules. There would be violence and bloodshed, but not as much as in the sagas.

The Vixen was not that book. There *was* no book like the one I imagined, and so, in the break I was taking from work, taking care of our children while Julia taught, I decided to write the book I had in mind, or try.

Baby Aurelia was two when I began.

I used everything I learned in college, everything I'd figured out from revising *The Vixen*. I worked when Evan was asleep, then when he went off to school; when Aurelia was asleep, then when she was in day care. When I mentioned the novel to Julia, I made it sound like something I was *thinking* about so she wouldn't be disappointed when I stopped after a few chapters.

I wrote slowly. I made charts and timelines of the lives of characters who vanished from the narrative and later reappeared. I needed to know how old they were, how they were related by blood and marriage, how greedy or generous, how hard-hearted or romantic, how each one responded to the murders and battles and feuds.

I hid the notebooks when Julia came home. I didn't want to disappoint her. I waited until the manuscript was finished before I gave it to her to read.

She read it in two nights. By then I knew her well enough to know that she was telling the truth when she said she loved it.

Through a publishing friend of Julia's, I sent out the book under an androgynous pseudonym: E. S. Rose. It found a champion, an editor who was comfortable with my desire to write under an assumed name. At first I was still hiding from Uncle Maddie and Warren, from whatever damage I imagined they could do to a book with my name on the cover. And maybe the pretending—pretending not to have written a book instead of pretending to have written one—made me think I might still understand Anya.

In fact I liked writing as E. S. Rose more than I would have liked it as Simon Putnam. It made it easier—made it possible—to *not be myself*, to let the story pour through me. Those moments of grace, of transcendence, were more satisfying than whatever celebrity Simon Putnam might have enjoyed.

The book found its readers, more than I'd dared to hope. E. S. Rose wrote five sequels, and, though there were many difficult moments, days of near despair, the truth was that I liked writing each book better than the last.

As I wrote, I thought of Crowley's stories, forever tainted for me by what he'd done. But they were still good stories, and I borrowed from them when I could. At first there was lots of revenge in my books. But over time I was less drawn to plots about murder and vengeance than to tales of rescue and reconciliation, of divine and human peacemakers, of spirits who swooped in to save my characters from the lion's cave, the sinking ship, the burning house. The Albanian sworn virgins reappeared as Valkyries in *The Shipwreck*, book number four. My readers were happy to think about something gathering them up in its powerful wings, plucking them out of the battle and taking them to an eternal feast in the Hall of the Gods.

CHAPTER 17

Eventually, my mother's headaches returned, a symptom of the disease that killed her. It turned out that the Harvard-grad Roosevelt-biography-reading surgeon had misdiagnosed her condition. It turned out that my mother's brain was not, after all, a piece of cake. This was before patients sued their overconfident doctors, but not before the doctors' secretaries sent flowers to the patient's hospital room, just in case there was any ill will.

When we believed that my mother could no longer see or move, when it was too late for heartfelt prayer or magical thinking, when we could do nothing but endure it, my mother slipped off her ring, the one that said *1931*, and with trembling fingers handed it to me.

It was like a fairy tale: I tried the ring on all ten fingers. It didn't fit over my knuckles. I was sad that it wasn't for me. I gave the ring to Julia, who slipped it onto the index finger of her right hand. My mother saw it and nodded.

"Take care of your father," she said.

"I promise," I said, at the same time as Julia said, "We promise."

My mother closed her eyes and didn't open them again.

When people ask Julia why she wears a ring that says *1931*, she flips the onyx over, and my mother's sweet face answers.

For some time I thought that we'd failed to keep our dying promise to her. I'd done a better job fulfilling Ethel's last wish. I'd tried to keep Ethel's name bright. But I couldn't save my father.

When my father stopped eating after my mother died, we assumed that grief was making him lose his appetite. The doctors agreed. Another fatal mistake. Too late, we learned it was something worse. A failure of the imagination: we couldn't yet imagine anything worse than grief.

I hardly remember their funerals except in isolated images, like snapshots of an event I missed. Everything was so clouded by sorrow that I hardly saw what Julia later reported: my relatives greeted me with the slightly bewildered, anxious faces of friends with whom we have lost touch and who don't know what they could have done to offend us.

I SEARCH FOR my parents in my daughter's face. In my dreams my mother and father are young and healthy. I wake from those dreams in tears. Not a day goes by when I don't think of them and miss them and wish they'd lived to see my children grow up.

I keep wishing I'd done something differently, though I'm not sure what. I should have visited them more often, more willingly. There is always that.

Sometimes I walk to the end of the snowy yard. Across the Hudson, and slightly south, shine the lights of Sing Sing, surprisingly bright and festive, less like a prison than a riverboat gambling casino. Sometimes, a trick of the darkness or the water makes the lights seem to blink on and off.

I think of that night, so rapidly fading into the past, when Ethel and Julius died. I remember our kitchen light flickering at that moment. Blink, a pause, then blink blink blink.

And I can hear my mother's voice.

Adios, amigos.

CHAPTER 18

Every summer, as soon as Evan was old enough, and then after baby Aurelia was born, Julia and I took the kids to Coney Island. At first we'd combine it with a visit to the grandparents, but after my parents died—within six months of each other—we still went.

The boardwalk, the beach, the crowds, the rides. Our pilgrimage. Hot dogs, cotton candy. Family fun. We rode the Wonder Wheel, the merry-go-round. The kids thought it was a cool place for their dad to come from.

Without discussing it, we took a circuitous route to avoid passing the dark rides. If we'd mentioned it, which we didn't, we would have said that it was for the children's sake. We didn't want them scarred for life, as we joked that I had been, by memories of the Cyclops's eye snapping in its socket.

The truth was: we avoided the rides to avoid upsetting Julia. I had told her about Anya and the Terror Tomb that first day, at Julia's house in Harlem. Even then I'd known: that was a mistake.

After we'd been married a while, I thought that the subject of Anya would have lost its power to wound Julia, but oddly, it grew stronger.

I didn't want to remind my wife of that brief, strange affair. I didn't want to be reminded. I almost felt as if I were being asked to choose between the two women. No choice was being offered. How could lasting love and a tranquil domestic life compete with strangeness and sex and mystery? How could presence compete with absence? Later,

I didn't like thinking about how many years had passed since then, or about the lost, innocent, unrecognizable boy who'd been in love with Anya.

I still thought about Elaine. Whenever I congratulated myself for remembering a birthday or a name, for packing something special that Evan or Aurelia might want in their school lunch, for figuring out what was bothering them and how to reassure them, I'd think that I had become the sort of person I'd imagined Elaine was. After a while, though, I had only a vague memory of what Elaine looked like.

But I had Anya's author photo. It was, like any photograph, an image of one moment, though we didn't know that then, when we believed it would last.

I tried not to think about Anya. She was the question that had no answer, the riddle with no solution, the one loss that, despite everything, I mourned when I was tired or nostalgic, vulnerable or saddened by the passage of time. Thoughts of her recurred, unbidden and unwelcome, like bouts of malarial fever. First it seemed impossible that I would never see her again, and then it seemed impossible that I ever would.

I searched for her from time to time, in phone books and later on the internet. Occasionally I thought I passed her on the street or in the subway. But always when I turned, she was gone, or had never been there. How foolish we are to assume that the lost will be found, the hidden revealed, the mystery solved, or even that we will figure out what to call the mix of emotions we feel when a passing stranger turns out not to be the person we hoped and feared to see.

ONLY ONCE, JUST once, I was sure that I saw her. This was in Grand Central station. I was on line at the ticket window. I was going to see a friend in Ossining. A dying friend. I was bringing bags of delicacies that Julia had helped me choose, even though we'd heard that neither my friend nor her husband was eating. Maybe I was doing something I hadn't done for my father, which put me in a particular mood: more available to ghosts. I was unhappy because of my errand, and because I was so far from the front of the long line.

I was transferring the grocery bags from one hand to the other when my fingers brushed against something furry, and I recoiled. A woman in a fur coat rushed by. It was the dead of winter.

Everything about the woman reminded me of Anya. It *was* Anya. Older. Still beautiful. But it was Anya. Definitely her. I would have known her anywhere.

She ran as gracefully as one could, on very high heels, up to another woman, also in fur, waiting for tickets near the front of the line. The line was so long it curved around. The two women were way ahead of me. I could see them laughing, talking, but only in fragments, like the stuttering frames of a silent film. Maybe it wasn't Anya. I couldn't imagine her having a friend. I kept craning my neck and rising on my toes, annoying the people around me.

As I said, the line was long and moving very slowly.

Maybe it wasn't Anya. Maybe I only thought I saw her because I was going to visit a dying friend. Or maybe because my friend lived in the town where Ethel and Julius died, not far from the asylum or rest home or theater set where I first met Anya.

Then I thought: It's Anya.

What if it was? I tried to imagine what I would say, how I would try to look. It never occurred to me to get out of line and go up and see if it really was her. I didn't want to lose my place, or maybe I suspected that I would be losing my place for nothing.

At last the women bought their tickets, and arm in arm, supporting each other on those ridiculous heels, rushed toward me. Maybe they were late for their train.

It wasn't Anya. I was sure of it now. The woman looked like her. Terrifyingly like her. But no. It wasn't her. I'd so wanted it to be her that I couldn't breathe. I thought I might die right then and there, my heart was slamming so hard. If I fell down dead on the station floor, Anya or Not-Anya and her friend would stop and join the crowd gathering around me. Or maybe they'd keep running.

I *wanted* it to be Anya, though I knew that it wasn't.

"Anya?" I said, as the woman rushed by. My voice sounded nothing like my voice. How could my heart have beat harder without suffering permanent damage? "Anya Partridge?"

The stranger looked at me and frowned. Both women shook their heads. What a stupid name.

Passengers hurried past me. The people on line were still on line. No one knew that I had seen Anya, that I hadn't seen Anya. No one knew what had happened and not happened. There was no one I could tell, no one anywhere. Not my wife, not my children. I was alone in the world.

My heart took its time slowing down. I waited. I bought my ticket.

I visited my friend. She and her husband thanked me for the food, for the delicacies, which they insisted I take home.

All that evening, I was impatient with Julia and the kids.

...

Once, just once, after all that time, Anya managed to drive a wedge between Julia and me. It was my fault. I had neglected to throw out the fur stole that Anya left in the nursing home, or whatever it was: an upscale mental hospital or CIA simulacrum.

I'd forgotten the fox pelt until I was going through some soggy cardboard cartons in the garage. Time and humidity hadn't been kind to the fur, and when I touched the pelt, it felt like a dead rat. I let out a yelp of animal fear. I was embarrassed in front of my daughter. I didn't want to remember looking into the fox's face as Anya twisted beneath me. I didn't want to touch it or recall the calculated witchiness, the fetishism, the time I spent under its spell, or how I'd found it in Anya's empty room.

Aurelia asked if she could play with it. I don't know why I said yes. At least it would have some use. I didn't think much about it. That was another mistake.

Julia must have known that it had belonged to Anya. She must have seen Anya wearing it. Or she remembered the detail from *The Vixen*. She threw it in the trash, and told Aurelia that it was crawling with mites and lice. Julia didn't speak to me for a week, and I had to slowly and cautiously work my way back into her good graces.

I wished that I could have told her that what I felt for her was so much deeper and more powerful than anything I'd felt for Anya, certainly for Elaine. I had never for one moment thought, as I did about Julia, that I couldn't live without them. I wished I could have told Julia that love was a stronger aphrodisiac than risk, longer lasting and with a lunar pull that flooded and ebbed over time.

Maybe she would have believed me. But she was still young, romantic, and jealous, and what she wanted—to erase everything I'd felt for any woman before I met her—was impossible. She wanted the past not to have happened, and I couldn't do that, nor would it have helped to mention that the past, the same past, was what had brought us together. To say that I loved her more than anyone would only have reminded her that *anyone* had existed.

...

The Wonder Wheel, the Tilt-a-Whirl, the Steeplechase, the Aeroplan-o, each ride had a minimum height and age that children had to reach in order to ride it. We mostly stuck to the rules with our kids. Though if they really wanted to go on a ride, we added a year and an inch, a harmless little lie that made us all feel closer: outlaws and rebels together.

WHEN EVAN WAS ten and five foot two, the legal age and height, he asked to go on the Parachute Jump. He'd been asking for years, and at last I agreed. I'd been hearing that they were about to shut down the ride because of safety concerns. That should have made us stay away, but instead it made it seem urgent. I thought about my father's warnings with detached bemusement: how ironic it would be if Dad turned out to be right.

Evan and I were strapped in together, and as we were hoisted up, I concentrated on not seeming scared, for my son's sake. I focused on breathing steadily. My boy was excited and happy. They kept us at the top for a while, to ramp up the fear and the excitement. People were already screaming, and their terror edged into my consciousness, like someone opening an envelope with the tip of a knife.

I wished I'd told Julia I loved her once more. I wished I'd kissed my daughter. I couldn't see them from the air. It was the middle of July, and the heat made the streets wobble and shimmer beneath us. Julia had thought the ride was dangerous. She'd been angry at me for doing something stupid. She'd whisked Aurelia off to get something to eat and spare our child the sight of her father and brother falling from the sky. Why hadn't I listened to Julia? Why hadn't I believed my father?

Goodbye, I thought. Goodbye.

But once we started our descent, I was no longer afraid.

As we dropped and dropped, I never doubted that things were under control, that we would land safely, that our parachute would open. We were weightless, deep in the ocean, looking up through jellyfish at the sun. Everything was beautiful except what we do when we forget our humanity, our human dignity, our higher purpose.

I held my son against me. His spine and his rib cage pressed into my chest, his bones as fragile as a bird's. I felt as if I had scooped up a baby bird fallen from its nest.

A baby bird fallen from its nest. The fear came back. I'd made a mistake. Because I gave in, because I'd ignored my instincts and intuition, because I'd forgotten my father's warnings, because I hadn't listened to my wife, because I'd wanted my son to think I was braver than I was, because of one reckless act, my son and I were going to die. Julia would never get over it. Aurelia would grow up without me.

I prayed to whatever was out there.

Shorter are the prayers in midair, but more heartfelt.

I prayed that if we landed safely, that after all this ended, after we'd plummeted through the air and floated down onto the ground, that if my son and I could just stand and brush ourselves off and go back to our ordinary lives, if we could just go on living, just this once, this day, this hour, if we could be allowed to keep what we had, just this, no more or less, then I promised that someday, I would write, as honestly as I could, the true story of the year when Ethel Rosenberg died and I so desperately wanted to save her. I promised the parachute that opened. I promised the sky that let us go. I promised the earth that heard my prayer and rose up to receive us.

ACKNOWLEDGMENTS

I'm endlessly grateful to my first readers, whose encouragement and suggestions improved this book in ways that I couldn't have imagined: Doon Arbus, Michael Cunningham, Deborah Eisenberg, Howard Michels, Judy Linn, Leon Michels, James Molloy, Scott Spencer, and Karen Sullivan. Thanks also to my editor, Sarah Stein; my agent, Denise Shannon; my publisher, Jonathan Burnham. Thanks to Padma Lakshmi, for her friendship and generosity. Thanks especially to Bruno, Jenny, Emilia, Malena, Jack, and Pablo for their love and support. And to Howie for everything, everything.

Dozens of books helped me understand the historical background against which this novel is set. Among them are *Legacy of Ashes*, by Tim Weiner; *The Cultural Cold War*, by Frances Stonor Saunders; *Finks*, by Joel Whitney; *The Rosenberg File*, by Ronald Radosh and Joyce Milton; *Secret Agents*, by Marjorie Garber and Rebecca L. Walkowitz; *We Are Your Sons*, by Robert and Michael Meeropol; *Invitation to an Inquest*, by Walter and Miriam Schneir; *A Conspiracy So Immense: The World of Joe McCarthy*, by David M. Oshinsky; and *Point of Order!*, by Emile de Antonio and Daniel Talbot.

ABOUT THE AUTHOR

FRANCINE PROSE is the author of twenty-one works of fiction, including, most recently, the highly acclaimed novel *Mister Monkey* and the *New York Times* bestselling novel *Lovers at the Chameleon Club, Paris 1932*. Her novel *A Changed Man* won the Dayton Literary Peace Prize, and *Blue Angel* was a finalist for the National Book Award. Her works of nonfiction include the highly praised *Anne Frank: The Book, the Life, the Afterlife* and the *New York Times* bestseller *Reading like a Writer*, which has become a classic. The recipient of numerous grants and honors, including a Guggenheim and a Fulbright, and a Director's Fellow at the Center for Scholars and Writers at the New York Public Library, Francine Prose is a former president of PEN American Center, and a member of the American Academy of Arts and Letters and the American Academy of Arts and Sciences. She is a distinguished visiting writer at Bard.

READ MORE BY FRANCINE PROSE

WHAT TO READ AND WHY

"Prose's writing sharpens, focuses. . . even thrills when she writes of the authors who move her most deeply. These essays on their own make the book worth reading and buying; they made me buy a couple of the books she most passionately endorses."

—*Wall Street Journal*

READING LIKE A WRITER

A Guide for People Who Love Books and for Those Who Want to Write Them

New York Times Bestseller

"Prose's little guide will motivate 'people who love books'. . . . Like the great works of fiction, it's a wise and voluble companion."

—*New York Times Book Review*

MISTER MONKEY

A Novel

"An indelible cast of characters. . . . In this strong, humane, and funny novel, Prose has treated us to an enthralling entertainment both on and off stage."

—*Boston Globe*

LOVERS AT THE CHAMELEON CLUB, PARIS 1932

A Novel

New York Times Bestseller

"Walk through the door of the Chameleon Club, and you'll be entranced by the way Prose plumbs the enigma of evil, the puzzle of history, and the mystery of valor."

—*Washington Post*

HarperCollins*Publishers*   HARPER ● PERENNIAL

DISCOVER GREAT AUTHORS, EXCLUSIVE OFFERS, AND MORE AT HC.COM.

READ MORE BY FRANCINE PROSE

MY NEW AMERICAN LIFE
A Novel

"Utterly charming. Savvy about the shady practices of both US immigration authorities and immigrants themselves, *My New American Life* is powered by a beguiling Albanian heroine and her hapless American employers. Entertaining, light yet not trivial, a joy to read."

—Lionel Shriver

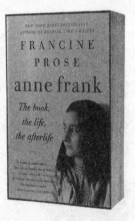

ANNE FRANK
The Book, The Life, The Afterlife

"A definitive, deeply moving inquiry into the life of the young, imperiled artist, and a masterful exegesis of *Diary of a Young Girl*…Extraordinary testimony to the power of literature and compassion"

—*Booklist* (starred review)

GOLDENGROVE
A Novel

"*Goldengrove* explores the intoxication and heartache of female adolescence…allowing humor and compassion to seep through the cracks of an otherwise dark tale."

—*San Francisco Chronicle*

HarperCollins*Publishers*   HARPER ● PERENNIAL
DISCOVER GREAT AUTHORS, EXCLUSIVE OFFERS, AND MORE AT HC.COM.

READ MORE BY FRANCINE PROSE

THE GLORIOUS ONES
A Novel

"[Prose] navigates serenely between the real and the fantastic, between the rational and the supernatural."

—*The New York Times*

A CHANGED MAN
A Novel

"Francine Prose has a knack for getting to the heart of human nature . . . *A Changed Man* moves ahead at a swift and entertaining pace . . . We enter the moral dilemmas of fascinating characters whose emotional lives are strung out by the same human frailties, secrets and insecurities we all share. Most telling is the way Prose cleverly draws a fine line between fanatics and idealists."

—*USA Today*

BLUE ANGEL
A Novel

National Book Award Finalist
New York Times **Notable Book**

"Screamingly funny... *Blue Angel* culminates in a sexual harassment hearing that rivals the Salem witch trials."

—*USA Today*

⊞ HarperCollins*Publishers*   HARPER ◯ PERENNIAL
DISCOVER GREAT AUTHORS, EXCLUSIVE OFFERS, AND MORE AT HC.COM.

READ MORE BY FRANCINE PROSE

GUIDED TOURS OF HELL
Novellas

"Francine Prose doesn't err. With a cool hand she wields the scalpel, dissecting hypocrisy, carving through self-delusion. Darkly delightful and ultimately illuminating."

—*New York Daily News*

CARAVAGGIO
Painter of Miracles

"Racy, intensely imagined, and highly readable. . . Prose brings to Caravaggio a fresh and unflinching eye."

—*New York Times Book Review*

THE LIVES OF THE MUSES
Nine Women and the Artists They Inspired

"In Francine Prose's exhilarating study of nine women who have inspired artists, you get to enjoy something rare: a book fo serious ideas that is also addictively juicy."

—*Boston Globe*

HarperCollins*Publishers* HARPER ● PERENNIAL
DISCOVER GREAT AUTHORS, EXCLUSIVE OFFERS, AND MORE AT HC.COM.